LAND OF ICY COLD AND FIERY FEVER

Megan saw signs of the gold rush even before she arrived in Dawson City. At the mouth of Bonanza Creek, the mud softened to a gravy-like consistency. Along a serpentine slough, not a tree, blade of grass, cranberry, blueberry, or salmonberry bush, or daub of moss had survived the gold-fevered invasion.

Then Dawson itself came into sight, and Megan paused, gnats swarming around her head as she stared in wonder.

Pioche, Nevada; Telegraph Creek, British Columbia; Coeur d'Alene, Idaho; Tombstone, Arizona—for all the mining camps and towns she had known, nothing had prepared her for this crazed carnival of greed.

She looked at the horde of men feverishly ripping at the earth until they dropped with exhaustion. Beyond them were the crude wooden shacks and ramshackle saloons, the squalid living quarters and the sordid brothels.

This then, was her golden chance, if she managed to survive. . . .

Suzann Ledbetter

KLONDIKE FEVER

A SIGNET BOOK

SIGNET
Published by the Penguin Group
Penguin Putnam USA Inc., 375 Hudson Street,
New York, New York 10014, U.S.A.
Penguin Books Ltd, 27 Wrights Lane,
London W8 5TZ, England
Penguin Books Australia Ltd, Ringwood,
Victoria, Australia
Penguin Books Canada Ltd, 10 Alcorn Avenue,
Toronto, Ontario, Canada M4V 3B2
Penguin Books (N.Z.) Ltd, 182–190 Wairau Road,
Auckland 10, New Zealand

Penguin Books Ltd, Registered Offices:
Harmondsworth, Middlesex, England

First published by Signet, an imprint of Dutton Signet,
a member of Penguin Putnam Inc.

First Printing, October, 1997
10 9 8 7 6 5 4 3 2 1

 REGISTERED TRADEMARK—MARCA REGISTRADA

Printed in the United States of America

For my sons, Joshua and Zachary,
who dare to dream big dreams
and have the courage and fortitude
to make them come true

Chapter 1

Megan O'Malley grinned as she tugged on her worn denim trousers. Other women might be thrilled to discover that an ensemble they'd shoved to the back of a chifforobe still fit—with a bit of English applied to the buttons, anyway. Megan's delight had more to do with sentimentality than vanity.

Twelve years ago, her hikes across untold miles of Alaska's wilderness with her infant son strapped on a backboard had left her britches' hems looking as if they'd been gnawed by a woodchuck. A mended rent above one knee reminded Megan of a mad, predawn dash to the claim office to register her moderate Alaskan bonanza. The whipstitched back seam lent evidence to a losing battle with a sharp stob.

Even without her white cotton shirttail tucked in the waistband, her "lucky" gold miner's trousers pulled tighter at the seat and thighs than they had in '84, but seven years of city living hadn't softened her as much as she'd feared.

She snapped the hasps closed on a pair of black silk galluses, the only Christmas present she'd ever given her best friend, Barlow P. Bainbridge. Frayed threads whiskered their edges. Just below her heart, a welted repair humped the fabric like a scar.

She turned toward the mirrored bureau, but only its ghostly outline remained. Sunlight and coal-oil soot had left phantom silhouettes shaped like the bedstead, wardrobe, and washstand on the cream-and-aqua wallpaper.

Megan's laughter echoed in the empty room. She'd bought her house goods dear and sold cheap, but the trunk securing what remained of her worldly possessions wouldn't need a weekly coat of beeswax, either.

"Having pretty things was nice while it lasted," she said to herself. "Except for all the scrub and polish, I think they owned me instead of the other way round."

She folded her cotton nightdress, wrapper, and slippers, put them in her reticule, then strode from the room without a backward glance. Her footfalls along the hallway and down the stairs sounded more like a stevedore's tred than a petite, forty-three-year-old lady's.

At her approach, Harold Dirkson pushed off from the newel cap and smiled up at her. "I hope you don't mind my letting myself in."

"Not a-tall. If a woman can't trust her lawyer, who can she trust?"

The portly barrister chuckled. "A rare attitude, and a most welcome one." He glanced around the cavernous front room and clucked his tongue. "Seattle will be gloomier than ever without you. I don't know how I'll bear it."

Megan felt a tug at her heart. She'd not miss the city's hustle-bustle, its noise, or sour smells, but surely would the friends she'd made.

"I haven't stayed this long in one place since I left Ireland when I was fourteen. I settled down for my son's benefit. I'm leaving for the same reason."

"Barlow David is a good boy, Megan. Thirteen is a difficult age. No longer a child, but not yet a man."

"Nor will he live long enough to become one if I don't pry him away from those toughs he's taken up with."

Harold challenged her with his eyes. "A strict boarding school or military academy would instill the kind of discipline he needs."

Megan shook her head. "It's me that spoiled the lad, and me that'll set him to rights." Grinning wickedly, she added, "A few weeks hence, Barlow David may be prayin' to every saint he's ever heard of to save him from his ma's clutches."

The attorney's palm stroked the back of her hand. "I've asked you to marry me a dozen times over the years. I don't suppose another would be charm."

Megan's throat tightened. She knew how lonely Harold had been since cancer had stolen his beloved wife. How easy it would be to let him take care of her and her son.

Lord only knew her sister Frances had all but fitted Megan for a beige lace gown and veil the last time she'd visited from San Francisco.

If only she could explain her reasoning in a way Harold would understand. Moments like these were when she missed Barlow P. Bainbridge the most. For fifteen years they'd scrapped and cussed and pecked at each other, but he would know without a word being spoken how desperately she needed to share one last grand adventure with the boy she loved so fiercely.

Leaning on the balls of her feet, Megan kissed Harold's brow. "I wasn't much older than Barlow David when I told a sea captain I wasn't the marrying kind. I reckon it still holds true."

His expression reflected disappointment, yet Megan knew he hadn't expected any answer but the one she'd given. "Then, besides posting your letter to Frances, is there anything else I can do besides say good-bye?"

"Brace yourself for a scorching reply from San Francisco," Megan advised. "It's a coward I am for boarding a ship before my sister knows I've gone north. She'll not be surprised the wanderlust has spirited me away again, but she'll not be a bit happy to hear it, either."

"I'll soothe her feathers the best I can and take care of any other business that might arise while you're gone."

The attorney held out his arms. "Come here, you

old gold digger. Mind your ribs, for this hug has to last me for a good while."

Megan held him tightly, rocking from side to side. His bushy sidewhiskers tickled her cheeks. "I do love you, you know, in a very special way."

"Yes, I do know. Just as you've loved the never-ending parade of grizzled, adoring prospectors who've streamed through this parlor since the day you docked in our fair city."

Megan stepped back, gazing at Harold wistfully. "Without you and Peg-leg Hank, Johnny Callahan, and Swifty MacBolland, I'd have been begging on street corners for me and Barlow David's daily bread."

"Nonsense. You're a giver, Megan O'Malley, not a taker." He kissed her cheek. "And if I weren't as complacent as a fat toad, I'd usher you up that gangplank myself. Seattle—hell, the entire country—is determined to wallow in a bleak, sluggish bog. It's depressing, I tell you, and there's no relief in sight."

"Swifty says what we need is a fracas or a frolic to get men's blood to boiling again."

"He's right," Harold said, "though I don't hold out much hope for either. Maybe if we can muddle through another three years, the new century will turn the tide."

Megan bent to retrieve her satchel from the step. As she straightened, her shoulders heaved with a deep sigh. "We both know I must be on my way."

He tapped a bowler atop his balding pate, his thumb and forefinger grazing the curled brim in a jaunty manner. "Good-bye implies a permanence I refuse to accept."

His voice caught, lowering it to a strained whisper. "Godspeed, Megan. I'll keep you and Barlow David in my thoughts and prayers."

With that, he spun on a heel and waddled out the door.

A jangling harness indicated his buggy's departure

from the curb. Megan paused at the threshold, her fingers curled around the door's oval brass knob for the last time.

Dust motes sparkled on the shafts of sunlight angling through the uncurtained windows. The faint burble of a little boy's laughter drifted through her mind. Behind it came an adolescent's hateful rant; his vow to run away where his mother would never find him.

Chin held high, Megan pulled the door closed behind her. An impetuous yank ripped a boldly printed foreclosure notice from its tack. The broadside skimmed across the porch planks and came to rest against a corner post.

The steamer *Abercrombie*'s passenger manifest had a cabin booked in her name. The ship was due to depart Seattle's harbor in a few hours, bound for Skagway, the gateway to the Canadian goldfields.

There was no time for self-recrimination and regret. She would be at the *Abercrombie*'s rail when its lines were cast ashore.

Chapter 2

An open stairwell beside Ike Meyer's pawnshop led to Beulah Livermore's brothel. Barlow David O'Malley wedged himself between the well's facings, his heels propped against the splintered jamb.

At a fraction shy of six feet tall and husky for his age, he could pass for eighteen if circumstances required it—and the lights were dim.

Two weeks earlier, Beulah had agreed to relieve him of his virginity, but even a Cyprian of ample proportions and experience can't trick nature into bestowing puberty at a moment's notice. To his everlasting gratitude, she slipped from between the sheets and into her silk wrapper without cracking a smile or patting his tousled head.

She offered to forgo her standard fee, but he'd insisted upon giving her ten of the five-hundred-dollar bank draft he'd stolen from his mother. Beulah thanked him, tucked the bills into her freckled cleavage, escorted him to the door, and kissed him as gratefully as she would a more virile consort.

The balance of Barlow David's ill-gotten gains had financed hotel rooms, drunken bacchanals with his newly acquired entourage, and meals at Seattle's finest chophouses.

For a giddy fortnight, B.D., as he preferred to be called, had been King of the Punks; the undisputed leader of a youthful gang that frequented and, often as not, wreaked havoc on the waterfront. He never dreamed that his popularity would evaporate the moment his pocket flattened.

Across the street, a scuffling, painfully thin figure caught his eye. B.D. looked away and tucked his chin as if settling in for a nap. Padraic Cummins and the rest of the punks had given him enough guff for one day. He didn't need an encore from "Twig" Loughlin.

" 'Ey, izzat you, B.D.?" Twig's voice grated like a nail pried from oak lumber. "Law-dee mercy. I ain't seen such a sour kisser since Frankie DeSmet got the clap."

B.D. chuckled despite his black mood. "I suspect that's one advantage to being broke. You can't catch the one-eyed weeper on credit."

"Your stake's done run out, eh? 'Tis a pity, sure enough. I was getting plumb partial to high living."

Rather than take his leave at the news, Twig squatted on his heels. "Don't s'pose your ma's got another roll stashed somewheres."

"Not with my name on it, she doesn't. Saint Megan has money aplenty for pick-swingers needing their bellies filled or a place to flop. But me? I'm just her misbegotten boy. If I want jingle, I can damn well earn it."

"I dunno . . . 'Least she don't whore for it, then drink ever' dime she lays her hands on. You ain't got no daddy to whip your ass for sport, neither."

The jagged gash at Twig's cheekbone testified to his last visit home; a squalid, one-room tenement flat that stank of rotted fish, raw sewage, and hopelessness. His father had lost an arm to a lumbermill's band saw, but the remaining fist was more than sufficient to batter a fifty-pound, ten-year-old boy.

"Yeah," B.D. said, "except at any given time, I've got a houseful of codgers playing father to me. I can't go to the outhouse without them checking my britches' buttons when I come back in."

Bitterness surged through him. He swung his legs around and crouched on the stoop. "I'll bet they've called me everything but a black-haired Irishman for copping that money. Two-faced bastards. They've been stealing Ma blind for years.

"First the silver disappeared, then the filigree knick-knacks, then piece by piece, they mined her jewelry box. Think she cared? So what if she hasn't bought a new dress since Cleveland was elected? If she isn't cooking and scrubbing up after those freeloaders, she's down at the Pioneers Club swapping stories with another bunch of bummers."

Twig flicked a pebble into the street. "Only seen your old lady once. Could tell right off she didn't want my shadow darkening her parlor again. Gotta admit, though, she's kept herself up real nice. Didja ever wonder if them boarders ain't getting more than supper and clean sheets?"

B.D.'s hand lashed out. He shagged a hunk of Twig's coat and jerked him so close their noses touched. "Are you implying that my mother's a slut, boy?"

"No—I, uh—dash it, I don't savvy that 'implying' stuff. Didn't mean nothin' bad I swear. M-maybe one of 'em's sweet on her or something—ya know?"

B.D. snorted, but loosened his grip. "They all are, my friend. To know Megan O'Malley is to love her, but her heart will forever belong to a couple of ghosts."

A door slammed. Ponderous footfalls thundered down the stairs. A stevedore with shoulders wide enough to scrape the flaking paint from the walls emerged from the gloom.

His lopsided leer was supposed to inspire envy. It would have a month ago, but for reasons B.D. didn't quite understand, he felt kind of sorry for the man.

As the obviously satisfied customer rounded the corner, B.D. shrugged and started off in the opposite direction.

"Okay if I tag along with ya?"

"I'm not bound for anywhere in particular, Twig."

"Damned if that ain't 'zackly where I'm headed. Besides, you can't just leave me twistin' about them ghosts—that is, if I ain't stepped in it again by asking."

"No secret," B.D. said. "You ever hear of Tombstone, Arizona?"

"Shit fire, I'm ignorant, but I ain't stupid. Must have been some gimcrackin' town whilst it lasted."

"My father, David Jacobs, was the editor of a newspaper there and—"

"Thought your right name was O'Malley?"

"It is."

Twig aimed a sidelong glance at him. His pale lips flattened as if to bar a question he knew would get his ears boxed.

"Ma was already wearing her bustle backwards when she agreed to marry her best friend, Barlow P. Bainbridge," B.D. said. "Apparently, Jacobs took enough exception to the idea that he plugged Bainbridge square in the galluses over his heart. Before the smoke cleared, another gent exacted an eye for eye and parted my daddy's eyebrows with a bullet."

"Well, I'll be damned." Twig stared into the middle distance for a moment. "How come your ma didn't want to marry your daddy 'stead of that other fella?"

"She did, and could have ten years earlier in Nevada. By the time her and Jacobs met up again in Tombstone, he had himself a wife."

Twig scratched at the lock of dark blond hair dangling beneath his cap's brim. "Women sure is peculiar, ain't they? Don't sound like either one of them jaspers did right by your ma or you, but you got their handles stuck on ya and she's still carryin' a torch."

"That's about the size of it. To hear her talk, besides Jesus and Moses, there's never been two better men to walk this earth than Barlow P. Bainbridge and David Jacobs."

"Hmmmph. Maybe it ain't so bad havin' a snake-eyed son of a bitch for a father and a drunk ol' whore for a mother. Hikin' myself outta the gutter ain't gonna take near as much tug as fillin' them ghosts' shoes."

B.D. ambled on, keeping his own counsel. The dense fog tumbling in from the ocean shrouded the city in a swirling gray veil. A clammy sheen glazed the ship-lapped facades of shuttered buildings. What had come to be known as the Panic of '93 had bankrupted legions of Seattle's shopkeepers and its swells alike.

Newspaper headlines promised that a recovery was well underway, yet every night the wharf teemed with unemployed factory workers, streetwalkers, opium-eaters, morphine addicts, drunks, thieves, and white slavers who profited from selling their human cargo into servitude.

The money that had separated B.D. from the tenderloin's derelicts was gone. Hunger clawed at his midsection. His parched throat begged for a tankard of beer. The image of his mother laying the table with a tureen of chowder, fluffy biscuits, and a pie made his knees weak.

The tidy clapboard house where she reigned wasn't much over a mile away. It might as well be a thousand. He missed her as much as he hated her, but there was no going back. Not now, anyway. The prodigal son would return in triumph, not in rags.

"Are ya really dead-busted?" Twig asked, ending B.D.'s woolgathering.

"Yep. Good ol' Paddy snatched my last sawbuck, bashed me around, then shoved me into an offal pit. Told me he'd have my cods for breakfast if I dared show my face in his territory again."

"So much for Irish kinsmanship, eh?"

B.D. grinned, but it sorely lacked for humor. "That Mick would've stolen the casks from the Blessed Madonna if he'd been at the manger that night."

Twig wrapped his arms around his belly. "It'd be nice if it was closer to Christmas right now. Folks get right generous to urchins, 'long about then. June ain't much good for nothin' 'lest you're a skeeter."

B.D. paused at the entrance to an alley. "We might find something worth chewing in one of those ash bins."

Twig lobbed a chunk of cobble at a pile of crates. Rats yipped and rustled for cover; their eyes glinting in the meager light.

A shiver crawled down B.D.'s spine. He'd starve to death before he'd wrestle a rat for his supper. On a steady diet of fish scourings and garbage, those that didn't succumb to rabies or strychnine could get as big as tomcats.

"I bet if we split up, one of us'll find a toff on the slum," Twig said. "How 'bout we make a pax to meet back here in an hour and divvy the take?"

B.D. hesitated. His fingers crabbed inside his coat pockets for a coin or a note he might have missed.

" 'Course, we could snag a Mr. Whiskers over yonder, skin 'im and roast 'im over a spit," the younger boy teased. "Pa says rat meat tastes jes' like chicken if you cook it right."

"Keep an ear cocked at the clock tower. I'll be here at the hour and gone by five past."

"That's the spirit." Twig peered up and down the street. "It's hell on lively this afternoon. If I don't bump into a wham-bam stumbling outta Beulah's, I'll hit a coupla dives down on the waterfront."

"I'm heading uptown. Paddy doesn't prowl where constables walk a beat."

Twig nodded and shuffled away. His cramped shoes with their soles flapping to the insteps accounted for his distinctive, side-of-the-foot gait.

A searing sensation in B.D.'s gut radiated through his loins. He jammed a fist in the palm of his hand, then turned and strode up the sidewalk.

Paddy Cummins's snide tone echoed in his mind. "Squall home to yer ma, Nancy-boy. Me an' the boys

never took you in to raise. Ya ain't got balls enough
to pick nothin' but her apron pockets, no how."

"I'll show you," B.D. muttered. "I don't need anybody to take care of me. And it'll be a cold day in
hell before I pay for anybody else's frolic again."

The low rumble of masculine voices slowed his pace.
B.D. surveyed the street, deserted but for jabbering
bums even less fortunate than he, then squinted at
stripes of light winking from a boarded-up corner
building.

A slim crack in the side wall afforded a bird's eye
view of the interior. Men in sack suits, flannel shirts,
and bibbed overalls occupied the narrow room's
benches. They spoke in monotones like mourners at
a wake before the kegs have been tapped.

On a makeshift stage at the far end, women pranced
and preened in sweat-stained pink tights and thigh-
high skirts. Lengths of gauzy fabric draped their bare,
floppy breasts, which they kneaded like bored bakers
readying loaves for the oven. Clumpy wigs, swipes of
scarlet rouge, and heavy applications of kohl failed to
camouflage the chorus line's pure, unadulterated
ugliness.

It was the most revolting, degrading scene B.D. had
ever witnessed. He couldn't imagine how any man
could sit through such an obscene display. His jawbone ground into damp wood and his eyelid scratched
for want of a blink.

The creak of unoiled hinges tripped his heart. B.D.
flattened himself against the wall, then sidled along it.

A top-hatted gawker staggered from the bawdy
house onto the sidewalk. Dabbing his brow with a
linen handkerchief, he aimed a furtive glance over
his shoulder.

B.D. shrank back and counted off a silent ten seconds. A cautious peek found the gent strolling away,
swinging an umbrella by its crook.

Exhilaration rushed through B.D. He fell in behind
the toff, mimicking Paddy's catlike stealth. Passing

drays and figures crouched in doorways gave him no
pause. On the waterfront, the Golden Rule translated
to a deaf, dumb, and blind minding of one's own business. Those who adhered to it tended to survive longer
than those who didn't.

The stroller breached an alleyway. B.D. broke into
a sprint. He sprang onto the man's back. His forearm
wrapped as tight as a garrote around his quarry's
throat.

Momentum sent both of them careening sideward.
The man's full weight slammed B.D.'s shoulder and
hip to the filthy cobbles. He struggled free, his fists
poised for a fight. The toff rolled over as if boneless,
his legs and arms splayed wide.

The steady rise and fall of his chest indicated that
he'd fainted rather than expired, yet an icy sweat trickled down B.D.'s ribs. He bent down to rifle the man's
jacket, waistcoat, then trousers pockets.

He extracted a gleaming silver money clip adorned
with an antique gold coin. Judging by the thickness of
the quarter-folded greenbacks, the take would net him
over fifty dollars. He stepped aside, then halted. The
toff stirred and moaned softly.

B.D. frowned at his proceeds. His thumb chafed the
coin's embossed surface. He'd swiped ten times as
much from his mother. Why the hell wouldn't his
elbow bend to pocket a stranger's loot?

He tossed it on the gent's mounded belly. "Aw,
keep it, you fat ol' pervert."

Whirling on a heel, B.D. took off at a lope. Boot
leather slapped the bricks; their reports chanting
"Nancy-boy . . . Nancy-boy."

He ran block after block, trying to outdistance a
taunt only he could hear. His lungs burned with the
wharf's briny stench. Paddy and the punks would leap
out in front of him at any moment, eager to carve up
B.D.'s cowardly hide and feed him to the rats.

Dizziness assailed him. His step faltered. He re-
bounded off a wall of barrels dividing the dock like a

staved redoubt. B.D. bent double, his palms anchored on his thighs. Every gasping breath coated his tongue with a rank, fishy taste.

Crunching footsteps startled him. Iron hands gripped his arms and wrenched them behind his back. The cloth clapped over his face muffled his cries for help. He grappled with his captors, but a sickly sweet pungency seemed to turn his very bones to butter.

Slavers, he thought as his head lolled to one side. He surrendered to the sensation of his entire body being submerged in a placid, warm pool.

B.D.'s fingertips grazed a canvas-wrapped railing. He needn't open his eyes to know he was in a bunk aboard a sternwheeler. Though he'd only been six years old the last time he'd heard an engine's relentless rumble and water swash over the paddles, the sounds were impossible to forget.

When he and his mother had left Juneau to resettle in Seattle, the ship's pendulum sway soothed him like a giant cradle. Now, with bile rising in his throat, B.D. gritted his teeth against the hull's cruel motion.

Bad enough to let himself be chloroformed and shanghaied as easily as a dim-witted greenhorn. Damned if he'd be sick all over himself and wear the stink for God knew how long. He shuddered despite the cabin's stifling heat.

Slavers didn't waste wormy hardtack and salted herring on the weak any more than cattle drivers nursemaided puny calves. The sharks would dine on any captives deemed unfit for sale.

Those hardy enough to survive the journey were sentenced to years of unpaid, muscle-tearing labor. Overseers strung up slackers and malcontents by their wrists and laid on the lash until blood dripped off their heels.

A different, but no less horrific bondage awaited the girls and young women whisked away by roving traffickers. For either gender, death afforded the only sure road to freedom.

Tears drizzled from the corners of B.D.'s eyes. Dear God, help me. Get me home and I'll mend my wicked ways—I swear I will. Give me a chance, Lord. Please, just one more chance. . . .

The door's string latch snapped up. He huddled against the rough wall; every nerve taut and tingling. The portal swung open. A booted foot stepped over the raised threshold.

B.D. goggled when his mother's oval, widow's-peaked countenance craned around the door's edge.

Chapter 3

Megan shuffled along the *Abercrombie*'s narrow passage. One palm slid along the wall for balance. The other supported a tray laden with a mug of beef tea, soda crackers, and a dollop of applesauce.

She hesitated outside the cabin door to brace herself for another unpleasant encounter. Barlow David's fury would diminish eventually. Even a thirteen-year-old couldn't muster enough energy to stay angry forever, even when it was somewhat justified.

She hadn't anticipated his fear of being shanghaied. The tenderloin and horrors it purveyed were foreign to her. "And if they'd stayed foreign to him," she said, "we'd have both been spared a fair lot of suffering."

The tiny compartment's fetid heat assaulted her the moment she pushed the door open. Their quarters were luxurious compared to the disease- and vermin-infested hold she, her sister Frances, and scores of other Irish immigrants crowded into to sail for America, but the odors and suffocating humidity belowships were all too similar.

Barlow David lay on his back, head cradled in his hands, staring up at the bunk bolted to the wall above him. His downy complexion contrasted sharply with the sizable pair of feet extending past the end of his berth.

"Here's something to remind your belly of what it was made for," Megan said, nodding at the tray. "It won't give your tongue much to crow about, but if it settles all right—"

"I'm not hungry."

"You were born hungry."

The cleft in his jaw deepened. "Get out of here and leave me alone."

Megan struggled to check her temper. Had she ever spoken to Selma O'Malley in that fashion, she'd have eaten her meals off the mantel for a week.

A camelback trunk afforded the only place to sit. Megan availed herself of it and laid the tray on her lap. By her son's theatrical groan, he expected the lecture to commence at any moment.

Rather than disappoint him, she said, "Think you're tough, do you? Well, before long, we'll both find out whether it's guts or guff you're so full of, me lad.

"Next time your feet touch dry land it'll be on Alaskan soil, but only for a day. From there, we're taking the trail north to Fortymile."

"Forty—what?" He rolled over and grimaced, the aftereffects of the chloroform obviously exacting punishment for his sudden movement. "I thought you were carting me off to boarding school."

"I am, in a manner of speaking," she said. "It's about time you learned that the true measure of a man is what he's got between his ears, not below his belt buckle."

She grinned. "It hasn't a thing to do with how long he can polish a bar rail with his elbows, either."

"Y-you know about that?"

"Just because I let you sow your wild oats doesn't mean I didn't keep a sharp eye on you while you were doing it. Hank and Johnny, the two blokes that toted you aboard, have been your guardian angels ever since you slammed out of the house."

His face flushed as red as a whorehouse's lamp shade. "Why? So they could butt in before I did something to tarnish your saintly reputation?"

His bluster reminded Megan of the graying colleen that stared back at her from the mirror every morning.

Except being on the receiving end of it did alter one's perspective.

"I'm no more a saint than you're the devil incarnate. Hank and Johnny stayed close in case Paddy and his gang parted your ribs with a shiv."

He snorted. "Made jumping me on the wharf and drugging me out with chloroform an easier job, too, didn't it?" His eyes narrowed to slits. "What kind of a mother stoops so low as to kidnap her own son, for Christ's sake?"

"The loving kind, Barlow David. Had you given me the chance, I'd have told you what was in store for us and why?"

"*Told* me, is right."

"Damn straight it is, boy. Smirk and sneer all you care to—it won't change a thing. Beyond money enough for our fares, supplies, and a bit set aside for a grubstake, we don't have a pot or a window to throw it through.

"Fact is, we'd have been standing on street corners waggling tin cups long ago if not for my friends keeping food on our table, then paying room and board for the privilege of eating it."

"You're lying . . ." The waver in his voice telegraphed the fear that she was not.

Megan knew she should have discussed their financial straits with him earlier. Pride got in the way, as did hope that the situation could be rectified without his ever being aware of it. Feeling like a failure was difficult enough without admitting it to her child.

How well she remembered watching her six-year-old son struggle to heft a shovelful of gravel into the sluice; his excited squeals when he spied a pinch of dull yellow grains caught in the Long Tom's riffles.

Old-timers who'd tramped across Alaska for decades swore there wasn't any gold for miles around the O'Malleys' camp. Said she and Barlow David were breaking their backs dredging a nameless creek with no prospect of yielding more than a thimbleful of flakes.

The boy hadn't appreciated their skepticism. When a rich deposit finally revealed itself, it was he who suggested naming their claim the Thimbleful.

He'd cried his eyes out when Megan decided to take the proceeds and repair to Seattle, but rumors of a proper school being established near their claim hadn't materialized. Though she'd taught him to read, write, and cipher, he needed more than the rudiments to make his mark in the world.

His exposure to the three *R*'s ended last month when Headmaster Stith told his most accomplished student he could pass a university entrance exam without ever cracking another book. Rather than motivate Barlow David, he decided he'd earned permanent freedom from blackboards, recitations, and debating the validity of Karl Marx's revolutionary theories.

"I know our mine's still paying," he argued. "The postman gave—uh, I mean, you're still receiving drafts from the Thimbleful's manager."

"The one you borrowed for your spree was the last, Barlow David."

Megan let that sink in a moment before continuing. "When the banks closed up tighter than a Cornish Jack's lunch pail, I had over ten thousand dollars stashed away. I'll not see a nickel of it again in this life.

"I pawned some geegaws and sold others outright to scrape by. What royalties we were getting ended a year ago when a New York syndicate sued for rights to The Thimbleful. Harold Dirkson fought them tooth and nail, but it didn't do any good."

"God Almighty, Ma. That whiny fussbudget couldn't wrestle a cockroach and win. Bet he charged a fat fee to lose the mine for us, too."

Megan shook her head. "Harold took the case pro bono, and told me from the start that we didn't have a Chinaman's chance of winning.

"There's been a territorial law on the books for years that says the foreign-born can't file a discovery claim. Those highfalutin robber barons used it to stop production, then steal The Thimbleful right out from under us."

B.D. grabbed a cracker off the tray and bit off a corner. He frowned as he chewed. "But if the mine is a lost cause and you can't legally stake another one, why in blue blazes are we going north?"

"Open your ears and listen, son. I've already told you, we won't be in Alaska longer than a day. Forty-mile is in Canada, where the government is more accommodating to foreign prospectors—Americans included."

"Sure enough?" he intoned sarcastically. "For Christ's sake, Ma, I'm not stupid."

Megan bit back a reprimand. She loved her son with her whole heart, but on occasion it was easier to understand why some animals devour their own young.

She'd delivered both sustenance and food for thought. Allowing him time alone to contemplate both before another shouting match commenced seemed the wiser course.

"My darlin' Barlow David," she said, scooting the tray beside him on the bunk, "like my da told me when I was a girl, 'May ye know half as much at twice your age.'"

Chapter 4

Megan waved farewell to the crewman who'd delivered her, Barlow David, and their plunder by scow from the *Abercrombie* anchored a mile offshore.

Then, arms outstretched and grinning like a child savoring her first taste of spun sugar, she whirled around on Skagway's graveled beach. Sucking in great lungfuls of the crisp, clean air fostered an odd sort of inebriation. She felt as giddy, carefree, and invincible as a twenty-year-old again.

Tears rimmed her eyes as she gazed at the rugged, white-capped mountains girdling the outpost. The lofty, spruce-flanked palisade was at once awe-inspiring and intimidating.

On this, the summer solstice, the sun would not dip behind their ragged peaks until almost midnight. It hadn't been intentional, but their arrival date seemed wondrously fortuitous.

"We're halfway to Fortymile, son. Eight hundred miles behind us and eight hundred to go."

B.D. plopped down on a crate, his expression the epitome of glum. "I thought you said Skagway was a town."

"It most certainly is. Captain Billy Moore platted it himself nearly a decade ago."

The boy scrutinized the forested inlet where the mountain-born Skagway River poured into the serene, shallow bay. He shrugged. "I give up. Where the hell is it?"

"Right here, Barlow—"

"B.D.," he corrected. "You promised, remember?"

Megan graced him with a bogus smile. "As I was saying, B.D., we are, at this instant, smack in the middle of the gateway to the Yukon."

"If you're joking, it ain't very damned funny."

"Well, it's hardly Seattle, but Skag—"

"A log cabin, three tents, a couple of jackasses, and a pack of mangy dogs do not constitute a town."

"Maybe not in the lower Forty-eight, but it does in Uncle Sam's Attic."

"I want to go home."

"You are home, Bar—B.D. Now, stop bleating like a *cheechako* and let's pay a call on Captain Billy."

He crossed his arms on his chest. "I'll stay here. If I'm lucky, the tide'll come in and wash me out to sea."

She trudged toward Moore's sturdy home. Each step grated the cobbled ground like coffee beans in a mill. A canine chorus erupted from beneath the overhang where stores were cached during the winter. One black-masked brute gave her pause until his tail thumped an enthusiastic welcome.

The absence of any two-legged greeters piqued her curiosity, as did the lack of response to her knock. She rapped again, in case the seventy-four-year-old mariner's hearing had failed.

No sound came from within, save a clock's rhythmic tick. She eased the cabin's door open a fraction to call, "Captain Moore?"

A musty odor and smells peculiar to bachelor quarters assaulted her nose. The hair prickled at the nape of her neck.

Two decades hadn't dulled the memory of finding Finley James's corpse in a cabin in the Cassiars. Snowblind and exhausted, she'd bumped into a bunk containing a marblelike object. Her fingertips rambled across its smooth, frozen contours before meeting the wiry beard that framed them.

Megan scrubbed her hand on her trousers leg, just as she had back then. Why did incidents she'd sooner forget flash in her mind unbidden while a mental list of goods needed from the mercantile vanished without a trace?

She dreaded what horrors might await inside Moore's domain, but pushed the door and let it swing wide. Leather hinges groaned as sunlight fanned across the room.

Megan peered around the jamb. "Captain," she said timidly, "are you in there?"

B.D. brushed past, sending her heart catapulting into her throat. He gave the interior a once-over, announced, "Nobody's home," then stomped outside.

"Barlow David O'Malley, if you *ever* skulk up on me like that again I'll tan your hide for shoe leather."

He chuckled wickedly. "Oh, so it plays a mite different when it's you about to lose your water?"

She drew herself up to her full five foot two, her dark eyes boring upward into his matching pair. "It should, and you damn well know it."

A lopsided grin crawled across B.D.'s face. With shadows deepening the hollows below his cheekbones and the breeze ruffling his wavy black hair, the boy's resemblance to his father bordered on eerie. The fleeting collision of past and present sent gooseflesh rippling up Megan's arms.

His palm grazed her shoulder, breaking the spell. "I really didn't intend to scare you." In a blink, his puggish scowl returned.

Megan tucked away his brief gesture of affection like a petal from a corsage. The rift between them cut too wide to mend in a fingersnap. Faith that it would must sustain her during the healing process.

He jerked a thumb at the tents staked in a semicircle around a campfire. "Whoever those belong to vamoosed in a helluva hurry. Stuff's tossed every whichway inside."

"Native packers, I'd reckon. Captain Moore hires out Chilkat tribesmen for trail guides and freight haulers."

He grunted. "I don't give a fig to know why they and their boss squat on this godforsaken beach. Where the devil has everyone gone—and why?"

Megan couldn't divine a logical answer. This was no time for a harbormaster to gad about the countryside; not when his profits were limited to June through late August, when weather opened the northbound trails.

She'd seen no evidence of mayhem, but for Moore to abandon his dogs and livestock to starve or be slaughtered by roaming wolf packs defied explanation.

"I suppose he and his packers could have trekked to Dyea for supplies, then tarried longer than expected," she said, as much to convince herself as her son. "The settlement is only a few miles away and has all manner of stores, shops, and a trading post."

B.D. knuckled his hips. "Then why didn't we land there, for heaven's sake?"

"Because what the Chilkoot Pass from Dyea lacks in miles, it makes up for in treachery." She added silently, not to mention a tempting complement of saloons, fancy women, and roadhouses.

"Fine and dandy, but where's that leave us, besides stuck in a ghost town too creepy for the ghosts?"

Though loath to admit it, Megan was as eager to leave Skagway as she'd been to dock there. But to bolt like rabbits, ill-prepared, and scant hours before nightfall courted disaster.

"We've no choice but to partake of Captain Moore's roof, bundle our supplies, and ready ourselves to hit White Pass at dawn. If he doesn't venture home by morning, we'll leave a note to thank him for his hospitality and cash enough to pay for the mule we'll need."

B.D. stared at the mountains for a long moment. "Simple as that, huh? Just three kinds of jackasses striking out for a leisurely, eight-hundred-mile stroll to Canada."

She laced an arm through his and hugged it to her bosom. "To be sure, there'll be rough spots along the way, but nothing we can't overcome."

He wrenched away. Apprehension clouded his features. "You're crazy, you know that? Why can't you be like everyone else's mother? Have lady friends over for tea and sampler stitching? Picket the courthouse to harp about temperance or women's suffrage or the vote?"

She hooked her thumbs in her galluses. "Because I'm not built that way, Barlow David. Never was. Never will be. I'm a prospector. There's no cure for it even if I wanted one. And hard as you try to fight what you were born to and me along with it, so are you, me lad. So are you."

Chapter 5

"C'mon, Paddy, you walleyed slab of buzzard bait." B.D. yanked the mule's lead. His shoulders ached from pulling the pack animal along the trail like a hunter drags a deer carcass.

He glared at his mother, who was unhindered by a four-legged shadow, thus marching gaily along a hundred yards ahead of him. Her definition of female emancipation didn't extend to superintending a contentious mule.

The animal's temperament became evident before they departed Captain Moore's one-man metropolis. While B.D. lashed supplies to a pack tree astride its back, the mule cocked a forehoof to bludgeon his shin, nipped a peach-sized hole in the seat of his trousers, then loosed a stream of urine of sufficient volume to douse a prairie fire.

B.D. called the beast everything except a mule, with "son of a bitch" taking precedence. He gave serious consideration to its permanent attachment, then realized although Saint Megan could outcuss a sailor on shore leave when her Irish flared up, she'd never brook such a profane moniker.

The synonymous *Paddy* not only sufficed, it amused B.D. so much he almost shared his reasoning with his mother. Trouble was, she'd have perceived his sudden gregariousness as a back-door invitation to let bygones be bygones. Which they most certainly were not.

"Rebellion sure does get tedious after a while," he

muttered. He glanced over his shoulder at Paddy. "Present company included."

Their first hours on the trail, such as it was, proved easier than B.D. anticipated. Other than a mild tautness in his calf muscles, the gradual incline hardly rated notice. Captain Moore or some other thoughtful pioneer had even fashioned a corduroy bridge where the swollen, milk-colored Skagway River bisected the sodden track.

Midway across it, Paddy balked at the timbers' slight roll beneath his hooves. B.D. pulled, wrangled, sweet-talked, and cursed, then dropped the lead and clomped to the other side. The mule followed, its muzzle held as high and aloof as a thoroughbred's.

B.D. could also have done without the gnats and mosquitoes harrying his eyes and nose, but the loamy, spruce-scented wind and feeling the river's surge to the bay reverberate in his chest revived long-buried childhood memories.

Once upon a time, Alaska had been more than his home. The forested foothills east of Juneau were a panoramic playground with enough nooks and crannies and wonders to stoke ten little boys' imaginations. In the course of one morning, he could be a pirate gazing out to sea from a granite prow, an Indian stalking elusive game, and a bald eagle scouring the countryside from the uppermost boughs of a fir.

Jaysus, he thought, next thing you know, I'll be swapping hindsighted yarns with Ma like those scruffy jaspers she ran with in Seattle.

"Plan to knit a cap with all the wool you're gathering, son?"

Not ten feet away, Saint Megan was holding down a boulder with her backside and smirking to beat sixty.

"What'd you stop for?"

"That." She pointed up the trail. "And a breather before we scale it."

A slate-cliffed hill erupted from the flats like a crouched, surly monster. The gentle, broad-cut grade they'd traversed narrowed to a slick rock ledge no wider than Paddy's haunches. Just looking at it made B.D. suck in his stomach muscles.

"Best let that mule have his head," his mother advised.

"Yeah, he's probably gone through there before."

"There's that, but I don't want him giving you flying lessons if he slips. Neither of you'd be much good at it."

He dismissed her warning with a wave of his hand. "You want to stand around fretting about it or get it behind us?"

"No rest for the wicked, eh? All right, let's move out."

Being rather long-legged for a petite woman, she'd scaled the lip's edge before her command fully registered in B.D.'s mind. Guilt nibbled at its recesses.

She wasn't as young as she wanted to appear, but stubborn pride wouldn't allow her to admit her need to sit a spell. Not to him, anyway. God forbid he should think her cast-iron constitution had rusted a bit.

"Onward and upward, Paddy," he said, "or she'll stomp clear to Canada just to prove she can."

Within minutes B.D. was trying to convince himself that sidewalks weren't much wider than the ledge's steep confines. The comparison soothed his jangled nerves until he negotiated a series of corkscrew curves. He glanced to the right. His heart plummeted to his boots. One misstep promised a screaming, five-hundred-foot free fall to the valley below.

Cold sweat broke across his brow. He gritted his teeth and shuffled on; the scrape of his boots lost in the rasp of Paddy's packs abrading the slate bluff.

The higher he climbed, the more the wind buffeted his body, threatening to hurl him into oblivion. Just as he reached the limits of his endurance, the trail leveled for a blessed few yards, then tilted downward. He glimpsed his mother as she rounded a switchback. Fearful he'd blunder into her, B.D. dug in his heels to slow his pace. A nudge brought the realization that several hundred pounds of mule and provisions were now bearing down on him, rather than straining to ascend the grade.

"Want me to step aside?" he yelled. "If you're in such a hurry, go around, you rabbit-eared bastard. I dare ya."

An eternity later, solid rock relented to even, albeit boulder-strewn, ground where his mother perched as prim as a schoolmarm on a fallen tree.

"Fair stretch of the legs, wasn't it?" she teased.

"Try it with a mule at your heels sometime. Breaks the monotony of simply hugging a cliff for dear life."

He knelt beside the river and cupped his hands for a drink. The water benumbed his teeth, but tasted as sweet as nectar at his wind-parched throat.

"This is as good a spot as any to make camp, don't you reckon?"

B.D. squinted at the sun. "Why? It can't be much past midafternoon."

"Seven or eight in the evening's more like it." She ambled toward him. "Can't risk galling that mule by keeping him trussed up too long at a stretch."

"Believe me, I've threatened him with worse."

She unhitched their bedrolls and a four-cup, graniteware coffeepot. Without being asked, B.D. swung off what she called the lunchbox, formerly known as her small, camelback trunk. Midas hadn't guarded his treasure any closer than she hovered over the victuals it contained.

She went about her housekeeping chores on a flat, vacant area adjacent to the trail while B.D. removed the rest of Paddy's burdens, then led him to drink his fill at the riverbank. The animal brayed at the icy deluge B.D. sluiced over its back, but Saint Megan swore the ablutions would prevent pressure sores from forming.

Thoughts of supper in progress started the boy's

stomach rumbling. He figured his mother intentionally allowed enough hours between meals to stanch complaints about the menu: soda crackers, jerked beef, tinned beans, and raisins.

"Better than broiled rat," he told Paddy. The mule responded with a peevish switch of his tail.

To shackle an animal reluctant to do much of anything beyond inhale, exhale, eat, and crap seemed ludicrous, but B.D. buckled the leather straps around Paddy's forehooves. Saint Megan would ask if he had and she doused a fib easier than a forked stick detected water.

He sauntered back to the campsite, leaving the mule to graze. Flames had already devoured the tinder and licked at the dry wood teepeed above it. B.D. couldn't help but admire his mother's efficiency.

"You did shackle the mule, didn't you?"

His eyes rolled skyward. "Yes, Ma."

"Might as well pull up a stump. No sense standing when you can sit."

"I know. You said the same thing last night."

She bestowed a withering look, then continued to scoop coffee grounds from a cloth bag and dump them in the pot. When boiled to her satisfaction, the inky brew would pack nearly as much wallop as a jigger of Forty-rod. She prided herself on it.

"How far are we from Skagway?"

She peered past him, her mouth going askew and puckery as folks' did whenever distance was the subject of conversation. "Twelve miles—maybe fifteen as a crow flies. Truth is, we're not making as good a time as I'd hoped."

B.D. swiped at the mosquitoes whining around his face. "Think I'm dawdling, do you?"

"Saints preserve us, if you're not tetchier than that ugly mule. It's not your fault the trail's boggy and cooked as a dog's leg, nor did I say it was."

Well, excuse me to hell and back, B.D. thought.

One minute you peck at me for not talking, and the next you hammer me for trying to.

"I don't know, B.D.," she continued, as if he were bothering to listen. "The longer I ponder it, the more it rankles my mind."

Despite a decision to sulk in silence, her tone compelled him to prompt, "Such as?"

"What we encountered at Skagway. More to the point, what we didn't."

She handed him a can of beans with a spoon jutting from it and several strips of jerky. "The pass is churned and rutted like the cavalry came through last winter. And that strewn cache back at the horse bridge? I'd wager my last dollar that it was discarded long before the thaw."

B.D. gulped down a mouthful of the salty meat, the ragged edges scraping his craw. "What difference does that make?"

"The rush to Juneau ended years ago. All that's traipsed across this country since then is die-hard argonauts, Indians, and trappers. They know better than flirt with a mountain trail before snowmelt."

Supper progressed and ended without their exchanging another word. As B.D. blew across his second, scalding mug of coffee, he wished his mother had kept her worries to herself.

Whenever he'd been bullied at school or rejected by a pinafored girl of his dreams, Saint Megan had wormed details of his tragedy out of him with the assurance that sharing his troubles would halve them.

It hadn't seemed to then, but by golly, it was sure working now. Hard as he tried to let night-bird songs and the river's music distract him, her "ponderings" chased around in his head.

A hissing noise startled him. Whitish smoke seethed from the fire where his mother had flung the dregs from her cup. Apparently, she'd finished her chores without his noticing.

"We'll let it burn out," she said. "Maybe it'll keep the gallnippers from bleeding us dry while we sleep."

"I haven't hit the blankets before dark since I was in kneepants. It took me forever to drift off last night."

She smiled at him as if he were still a member of the sailor-suit set. "Keep feisting around until midnight and you'll walk on your knees before the week's over."

"Uh-uh. Well, maybe if you included water in your coffee recipe, I wouldn't be as blinky as a barn owl."

"Son, if you didn't have something to grumble about, would you grumble about that, too?"

"Judging by what I've heard, that should put you in mind of my dear old dead namesake, Barlow P. Bainbridge."

She blanched as white as her shirt collar. "He and I squabbled aplenty, but not for meanness's sake." Her voice wavered with emotion. "Never once did he hurt me like you just did. He doesn't deserve the insult and neither do I."

"Is that a fact? Then tell me what I've done to deserve getting hauled aboard a steamer, dumped on a deserted beach in Alaska, and made to hup-two from here to God knows where at your bidding?"

He leaned forward, the fire's heat matching the inferno raging inside him. "Ever try to compete with a couple of ghosts? Have the names of two paragons you never knew—never as much saw pictures of—stuck on you, then try to live up to their martyred memories?

"You tell me I look just like David Jacobs. That I talk like Barlow P. and have his horse sense. Fine. Great. All that means is I'm at best, half the man they were and just being me damn well isn't good enough."

"No, it doesn't—"

"The *hell* it doesn't. For all the proposals I know you've gotten, no man on earth has a prayer of replacing Jacobs and Bainbridge in your affections—including me."

"No, son." Tears coursed down her cheeks; the drops glistening on her mackinaw before the wool absorbed them. "I've loved you since before you were born and it's you that leaves no room for anyone else. I was wrong, I guess, to talk so much about Barlow P. and David, but it's kept them alive for me and I hoped it would bring them alive to you."

"Oh, it does," he said. "One squats on my left shoulder; the other on my right. I can't draw breath without feeling their weight."

"And you despise me for placing it there."

He shrugged. "Part of me does."

"What about the other part?"

"You're my mother. When I'm not so angry I could throttle you with my bare hands, I do care about you. Only your footsteps are impossible to walk in, too. So, what do you do? Cart me off to where you throw the biggest shadow."

Her dark eyes bored into his. The tears had dissipated and he was thankful they had. Some women turned them on and off like twin spigots, but not Megan O'Malley. Making her cry made B.D. feel more despicable than Padraic Cummins. Seeing that Irish glint return relieved his conscience.

"Tell me, then," she inquired haughtily, "have I once, in all your thirteen years, done anything to please you?"

"Yeah, Ma." He grinned and added, "Though not much within the last month."

Obviously his mother was in no mood for sarcasm, for she asked, "Would hightailing it back to Seattle make you happy?"

B.D. considered the question at length. Saint Megan hadn't cornered the market on stubborn pride. If he lied and said yes just to spoil her grand adventure, they'd be climbing that damned hill in reverse at dawn. But a no implied that while he resented her method, coming north wasn't such a bad idea. She'd trapped him like a hare in a gin and they both knew it.

"For the moment," he hedged, "a stroll up yonder followed by several hours between my blankets will do me just fine."

"We haven't settled anything."

"Nope."

"I can't promise you won't hear another mention of you-know-who."

"Wouldn't believe it if you did."

Raised eyebrows signaled her surrender. "Then I'll bid you good night, but do be careful traipsing around up there."

He dodged between boulders the size of steam locomotives, then headed for a stand of poplars clinging to the hillside. As he unfastened his trousers, he gandered around, then chuckled. "Yeah, well, old habits do die hard."

Above the splatter of evening dew came a rustle from the sprigged brush to his left. While B.D. hummed a few bars of "Beautiful Dreamer," a casual glance over his shoulder revealed precisely what he hoped—nothing. A bear, on the other hand, would have constituted something.

One balmy summer afternoon when a hungry grizzly lumbered into their diggings near Juneau, Saint Megan cut loose with both barrels of a .50-caliber shotgun. The barrage had only stunned the scavenger, but its report scared B.D. spitless.

His mother scooped him up and ran for their cabin, the enraged bear snarling at her heels. It had taken the combined firepower of three prospectors working a neighboring claim to kill the slavering beast.

A snort yanked B.D. back to the present. It wasn't easy to resecure his trousers and hasten to camp at the same time, but he managed. Any one of a hundred furry voyeurs could be watching me, he assured himself. Harmless, most of 'em, except to each other.

His mother's blanket-wrapped form didn't move a

muscle at his approach, but B.D. knew she wasn't asleep. Hens never dozed until their chicks were tucked in the nest.

He stretched out atop his pallet and clasped his hands under his head for a pillow. He stared up through a branched canopy, his heartbeat still thrubbing in his ears.

To hear his mother tell it—which he inevitably would, repeatedly—to sleep out under the stars was the jolliest of good shows.

Per the Gospel According to Saint Megan, having one's extremities lanced by insects and wondering what nocturnal, man-eating beast lurked in the bushes built the kind of character people accustomed to feather mattresses, window screens, and civilization in general could never attain.

He rolled over on his side. Aw, it's her skull-and-crossbones coffee that's got me jittery as a lawyer on Judgment Day, he thought. Damn stuff'd make a corpse jump to conclusions.

Chapter 6

The fire's pert crackle nudged Megan from a sound sleep. It should have died to embers hours ago.

She opened her eyelids a fraction. Flames scorched a pile of birch limbs' parchment bark. Beyond them, B.D. lay curled in his blanket like a katydid in a cocoon.

Her hand snaked between the folds of the mackinaw beneath her head. Her fingers closed around the short-barreled Colt's walnut grip. She silently thanked Peg-leg Hank for his hours of patient instruction.

Megan raised up cautiously and surveyed the campsite. Peaceful as a churchyard. Near the river, Paddy gnashed a mouthful of grass, yet his ears were cocked forward.

The Colt's cylinder clicked as its empty chamber revolved to position a loaded one. Megan held it at ready and crept toward the riverbank.

Paddy craned his neck. A wet sniff preceded him returning his attention to a spot sheltered by brushy outcroppings.

A droopy sombrero appeared to rest atop a pair of yard-wide, flannel-clad shoulders. The fabric strained around the intruder's forearms and across his back. He stood up gingerly as one did when knee joints must be coddled into cooperation. Their balkiness was understandable. The man was all of six foot eight and easily weighed three hundred pounds.

He started up the slope; an awkward, backsliding enterprise. River water sloshed from the coffeepot he carried. A pair of moccasins hung from his neck by their laces.

"Stop right there, mister." Megan aimed the pistol dead-square at the fourth button on his shirt.

A toothsome smile gleamed against his coal black skin. "Lawsy mercy, ain't it a beautiful mawnin', ma'am?"

Her mind went blank. She hadn't known what response to expect, but didn't anticipate a remark on the weather. "I—uh, yes, I suppose it is."

He crab-walked to level ground. "No need for that cannon you got. I don't mean you and the boy no harm."

"That's nice to hear, but how should I know if it's bona fide?"

His laugh rumbled like tenpins falling on hardwood. "Well, if I did, Saint Peter would've had to woke you up to usher you through them pearly gates."

She considered that and his gleeful expression. Big didn't necessarily mean dangerous. Fact was, most of the sidewinders she'd known were of the sawn-off persuasion. "I reckon tha—"

"What the hell's going on?" B.D. bellowed, rushing up behind her. "Who's the . . . Jay-sus criminy, Ma. You're packing a *gun*?"

"Simmer down," she said, lowering the Colt. "The excitement—little there was of it—is over."

The impulse to spin the cylinder to its empty chamber with the panache of a Wild West show's actor proved irresistible. B.D.'s chin dropped as far as his jawbone allowed.

"This gentleman will—"

"Gamaliel Ramsey, ma'am."

"Mr. Ramsey is about to put the pot on and tell us where he came from and why." She looked toward their visitor. "Isn't that right?"

"Yep, that's what I'm agonna do here, directly." He strode past and headed for the fire.

"Grounds are in the trunk," Megan called after him.

B.D. grabbed her arm. "You really are crazy, letting that hoss sashay into camp without a by-your-leave. And since when did you start carrying a pistol? Last I knew, you wouldn't touch one. Wouldn't allow one in the house."

"Let go of me."

"Not until you—"

"I am not one of your dock rat friends, Barlow David. Nor will I be treated like one."

He glared at her, but relaxed his grip.

Megan proffered a curt nod of appreciation. "I'm sorry your day began with a fracas, but as Mr. Ramsey said, if he wanted to hurt either of us, he could have before we knew he was about."

"Oh, so since we weren't murdered in our—"

"*Shut up and listen.* I do have a gun, he knows it, and if need be, I'll use it. While he's still drawing breath, we *will* give him a chance to explain himself and we *will* be civil for the duration of it. Do I make myself clear?"

If looks were bullets, the one her son bestowed would have riddled her with unnatural causes. "Yes, Mother."

"Then, let's join our guest before the pot boils dry."

He batted her gun hand. "Not yet."

A blistering retort dissolved into a sigh. "I'm a hypocrite to be sure. There, I've admitted it." She hefted the Colt. "Hard to believe something that doesn't weigh more'n a ripe melon could take your father and my best friend away for all eternity."

Her eyes searched his face. "But if it keeps harm from coming to you, it's worth feeling sick every time I touch it."

B.D.'s lips parted, then closed. She knew a thousand questions he'd never asked whirled inside him, but this wasn't the time to resolve them.

"Mr. Ramsey's waiting."

"I know, Ma. Somebody always is."

He struck off for the campsite with Megan close

behind. They found their guest sitting Indian-style on the ground. Both bedrolls lay atop the trunk; their ends cinched and ready to pack on Paddy.

Ramsey reached for the pot, poured two brimming cups of coffee and offered them up by their rims like a backwoods butler.

"No, thanks," B.D. said. "Stunts my growth."

Megan slipped the Colt's barrel inside her waistband. She felt like a second cousin to her old friend Wyatt Earp, but better to be cautious than stupid.

She squatted by the fire and lofted her cup. "Nothing smells finer than fresh coffee in the morning. Here's to you, Mr. Ramsey."

"It's me that's beholden, for not running me off." He took a sip, squinting against the steam. "And it'd please me no end if you'll just call me Gamaliel."

Megan's introduction of B.D. and herself brought a pensive expression to Gamaliel's blocky face. He snapped his fingers. "My, oh my, pinch me so's I knows if I'm dreaming. Ain't no way this ol' buck's palavering with the Angel of the Cassiar."

"That was twenty years ago, and I wasn't the only one who helped those sickly miners at Eight-Mile Creek."

"Don't matter how long it's been." He cocked his head. "You remember a fella, name of Jerusha Howell?"

Megan nodded. The image of the husky sourdough with scurvy lesions ravaging his body was vivid as the day she, Barlow P., Buckskin Pete Vladisov, and their native guides arrived at the stricken camp.

"Well, Jerusha and me worked together in a mine down in Dakota Territory. Him and a coupla others got caught in a cave-in. We prized Jerusha out, but he was busted up real bad."

Gamaliel's voice faltered. "Last thing he said was, 'If only Megan O'Malley was here, I'd get well.' "

"God rest him," she whispered.

B.D. ruckused around noisily. "Guess it comes as

no surprise that you're a miner. Ma attracts them like hummingbirds to a trumpet vine."

Gamaliel chuckled. "Ain't the easiest way to make a living, but it shore beats the cane fields. Got my fill of that ordeal when I was a little shaver afore the war."

"No insult meant," Megan said, "but you're mighty big for a pick-swinger."

"I'm a carpenter by trade. Mostly I hewed shoring timbers. Did some blasting, too, but there's something about being in a hole whilst you're blowing it to kingdom come that makes a man kinda jumpy." He winked at B.D. "Know what I mean?"

The boy frowned. "No, can't say I do."

"Sorta like you were up yonder in them trees last night. Lawsy mercy, I seen polar bears with more color to 'em than you had."

Megan took a demure sip of coffee. Her son's return to camp had seemed hasty, not to mention rackety, but she'd assumed it was intended to aggravate her.

"Jaysus, why didn't you say something, instead of just spying on me?"

"Figgered if I did, you'd keel over and die right there on the spot. Weren't totin' no shovel to bury you with, neither."

Judging by the angry flush rising on B.D.'s face, Megan thought it wise to change the subject. "So, where are you bound for, Gamaliel?"

"Same place y'all are, I suspect."

"Fortymile?"

He goggled at her then burst out in raucous laughter. "I heard you was a caution, Miz Megan."

She and B.D. exchanged perplexed glances. "I, uh, guess we missed the joke."

Seeing that she was serious, Gamaliel sputtered like a donkey engine running out of fuel. "You truly don't know nothin' about Dawson City, do you?"

"Never heard of it."

"Where'd you come up here from?"

"Seattle. We landed at Skagway the day before yesterday."

"That explains it. Dawson didn't get born till last fall. By the time word spread about the strike at Rabbit Creek, the rivers'd done froze. Quite a few hashed it afoot, but Old Man Winter put a kink in the grapevine betwixt there and the coast."

Megan shook her head. "You're either going to have to back up or slow down. I'm losing you in the fog."

His gesture at the coffeepot indicated a desire for a refill. At her smile, he began pouring and talking at once.

"Round the middle of August, Lyin' George Carmack paddled into Fortymile with his Injun brothers-in-law jabbering about a strike at Rabbit Creek. That's betwixt Fortymile and Ogilvie and pert near where the Klondike and Yukon rivers meet.

"Naturally, nobody believed him at first, but it turns out ol' Lyin' George weren't lyin'. It's on the wind that a steamer with a full ton of gold aboard left Dawson when the river busted up a coupla weeks ago."

He chortled. "Don't know if it'll drop anchor in Portland, Seattle, or Frisco, but every man and his dog'll know about Dawson City by the day after."

Megan recalled Swifty's remark about people needing a fracas or a frolic. How he, Johnny, Peg-leg, and several others were en route to Mexico, spurred by legends of a lost mine and determined to shake off their doldrums. The news of hundreds of thousands of dollars worth of dust snubbing up to a stateside harbor could surely do the trick.

"Cap'n Billy's happier than a goose in a millpond," Gamaliel continued. "After swearin' for ten long years that's there's gold in the Yukon Basin, the old salt finally proved right."

"You've seen Captain Moore recently?" Megan asked.

"Yeah, him and me and a bunch of Chilkats packed

a load into Skagway yesterday. Fine gent, the cap'n. He knowed I lost my grubstake in a crooked faro game the night before at Dyea. Give me a tow sack full of tinned goods on tick so's I could hit the trail north. Shoot, everybody livin' within five hunnert miles of Dawson last winter is already there."

Megan waffled between skepticism and excitement. The mother lode was the prospector's unicorn. No sourdough had ever seen one, but devoutly believed in its existence. Although billed as such, the California, Arizona, Nevada, and Dakota strikes were merely hoofprints. A genuine El Dorado had yet to be discovered.

Or had it?

She turned to B.D. "What's it to be? Back to Seattle, to Dawson City, or further downriver to Fortymile?"

"Why are you asking me? I didn't get a vote on coming here in the first place."

"Very well," Megan replied evenly. "Then I suppose inviting Gamaliel to come with us, if he's a mind to, is no concern of yours either."

B.D. sat up stiffly. "Now that's a horse of a different color alto—" His bray rivaled Paddy's for rudeness. "Hey, that's a good one. Bet ol' Gamaliel eats like a horse and you can't argue that he's . . . a . . . different . . ."

That her scowl muzzled her son in midinsult didn't lessen Megan's fury. "Pack up the mule. We've burned enough daylight."

"I didn't mean to—"

"Now, B.D."

He scrambled to his feet, muttered, "Beg pardon, Gamaliel," and stalked away.

Megan sighed. "Precious little compensation for bad manners."

"Aw, don't fret, Miz Megan." Gamaliel looked more embarrassed than she felt. "The boy does lean a mite toward sullen, though, don't he?"

"He hasn't always. I guess growing uppity is part and parcel with growing up. Leastwise it is in B.D.'s case."

"May be, but he shore ain't taken a shine to me."

Her lips curved into a wan smile. "He's too angry at his mother, the world, and himself to show much fondness for anything. Coming north was a gamble I had to take. I'd hoped the peace I've always found here might be visited on my son. Selfish, I reckon, but to mend what ails us, I had to bring him where I feel most at home. Truth is, we never should have left."

"Well, right, wrong, or indifferent, Miz Megan, y'all are back here now. And if you're sure it wouldn't discommode you overmuch, I'd be plum tickled to throw in with you."

She stuck out a hand. "Dawson or bust?"

His laughter startled the birds from their branches. "Lawsy mercy, I'm agoin' to the Promised Land with an angel by my side. Good omens just don't come no stronger than that, by cracky."

Chapter 7

The drizzle began two days later.

The sun, reduced to a glutenous yellow stain by clouds as dingy as old cotton batting, shed no more light than a candle in a cathedral.

Skagus, the Indian word for the incessant north wind from which Moore's bayside town derived its name, moaned through White Pass like a demon bent on driving intruders on its domain completely mad.

Megan, B.D., and Gamaliel trudged on. By no logical definition could the slough they followed be called a trail. They picked and stumbled their way over and around boulders, thanking God they had only two legs, while pitying the mule its four and the burden it carried.

At the crest of Porcupine Ridge, a ribbon-slender, nearly perpendicular aberration with corkscrew twists and turns, the prospectors had looked southward at the bluish hills guarding Skagway and the triangular slice of Lynn Canal's jade green waters that skirted them. The panorama's magnificence stirred their very souls. Yet B.D. spoke for all three of them when he said, "We shouldn't be able to see where we started from. It oughta be too far. Miles and miles too far."

To the north lay another hill, then another. Whether pushing upward or skidding down, they slogged through tree roots, thorny devil's club vines, and ankle-deep mud. Day after day, the rain-slick roller-coaster terrain tried their endurance; their strength of will; their courage.

At night, they huddled around a smudgy fire long enough to wolf down a meal. B.D. no longer complained about daylight robbing him of sleep. It was all he could do to keep his eyes open long enough to fill his belly.

Now as they ascended Summit Hill, Megan's lungs begged for more air than the thin atmosphere could provide. Canted forward against the incline with her chin on a plane with her knees, she counted each shuffling step.

At four hundred and nine, knifelike cramps ripped her thigh and calf muscles. Only five hundred and ninety one to go—give or take a few feet, she thought. Buck up, old girl. You're almost halfway to the top.

Because Gamaliel had learned on Porcupine that to look backward risked losing his precarious balance, at regular intervals he called over his shoulder, "Faring all right, Miz Megan?"

Her answer never altered from a lying, "Fine. You?"

"Strugglin' a bit."

She appreciated his honesty. A man his size forced into a dowager's crouch for hours on end must be in agony. Never before had her petite stature seemed such a blessing.

Megan sucked in a deep breath to continue their bucket brigade style of communication. "How about you, son?"

Silence yawned like the river canyon below before she heard B.D. croak curses and Paddy's hooves scrape stone. Megan tested a jutted root for soundness, then nestled her back in a crotch in the rocks.

A good twenty-five yards behind her, the mule let out a piercing bray. B.D. pulled with all his might on the lead. His heels backpedaled in place.

He bellowed in frustration and he hurled himself against the embankment, beating the wall with his fists. "The trail's too damned steep."

"Gamaliel," Megan yelled. "Paddy's played out."

A faint but fervent "Aw, shit" drifted from above. It expressed her sentiments precisely.

She grasped stobs and frail willow trunks to ease herself down toward her son. He sat slumped beside the panting mule; his mud-streaked face a picture of vexation.

Before she said a word, he snarled, "It ain't Paddy's fault. A mountain goat'd be hard-pressed to make it through."

"For heaven's sake, B.D. You're ungodly quick to get your hackles up before there's any cause to raise them."

"Yeah, well." He reared back to pitch a rock over the ledge. "Just wanted you to know he tried, that's all."

The animal's head hung so low its breath bored conical hollows in the chocolate-colored gumbo. Froth dribbled down its rope lead. Bloody rivulets seeped from gashes in its legs.

"You wondered why Captain Billy stocked mules," Megan said. "I reckon you know now. A horse couldn't hash it this far, much less to the top."

Gamaliel skidded to a halt behind her. "Question is, can we take on some of Paddy's load? The weight is what's swamped him and his feet's gotta be tender as boils."

B.D. grunted. "If our stuff's too heavy for a mule, how do you propose we carry it up there?"

"Real slow and careful, boy," Gamaliel drawled. "I suspect that working ol' Paddy to death'll kinda put a damper on how much he can tote anyhow."

B.D. shot him a scathing look. "You're about as funny as a crutch, you know that?"

"Been accused of worse." Gamaliel's cracked lips could still manage a grin. "Got a coupla rules I live by that my mammy taught me afore I shucked my tricornered britches.

"One, if you ain't got nothin' nice to say, keep your mouth shut until somethin' comes to you. T'other is that there's only two moods worth havin'—good 'uns and bad 'uns. Anything in-betwixt is jes' fence-straddlin'."

"By any chance," B.D. inquired, "was your mother Irish, too?"

Gamaliel laughed heartily for the first time since he'd thrown in with the O'Malleys. It did Megan's heart good to hear it.

"Lawsy, boy, you're a caution your own self when you want to be." He glanced at the mule, then added more soberly, "I reckon Paddy don't appreciate me doin' the hee-hawing, though. Let's get him unhitched afore he falls down."

While they accomplished that chore, Megan availed herself of a flat rock to rest upon. She figured Gamaliel would set aside the lightest items for her pack when he redivided the stores. If he tried, she'd divest him of that notion in a finger snap. Being female didn't excuse her from the hardships of the trail or the responsibilities thereof.

She blinked against the chill mist to stare at the track that seemed to ramble forever before it vanished into the cloud cover. How she'd bear up with an extra twenty-five or thirty pounds strapped to her back remained to be seen.

To have necked a sled across the Cassiars with four hundred pounds of provisions aboard paled in comparison. The mission of mercy had been fraught with danger and physically exhausting, but it was infinitely less taxing to pull weight over snow than pack it up a slope. Then again, much as it pained her to admit it, having celebrated only twenty-two birthdays at the time might have been a factor as well.

The clanks and rattles of supplies being flung to the ground brought her attention back to the men's labors. Gamaliel had repositioned her lunchbox and the heaviest bundles on the pack tree.

He clucked his cheek, encouraging Paddy's attempt to scale the slippery morass that held him captive. The mule lunged forward, his forehooves churning like pistons, then bogged again.

B.D. halved the load to no avail. Not until Paddy's back was free of everything but the trunk could he take a step without sinking to his hocks.

The onlookers had cheered the mule's valiant efforts, but realized the predicament it created.

"We can't haul that much in one trip," Megan said.

"No, ma'am, we can't. It'll take two, maybe three loads apiece."

"How about rigging a travois?" B.D. asked. "I've seen paintings of Indians dragging an entire village on them."

Gamaliel chafed his jaw. "That'd plumb be a stroke of genius if we was striking out across Nebraskie or Kansas."

B.D. drilled a boot toe in the muck. "Knew it was a stupid idea the minute I said it."

"Nope. Ain't a fraction as stupid as Ben Franklin fishin' for lightning with a kite string, but there's a passel of e-lectrificated city folks that's awful beholden he got a nibble of it that night."

The boy's frown relaxed to bemusement. "Then if the only way we can heft Ma's dry-goods emporium and mercantile store through the pass is by to-ing and fro-ing like ants, we might as well do it." He winked at his mother. "None of us is getting any younger, you know."

After fortifying themselves with jerky, cheese, and raisins, they left the mule behind to rest and forage. Gamaliel took up his seventy-five-pound pack. Megan and B.D. strained under a third as much.

Rather than ambulate in the traditional manner, mud and their added burdens fostered a gait similar to a dog dragging an injured leg to meet the good one. Despite Megan's wool mackinaw, the tins in her pack grated her spine like so many lead doorknobs. She tried wedging her hands under the tow sack, but came a whisker from sprawling facedown in the muck.

Is it a weak sister you are or a sourdough, she taunted silently. Why not give it up and let the men coddle your creaky bones to the goldfields?

Megan's fingers balled into fists and she jutted her jaw. She lost count of her steps during the delay with Paddy. She began again at one. The mental tally hardly distracted her from various self-inflicted tortures, but lent a measure of hope that her misery was only temporary.

What she couldn't track was time, though she knew several hours must have passed since they'd broken camp that morning. As she searched out the sun, she glimpsed another mountain's snow-patched flank looming beyond the trail.

Megan shagged a root, pointed ahead, and shouted to B.D. "Saints be praised. We're almost to the summit, me boyo."

He anchored his haunches against an outcropping and squinted in the direction she indicated. His grin faded immediately. "Look to the left, Ma."

She scrambled a yard or so higher. Gamaliel was rounding a bend in the accursed trail just short of the precipice she'd thought indicated its end. Rain pattered her face as she craned her neck to see where it led. Unless Mother Nature was playing yet another cruel trick, the crest of Summit Hill was still five hundred almost vertical feet away. And upon reaching it, they'd shed their packs and begin the descent to fetch the second load.

Megan released her grip on the root. She stooped over, adjusted her pack, and took a step forward. Through clenched teeth, she growled, "Fifty-one."

Chapter 8

Megan stared over the lip of the precipice. She swallowed hard to subdue the nausea inching up her throat.

Paddy's mangled carcass sprawled at the bottom of the canyon four hundred feet below. The mule's neck hooked around a stump; its body twisted in the opposite direction. Skagus had carried away the animal's screams, yet Megan could still hear them.

An arm hugged her around the shoulders. "He was just a mule," B.D. said. The quaver in his voice belied the harsh epitaph.

"How did he fall?" she asked.

"It happened so fast, I don't know exactly. His back legs must've slipped off the ledge, then his own weight pulled him over."

She shuddered. "Thank God you had time to turn loose of the lead."

The smashed trunk and its contents were broadcast down the hillside; most of it ruined and all of it irretrievable. Megan knew better than to pack their entire food supply in one container, but it was an egregious loss nonetheless.

B.D. urged her away from the grisly scene. "C'mon, Ma. We'd best move on."

Gamaliel gazed northward, his elbows propped on a pump-organ-sized rock, and hame-jawed face composed, but pensive. He must have heard their approach, for he said, "That crookedy track yonder is Cut-Off Canyon. From there we gotta climb Turtle

Mountain, cross the Tutshi Valley, then clamber up another mountain pass afore the land levels off considerable."

"How do you know the landmarks?" B.D. asked. "You told us you'd never been on this trail."

"I ain't, but I listen good. Them pioneers in Dyea laid out a pretty fair map with their bar-dog tales. 'Leastways, good enough to divine what's where."

He scratched at a scarlet welt on his neck. " 'Course, them callin' White Pass a highway to the goldfields is the biggest whopper I've heard since the carpetbaggers swooped down to promise us six hunnert acres and a plow mule."

"With that much hard road ahead," Megan said, "can we manage without Paddy?"

"Been cogitatin' that very thing. The boy's idea of rigging a travois is lookin' shinier all the time."

"We'll also be on short rations from here on out," she warned.

"When I left Skagway, I figured on shaggin' fish and pickin' berries for my vittles. Why, Injuns has tramped through here since afore Moses split the sea without nary a sack of meal nor a fryin' pan amongst 'em."

Megan squinted against the drizzle tickling her eyelids. Despite ongoing boundary disputes, Canada considered White Pass the threshold to its westernmost province. Whether Gamaliel and B.D. were aware of it or not, they were poised on the brink of the British Columbian wilderness.

The canyon stretching as far as the eye could see was little more than a winding, slender cleavage between mountain ranges. Snowy streaks and jagged shadows striped the pocked granite carapaces. Unruly battalions of trees marched the knife-edged ridges and fissures gouged by glaciers a millenium ago. Along an eastern slope, a family of mountain goats ambled along its sheer facade as nimbly as housecats pad across a porch rail.

The vista exuded a mystical, reverent grandeur. Its

majestic arrogance forbad trespass by the foolhardy, yet beckoned those courageous enough to endure its tyranny.

Megan scanned the horizon and realized she'd either forgotten or intentionally dismissed that in the hinter regions to measure distance in terms of mileage had no more meaning than to gauge seasons by a calendar. At most, only twenty-five miles separated them from Captain Moore's snug cabin, but a week had passed since she'd rapped on its door.

The splintered swath in the brush where the mule careened off the ledge sent a chill racking down her spine. The hardship and peril she'd already subjected her son to made her sensical reasons for leaving Seattle seem criminally nonsensical.

"It isn't too late to turn back," she said. "The way our luck's running, one of us might be the next to make the Grim Reaper's acquaintance."

"Uh-uh," B.D. said. "No way, no how. I didn't bust my tail to get this far just to about-face and bust it the same way twice."

"But we're still hundreds of miles from Dawson."

"So why are we standing around fussing instead of closing the gap?" he countered. "Jaysus, it was your lunatic notion to hie up here. It's not like you to just shrivel up and quit."

Megan knuckled her hips. "Who said anything about quitting? And since when are you hell-bent on getting to the Klondike?"

"Actually, I sort of surprised myself a minute ago." He shrugged. "I've been exposed to gold fever long enough. Maybe I finally caught it."

"Or maybe if I said 'up,' " Megan retorted, "you'd grab a shovel and start digging a hole."

"Could be."

Gamaliel cleared his throat. "If y'all is done tormentin' each other, I suggest we get off this here mountain afore winter sets in."

Megan glanced from him to B.D. "First man that

complains about the grub, the packin', or the rigors
will get his ears scalded."

"How about you?" B.D. teased. "Or is this one of
those women's perogatives that gives you the right to
change the rules as you see fit?"

She jabbed him playfully. " 'Tis the voice of reason,
I am—a devil's advocate. Every expedition needs
one."

"Yeah," he muttered, sidling away, "kinda like
every miss needs a mister."

Five days and twenty-five miles later, the trail
veered west and the mountains' jagged rampart re-
treated. The rain had finally ended, but beneath a canopy of spruce and hemlocks, the sky's clear blue was
only a backdrop for a kaleidoscopic array of
multihued greenery.

Moss-blanketed deadfalls humped the forest's dap-
pled floor like buffalo carcasses left to rot where
they'd fallen. A stringier variety of moss whiskered
tree branches, while a third draped itself in shapes that
eerily resembled stretched muskrat and otter hides.

Gamaliel, B.D., and Megan stood shoulder to shoulder, gripping the handles of their respective travois
and gawking at their musky surrounds.

The yeasty-sweet odor peculiar to decomposing veg-
etation wasn't unpleasant, but seemed to clog Megan's
lungs. Moisture oozed from lichens; their forms and
colors ranging from greenish doughy wads to crusty
layers that resembled peeled gray paint.

"Reminds me of bayou country," Gamaliel said in
a sepulchral tone. "Nary the only thing missin' is the
gators."

From the corner of her eye, Megan saw her son
glance about as if a snouted reptile might be sneaking
up unnoticed. "Spooky as hell," he said. "I didn't
know glaciers and swamps could neighbor one
another."

"Barlow P."—she snorted inelegantly, then blundered on—"he called British Columbia Mother Nature's kitchen, where she cooks up blizzards, volcanoes, swamps, earthquakes, floods, and all manner of calamities to serve up elsewhere in smaller portions."

"Not a bad analogy," B.D. allowed.

A hermit thrush's slivery music echoed from within the verdant cavern. Water droplets tatted Megan's head as a red squirrel with a spruce cone in his teeth scampered from limb to limb.

She took a couple of tentative steps forward. The spongy ground gave a mite, but after traversing miles of stony terrain, the buoyancy felt rather delightful.

"It's sound enough, I'd reckon," she said, "only I'd advise you heftier sorts to pay heed to where your feet are landing before you plant them."

"Listen to your mama, B.D.," Gamaliel stressed, probably due to the smirk on the boy's face. "Last thing we need is for you to bust a leg."

"Is that so? Well, I learned to walk without a father to tell me how and I damn sure don't need you bossing me like one."

A rude sucking noise disturbed the quietude as he stomped off. A rock bucked his travois sideward. He righted it without a backward glance.

Gamaliel spoke before Megan had the chance. "Don't go apologizin' for him, ma'am. Ain't no skin knocked off my nose. Fact is, I suspect you've waved the white flag at too many of his battles already."

Defensive remarks sprang to her lips. She shook her head. "I could argue, but I'd only be fooling myself."

He laid a comforting hand on her shoulder. "Ain't no cause to get daunsy, neither. Mamas is s'posed to take up for their cubs."

"They're supposed to teach them to fend for themselves, too. That's the part I can't muster very well, it seems."

Gamaliel indicated they should fall in behind the rapidly disappearing B.D. His throaty chuckle accompanied the swish of their travois across the sodden moss.

"Jes' goes to show," he said, "that acorn ahead of us didn't fall far from the tree."

"Beg pardon?"

"You and the boy. If y'all ain't thrashing each other, you're thrashing your ownselves for somethin' or t'other. Frettin'est white folks I ever did see."

"The bane of the Irish, I'm afraid. Our kith and kin are renowned as jolly warriors and melancholy balladeers." She smiled. " 'Tis hopeless we are, but nobody carries more hope in his heart than a Mick."

Gamaliel aimed a perplexed look at her. "Ma'am, if there's a lick of sense in what you just said, I ain't tasting it."

"My da told me you've got to be Irish to understand the Irish." With the tumbling brogue she usually stifled due to B.D.'s remonstrations, she recited Saint Donatus's beloved lines:

" 'Tis said that western land is of Earth the best,
that land called by name Scotia in the ancient books:
an island rich in goods, jewels, cloth, and gold,
benign to the body, mellow in soil and air.

The plains of lovely Ireland flow with honey and milk.
There are clothes and fruit and arms and art in plenty;
no bears in ferocity there, nor any lions,
for the land of Ireland never bore their seed.

No poisons pain, no snakes slide in the grass,
nor does the chattering frog groan on the lake.
And a people dwell in that land who deserve their home,
A people renowned in war, and peace, and faith."

A discomfiting silence fell over the marsh, broken only by the muffled sounds of their passage through it. The Celtic pride and pure joy that swelled within when she repeated the bishop's immortal stanzas yielded to embarrassment at having indulged herself.

Like thousands of greenhorns with naught in their pockets save lint, who held their dreams to their bosoms as tightly as drawstring bags of Irish soil, Megan knew when she left her homeland thirty years ago that she'd never return.

Her son was born an American, as was Gamaliel. Neither could, nor would ever understand why a resplendent, lilting tenor crooning "Danny Boy" brimmed every Irish eye with nostalgic tears.

"You're truly blessed, Miz Megan," Gamaliel said softly. The profound sadness etched on his rawboned features gave her pause.

"My front name comes from the Bible. The Ramsey's for the man that owned me. 'Twas born in Florida, same as my mama, but my gramma's in Alabama somewheres—or was, last we knew.

"Don't know much of nothin' about my daddy, 'cept that he was a big 'ol buck. Uppity too, I hear. He lit out north, but Mamma was too near birthin' me to go with him."

Gamaliel's chuckle was the kind people expel when they've revealed more than they intended, but can't stop themselves from making a complete breast of things.

"That's as far as it goes, Miz Megan. I don't know any verses 'bout Africans or which part my kin come from. Don't even know what kinda folks they was or if they's any left."

"Does it bother you?" Megan asked. "The not knowing, I mean."

"Never thought much about it till now." He swung wide around a squirrel midden; a knee-high mound of shucked spruce bracts where the creatures stored their winter food supply.

"Naw," he decided. "I reckon ignorance is kinda like

the cricks I get in my bones when winter blows in. Can't do nary a thing to change it, so there ain't much use in gnawin' on it just to pass the time of day."

"You're a smart man, Gamaliel."

His jubilant grin returned with a vengeance. "Well, make no mistake, you ain't half as dunce-headed as that boy thinks you is, either. He just ain't smart enough to know it, yet."

They tramped on in a companionable silence for an hour or more. As suddenly as a lantern brightens a cellar, the forest opened into a sunny, albeit moorish, clearing. An undulating, mossy carpet of pink bog laurel, blooming rosemary, yellow lousewort, and other dainty blooms surrounded the muskeg's dark pools. Stunted lodgepole pines with their branches contorted in macabre disarray sprouted every few yards like hobgoblins capering in a graveyard.

Megan's nose wrinkled at the strong odor of skunk cabbage; an aptly named perennial if ever there was one. The smell didn't appear to bother B.D., for he was squatted at the rim of the bog with a canteen in one hand and a piece of jerky in the other.

"Took you two long enough," he said.

"Had I known you were plundering the supplies, I'd have stepped along sharper."

B.D. wrenched a bite of meat from the strip. "Gee, Ma—" his lips smacked rudely—"growing boys do get hungry more than twice a day."

"And when they do, it's forever the choicest morsels they scrounge from the larder, too."

She turned to Gamaliel, who looked entirely too amused by her son's insubordination. "Do you want a proper dinner and a rest or should we push on?"

"If it's all the same to you, my druther's to keep on till we reach the lake. Me and the boy can net a mess of pike—"

"What lake?" B.D. asked. "And what are we supposed to do when we get there? Swim across?"

Gamaliel leaned over to stage whisper, "You didn't tell him, Miz Megan?"

"Tell me what?"

"No, I thought I'd cross that bridge when we came to it. So to speak."

"Oh-h-h, he ain't a-gonna like it."

"I damn sure don't," B.D. thundered, "and I haven't heard what it is, yet."

Megan winked at her coconspirator. "Nothing to raise a donnybrook over, to be sure. All we have to do is build a little raft, launch it on Lake Bennett, then sail a ways along the Yukon River to Dawson City."

The boy glanced from Gamaliel to his mother and back again. "A little raft, you say?"

"Just big enough for us three and our possibles."

"And we're going to float down the Yukon on it."

"Pretty as you please, my boyo. It'll be a grand ride."

"How far?"

Megan hedged. "Well, it'll take a few days . . ."

"How far, Ma?"

"Best I reckoned with an old map and a ruler, Fortymile was a scootch shy of nine hundred miles, so Dawson ought to measure about eight-fifty." Smiling sweetly, she inquired of Gamaliel, "Does that sound about right to you?"

"Pert near, give or take a mile or five."

B.D. grumbled around a mouthful of food, "Build a little raft, she says. Climb aboard and float what constitutes the length of California's coastline, she says. Why, nothing to raise a donnybrook over, she says."

He leaped to his feet and stuffed the packet of jerky and the canteen into his tow sack. "I take a notion to run away from home and what happens? I'm induced to shinny up and down a coupla mountain ranges. Ford the damned Skagway River a dozen times. Wade a swamp or two, meet up with a Nigra taller than a friggin' oak tree, and for a finale, I get to be Huck Finn of the Yukon, that's what."

Chapter 9

B.D. held the jerry-rigged rudder with one hand and flipped up his coat collar with the other. The north wind had a sharper bite to it on Lake Bennett than it had on the trail.

He shifted his feet to relieve the ache behind his knees. Standing in place to steer the raft was strangely similar to riding a horse, if he could only get the hang of letting his body sway with the current instead of fight it.

"Lawsy mercy," Gamaliel said yesterday as they water-tested their homely craft. "Ain't she a beauty?"

B.D. had regarded the eight-by-ten-foot shipwright's nightmare and reserved comment. But by golly, when Gamaliel played the line out a few yards, the raft bobbed gently atop the waves washing ashore. "I don't believe it."

The strapping Negro looked as happy as a kid with a puppy on a string. "You just gotta have faith, son. It's the onliest thing that'll get you through this life."

"It isn't faith keeping that rig afloat."

"Shore enough is. You didn't work like a fieldhand axing all them trees, nor lashin' 'em tighter'n ticks, nor chinckin' the cracks with moss for sport, did you?"

"No-o-o." Although watching his burly construction supervisor heft a half-dozen felled logs as easy as matchsticks did banish any notions he'd had of shirking.

"All righty, then. You prob'bly had doubts, but

'twas faith that you were doing the best you could that got the job done and done right."

B.D. knew when they'd shoved off that morning that being awarded control of the rudder was an honor. Saint Megan had certainly beamed approval when Gamaliel suggested it.

Of course with B.D. manning the helm—sort of— the passengers were free to loll against the bundled goods tied amidships and have themselves a jolly good cruise.

The stalwart navigator relaxed his vigilance long enough to regard his mother and the man seated beside her. B.D.'s grip tightened around rudder handle's sap-sticky breadth.

Gamaliel was smitten with her. During the days they'd spent camped beside the lake, subtle observations had changed B.D.'s suspicions to fact. Apparently she remained oblivious to the hound-dog eyes that followed her every move, but B.D. knew the symptoms of lovesickness when he saw them.

The very idea should have aroused his anger. What he knew about the Civil War and Reconstruction was gleaned from a history text, but three decades hence, any Nigra that dared make eye contact with a white lady on the street invited a flogging, if not worse.

Trouble was, B.D. liked ol' Gamaliel. Liked him better than any of the strays his mother dragged home from the Pioneers Club, and certainly more than prissy Harold Dirkson.

He surveyed the lake's choppy blue surface, but his mind stayed on the couple talking and laughing at the bow—assuming the term applied to a raft.

B.D. remembered reading a florid account in the *Seattle-Intelligencer* about a train trestle's collapse and the wreck resulting from it. One survivor, a seven-year-old girl, had been pulled from a burning coach unscathed, but sheer terror had turned her long black hair a permanent, snowy white.

He stared at the swath of ebony skin between the

brim of Gamaliel's sombrero and his flannel shirt and thought, if only you could believe half what you read in the newspaper. . . .

B.D. chuckled to himself. Nah. It wouldn't matter if by some miracle Gamaliel woke up a pure-de-albino tomorrow morning. Saint Megan needs a husband about as much as a lion needs a tamer and a cage.

The raft lurched forward as if propelled by an unseen hand. Gamaliel swiveled around and shouted, "Ain't no time to fall asleep at the switch, boy." He pointed toward the rapidly narrowing passage. "Canyon ahead."

A roar like unrelenting thunder rumbled in B.D.'s ears. The rudder jerked left, then right. He grabbed it in both hands, but gained scant control over the force of the suddenly raging current.

Along both banks, boulders and crags erupted from what had been strips of sandy beach a few heartbeats ago. Sheets of icy spray drenched B.D. to the skin. Water sluiced over the logs with every buck and swerve. Chunks of moss pried loose, washed over his boots, and disappeared in their wake.

"Tie up." Gamaliel tossed back one of the ropes they'd anchored to the raft's underpinnings. B.D. tried to catch it, but the line fell short.

His mother hollered, "Get a hold, or you'll slide off."

Afraid to let go of the rudder, he stretched as far as he could, reaching for the cargo rope. His fingertips grazed the prickly hemp. He couldn't get a grip.

B.D. squeezed his eyes shut and lunged. The raft bucked to starboard. His leather-soled boots skated over the humped logs. He clawed frantically for a hold.

An iron hand manacled his wrist. B.D.'s face slammed burlap. The raft settled into a trough with a *whump* that nearly ripped his arm from its socket.

He forced his fingers behind a cargo rope and hugged his body tight against the stacked bundles.

"We're 'bout out of it," Gamaliel assured from above him. "I won't let go till we is."

The current becalmed as quickly as it had kicked up. Behind them, the water's lusty roar diminished to a low moan.

B.D. climbed to his feet on legs as wobbly as a fawn's. He tasted salt and nuzzled his shoulder. Blood streaked the cloth. He almost laughed.

Once upon a time, for Padraic Cummins to bust B.D.'s nose in a saloon free-for-all would have seemed glamorous as hell. It didn't hold a candle to bustin' it while shooting a stretch of rapids. Better yet, that punk'd shit his britches at the mere thought of hurtling through a canyon on a raft.

Gamaliel peeled his fingers away. A row of ruddy imprints marked B.D.'s skin. "Hope I didn't hurt you tryin' to help you, son."

He flexed his wrist, stalling until the tautness in his throat eased somewhat. "All I can think of to say is thank you. Plumb pitiful, considering you saved my life."

"Aw, spared you a dunk in the lake, mostly."

"How about you, Ma? Appears you sailed through like a trouper."

She grinned as wide as a child. "Other than you scarin' the bejesus out of me, it was the grandest ride I've had in years." Her glance averted to their drenched supplies. "Except everything we own got soaked in the process."

"Yeah, well we may eat supper off the bottom of the lake if we don't pull in and replace those moss plugs," B.D. warned. "Water's splashing up from below on this side."

He took a step toward the rudder—at least, where it used to be. "Jaysus, the poor girl got her tail docked. How will we steer to shore?"

Gamaliel wrung the water out of his sombrero. "Good question."

"I told you boys to cut a barge pole, but you wouldn't listen."

"Oh, and it'd be a bare-knuckled cinch if we had one, too," B.D. said. "Hell, the water's only about thirty feet deep here."

Gamaliel sidled between the cargo and the raft's edge presumably to see for himself that the rudder was gone. The craft tipped sharply to port. B.D. and his mother skidded sideward, flailing for handholds. Gamaliel scrambled back to the center with surprising agility.

"Sor-ree. Didn't expect to cattawampus the whole shebang."

"I'm glad you did," B.D. said. "You solved our navigation problem for us."

Gamaliel brow furrowed. "I did?"

"I know what you're thinking, son. If he plants his weight in the right spot, the ballast'll turn us inland again."

"That's what I hope, anyway."

"Worth a try, but you runts'd best grab aholt of something stout afore I make a move."

Tacking crosscurrent without catching a swell and capsizing proved easier divined than done. The raft drifted a mile or more before its curving trajectory brought them within wading distance of the beach.

Gamaliel leaped off into armpit-deep water. "Throw me a line, Miz Megan."

B.D. feared the current's pull was too strong for even a man of Gamaliel's size. He snatched up a second rope and jumped in to help.

His feet smacked the cobbled bottom—which was about a foot further down than he was tall. He launched himself to the surface and broke through just in time to hear Saint Megan and Gamaliel laughing like front-row spectators at a Christy Minstrels show.

Cursing to himself, he dove under and fishtailed the length of the line, then tried standing again. The water lapped at his waist. And Mary, Mother of us all, was it ever *cold*.

"Funny, eh?" he sputtered, yanking on the rope. "Oughta flat be . . . a gut-buster when I . . . catch pneumonia. Serve you both right . . . if I up and . . . die on ya."

The raft scraped what might pass for sand in Canada, but was nearer the consistency of gravel with a full complement of rocks mixed in to ensure difficult walking.

Gamaliel swung Saint Megan from the raft as if her limbs were painted on. B.D. swiped the dripping hair off his face and bent to dally the rope around a stump.

Footsteps crunched behind him. "While I get the fire going," she instructed, "you shuck out of those wet clothes."

"I forgot to pack an extra breechclout."

"Oh, don't have a snit just because we chuckled a mite. You'd have done the same."

B.D. stood and crossed his arms at his chest. "Peculiar how being the one freezing my ba—er, my butt off effects my sense of humor."

"Well, at least you got a bath out of it. I'm so ripe I can hardly stand my ownself."

He glanced at the lake. "Don't tempt me, Ma."

"You wouldn't dare."

"Oh, how I wish you hadn't said that." He scooped her up in his arms and jogged toward the water.

His mother beating his chest with her fists, bellowing, "Put me down. Dammit to hell, I mean it. Put me—GAMALIEL!"

"Lawsy, what the—"

"Heel, big fella," B.D. warned. "I'm not gonna hurt her." He waded out thigh-deep and began swinging her like a babe in a cradle. "One . . ."

"So help me, Barlow David—"

"Two . . ."

"Please, please don't—"

"Thr—" He stopped in midswing. "Well, seeing as

how you said please, what's it worth to you to stay
dry?''

"That's blackmail."

"Yep."

"I won't—" A shift in his hold brought a high-
pitched, "All right, what do you want from me?"

He looked into those smoldering black eyes and answered softly, "Credit for having brains enough to
peel off my wet clothes without being told to."

Her mouth fell open. She blinked like an owl on a
branch. "That's the silliest thing I've heard in all my
born days."

"Think so? Then why didn't you tell Gamaliel to
shed his? He's as wet as I am."

"Because he's a grown . . ." She sighed, then
reached to caress B.D.'s face. "I understand, son.
Truly I do. But same as not mentioning certain names,
I can't promise I won't mother you too much sometimes, even when you're old enough to have children
of your own."

"Wouldn't believe it if you did," he said. He
wheeled to slosh back to shore. "Just wish you'd spoken your peace a tad quicker. If I don't shuck these
frozen drawers, you don't stand a snowball's chance
of ever being *anybody's* grandma."

Chapter 10

A rumbling sound chilled Megan to the bone. She'd cozened herself into believing the rapids they'd braved were a lark; a thrilling, brief episode of death defiance worthy of permanent record in her mental scrapbook. The chain of wind-spanked but serene inland lakes north of Bennett contributed to her hope that the worst was behind them.

But that ominous roar could not be denied. Nor could the black basalt walls closing in be dismissed as an optical illusion. Miles Canyon. Any prospector who'd roamed the Klondike had heard stories of its treachery, yet like other legendary landmarks, few could pinpoint its location.

Clarity wasn't sacrificed in their descriptions of running that soot-colored gauntlet and they never failed to mention that the canyon was but a prelude to a stretch called Squaw Rapids, which preceded the granddaddy of them all: White Horse Rapids.

Megan nudged B.D., who was slumped against the pile of tow sacks. "Wake up, son. I'm afraid we're in for it."

"Huh?" He smacked his lips, then regarded her with bleary, bloodshot eyes. "Whassa matter?"

"Miz Megan, I ain't likin' what I'm hearin'. You and the boy best saddle up."

Either B.D. heard the rumble or Gamaliel's warning, for he bolted upright and squinted into the distance. "Want to ride it out standing or sitting?"

"I'll stand."

Megan pulled herself up, wincing from the pain of ever stiffening muscles and joints. Her workload had been confined to basic housekeeping chores since they arrived at Lake Bennett, but fatigue plagued her like a convict dragging a ball and chain—an ironic analogy, considering the small pouch she'd concealed under her voluminous and insufferably hot mackinaw. The drawstring bag she'd fashioned from a cornmeal sack and lined with a scrap of oilskin contained their cash—in coin rather than vulnerable bank notes—the Colt, and extra cartridges.

While B.D. lashed her and himself to the bunkered towsacks, Gamaliel tied down the new, removable rudder he'd rigged. Her gaze met his and locked. His feeble attempt at a smile better resembled a grimace. "It's gonna be all right, Miz Megan. Me and the boy has got us an angel on—OmiGod . . ."

The river bent sharply left. A whirlpool caught the raft and spun it in a dizzying circle. Black rock flashed to blue sky—to black—to blue again. B.D. groaned and covered his mother's hand with his own.

They were forced from the vortex by the sheer velocity of the current. Cresting waves tossed the raft like a feather in a breeze. Megan ducked away from tree roots pinned against the gorge by the rushing torrent; the gnarled, woody claws as lethal as hawks' talons.

"Look out," Gamaliel hollered. He shoved B.D.'s head down a split second before the raft glanced off the cragged bluff.

A corner of the raft clipped a rock as it negotiated another hairpin curve. The momentum wheeled the craft half around. Now faced forward, Megan didn't have time to sound a warning before the gorge funneled to a thirty-foot width. Water churned through the bottleneck at breakneck speed.

By some miracle, the raft shot through the gap. It sailed airborne for a heart-stopping second, then nosedived. A wall of water broke across Gamaliel's back and crashed into B.D. and Megan.

Perpendicular cliffs gave way to a spruce-studded bank. A terrifying boulder-strewn obstacle course cleaved the soapsudsy current.

"Gamaliel," Megan yelled, "you've got to tack us through."

He fumbled with his safety line's knot. The wet hemp had pulled too tightly to pry apart. His hand whipped to his belt scabbard. Sunlight glinted off a knife blade.

"No!" B.D. shouted.

"Gotta."

Gamaliel sliced the rope in one stroke. He scooted to the side of the raft with nothing but a cargo line to hold on to. The raft tipped and took a sharp bank to the left. Its underside scraped over a partially submerged rock, but didn't hang.

"Center," Megan commanded, her eyes focused on several boulders clustered like eggs in a nest. "Left—now!"

Gamaliel zagged toward B.D. The boy grabbed for his sleeve and held fast. The raft skimmed past the deadly formation with an inch to spare.

"Back—go back," she shouted. "We're clear if we can catch this trough and ride it out."

As he complied, Megan offered up a prayer that she'd gauged the river's course accurately. She thought it had been answered when the foamy sluiceway hurled them past a field of jagged rocks. She allowed herself a sigh of relief.

It died in her throat.

A demonic pounding reverberated in her chest. The raft surged forward, swaying like a pendulum. Wave after wave crashed over the logs. Water swirled above Megan's ankles.

White Horse Rapids. God help us all.

The sloping shore whisked by in a blur; overhanging boughs near enough to touch. Churning whitecaps broke on all sides, swamping the raft only to heave it skyward again.

B.D. and Megan slammed together and lurched apart like rag dolls. The rope tether binding her waist felt as if it were sawing her in two.

A crosscurrent sent the raft careening broadside, the river alternately launching them free of its fury, then almost swallowing them whole.

Megan glimpsed a log shooting toward them from behind an instant before a spine-jolting drop into a trough. Sheets of water pummeled her, filling her nose and mouth. A swell vaulted the raft from the torrent.

She forced her eyelids open a crack. Not a log—a canoe. Headed straight at us. Crash. Going to crash.

A whitecap curled over them from starboard, shoving them into an enormous whirlpool. Spinning clockwise in its vortex, the current spit them out again into an eddy rotating in the opposite direction.

The canoe plummeted into the whirlpool. Its two oarsmen dug in against the undertow, battling its cyclonic whorl.

A leftward swerve wrenched Gamaliel from the pile of tow sacks he'd clung to. He staggered backward. His hands clawed at the air. He toppled into the water and disappeared.

The raft surged from the eddy, whipped sideward, then smashed into the rocky bank. Wood splintered. The deck cracked and split in half. The canoe skirred over the edge Gamaliel had fallen from only seconds earlier.

Megan screamed his name, struggling to loosen the safety line. Her vision fogged by the spray, she saw nothing but gyrating glimmers of aqua and white.

"Hang on," one canoeist yelled as he scrambled from its stern. "We'll help you."

Megan pointed to where Gamaliel had vanished. "Help him, for God's sake, before he drowns."

Both men leaped onto the beach; B.D. at their

heels. They clambered between and over boulders, following the shoreline's inward curve.

Megan kicked the stacked towsacks. Her waterlogged fingers were too numb to manipulate the knot. B.D.'s voice calling for Gamaliel echoed faintly over the splashing waves.

She swallowed the scream welling in her throat, prying and tugging until the rope's intertwined strands began to loosen.

A thud sounded behind her. The raft tilted sharply. Her feet slipped out from under her. She fell to her knees, shagging the rope and rolling sideways in the same motion.

"Miz . . . Meg—" Gamaliel collapsed, sprawled half on and half off the raft. His shirt hung in tatters. Blood streamed from a gash at the back of his skull. If she hadn't known better, she'd swear he'd been mauled by a grizzly.

Megan scooted beside him, anchored her heels against an outside log, and grabbed his belt in both hands. She pulled with every ounce of strength she possessed and lugged him aboard. Water gushed from his mouth, but he didn't regain consciousness.

"B.D.!" Get back here on the double!"

A hasty examination determined that Gamaliel's head wound was the most needful of immediate attention. His dark skin intensified the cut's gaped, rosy furrow and the ribbons of crimson pulsating from it. Megan wrung out her neckerchief, folded it, and clapped it to the gash.

White Horse may have chewed you up and spit you out, she thought, but I'll get you back on your feet in no time, old friend.

B.D. clattered to a halt near the water's edge. "How in the hell did he wind up here?"

"I don't know. All that matters is that he did."

B.D. jerked a thumb at the taller of the two canoeists. "He says they spied a cabin on the ridge just before the whirlpool caught them."

The man nodded a greeting. "Nathan Kresge, ma'am, and this is my partner, Nels Peterson. We're the sorriest boatswains this side of Pennsylvania, but stout enough to carry him to higher ground."

Megan scanned the slope. A footpath snaked down its brushy facade. "Big as he is, it'll be a trial hefting him that far."

Nathan eased onto the raft the same way a more youthful B.D. once scaled a seesaw's beam. The former daredevil and Nels Peterson followed suit.

"Ma'am, if you'll lead the parade," Nathan said, "we'll follow as quickly as we can."

Despite the gravity of the situation, Megan smiled at the young man. Never had she heard a request to get out of the way spoken with such tact.

She removed the blood-soaked compress and rinsed it in the river. "Kindly raise his head a fraction so I can bind that cut."

Her crude attempt at first aid accomplished, she sidled past the litter-bearers. B.D. squeezed her arm gently. "Don't worry, Ma. It'll take more than a bump on the noggin to kill that ol' hoss."

She waited on the bank, watching the three young men grapple with their heavy burden. Having rolled Gamaliel onto his back, Nathan and Nels interlocked their hands beneath him to form a human sling while B.D. positioned himself between his legs to yoke his ankles.

Gamaliel's head dangled like a caribou tied to a tote pole. Megan considered trying to cradle it in her hands, but feared the pressure might increase the bleeding.

She hastened to the top of the hill and jogged toward an elongated, roofless log structure surrounded by a moat of tree stumps. "Hello the house."

A scarecrow-thin man clad in a grimy Union suit and knee-high rubber boots leaped out the door, gawked at her, then raised his face and arms to the heavens.

"Thank you, Jee-sus," he bellowed. "It sure took You a spell, but my prayers have been answered."

"You asked Him for a bust-up on the river?"

His joyous expression wilted. "Is that what brung you here?"

"Afraid so."

A bushy eyebrow shot up. "You're posi-lute-ly sure you ain't one of them Divine Interventions Reverend Throckmorton jabbers about?"

"It's sorry I am to disappoint you, mister, only my friend's hurt pretty bad and we need your help."

His bony shoulders sagged. "Just my luck to ask for a sweetheart and get a damsel in—" His hands fluttered every which-way, then he whirled and sprinted into the building.

Above its topmost log, she saw his fiery red head advance to a corner. He vanished for a moment, reappeared, retraced his steps, and burst out the door, adjusting the straps on a pair of bibbed overalls.

"A thousand pardons, ma'am. I done forgot myself in the excitement." He stared past her. "Hmmm. That big galoot looks plumb temporary, all right."

Megan glanced over her shoulder. B.D.'s teeth were bared and his neck corded from exertion.

"Tell them fellers to lug him inside to my bunk. Won't be the first time a saloon's doubled for a hospital."

"Thank you, Mr. . . . ?"

"Plew James the Second. Comes for having a mountain man for a grandpap and a pappy too scared of him to flout tradition."

Megan provided her name, then relayed James's instructions. Sweat flipped off B.D.'s chin when he nodded.

James's rickety cot was shoved in a corner and ringed by splayed books, dirty dishes, and tin can spittoons. Without a by-your-leave, Megan snatched it away from the walls and smoothed the moth-riddled blanket. "Don't turn Gamaliel loose till we're sure this contraption won't collapse under him."

From shoulders to knees, the canvas bound him like a split sausage casing and his lower legs splayed over the dirt floor. He was shivering so hard, his teeth clacked.

"We must get him warm," Megan said and started unbuttoning his wet shirt. "Mr. James, I'll need all the blankets or tarps you have. Nathan, Nels, stoke the fire and put the kettle on to boil, please. B.D., I believe there's a spare shirt in his pack."

"Good," he said. "We'll see to Gamaliel while you fetch it."

"What do you know about caring for an injured man?"

B.D. pulled her away from the cot. "More than you're going to know about this one."

Megan stamped her foot, struggling against his hold. "He doesn't have anything—"

"I know, Ma." B.D.'s voice raised to a singsong brogue. " 'Tis true, I've nursed men, embalmed them, fed them, scolded them, acted as Mother Confessor, and fought my own with them and nary a one has anything I haven't seen a hundred times before."

"There, you have it."

He hustled her across the room. "And out you go until you're sent for."

Megan's Irish temper fueled her feet. Gamaliel's pack banged her shins at every stride as she maneuvered through the stump-littered yard.

Plew James slouched in the doorway of the saloon. "Where's the fire, ma'am?"

She motioned for him to step aside. "Excuse me, please."

"Huh-uh. Not till your boy gives the word."

"This is an outrage."

"Less of one than a lady sashaying where there's a fella stretched out as nekkid as the day he was born."

"Jesus, Mary, and Joseph," she said, her tongue dicing each syllable. "It's women that are supposed to be champeen prudes."

The stogy he gnawed on twirled between his lips. "Well, I can assure you, Megan ol' pet, that ain't the area of his anatomy that's keeping me here, and you there, for the time being."

A feeble groan sounded from within.

"Damn your skinny hide, if Gamaliel dies—"

Plew tut-tutted in a most patronizing manner. "Oh, now, if that's what's put the bees in your bonnet, let 'em fly away home. He looks like the business end of a meat grinder, but no bones are broke."

"How would you know?"

"Used to be a taxidermist by profession," he drawled, "before I became a wastrel by choice. Didn't take long to get more pro-ficient at my avocation than I ever was at my vocation."

Megan couldn't check her bemused smile. Hard as she tried to stay angry at their gristle-and-guff host, his patter had a certain charm to it.

"You're not spoofing me, are you? About Gamaliel, I mean."

"No future in it. If I did and he made a liar out of me by pro-ceedin' to expire, you'd tear into me like a wolf on a moose calf."

Plew grinned around his cigar. "Any ol' girl that ain't inclined to marry me, I ain't inclined to let bury me. Fair enough?"

B.D.'s snide tone intervened. "C'mon in, Angel. Gamaliel's ready to be tucked under your wing."

Plew bowed and stepped aside. "My castle is your castle, ma'am. For how-some-ever long you need it."

Megan hurried over to the injured man. With blankets and hides piled atop him from chin to knees, he resembled an enormous upended turtle.

His puffy eyes were open and he did his best to greet her with a smile. "Same as I told these boys and Mr. James, I'm powerful sorry for all the trouble I'm causin'."

"Hush that silly talk. Taking care of one another is what friends are for."

Steam wafted from a dishpan beside the cot. The clean rag folded over its rim garnered her approval. Beside it, strips torn from Gamaliel's ruined shirt had been rinsed out and piled in a crockery bowl of bandages.

"We looked him over and washed what's not showing," B.D. informed. "He's scraped and bruised to beat Billy Thunder, but that conk on his head is the worst of it. Left it for you to minister to."

"No tenderness about the ribs?"

"Lord, yes, he's tender—nose to toes. But no pain in his chest when he breathes. Honest, Ma, me and the others poked and prodded every inch of him."

"When Gamaliel's fit to live, it's you three he'll have to thank for it."

"Not hardly," Nathan said, "since we're the ones that got him hurt in the first place."

She flinched as she wrung scalding water from the rag. "True enough, you and Nels won't be giving canoe lessons to the natives anytime soon, but Gamaliel fell in before you crashed into the raft."

"Tried to tell 'em that, Miz Megan. Thought I was home free till we smacked that second eddy. It knocked me Virginny reelin', for sure."

"Well, Hoss," B.D. said, "unless you need us to protect your virtue, Plew told us we'd better unload the raft and pry the canoe off it before everything floats to Dawson City without us."

"I've heard all of that song I care to, B.D.," Megan warned. "Do as Mr. James says and be quick about it."

He snickered and started for the door. "Plew did have another suggestion, Ma. Actually, it's closer to an order."

"Oh?"

The wastrel piped up, "I guess you plan on bunking here until morning?"

Unsure of the intention behind Plew's inquiry, Megan replied, "Yes, if it's agreeable to you. Soon as

I see to Gamaliel, I'll rustle up a hearty supper for everyone in exchange."

"Sounds like an even swap. Then I'll escort you to the Throckmortons' cabin and bid you good night. Wouldn't be seemly for a lady to sleep here with us gents, don'tcha know."

She eyed her son, the canoeists, and Plew James in turn. Intuition told her a conspiracy had hatched while she retrieved Gamaliel's pack.

Scruffiest flock of mother hens on God's green earth, she thought. And it won't do a lick of good for me to start squawking, either.

"Who, might I ask, are the Throckmortons and what makes you think they'll take kindly to boarding a stranger?"

Plew grinned as wide as the devil himself. "Well, now, they're the reason I'm building my saloon here. The Reverend and Missus T. are Church of England missionaries and were plumb devoid of sinful behaviors to preach against until I happened along. Fine folks, mind you. Just turned a mite strange. He's tighter than bark on a tree and she's . . . well, *fervent* is the best word for it, I'd reckon."

Megan had encountered her share of evangelists and gotten along with all, save one, but Plew's description left her on the low side of eager to make the Throckmortons' acquaintance.

"You'll be more comfortable in their cabin than here, Ma," B.D. wheedled. "No sense denying that you're tired to the bone, either."

"I won't." She dabbed Gamaliel's wound with the rag. " 'Long as you don't deny that the whiskey, cards, and stogies are due to appear about five minutes after I'm tucked in at the parsonage."

B.D. sputtered, "How in blue blazes could you possibly know . . . ?"

Plew burst out laughing. "She didn't, kid. In poker parlance, you've done been bluffed by a gen-you-ine slicker."

Chapter 11

Megan awakened to the same monotone that had lulled her to sleep the night before.

Mrs. Throckmorton, who apparently surrendered both her first and maiden names at the altar, sat slumped beside the hearth reading Dante aloud, and in the original. Megan assumed the missionary had retired during the wee hours, but neither her posture nor her endless literary recital lent any indication of it.

A survey of the parsonage found no sign of her rheumatic, Moses-bearded husband. For that Megan was thankful. The reverend's raisin eyes and hawklike demeanor were more disconcerting than his wife's passion for brimstone prose.

To say he'd welcomed Megan to their humble abode would strain the Ninth Commandment. Her stogy-chomping escort's probable disregard of all ten didn't raise Megan's estimation in Reverend Throckmorton's eyes either.

Upon giving her a grim once-over, the missionary asked, "Do you know Jesus?"

"I do," Megan replied, "though my faith does portend a closer acquaintance with His Mother."

Plew's cigar had gyrated and he chuckled his approval.

By the harrows etched around his mouth, Reverend Throckmorton hadn't cracked a smile for a half century and had no intention of gracing a Catholic with one. He'd jabbed a forefinger at a straw mat in the corner, the poor box nailed inside the door, then whisked past them, muttering, "I will not burden you with listening to my evening prayers."

"Hospitable, ain't he?" Plew said. " 'At kind of fervent's enough to make a heathen hope there's a heaven waiting him on the other side. 'Course, the idea of a huge flock of Throckmortons roosted there already don't give much incentive for going, neither."

Now, while Megan yawned herself fully awake, she stretched this way and that to work the kinks from her muscles. The log parsonage's dearth of creature comforts certainly testified to her hosts' devotion to penury.

Eating utensils consisted of a knife, two tin plates, and an iron cup. The three packing crates and an empty nail keg that sufficed as furniture reminded Megan of the squalid San Francisco flat her sister and brother-in-law once occupied.

Except circumstances forced Frances and Oran's temporary decline to a hand-to-mouth existence. And there hadn't been any notions of piety expected or gained from it.

Takes all kinds, Megan thought, easing from beneath the threadbare blanket. Mrs. Throckmorton took no notice of Megan folding it neatly atop the mat, gathering her belongings, or the hard coin's thunk into the alms box. Save the birds' songs and the river's hum in the distance, no sounds of civilization intruded on Megan's stroll from the parsonage to Plew's saloon-in-progress.

Plew's concern for wild animals invading his premises was evinced by the wide-open door. "B.D.?" she called softly. "Mr. James?"

"They's all down to the river," Gamaliel drawled from within. "Nobody to home 'cept puny ol' me."

Megan tossed her possibles on a bench drawn up to a table. The lack of a roof hadn't dispelled the reek of raw whiskey, cheap cigars, and wet wool.

A twine clothesline sagged across one end of the room. Apparently the men had thrown their wet garments at it, rather than exhaust themselves draping each article over it.

The cot had been shoved back into its corner. Gamaliel sat propped against the wall, his jowls as droopy as a kicked pup's.

"And how are you faring this grand morning?" she chirped.

"Tolerable well." He picked listlessly at the blanket wadded beneath him. "Head's pounding like a smithy's anvil. Breathin' deep sends a hurt clear to my heels. There's this stitch in my side that's pesterin' me fierce. But other'n that, I'm jes' dandy, ma'am. Don't you fret for me."

His mournful list of miseries was so similar to an elderly dowager's "organ recital," Megan had to stifle a chuckle. Had the good Lord erred and given Adam a womb, Cain would have been an only child.

"I'm a-thinking what pains you most is being stuck here by your lonesome," she said.

"Hmmph. Ain't too stove-up to help mend that canoe, shore enough. Don't take much to spread pine-pitch over holes, you know."

She gestured for him to lean forward and unwound the bandage that encircled his head. The gash was free of pus; the skin around it swollen, but not inflamed as it would be if infection were setting in. Nor did her fingertips detect any hint of fever.

As she rewrapped the wound, she said, "I never hung out a shingle, but I've done plenty of doctoring in my day. You're healing nice enough, but your skull has a dent in it big enough to put my fist in."

"Yeah, that's what B.D. told me."

Wriggling into a comfortable slouch, Gamaliel nodded toward a barrel-back chair. "If you ain't in no hurry to run off, I s'pect we got some talking to do."

"Oh?" The four oak legs plowed furrows in the dirt floor as she dragged it beside the cot. "Is something wrong?"

"Nah, we just gotta agree on changin' our plans a

mite. Now I don't mean to tell tales outta school, but Nels and Nathan has got your boy chompin' at the bit to get on to Dawson City.

"Turns out that Nathan's a geology student from a highfalutin Pennsylvania university. Got a headful of book learnin' he's determined to put to use. B.D.'s eyes almost frogged outta their sockets just listenin' to them three-dollar words Nathan was spittin'."

"More power to him," Megan said, "especially if it means an end to B.D.'s grumbling."

Gamaliel grinned. "If their plans don't get scuttled, you won't hear it next time he grouses anyhow."

"I don't understand."

"Them three hooligans thinks they can flimflam you into staying here with me, whilst they set-paddle for Dawson to make their fortune."

"The devil you say?" Megan snorted. "And I suppose they were counting on you keeping their scheme a secret?"

"Lawsy, ma'am. Them boys and Plew was having such a rollickin' ol' time spending money they ain't even made yet, they done forgot I was here."

"Take heed then, my friend—B.D. is bound to pitch six kinds of screaming conniptions when Kresge and Peterson pull out without him, but we'll simply have to endure it. You're in no shape to ride a raft downriver and won't be for several days."

Gamaliel's fingers drummed his thigh. "Finally we're comin' to what really needs the palaver put to it."

"Which is?"

"You and B.D. leavin' me here to mend and goin' on with—"

"Absolutely not."

"Kinda expected you'd say that, Miz Megan. But seeing as how I did some serious thinkin' about this, would you hear me out?"

"It won't change my mind."

"Prob'ly not. I just figger if a man thinks real hard

on somethin', he oughta get more out of it than a headache."

"You're right. The least I can do is listen."

He racheted a bit straighter on the cot. "I'm told the raft got smashed to kindling. If'n us three sticks together, we'll have to build a new one afore we can go anywheres. I don't begrudge the work, but it'll be a day or two afore I'm up to it. Add a couple more to finish the job and we're lookin' at squattin' on Plew's property for pert near a week."

Megan bemoaned the thought of boarding with the Throckmortons for that long. Between the reverend's dour silence and his wife's monotonous diatribe, Megan would be a raving lunatic in half that time.

"On the other hand, them boys' canoe is big enough for you, B.D., and most of the provisions. Makes better sense for you two to head on to Dawson City whilst I swap out my board helping Plew roof this place. Shouldn't be no problem for me to hitch a ride later on a mail scow or supply steamer."

"If B.D. and I join in the barn raising," she argued, "the three of us can go north together."

Gamaliel's frustration was evident. "I ain't tryin' to tell you how to raise your son, Miz Megan, but just once, wouldn't it be wise to let his horse lead the parade 'stead of yours?"

Chapter 12

Megan floated downriver, her arms winged on the canoe's gunwale in blissful repose. A folded blanket atop a scrap of oilcloth provided a dry, padded seat for the journey. Piled tow sacks supported her back as comfortably as a parlor chaise.

She'd rarely spent any waking hours—much less three days' worth—with nothing to do beyond watching the world and the clouds above it drift by. Expecting her enforced leisure to ignite a serious case of the fidgets, she was astonished by how quickly she'd become as carefree as Cleopatra aboard a barge.

Nels and Nathan, her trusty oarsmen, allowed the current to carry them along at a spirited pace. B.D. knelt behind Nels at the bow, his gaze continually sweeping the gray-green water for submerged boulders and deadfall. Megan wondered if the serious young Swede had guessed that her son's diligence came from a sore desire for a turn at captain.

Her contented reverie ended when B.D. informed over his shoulder, "Batten down, Ma. Whitewater ahead."

The words were no sooner spoken than she felt the current quicken. Plew had told them the Five Fingers and Rinks Rapids lay midway between his town site and Dawson City and swore they "were tame as porch dogs" in comparison to White Horse's heart-stopping stretch.

Megan gripped the gunwale and hoped the saloonkeeper wasn't prone toward understatement.

The canoe cut its share of didoes as it danced through the frothy rapids, but other than getting soaked to the skin in the process, Plew's description proved accurate.

Nathan chuckled. "No hill for us climbers, eh, Mrs. O'Malley?"

She squirmed around to peer over the supplies. "Haven't I told you a dozen times that Megan will do? The other makes me feel older than Methuselah's grandma."

A toothy grin gleamed against his sunburned skin. "I'll try, ma'am, but my mother's such a stickler for comportment, she'd swoon if she ever heard me address a lady of maturity in the familiar. The instant she recovered her wits, believe me, there'd be hell to pay."

"It's none of my business, but how did your mother react to your traipsing off to the Yukon?"

Nathan removed a hand from the oar handle and scratched at his whiskers. The downy sprigs didn't show much promise of ever becoming a proper beard and at this stage only made his face look in need of a good wash.

"I can't say for sure, since bravery took the hindmost to self-preservation," he admitted. "When Mother found the note I left, every neighbor within hollering distance probably knew the gist of it before she reached the 'Love, Nathan' part."

Compelled to defend a sister-in-maternity, Megan replied, "It's a scoundrel you are, Nathan Kresge."

"So I've been told, ma'am. On numerous occasions."

She settled back into her cozy nest recalling the stormy scene that preceded B.D.'s jamb-rattling exodus from their Seattle home. He'd done his level best to cut her apron strings permanently, whereas Nathan had judiciously untied them.

Their methods differed, but there must be something inherent in those of the male persuasion that

unless distance was put between them and the women
who bore them, they'd spend their lives as mollycod-
dled sissies.

Megan chuckled softly. Come to think of it, every
milksop she'd ever met had been either uncommonly
fond of his mother or excessively afraid of her. But
Jesus, Mary, and Joseph, she thought. I didn't raise
that boy to hang off my arm like a reticule for the
rest of our natural lives. Other than himself, there's
no one on earth that wants him grown and gone more
than I do.

"In due time, of course," she murmured, then
smiled at her own hypocrisy. "And not a moment
sooner."

She'd been too busy woolgathering to notice waves
slap the hull or the canoe's curve toward shore. A log
trading post squatted amid the trees a hundred yards
from the water's edge.

"Is it a free meal you boys are after or to get shed
of the last one?"

Lord only knows, she added to herself, if there'd
been room enough for a backhouse aboard, we'd have
made Dawson City before sundown last night. Apparently, Plew's home-cooked hootch packed a unexpected wallop.

B.D. swiveled on the balls of his feet. "If you must
know, it's both. Any objections?"

Megan puckered her lips and looked skyward.
"Well, now, best I can figure, it's almost the end of
July and we're no more than a couple of hundred
miles from Dawson." She paused, tapping a finger
against her chin. "Yes, even at this rate, we should
make it before the September freeze-up."

The canoe juddered with Nels's and Nathan's laughter, but it was obvious that her son found scant humor
in the remark.

"Glory be," she said, "if you're not giving a fine
imitation of Reverend Throckmorton's scowl. Cheer
up. Life's too short to spend it all pickle-pussed."

"Far as I'm concerned, there hasn't been a short day in the lot since we left Seattle."

The canoe tipped with his abrupt return to position. "Nor will there be, as long as that chip's gouging your shoulder."

"Damn it, you just always have to have the last word, don't you, Ma?"

A kinder woman would have let matters rest. Megan couldn't resist adding, "Yes, son. I reckon I do."

It came as no surprise when their craft's hull scraped ashore that Nels's hand was the one extended to assist her. The flaxen-haired young man had enough compassion to grimace at the crickety noises emitting from her joints.

She smiled up into his owlish blue eyes. "May ye live long enough to feel the years in ye bones, me lad."

"It sounds kind of painful."

"No worse than a skeeter's bite." She squeezed his fingers before releasing them. "And a far sight more tolerable than the alternative."

They started after B.D. and Nathan, but all four halted abruptly when a lithe native woman bore down on them waving a pair of small freshly laundered flour-sack drawers.

"Mika coolie." Her shooing gestures served as a translation. *"Mika coolie—scat."* Her waist-length hair fanned out like glossy black wings, but her squared features were as rigid as bronze marble.

A barrel-chested, brown-haired man lumbered out onto the porch. "Simmer down, Kate. If you're determined to hang something, please start with the wash."

She stalked away, the tone of her mumbled comments lending a definite blue shade to the syllables. Megan didn't need familiarity with Kate's native tongue to know a cussing when she heard one.

"Sorry to tell you, folks," the man said, "but this post is closed. We moved to Fortymile last spring, then

Dawson City. Only came back to gather the treasures I left behind."

"We're more in need of stand-up time on solid ground than anything," Megan said.

"I know that feeling, sure enough." He staggered when a copper-complected cherub poked her head between his legs and wrapped her arms around his knees.

The little girl's bowed lips parted in a sunny smile and she giggled at her own orneriness. *"Klahowya,"* she chirped. *"Klahowya—klahowya—klahowya."*

Her father tapped her gently on the head. "That's enough how-do-you-dos, Graphie Grace. Go help your mama."

Obviously delighted by the suggestion, she waddled off the porch with the slewed, flatfooted gait common only to the very young and the elderly.

"Your daughter is the most beautiful child I've ever seen," Megan said. "She'll break hearts long before she's old enough to know why."

"If her antics don't stop mine from beating first, Miss . . . ?"

"O'Malley." She promptly introduced B.D. and her soggy travel companions.

"That name is the stuff of legend here in the Yukon, ma'am." He tugged an end of his droopy moustache. "I'm not the kind to blow my own bugle, but I suppose George Washington Carmack is, too, or soon will be."

"Lyin' George?" B.D. blurted.

"I've been called worse," Carmack replied drolly. "And I'll admit a growing fondness for King of the Klondike."

Megan's toes curled inside her boots. "Then the rumors are true?"

"Beyond any sane man's wildest dreams, ma'am. As a matter of fact, a dream started it all."

Her mind spun with a hundred questions, but B.D.'s

scornful attitude toward prospectors' yarns made her hesitant to ask them.

Darned if B.D. didn't pluck the words from her own mouth when he said, "I'd give my right arm to hear the story straight from the horse's mouth—that is, if it wouldn't be a bother."

"A bother?" George echoed. "Why, do you think John the Baptist ever tired of telling people about the loaves and fishes? Bonanza Creek is the closest this orphaned son of a forty-niner will ever get to a miracle."

He waved them inside the trading post. "Coffee and a piece of floor is about all I have to offer. As soon as my brother-in-law arrives, we're gone for good."

"I've never turned down a cup of coffee in my life," Megan said. "And a floor without water gurgling under it sounds grand."

Like cowhands around a campfire, the visitors piled down in a semicircle between the dusty counter and the hearth while their host pawed through a carton to retrieve four dented tin cups and a cracked shaving mug.

Nathan whispered to Nels, "Professor Glenhaven is going to pop his garters when I turn in my thesis report. To take a sabbatical and stumble onto an honest-to-God gold rush is beyond belief."

"Sabbatical, my eye," Nels said. "We're going to be rich, partner. Why even go back to school?"

"Ignorance is far from bliss, gentlemen," George said in a lecturing tone. "I was eight years old when the Transcontinental Railroad's spike was driven at Promontory Point. An amazing achievement then, but who could have imagined the advent of submarines? The telephone? Airships—even a combine harvester?"

While three youthful pairs of eyes exchanged impertinent glances, Megan looked at the thigh-high, string-tied bundles of *Scientific American* magazines and *Review of Reviews* lining one wall. Pyramids of leather-bound books with gold-embossed titles bunkered an organ resting whomper jawed in the corner.

"Does your wife play?" Megan asked.

"No, she just plays hell when I do."

Distributing the tinware among them, he reserved the soap receptacle for himself. "As soon as Graphie Grace can reach the pedals, I'll start teaching her musical scales."

"That's quite a handle for such a tiny girl," B.D. said.

Carmack's nose wrinkled when he sucked down a mouthful of coffee. By the bubbling ring inside the mug's rim, dregs of its original purpose remained inside.

"Her mother is Tagish and I never could pronounce her tribal name to her satisfaction, much less our daughter's. Rather than be lambasted every time I tried, I call my wife Kate and changed Ah-gay to Graphie Grace after a character in a book I admired."

A lump formed in Megan's throat, unbidden. Her misty gaze traced B.D.'s face; his coloring and angular features familiar, yet unique unto himself.

"I've only known one other man who held books in such high esteem that he'd call his private library his treasures," she said softly.

"I couldn't discard them, that's for sure. Kate and her brother Jim think I'm crazy. We're rich, they say. I can buy a shipload of books with the profits from one day's diggings and likely will, but new isn't always better."

"What type of gold deposit did you strike, Mr. Carmack?" Nathan asked.

"Once the men I hired burrowed down to bedrock, the hundred-and-fifty-dollars-a-pan kind, mostly. Some washed a bit fatter and some leaner, but it all started with just one shotgun cartridge full of flakes."

Megan set her cup down on the puncheon floor and leaned forward eagerly. Nels, Nathan, and B.D. were all but drooling for George to continue.

The King of the Klondike's twinkling blue eyes tacked left to right. His brushy, dog-tail mustaches failed to hide a widening grin.

"It's a cruel man you are, George Carmack," she teased. "You've got these poor lads wound tighter than a two-bit watch."

"All right then, hard as it is to believe"—he winked at B.D.—"what I'm about to tell you is the God's honest truth. On a clear June night one year ago, I dreamed I was sitting on a creekbank watching grayling struggle up the rapids. Lo and behold, a monstrous king salmon armored in gold nuggets shot upstream in their wake and scattered the smaller fish.

"At the time, it seemed reasonable to interpret my vision as a sign that the fishing would be exceptionally good—a matter of great import to we who depend on the river's bounty for sustenance.

"My brother-in-law, Skookum Jim, and his nephew, Tagish Charley, agreed to accompany me on the expedition, thus we proceeded up the Klondike River. Now, I've dabbled at prospecting since I arrived here in '85, but thoughts of gold never crossed my mind, nor can I explain why we put in at the mouth of Rabbit Creek to wander inland."

George smiled and shook his head. "Why we slogged through the muck despite swarms of gnats and mosquitoes hectoring us to the brink of madness defies explanation, as well. We did, however, until darkness prevailed on us to make camp."

"That's when you found the mother lode?" Nels prompted when the storyteller paused an instant to inflate his lungs.

"Purely by accident, I assure you. Jim was rinsing a dishpan when he spied flaky slabs of rock in the streambed. Gold was wedged between the layers like honey in a biscuit."

Carmack motioned to Megan. "If you dipped a pan in a stream and washed out pay dirt, how much would it take to bring tears to those lovely Irish eyes?"

"Back in the Cassiar, a nickel pan got me dancing a merry jig. With a purse not stretching nearly as far these days, I reckon a ten-cent pan'd do it."

"And a full quarter ounce?" Carmack asked. "In a single pan?"

"Why that's—that's four dollars if it's a penny," she wheezed. "I've only swooned once in memory, but I'd wilt like a lily in the desert at the sight of it."

"Four dollars' worth?" B.D. said. "Doesn't sound like much of nothing to me." He pointed at his mother's prized calf-high leather boots. "Bet those godawful clodhoppers cost more than that."

Megan fumed silently, *as a matter of fact I paid five and change for them*, but devil take me if I'll admit it. Instead, she admonished, "Glory be, son, have you forgotten all you ever knew about prospecting?"

"I was six years old, Ma. How much do you expect me to remember?"

Nathan cleared his throat. "No disrespect intended, but could you two quit squabbling so Mr. Carmack can continue?"

Megan felt her cheeks flush with embarrassment. "My apologies for the both of us."

"Accepted," George said, "though unnecessary since I'm wedded to the queen of Cain-raising. Kate scared the liver out of Ed Conrad last winter. He heard her screams and came a-running to prevent murder from being done. Ed didn't know that yowling like a tomcat is just Kate's way of getting my attention."

Nathan prompted, "I take it that you and your comrades wasted no time staking your claims."

George signaled a pause while he emptied his frothy brew in one gulp. Megan sat back, sucking in her cheeks to keep from laughing at the beads of perspiration glistening on the other listeners' brows.

The soul of a thespian lurked in any born prospector and George Washington Carmack was no exception. Surrounded by an entranced audience, he'd milk every drop of drama from this, his life's one sweet moment of grandeur.

"On the seventeenth of August, eighteen and ninety-six, to be exact," he began, "and a Monday, as I recall, I whacked the top off a spruce tree, squared its stump, and penciled a notice of discovery on its meaty white interior. We then stepped off Number One Above Discovery for Skookum Jim, Number One Below for me, which was my rightful due as original claimant, and Number Two Below for Tagish Charley.

"The three of us, staggering like giddy drunkards without benefit of spirits other than joy, took to the river to spread the news to all we saw on the way to Fortymile to register our claims at Acting Commissioner Constantine's office."

"Jaysus criminy," B.D. said, "if I'd found that much gold, I'd have clamped my mouth shut so tight, folks would have thought I had lockjaw."

When Nels and Nathan added muttered agreements, Megan asked, "Oh, is that a fact? You'd have filed your discovery and secondary claim and left no one the wiser."

"Damn straight, I would. Any recorder's office has bales of registries that never wind up paying squat."

"And what then would you have done with your blinking fortune, son? Gold makes a poor meal and you couldn't spend an ounce of it without raising suspicion. Ask Mr. Carmack if you don't believe me—to scrape it out of one hole only to cache it like a miser in another is plumb foolishness."

B.D. favored her with a well-practiced scowl. "I wasn't hankering after a civics lesson."

She bit back a sarcastic reply, preferring to enjoy her victory. Her son had been known to argue until the veins blued at his temples, but did on occasion have sense enough to realize when he was licked.

"Sad but true," Carmack said. "A stranger's opinion is always easier to swallow than a mother's or father's. Yet hogging a bonanza *is* a fool's paradise for another simple reason: Canada's Dominion Lands Mining Regulations permit any miner over the age of eighteen to stake a claim, but unless he's the discoverer and allowed two, the rules are strictly one per customer. Plus, had I laid claim to another parcel in the Yukon district sixty days before our find at Rabbit Creek, Commissioner Constantine wouldn't have allowed me to register it at all."

Nels poked Nathan with an elbow. "Think of it. We'd faint dead away if we were paddling along and got word that a bloody fortune awaited around the next bend."

"Even if the town crier was known far and wide as Lyin' George?" Carmack's throaty chuckle held a twinge of bitterness. "I'll admit I did expect a warmer reception than the one we received at Fortymile."

"No one believed you?" Nathan asked. "That's incredible."

"Once my wounded pride had a chance to scab over, I better understood their skepticism. Rumors take wing faster than snowbirds in this country and ninety-nine-point-nine percent of them are pure hooraw. I should know. I've chased after a few of them.

"When Jim and Charley and I waltzed into Bill McPhee's saloon all big-eyed and blabber-mouthed, an ancient mariner named Salt Water Jack duly announced that Rabbit Creek wasn't rife with rabbits, much less gold.

"Another said the valley was on the wrong side of the Yukon. That it was too wide to contain gold-bearing bedrock, and furthermore, the willows didn't lean the right way. Finally Cannibal Ike declared our claim site to be nothing but moose pasture—the ultimate disparagement."

This time, his shoulders shook when he laughed. "The marvelous irony of it all is that they were right. No sourdough worth his salt—myself included—would have given that swampy, insect-plagued, sultry slice of hell on earth a second glance. But to three fisherman searching for a monster king salmon's lair, it was, no pun intended, a dream come true."

His listeners hardly blinked for a long moment, unwilling to break the spell he'd created and giving what they'd heard a chance to take root in their minds.

"Judge!" Kate hollered from the yard. Her exasperated tone indicated that it wasn't the first summons she'd issued. *"Mika chako tika mika."*

George whispered, "Obviously, I'm not the only family member who can't wrap my tongue around a foreign name."

He frowned as he gained his feet to answer his wife's summons. "Kate doesn't deserve that kind of behind-the-hand teasing," he said, as much to himself as his guests. "Neither the Tagish nor most of the coastal tribes can pronounce the letter *r.*"

"J-u-udge!"

"I'm coming, dear."

Nathan slapped his knees. "Don't know about the rest of you, but I'm itching to get to Dawson City more than ever. What say we avail ourselves of the post's facilities, break a snack out of our stores, and hit the river?"

All three young men scrambled up and raced out the door, leaving Megan to stare after them. Unsure how to dispense with the cups they'd drunk from, she put them on the counter beside George's. Considering the Carmacks' newfound wealth, they were all likely destined for the burn barrel. She was a yard shy of the threshold when George bustled back inside and bumped into her.

"I do beg your pardon, ma'am. I wanted a private word with you and almost trampled you in the process."

"What about, Mr. Carmack?"

"Well . . ." He shuffled in place, then glanced over his shoulder. "I intentionally ended my story somewhat short of its conclusion. Perhaps I shouldn't have, but I just couldn't bring myself to knock the stars from your son's and those other two fellows' eyes."

Megan's belly constricted as one's does whenever it's clear that very good or very bad news is in the offing. She let her expression ask the obvious.

"Because you're a pioneer—a mining expert, some say—it shouldn't surprise you to learn that every claim along Rabbit Creek, which I renamed Bonanza Creek and a rill branching from it called El Dorado, were staked within a fortnight of my original discovery."

"Every single one?" she inquired with a gasp.

"For all the naysaying at McPhee's saloon, those bar-dogs knew by the color and consistency of my ore sample that it hadn't come from Indian, Miller, Glacier, or any of the creeks they'd panned for years. One boat after another snuck out before darkness fell. By the next morning, nothing that'd float could be found at Fortymile."

George shook his head slowly, as if he still couldn't quite grasp the rush one cartridge casing full of gold had ignited. "Before week's end, Joe Ladue had loaded a raft with dressed lumber and floated his entire sawmill from Ogilvie to the confluence of the Yukon and Klondike rivers. Ladue platted town lots and streets, threw together a combination saloon and living quarters, and named his instant boomtown Dawson City after George M. Dawson, the Canadian geologist.

"I've never seen anything like it before, Miss O'Malley, and never expect to again. The frontier grapevine roared as loud as a high-ballin' locomotive. All last winter, men walked, sledded, even crawled to Dawson from every direction. Even they were too late. Other than some fractions that fell open after a survey last January, those creeks' claims were spoken for a year ago."

Every negative emotion known to the human heart stabbed at Megan's like blows from a dagger. She didn't have enough money to return to Seattle on. No hope of claiming a piece of what might well be the richest chunk of real estate in the world. B.D.'s distrust of her was only beginning to fade. He'd never believe she hadn't known about the original strike and had stolen him from his home just so she could say she'd been a part of the biggest gold rush in history.

"What you're telling me is that we'd better turn tail for Skagway before the river freezes over."

"By reputation, I don't think it'd do any good if I did."

She graced him with a feeble smile. "Yours? Or mine?"

"Dear lady, it wasn't me who once told an interfering army captain where he and his troops could go and precisely how to get there."

"If not to discourage me," she asked, "why did you bother giving me chapter *and* verse?"

"Two reasons. The first, because you're the one who'll have to comfort those young men when they find out the golden goose is barren. As for the second, it's rankled me for quite a spell to leave this snug cabin to fall to ruins.

"But I promised Kate, Graphie Grace, Jim, and Charley that we'd winter in Seattle—live it up like the kings we're supposed to be. Our passages are already booked on the *Roanoke,* but in the meantime, if you're interested, I believe I can persuade those bull-muscled Indians to disassemble this edifice and float it to Dawson City."

"What would I do with it? I'll tell you for true, I don't have enough to buy that counter over yonder, let alone the entire building."

"Open a store—a flop house—a saloon, for all I care. When we return next spring, I'll collect a fair share of your profits in rent. Good Lord, do you think I don't know you nickle and dimed every miner in the Cassiar to help fund the Sisters of Saint Ann's Hospital in Victoria?"

"But that was twenty—"

"Proverbs 11:25," George interjected. " 'He that watereth shall be watered also himself.' I'd be honored to provide that dousing in return, if you'll accept it in the spirit with which it's given."

"I—you—glory be, how could I refuse something all prettied up with a ribbon of Scripture?"

"You can't," he said. He steered her toward the door. "Now before those gold-fevered lads shove off without you, I'd say we should make haste for the bank."

Megan broke into an awkward trot to keep pace with his strides. She glimpsed Kate and Graphie Grace and waved good-bye, but the flailing gesture probably looked more like one of surrender.

As they approached the canoe, George rattled off further instructions at a dizzying clip. "Seek out Minnie Walentine's boardinghouse in Dawson, so I'll know where to find you when we arrive with the cabin. Joe Ladue won't be back in town for a while, but he won't mind my commandeering a vacant lot. Just relax, familiarize yourself with Dawson City, and don't worry about a thing. I'll see you in a few days."

"Jaysus, Ma," B.D. said, "you look as green-gilled as you did after we smashed the raft."

"I-I suspect I do."

"Well, it's smooth sailing from here on to Dawson City," George assured her. A glance at Kate, who stood on the porch with an unmistakable warpath expression on her face, started him backpedaling.

"Unless you put in at Fort Selkirk," he said, "you should be in Dawson City by midday tomorrow."

"Thank you, Mr. Carmack," Megan called. "For everything."

He blocked his wife's line of vision with his body, but waggled a thumb in her general direction. "Uh, don't mention it, Miss O'Malley."

Megan assured him with a subtle nod, then turned to board the canoe. Her head spun from the events of the last couple of minutes and she faltered, hopping away from the craft with the grace of a one-legged turkey.

"Ma . . ."

"I *am* hurrying, B.D."

"No, hold up a second, will you?"

"Why?"

"I just want you to do something for me." He cupped her elbow and escorted her several yards away from the canoe.

"For heaven's sake, what's this all about? Nathan and Nels are fawnching to shove off."

"We're not more than a couple of hundred miles from the mother lode, right?"

Megan hesitated. "I suppose you could say that . . ."

"And Nathan and Nels were already partners when we met them, right?"

"As I recall, they joined up before they left Pennsylvania. Why do you ask?"

"Because that's what I want from you, Ma. A partner's handshake. Same as you'd give any other man."

"Lord above, Barlow David, wherever do these foolish notions come from? You're my own flesh and blood!"

She started for the canoe. "C'mon now, we've kept the others waiting long enough."

B.D.'s lips flattened into a thin, pale line. He brushed past her; his reckless leap behind Nels almost capsizing the top-heavy craft.

Chapter 13

I can't fathom why the Yukon River isn't named The Republican, B.D. grumbled to himself. It's damn sure crooked as one, rambles on forever, and appears to be going nowhere.

At times, the water's surface tricked him into believing they were either not moving at all, or drifting backward, and the wooded shoreline offered few landmarks with which to gauge their progress.

Now and again, native fishermen whisked past in animal-skin canoes. The fresh-netted fish heaped from stem to stern exuded an oily stench that lingered long after the slap of paddles faded away.

The Indians' stoic expressions didn't reflect the size of the bounty they transported. To catch, dry, and hoard enough food for a village's winter survival was serious business. The one quirk the white man possessed that natives could not understand was his impetuousness. Old-timers knew better than to trust Providence to provide sufficient nourishment, but every spring the frozen, emaciated remains of fools who'd disregarded their dire warnings were found in barren shacks and along creekbanks.

A few boatloads of that breed had sailed past them, too. They stared straight ahead, setting their oars with military precision like last-place skullers determined to cross the finish line, but knowing full well the race's spectators will have all gone home before they got there.

A string of low-lying islands, as gnarled and narrow

as an ancient pianist's fingers, broke the river's monotony somewhat. Stands of spruce and white birch trees dotted the archipelagos. When B.D. realized he was entertaining himself by counting them, he questioned his sanity. Only a lunatic would try to decipher distance by the number of trees he passed by.

He knew his restlessness came from anticipation, but like a doctor's diagnosis, to recognize a condition did nothing to alleviate its symptoms. His mother's attitude provided secondary aggravation. Saint Megan hadn't noticed that her only issue hadn't spoken to her since they left Carmack's trading post. Revenge tasted not a bit sweet when its object remained oblivious to it.

After darkness had forced them onto a beach for the night, B.D. had coerced Nels into remarking on his ill humor and inquiring why he appeared upset. Nathan, who hadn't been coached, offered an opinion that B.D. must be worried about Gamaliel, but shouldn't be, since his overnight partnership in Plew James's roadhouse would surely reap easier dividends than panning for gold.

Throughout the discourse, Saint Megan, the soul of single-mindedness, ogled the cookfire as if her ears were stuffed with cotton wool. It hadn't taken a genius to see that something was gnawing at her craw, too.

B.D. altered his position in the bow to relieve the numbness in his legs. *Like I give a rat's ass what she might be fretting about. Sure as milk makes butter, it's a maudlin memory of the good old days when Bainbridge and Jacobs were alive, and I wasn't.*

"You're not getting sick, are you?" Nels asked over his shoulder.

"Never felt better," B.D. said. "Why?"

The bemused Swede swung his paddle to his right. "My Aunt Lorraine gets dyspepsia. All that grunting you're doing sounds as bilious as she does."

B.D. cuffed Nels's arm. "Keep it up, Peterson, and you'll be wearing that oar like a tail."

"I'll thank you to stop the horseplay," his mother commanded from her amidships throne. "Capsize this canoe and I'll take a switch to the both of you."

Would the woman never learn? B.D. mused. To dump her in the drink for the sheer hell of it hadn't occurred to him until she suggested it. And the threat of a few lashes with a birch rod sure wouldn't stop him if he were so inclined.

"You're grunting again," Nels singsonged.

"Shut up and row."

"For Dawson City?"

"Aw, it's such a lovely day, why don't we drift on down to Frisco? Or better yet, Mexico. It's warmer there, I hear."

Nels speared the air as they rounded a bend. "But *that's* where the gold is, my friend."

B.D. leaned to his right to see around Nels's blocky blond head.

A flotilla of docked steamers appeared to shepherd a jumble of boats, skows, rafts, and canoes onto a marshy beach. Dingy canvas tents and log buildings of every size and description littered a humpbacked rise overlooking the river.

Above Saint Megan and Nathan's excited yammering, B.D. asked, "You sure this is Dawson City?"

"It about has to be," Nels answered.

A crude, wood-whittled rendition of what B.D. assumed to be a fish rested on a tall pole sunk in the bank. Best he could tell, it was supposed to act as a wind vane, except its head was aimed due west, whereas the wind whistled along from the north.

Shorter posts supported a line of boxlike affairs and halved boats clam-shelled atop each other. Regardless of design, a homemade ladder canted against each structure. Their resemblance to photographs of Indian sky graves gave B.D. the willies until he recalled the cache he and his mother had built at The Thimbleful to protect their supplies from foraging animals."

Passengers streamed down two riverboats' gangplanks and were immediately swallowed up by the crowd milling on the bank. The newcomers laughed and gestured eagerly, but the resident congregation seemed content to scuffle up and down the shoreline.

B.D. cupped his hands to yell, "Dawson City?"

A gent in a mangy fur hat shouted, "Nope—Klondike City."

The codger beside him cackled. "Us what don't put on airs jes' calls it Lousetown." He gestured downriver. "That's Dawson, yonder, but the whiskey and the wimmen's cheaper on this side o' the tracks."

Nels and Nathan dug in their paddles to swing back into the current.

"Thanks," B.D. hollered. "I'll keep that in mind."

"That's precisely where you'll keep it, son," his mother warned.

The Klondike River's wide mouth divided Lousetown from their intended destination. Dawson City sprawled along its northern bank and more or less faced the Yukon River.

The town skirted a rather ominous, bald-peaked mountain with a mammoth, dressed moosehide-shaped scar on its rugged flank. B.D. forced his gaze toward the town proper. It returned immediately to the strange mark emblazoned on the mountainside.

The dives and bawdy houses he'd frequented during his sally with Paddy's gang were reputed to be evil—the crux of their attraction, truth be known. Wickedness abounded on Seattle's waterfront, but B.D. suddenly realized he'd been more of an observer than a participant, much less a devotee.

But here, as he stared at that branded mound of rock, B.D. sensed an oppressive malevolence. Watching. Waiting. Beckoning.

B.D.'s stranglehold on the gunwale sent needles prickling through his hands and fingers. He welcomed the discomfort. It distracted his imagination from the childish tricks it was trying to play.

Tearing his eyes away from the mountain, he muttered, "Nancy-boy."

"Excuse me?" Nels said.

"Uh, I said, that steamer looks to be pulling away from shore."

"Nathan's j-stroking to take us in downriver from it." Nels swiveled half around. "But that isn't what you said."

"Don't pay me any mind, bub. I'm delirious with gold fever."

No sooner than the canoe nosed to shore, a gaunt, jug-eared fellow splashed out, grabbed the bow, and gave a mighty yank.

B.D. toppled backward, landing squarely on his mother's booted toes, which jabbed his haunches like twin bayonets. "Yee-ow-w-w-w. Jaysus Chri—"

"Welcome to Dawson City, folks," the volunteer dockhand drawled.

Saint Megan giggled as she pried her feet from beneath B.D.'s posterior. "Now you know why I paid a premium for these clodhoppers, son. Hobnailed soles and custom, hard-rubber reinforced toes."

"All the better to geld me with."

"Welcome to Dawson City, folks," Jug-ears repeated in a louder voice as he wound their bowline around a stob. He reached to assist Nels and B.D. from the canoe, then twitched into a sort-of curtsy before helping the lone lady ashore.

"Spare-ribs Jimmy Mackinson's the name, ma'am, and you're lucky to make my acquaintance. I'll swear that on the Bible, yes-sir-ree I will. Best friend a greenhorn'll ever find amongst this den of scoundrels. That's me. Swear to it."

"You're about two ticks from being sweared at, *friend,*" B.D. threatened as he massaged his tender hindquarters. "My mother was the first white woman to venture across British Columbia. We damn sure don't need you along for this ride."

Mackinson's Adam's apple flumed up his throat like

the counterweight on a carnival's strongman platform. "Well, I'll be hornswoggled."

"But we don't plan to be," Saint Megan replied.

"Honest Injun, ma'am, I ain't tryin' to cozen you. I can show you around and'd be right proud to, especially seeing as how you're a pioneer and all."

"Uh-huh," Nathan grunted. "What's the going rate on Samaritanism in this boomtown?"

"How about you decide that when we're done? I won't lie to you later nor start now. Ain't nary a thing here that don't cost the world, except maybe hope. That's what I'm a-selling."

B.D. squinted at him. "I thought you were angling to be our guide?"

"I am." Mackinson's grin exposed a set of picket-fenced teeth he could strain cream with. "And I *surely* hope it earns a dollar or three for my supper. Been sniffing fumes outside the Palace Restaurant since Tuesday. It lays a fine table in my mind, but t'ain't real filling behind my belt."

B.D. groaned inwardly and reached for his pack. Nothing short of sudden death would prevent his mother from taking pity on a starving wretch.

"What'll we do with our supplies while we take the tour?" she asked, right on cue.

"Leave 'em where they lay, ma'am."

He pointed to a group of log buildings beyond Dawson's commercial district. The Union Jack furled in the breeze above the brush-fenced compound.

"That's the North-West Mounted Police barracks under the command of Inspector Charles Constantine. Him and his thirty constables don't brook stealing, murdering, or shenanigans of a general nature. The mounties being the only ones allowed to carry guns pretty well puts the quietus to those of an outlaw mentality."

"Hear that, Ma?"

She fixed him with a stony glare. "I'm not deaf, B.D."

Before he could argue that opinion, she tendered introductions, then grasped Mackinson's arm.

"Rained a couple days back," he cautioned. "Take care. The ground's a skootch mushy."

B.D. claimed their guide's left side, leaving Nels and Nathan to bring up the rear.

Dozens of boats tethered adjacent to their canoe were rigged with makeshift clotheslines running stem to stern. Others used bracketed poles to fashion tent-like affairs from draped blankets. More enterprising river dwellers hawked everything from snowshoes to long johns from what constituted a floating bazaar.

The O'Malley party struggled forward, each step sinking them ankle-deep in chowdery mire. Extrication set off a chorus of sucking noises. How tent stakes took hold in the brackish soup was a mystery to B.D., but row after row of peaked canvas homesteads testified to the feat. Stacked cordwood rested beside one with a hand-lettered placard that read: COWELD WIN-NER AHED, STOV WUD, 40$. BY NOW OR REEGRET IT LADER.

A slope divided the shore from the town proper; a minor obstacle but for the soft terrain.

"This here's Front Street," Spare-ribs announced. "Some calls in Main 'cause it's the busiest and the only one, but Joe Ladue who birthed this fair city named it Front on account of it fronts the river."

"Isn't it a little unusual to have a cabin squat-centered in the middle of the road?" B.D. inquired.

"Not when it belongs to the town's founding father. Ol' Joe might have been a touch orrey-eyed when he surveyed last fall, but that's where he put it, so that's where it'll stay.

"Ladue don't live there no more, though. Sold out to a bakery and moved into that fancy clapboard saloon he built." Spare-ribs chuckled. "Easier for a feller to live high on the hog if'n he owns a sawmill."

B.D.'s head whipped this way and that trying desperately to take in the sights. His nostrils filled with an ungodly mixture of yeast bread, fried meat, wood smoke, manure, overripe fruit, hot grease, and curing hides.

Discordant renditions of "A Hot Time in the Old Town," "Streets of Cairo," and "Oh, Dem Golden Slippers" blasted from saloons. Hammers, handsaws, and the sawmill's strident wails added off-tempo percussions to the fray.

A teamster stood on a freight wagon sunk to its hubs and cussed the two-horse team trying to swim through a slough of hock-deep chocolate brown sludge.

Upturned roots and stumps in the roadbed further complicated the traffic flow. If not for the boardwalks, pedestrians would bog to their knees the moment they stepped from a doorway. Dogs too frail for sled duty meandered between the people's legs while packs of wolf-eyed mongrels trotted along with their tails aloft in a proprietary manner.

The Barnum & Bailey array of humanity promenading Front Street mesmerized B.D. Other than the conspicuous absence of those of the Oriental persuasion, the entire world and every eccentric in it seemed to have converged on Dawson City.

It didn't take long for him to distinguish greenhorns by their tailored garb or dye-bright flannels and stiff jeans. The old-timers—a distinction irrespective of age—were a uniformly patched and mended lot, which probably explained their nods at B.D.'s similarly attired mother.

All were stoop-shouldered and gimlet-eyed from countless hours crouched over a streambed, panning and peering and praying to find dull yellow grains amid worthless silt. The argonauts' weather-beaten faces reflected a keen dislike of civilization as well as their resignation to it.

For obvious reasons, knee-high rubber boots with buckles jingling like spur rowels constituted both groups' footwear of choice.

Now and then, a woman strode past, but few would, by any stretch of B.D.'s imagination, be described as demure. One in particular, a one-eyed, broad-beamed denizen, parted the masses with the gentility of a pile driver.

Spare-ribs murmured, "That's the Grizzly Bear. If'n you ever venture into a dance hall where she's at, best skedaddle quick. She's wild for young boys, but if'n you don't buy her a drink, she'll wrap them fat ol' arms around you and hug you till your heart busts."

B.D. grimaced. "Thanks for the warning."

"What are you two whispering about?" his mother asked.

To B.D.'s everlasting gratitude, Spare-ribs said, "Bears. I warned your son not to get close to 'em. They's dangersome beasts."

Saint Megan's brow wrinkled suspiciously, but she didn't belabor the point.

The dignified muzzles of a pair of Great Danes preceded a gander at the buxom matrons controlling their leads. Both women were attired in galoshes, a wide-brimmed sombrero, a striped sweater, blue serge knickers, and a holstered cartridge belt complete with a big-bore revolver. The taller of the two, however, had a parrot perched on her shoulder.

B.D. nudged their guide. "I don't suppose there's any details worth mentioning about them?"

"Why, that's Mrs. Mary Hitchcock, the famous admiral's widow and her companion Edith Van Buren, ol' Martin's niece. They're just here for the summer and ain't near as batty as they look. Done pitched a honkin' huge circus on the far side of the river and's got it crammed full of birds, a portable bowling alley, a movin' picture machine, and a ton of patty-fo-grass and other fancy-pants vittles."

"I thought you said only the mounties could carry guns," B.D. said. "What are they packing? Pea shooters?"

"Would you want to tell them gals what they can do and what they can't?"

"Nope."

"Well, I don't feature Captain Constantine does either."

B.D. whistled softly. What a place this is. Can't be another like it anywhere, and it didn't even exist a year ago.

"I don't figure the establishments over yonder hold any appeal to you, ma'am," Spare-ribs said, "only they's kinda landmarks hereabouts and I'd be dere-licting my duty if I ignored them."

"I spent enough time in Tombstone to know money attracts vice like black wool does lint, Mr. Mackinson."

"Please, ma'am, it's Jimmy to my friends. Ain't got many of them, but not for lack of trying to be one."

The poignant note in his voice gave B.D. pause. What met the eye was skin and bones holding up a cap and a threadbare shirt and trousers, but there was more to Jimmy Mackinson than a jaunty manner and an instinct for picking a softhearted woman from a clutch of new arrivals.

Come to think of it, that's true of everyone I've met since this harebrained journey began. Gamaliel, Plew James, Nels Peterson, Nathan Kresge, George Car-mack—gold-hungry dreamers and schemers to the nth degree, the same as . . . B.D. stopped dead in his tracks. The same as every sourdough that took squat-ter's rights to our house in Seattle. Only why did I resent them, and enjoyed the company of every one I've met on the trail?

Fingers closed around B.D.'s elbow and tugged him sideward. "Don't you stray off on me," Jimmy said. "I got a steak and fried taters ridin' on keeping you folks safe and sound and I'd appreciate it if you'd wait till sundown to start sleepwalking."

"Sorry, I—"

" 'Lest y'all are blind," Jimmy said more loudly,

"you can see by the signboards that we're comin' up on the Klondike, Dawson City, and Green Tree hotels. The 'Brewery' one gives a fair idea of what that neighborin' building is, and the Pioneer, Moose-horn, and Dominion sell squeezed corn by the glass at a buck a throw. The Palace is a restaurant, but I've been told the vittles sniff finer than they swallow. Joe Juneau's place has—"

"Joe's here?" Saint Megan said. "There can't be but one man in the country with that name."

"I shoulda expected you'd know each other. He owns that round-the-clock eatin' house wedged between the Horseshoe Saloon and the commission outfitters' store, if you want to trade howdies."

"Not until I've had a bath and run a comb through my hair. Joe must be in his midsixties—too old to risk scaring him to death."

"Well, I ain't seen no windows break when we ambulated by," Jimmy said. "Believe you me, there's a passel of females in this town that'd take 'ugly' for a compliment."

B.D. had almost forgotten about Nels and Nathan until they burst out laughing.

"Might I remind all of you gentlemen that you can't judge a book by its cover?"

Jimmy and B.D. exchanged sidelong glances. The chortling behind them sputtered to muffled coughs.

"As I started to ask," she continued, "are you familiar with a boardinghouse owned by a lady named Minnie Walentine?"

"Yes, ma'am. Matter-of-factly, it's only a coupla hops, a skip, and a jump up the street."

"Is it clean?"

"Yes, ma'am."

"Reasonably priced?"

"Yes, ma'am."

"Why are you so short-winded all of a sudden, Jimmy? Is her house usually full up? Or worse yet, always empty?"

He worried his lip for a moment. "If she's full, chances are she won't be along about nightfall."

"Why?" B.D. asked. "Does she let rooms by the hour or something?"

"Not exactly on purpose, she don't. Miz Minnie just won't abide owl hoots. Them that comes in smellin' of anything but witch hazel goes right out again with her shoeprint decoratin' their backsides."

That seals it, B.D. thought. Eavesdropping on his mother's reply wasn't necessary. Come hell or high water, there'd be two O'Malleys registered in Miss Minnie's guest book within the hour.

He glanced over his shoulder at Nathan. The geologist shook his head and mouthed, "No way, kid." The smirking traitor then said, "Uh, since me and Nels are heading up to the creeks in the morning, a hotel would suit us better. Any suggestions?"

Jimmy chafed his knobbed chin. "They're slapping new ones up as quick as the mills spit out lumber, but rooms is still scarcer than hen's teeth. Best you start inquirin' at the far end of Front and keep on till you get lucky or run outta road. Worst comes to worst, that canoe'll rock you boys like a cradle."

"Is that why you're camped in one?" Nels asked.

"Naw. Couldn't let a room anywhere if I wanted one. Tried to back when I had spare cash, but them clerks said my bones'd slice their sheets to ribbons. That's how Spare-ribs got stuck on me. Used to rile me some, but I've gotten kind of fond of it."

B.D. said, "I'd take a boat any day over Mrs. Walentine's House of Virtue."

"Shhh," Jimmy hissed. "Here, 'tis, and Minnie ain't hard of hearing."

The two-story, ship-lapped house sat back from the boardwalk far enough to accommodate a railed footbridge. Its recessed corner entrance created a boxy porch, with the overhanging upper level braced by a spindled post.

White lace curtains adorned a six-paned window

that had been set inordinately high in its facade. A pair of rectangular sash windows overlooked the street from the second level.

Prim as a schoolmarm, B.D. thought. He glared at the card advertising a room available by day or week clothespinned to the door.

Saint Megan clapped her hands. "Why, it's lovely. The nicest house in town, I'll warrant."

"Yeah, I s'pect so," Jimmy hedged.

"I guess this is where we part company, Miss Megan, B.D.," Nathan said. "If you'd care to hike up to the mines with us in the morning, we'd be glad to have you along."

Oddly, her entire body sagged as if the weight of the world just dropped on her shoulders.

"Ma? Are you all right?"

"Yes—of course, I am." She straightened to her full five feet and change. "Weary, and craving a long, hot soak, but I'll be raring to go at dawn."

"Wonderful," Nathan said. "We'll call for you at first light."

He took a roll of money from Nels's hand that was thick enough to make the larcenous imp in B.D.'s head lick his chops. Nathan peeled off three bills and thrust them at Jimmy. "For a job well done, friend. We surely were fortunate to make your acquaintance."

Their stunned guide stared at the money, his fingers quavering like a spider's legs.

Nathan grabbed Jimmy's hand, turned it palm up, and pressed the money into it. Before it closed into a fist, B.D.'s mother laid a stack of coins atop it.

"No, no . . . this is too much." Tears rimmed his eyes. "I can't take what I ain't earned. That's charity."

"Oh, but you did earn it," Nathan said, returning the balance of his stash to his Swedish banker. "Next time we meet, I expect to see that belt loosened a notch or two."

"Don't think I ain't grateful . . ." Jimmy shuffled anxiously. "How 'bout I run back to your canoe and wait for you there? If'n you get a room, I'll carry your gear to the hotel for you."

Pivoting toward the O'Malleys, he added, "I'll tote your belongings to you folks, too, directly."

Nathan said, "No, just put yourself on the business end of a fork—"

B.D. silenced him with a subtle headshake. "That'd be a great help, Jimmy. I know Ma's worried about her belongings, and that'd save me a half dozen trips between here and there."

Their guide's homely face practically glowed. He crammed the money into his trousers. "Be back afore you know I'm gone." He took off at a sprint, jacket tails flapping.

" 'Twas a kind thing you did, son, letting him feel he'd truly earned his keep. I'm proud of you."

Warmth suffused B.D.'s cheeks. Unable to meet her gaze, he said, "Hell, if Jimmy wants to play pack mule, who am I to argue?"

"We'd best be off before he faints from hunger," Nathan said. "Rest well."

B.D. motioned for his mother to step ahead of him onto the footbridge. Her light rap on the door was answered so quickly he knew the landlady had been spying on them through her prissy curtains.

He'd expected Canada's answer to Carrie Nation to be equally she-ox-sized. Instead, a petite, elderly lady peered out at his mother and inquired, "May I help you?"

"Mrs. Walentine?"

"I'm Minnie Walentine. Have you come about a room?"

"Yes, for me and my son. George Carmack thought you might have one available."

"Do come in and make yourself at home."

B.D. followed his mother inside, trying not to stare at the neatly bunned, elfin creature who made Saint Megan look statuesque by comparison and made him feel huge and clumsy.

Mud splattered the rag rugs in his mother's wake. "Jay—er, Ma, we're dirtying the floor something fierce."

She cast a rueful glance at her boots. "Oh, Mrs. Walentine, I'm terribly sorry."

"Think nothing of it, dearie. Cleanliness and godliness go hand in hand, but I don't believe He anticipated the condition of Dawson City's streets."

While introductions were made and particulars exchanged, B.D. gandered at the unusually Spartan parlor. Until now, he'd thought his mother was the only female who shunned the notion that a room must contain enough furniture, potted plants, and bric-a-brac for three of comparable dimensions.

He nodded an approval at the sturdy horsehair settee flanked by pie-crust lamp tables, a capacious armchair and ottoman near the window, and stacked barrister's bookcases with a duke's mixture of classics, popular novels, and standard reference works. The fussy drapes and a split-oak basket full of unfinished needlework projects were the only feminine touches—besides a level of housekeeping few men would attempt, let alone maintain.

"Are you listening, son?"

"Hmmph. You know I wasn't or you wouldn't have asked."

She favored him with a catty smirk. "Before Minnie shows us to our room, she wants to explain the house rules."

"They're not unreasonable," the landlady said. "If all the newcomers swarming in didn't act as if they'd jettisoned common courtesy at the border, they wouldn't be necessary."

Lord, if she and Ma aren't birds of a feather, he thought. *Bad enough to have one pecking at me night and day. What did I ever do to deserve a matched pair?*

He clasped his hands behind his back and feigned

the same hanging-on-your-every-word expression that his schoolmasters had eaten up with a spoon.

Minnie responded with an ornery grin that said he wasn't fooling her for a second. "Breakfast and supper are served at six. I insist upon scrubbed faces and hands around my table. Come in late and you're welcome to whatever's left on the stove, but you'd better leave my kitchen the way you found it.

"I don't allow tobacco in any form. It's messy and is a fire hazard. No liquor, either. It dulls good judgment, upsets digestion, and induces the tin-eared to sing opera at the top of their lungs.

"I bolt the door at nine. If you're on the wrong side of it, don't bother me to whine excuses. I've heard them all and none have cut the mustard.

"Guests must bathe on Wednesdays and Saturdays. Soap and water are cheap. Replacing lousy mattresses and linens is not. Tub's in the kitchen where privacy is assured. Again, no excuses."

Minnie cocked her head. "Any questions?"

B.D. stammered, "No, ma'am."

The hem of Minnie's navy cotton skirt swept the floor as she led them up the stairs. The treads squeaked softly under her and his mother's feet, but howled under B.D.'s weight.

Minnie cackled. "Just so you'll know, my room is off the kitchen and I'm a very light sleeper." She marched down the upstairs hall and opened the second door on the left. "Small, I'll admit, but cozy, I think."

Two narrow iron beds elled in one corner, with a mirrored chest of drawers, a washstand, and a rocker and lamp table claiming the balance of the floor space.

Minnie held the washstand's tin pitcher to her nonexistent bosom. "I'll fill this so you can freshen up before supper. B.D., if you'll man the pump later, I'll fetch the tub from the back porch, so you and your mother can avail yourselves."

"Be glad to. I'm beginning to feel like I was born in these clothes."

"Then I'll leave you to settle in and relax." Their landlady bustled out, closing the door behind her.

Saint Megan began flitting about, pulling open drawers and patting the furnishings as women were wont to do. B.D. sidled between a bed and the rocker to gaze out the window.

His breath caught in his throat. He jerked the tabbed muslin curtains closed.

"What did you do that for, son? It's gloomy as a cave in here now."

"My eyes are sore from the glare off the water."

She peered at him curiously. "Funny you didn't mention it before."

He plopped down in the rocker and crossed his arms. No, Ma, he countered silently, what I didn't mention is that moose-scarred mountain and how it makes my skin crawl just looking at it. And I'll stumble around like a snow-blind sled dog before I'll let it watch me through that window, day and night.

Chapter 14

"You didn't need Nathan to tell you that, did you, Ma?" B.D.'s fist slammed the footbridge's rail. "You already knew both creeks were staked last year."

Megan felt trapped. Nauseous. As contemptible as her son's face accused her of being. Meaning well didn't excuse lies of omission.

Even in the dim early-morning light, Nathan and Nels looked stricken. Swollen wattles under their eyes bespoke a sleepless night. They'd undoubtedly spent it discussing how to break the devastating news imparted by a patron of the Yukon Hotel's saloon.

"George Carmack told me as much, yes," she admitted. "I don't know whether I didn't believe him, didn't *want* to believe him, or simply kept quiet to protect all of you."

"From what?" B.D. roared. "You knew we'd find out once we got to Dawson City."

"Don't yell at her like that," Nathan said. "She was wrong and knows it, but she's still your mother."

His rise to her defense only intensified Megan's guilt. There was a strange sort of justice served by being hollered at. Nathan's admonition made her wish she could crawl into a hole and pull the dirt over her.

Yesterday, she'd vowed to tell B.D. the whole truth after supper. Minnie's rib-sticking fare and pleasant conversation had put him in such good humor Megan decided to delay until after they'd bathed.

The steaming soak in the oval copper tub had

turned her bones as soft as the *Pears'* soap cake from Minnie's private stock. Having climbed what seemed like a thousand stairs to the second-floor landing, Megan had neither the strength nor desire to apprise her son of the grim ending to George's story.

"It was more than wrong," she said. "It was cowardly not to tell you boys the truth, but what's done is done."

"Funny how that kind of hogwash always lets adults off the hook." B.D. sneered. "Sure as hell doesn't work for their children."

"Gives you something to look forward to, then, doesn't it?" Megan shot back. "Now do you want to stand here tongue-lashing me the livelong day, or follow me to the mines for a look-see?"

Nels lifted his wool cap to fingercomb his hair. "Maybe I'm a glutton for punishment, but I didn't travel four thousand miles to roam Front Street with the dogs."

"Who knows?" Nathan said. "All may not be lost. We heard that a newspaperman named William Johns sold half of his Twelve Below Discovery on the Eldorado for five hundred dollars right after he claimed it. Took twenty-five hundred for the other half just before Christmas and called the buyer crazy for offering it. Johns went stateside before it started coughing up tens of thousands in gold. It's turned out to be one the richest on the creek."

Nels piped up, "Just because the claims are spoken for doesn't mean we might not find another tinhorn itching to sell or take on partners."

Megan challenged B.D. with her eyes. Her son's stony features mirrored the internal battle being waged. Much as he might want to punish her, absenting himself from the excursion punished no one but himself.

Striding up the boardwalk sufficed as his answer. Megan urged Nathan and Nels to fall in behind him. For her to take the subservient hindmost position wasn't as symbolic as it may have appeared. Like railroad brakemen once rode in the caboose between whistle stops, putting distance between herself and their human train's engineer eliminated an ongoing tussle for sway.

They left Dawson City and its raucous commercial district behind and began the snail's-paced two-mile trudge along the Klondike River.

Indians called the watercourse, known as the finest salmon stream in the Yukon, The Thron-diuck, meaning *hammer water*. To white men's ears, the native's pronunciation sounded like one's windpipe collapsing by virtue of a noose, hence the bastardization of Klondike.

The foot-, hoof-, and paw-tilled strip adjacent to its bank presented a mean challenge to all who relied upon it. To call it a road was a finer example of embroidery than the samplers in Minnie Walentine's sewing basket.

Megan stepped aside to allow an ore wagon's passage. The two-horse team's ribs corduroyed their hide and their fetid breath fouled the air. She'd seen enough signboards to know that pound for pound, dray animals were cheaper than the hay and grain necessary to feed them properly.

As she watched the animals strain against their collars, she decided that their pack mule's mortal misstep was more blessing than tragedy. Had Paddy survived the raft-borne leg of the journey, he would have shared the horses' fate.

The driver tipped his slouch hat. "Sorry if I splashed ya, ma'am. Used to gig catfish outta ruts shallower than these when I was a boy."

Her sympathy expanded to include the jocular teamster. He didn't have any more meat on him than his horses. She waved him on, then retook the road when the wagon lumbered past.

True enough, her dream of returning to the north country had omitted the ugliness that coexisted with

its awe-striking splendor. She recalled that a scholarly
gent named Spencer had coined the phrase 'survival of
the fittest.' Its original application had vanished from
memory, but she couldn't imagine a more appropriate
adage for the Yukon.

"Are you faring it all right?" Nels called, ending
her reverie.

"Fine," she answered. "Don't tarry on my account."

At the mouth of Bonanza Creek, the mud softened
to a gravylike consistency. Along a serpentine slough,
not a tree, blade of grass, cranberry, blueberry, or
salmonberry bush, or daub of moss had survived the
gold-fevered invasion.

The shell of a building under construction occupied
one ridge. Why anyone would choose such a bleak
location for a commercial enterprise was a mystery
to her.

"Moose pasture is right," she said as she yanked a
boot out of the brackish ooze.

With her mouth clamped shut against the gnats
swirling around her head, Megan added, never have
kinder words been used to describe a blessed swamp.
And Mother Mary forgive me if I wouldn't make a
deal with the devil himself to own a piece of it.

Megan noted with satisfaction that B.D., Nathan,
and Nels were bogged down as badly as she was. Feet
splayed wide, torsos pitched forward, and posteriors
thrust out for balance, they waddled around a bend
like three lead-shackled ducks.

B.D. stopped abruptly. The other two stumbled beside him and stood with their arms hanging limp at
their sides. She understood why the moment she
joined them.

Pioche, Nevada; Telegraph Creek, British Columbia; Coeur d'Alene, Idaho; Tombstone, Arizona—for
all the mining camps and towns she'd frequented over
the last quarter century, nothing in her realm of experience prepared her for this crazed carnival of greed.

Tents and log shacks rambled helter-skelter as far

as she could see. Ditches to divert water into flumes interlaced the denuded valley's slopes. A ragtag army shoveled mountains of white gravel slag and clay into the sluices like human machines. The force of the water would separate the dross from the heavier placer gold, which would cling to the riffles and matting at the end of the sluice.

Smoke curled upward from lateral shafts burrowed into the permafrost; the miners hired to tunnel into the earth's rich bowels accomplishing their bone-chilling task by candlelight. Windlasses were mounted above the glory holes to hoist frozen clay from the manmade caverns by the bucket load.

Megan glanced at her stunned companions and burst out laughing. "Did you think digging for gold was the same as digging radishes from a kitchen garden?"

Nathan stammered, "Three years of studying geology and I had no idea it was anything like this. Those men—they never stop. Never so much as pause to catch their breath."

"They're as crammed together as corncobs in a crib," B.D. said. "How can they know what belongs to who?"

Nels shook his head. "I don't know, but something tells me that inching over on your neighbor's claim wouldn't go unnoticed."

"Naw, it woun't," boomed a voice behind them. "Not if 'twas mine, I'll have you."

Megan spun around, her startled gaze level with a nugget-encrusted belt buckle. Though no taller, the speaker would have made two of Gamaliel.

A thatch of brownish black hair cloaked his massive brow and a handlebar moustache of comical proportions hung over his lip like an awning.

"I am the King of the Klondike," he declared in a halting burr. "Big Alex McDonald, that is me."

"Sorry, bub," B.D. drawled, "but we met the real king a couple of days back."

McDonald's bluish jowls slackened. His dark eyes switched thoughtfully from corner to corner. "Naw, naw, I am the king here. The other fellow? He lies."

"Well, I don't reckon George Carmack would take kindly to being called a liar anymore," Megan said.

"George! My friend, he is. Everybody's my friend, but naw, he is not the king." A chuckle rumbled up McDonald's chest. "A prince, maybe."

Judging by their expressions, Megan's companions were as intrigued by the gargantuan fellow as she was. "Do you have a claim here at Bonanza?"

"Only one, but tomorrow, perhaps more. Today I have shares in nineteen—naw, 'tis twenty-two of them, at Eldorado."

He hoisted upturned palms. "I trade for this piece, for that piece. Lay a fraction of another. It makes me rich."

"How do you keep track of them?" Nels asked.

McDonald thunked his temple with a forefinger. "'Tis all in my noggin, laddie. From the first trade of flour for half of Thirty Eldorado to the five thousand I borrowed against lays of Six Below Bonanza, Twenty-seven Eldorado, and a mortgage on Thirty."

Megan's head swam just listening to him. Swear to everything holy, the enormous speculator didn't appear bright enough to buckle his overshoes by himself.

"If it's not being too nosy," Nathan said, "what's that 'lay' you mentioned? I'm supposing it isn't the same as a mortgage?"

Big Alex beamed as men did when a conversation centered around their favorite topic. "Naw, t'ain't. 'Twas me that learned these pioneers the difference." He rubbed his jaw as if collecting his thoughts. "A lay is a lease of sorts. Can be a fraction of a full claim or a fraction of a fraction. The lay holder, he works it and pays the owner—that being me—a percentage of his take."

"Then you don't mine your holdings?" Megan asked.

"Why should I, if men pay me for the privilege to own it?"

He laughed long and loud, yet not in an arrogant manner. "It's them that tunnels like gophers. Buy lumber for flumes and sluice boxes that costs more than mahogany in the east. They are happy getting rich. I am happy being rich."

"We'd be happy to take one of those fractions off your hands," B.D. said. "If you have any to spare."

"No."

Megan repeated. "No?"

"I always say no. Then, I think."

Nels scratched his side-whiskers. Nathan jingled coins in his trousers' pocket. B.D. fiddled with a button on his shirt.

Megan found herself surrounded by three men who were twitching as if plagued by St. Vitus' dance, and another using the sky as a slate for ciphering mental arithmetic.

They all jumped when Big Alex said, "Thirty-five percent of thirty-five feet of Seventeen Eldorado."

His announcement set Megan's mind to calculating. The maximum legal claim was five hundred feet square, which meant the entire fraction measured a hundred seventy-five feet, so their lay of it would be . . .

"Glory, that's only twelve and a quarter feet wide," she said. "We couldn't stand shoulder to shoulder on it, much less mine it."

"Ho ho. 'Tisn't near the smallest on Eldorado. William Ogilvie's survey last January made a wee adjustment to Jim White's claim between Thirty-six and Thirty-seven. The lout thought he could carve a sliver between them, and lo, that he did."

Big Alex's kettle belly joggled like puppies in a towsack. "For his scheming ways, ol' Jim will forever be known as Three-Inch White."

Nathan glanced at Megan, then at the speculator. "Twelve and a quarter feet, you say?"

"That it is. But a bigger fraction may come to me tomorrow or next week. Might not, too."

"How much?" Nels asked.

"Twenty."

B.D. inhaled sharply. "Twenty *dollars*?"

Big Alex's rubbery lips stretched into a huge grin. "Naw, naw, 'tis twenty thousand, young man. In gold."

He noted B.D.'s crestfallen expression. "Not cheap, but not robbery. Ask Mr. Ogilvie. He told Rupert von Euler that his eighteen-foot lay on One Below Bonanza could pay out two and a half millions."

"We don't have anywhere near that kind of money, Mr. McDonald," Megan said.

"You can borrow. When I came here, I had no cash—only supplies to barter. Before the spring clean up, I had notes of one hundred fifty thousand falling due. My lay holders washed plenty enough to pay the debt and more. Lots more."

Megan shook her head. "Even if we had collateral, which we don't—"

"Isn't that what prospecting's all about, Ma? A huge make-it-or-die-trying gamble?"

"Not that huge, kid," Nathan answered for her. "Tack a fat chunk of interest onto that sum and you've got a number with more zeroes in it than a primer."

B.D. flung an arm out toward the valley. "Then how in bloody hell are those scarecrows over there becoming millionaires, Ma? You told me yourself that Dawson City's crawling with 'em!"

In as calm a voice as she could muster, she said, "Because they got here first, son."

Chapter 15

After Big Alex's lumbering departure, a pall descended over Megan, B.D., Nathan, and Nels. The bleakness enshrouding them leeched their hopes and dreams.

They shuffled about, refusing to meet each other's eyes. Like mourners at a funeral, to feel despair grip one's own heart wasn't nearly as grievous as seeing its effect on others.

Megan realized their anguish came from a different source from her own. They envied McDonald and the original claim holders their wealth—more accurately, the power it bestowed.

She understood the misery churning inside them because she'd come to America obsessed with striking it rich for that identical reason. As if she could read his mind, she knew B.D. was trying desperately to finagle a brilliant scheme to get his hands on that twenty-thousand-dollar lay.

How could she explain that it wasn't the money—the inability to buy McDonald's fraction—that tormented her? Even if she had such a sum tucked under a mattress, she'd sooner invest it in a restaurant or a mercantile.

There's two kinds of people in this world, she mused. Those who want to *have* and those who forever seek. Most fall into the first category. Prospectors are among the second.

Ed Schieffelin had been a seeker. He'd fought marauding Apaches, the army, and a legion of nay-sayers to comb Arizona's San Pedro Valley for the silver lode he believed he'd find there.

In 1879, the city of Tombstone was born around Schieffelin's Lucky Cuss mine. Its discoverer became an overnight multimillionaire and spent his proceeds like water for a time. Ed had so much money, it ceased to have any value.

Five years later, Tombstone's Silver King was exploring the Yukon River, convinced that a mineral belt encircled the earth and that he'd find it if he looked long enough.

Megan read Ed's obituary just before she left Seattle. His body had been found near his remote Oregon cabin. A probable heart attack according to the newspaper account which noted the chunks of high-grade gold ore scattered around his corpse and speculated that perhaps the excitement of his discovery had killed him.

His passing saddened her, yet she knew Ed died happy. Forever the seeker; never content to just find and have.

That's why she had no interest in McDonald's fraction. Someone else had found it. Felt the indescribable euphoria of seeing those first grains of gold form a dull yellow smile along the pan's creased bottom.

She studied B.D.'s face and asked herself, which category does he belong to? Is he his father's son? Or mine? She looked away, fearful of the answer.

Knowing someone must break the stalemate, she said, "Before you all drown in that funk you're wallowing in, may I remind you there's more than one way to skin a cat."

B.D.'s head jerked sideward. "You've figured out where to get the money?"

"Not in one fell swoop, but I know how we can earn it."

"Jaysus, Ma. It'd take the rest of my life to make that much in wages."

"That it would."

She sat down on a stump and watched a pair of burly shovel stiffs reduce a towering slag heap one scoop at a time.

"So, are you going to tell us your grand scheme, or what?" he asked.

"Not unless you all truly want to hear it. I'm too old to waste air on deaf ears."

Nels and Nathan exchanged glances, then shrugs. "We don't have a train to catch. How about you, B.D.?"

"I wish."

Megan rested her forearms on her knees. "Besides not telling you about the claim situation, I left another tiny detail out of my talk with George Carmack. Now, I don't know the man well enough to take his word for gospel, but he said he'd float his trading post downriver for us to use and reassemble it on one of Joe Ladue's vacant lots."

"Use for what?" B.D. sneered.

"A free roof over our heads for starters," Nathan snapped back. Criminy, a cabin in town is worth anywhere from five hundred to a thousand dollars and that doesn't count the land to set it on."

Her son's jaw fell as slack. "You're joshin'."

"Not hardly, but I have a feeling your mother doesn't plan to simply homestead in it."

"More years ago than I care to admit," Megan said, "Big-Nose Kate Elder—"

"You knew Doc Holliday's woman?" Nels asked.

"I did, and she was a fine lady, regardless of the stories you may have heard."

"No insult intended, ma'am," Nathan said, "but you truly have been around the Horn a few times, haven't you?"

Megan winked. "The winters do drag on up here. Beg me a little and I'll tell you some thumping-good tales when the snow starts flying."

She cleared her throat. "As I was saying, Kate gave me a piece of advice I've never forgotten, which is, any service a man doesn't have that he'll pay to get means money in the till."

B.D. pawed at his chest and staggered backward. "Good God Almighty, me dear ol' mum's fixin' to open up a whorehouse."

"Dire straits as we're in, I might consider it if there was enough profit in it."

"All right. What, then?" B.D. asked.

"I'm not sure until we scout some more, but I'm a-thinking that a place with all the comforts of home—a table for writing letters, books, newspapers, fine cigars, homemade sweets—all manner of comforting things, might be enormously popular."

"I don't know," Nathan said. "You'd have stiff competition—no pun meant—from the bawdy houses, dance halls, and saloons."

"Like I said, the winters here drag real slow," she argued, warming to the idea even as she hatched it. "Much as these adventurers wanted away from hearth and home when they came here, I'll wager they hanker for a touch of it. Or will, when the ice and dark months close in."

B.D. countered, "But what about us? I can't speak for Nels and Nathan, but sweeping floors and emptying spittoons doesn't appeal to me."

"One step at a time, son. If George comes through, we'll take it from there."

"Uh-huh." His chin rumpled like a banker evaluating collateral. "I do believe all this thrashing you got us to doing was to take our minds off that lay McDonald offered."

"No, not entirely."

Nels snorted. "Well, it worked."

"Darned if it didn't," Nathan agreed. "A few minutes ago I was fawnching to pitch rocks at those lucky devils over yonder. Now I wouldn't mind wandering around awhile longer."

"Fine by me," B.D. said. "Soon as you pass that canteen around and dole out the victuals you're toting."

Megan couldn't have asked for a better sign than an impromptu picnic. Barlow P. once told her when a man's off his feed, it's because his mind is too busy chewing on something.

The menu consisted of tough biscuits, smoked sausage, and apples, washed down with great gulps of lukewarm tea. Around a mouthful of fruit, B.D. proclaimed, "Am I ever glad you had the smarts to bring food along, Nathan. My belly was beginning to tickle my backbone."

"Actually, it was my idea," Nels said. "My partner, the college-educated Mr. Kresge, was in such a hurry to hit the road he almost forgot to put his trousers on."

"Thank you so much for setting the record straight, Mr. Peterson, though as I recall, someone had to remind you to button yours."

A quarter hour later, the four were again in single-file formation, only this time, with Megan in the lead.

Slag piles, tunnel mouths, flumes, cart tracks, timbers, and living quarters spread across the valley's floor and up its flank. She angled toward the ridge bounding Bonanza Creek on the west rather than pick their way around the impediments and probably raise the miners' hackles in the process.

The mud relented to more solid ground at that elevation, but the ruts gouged by winter wood being dragged to the camps could twist an ankle in a finger snap. The further they walked, the more apparent it became that the faces staring up at them changed, but the monotonous shovel-hoist-cart-wash routine did not.

When night fell, the laborers would straggle to their tents, rustle up a meal of beans, salt pork, and flapjacks, then collapse in their bunks. Few would shuck their mud-splattered clothing. Why bother, when ten hours later they'd take up their picks and shovels again for another day's work?

"Helluva life for a millionaire," B.D. muttered.

"Most are probably hired hands," Megan said. "Besides the company we had at Eight-Mile Creek, I've only known three prospectors that hit a pay streak and did the placering themselves."

"Who?"

"Me, Barlow P. Bainbridge, and a wee sprig of a lad that goes by the name of B.D. O'Malley."

"Hmmmph. I wouldn't call what I did in Juneau mining."

"Oh? What would you call it?"

He didn't respond, which pleased her. She hadn't included him in that short list to put a pearl in his oyster and intuition told her he knew it.

Her boot plunged into a furrow. She pitched forward and sprawled in the dirt.

"Jaysus, Ma." B.D.'s hands slipped under her arms to help her up. "Are you hurt?"

"I hope not." She shifted her weight to test her ankle's soundness. "Breaking a leg would give you too good an excuse to shoot me."

"Like I need another one?"

"You did take a nasty tumble," Nels said.

"Trust me," B.D. said, "as long as her mouth works, she's finer than frog's hair."

Megan bent to brush the dirt from her britches. She stopped in midswipe to stare at Nathan, who pawed at the rut like a hound after a bone.

B.D. followed her gaze. "What the devil are you doing, bub?"

Without raising his head, Nathan panted, "Ignore me. Talk among yourself. Anything. Just don't stand there gawking."

B.D. and Nels traded befuddled expressions, but turned to face Megan.

"What's he doing, Ma?"

"You saw him, same as I did."

He angled his head toward Nels. "Your partner given to this sort of thing?"

"Not that I've noticed."

"What's he doing now, Ma?"

Megan peeked between him and Nels. "Scooping pebbles into his pack."

"He's *what*?" Why?"

"I don't know, B.D. Why don't you ask him? He's standing right behind you."

Nathan grinned. "You three are the worst actors I've ever seen."

"Not much of an insult, coming from a lunatic," B.D. said. "What are you collecting rocks for? Ballast?"

"That may be all they turn out to be, but I don't think so."

"Nathan . . ." Nels prompted.

"Yeah, I'm stalling, but so help me, a single solitary one of you lets out a yelp and I'll bash you with this pack."

He took out a handful of white gravel. "Miss Megan, if we were down there instead of up here, where would you say this came from?"

She squinted at the peculiar stones. "Well, judging by how round they are, I'd guess the creekbed." A chill shot through her. She surveyed the valley's opposite slope, then the milky pebbles in Nathan's hand.

"Jesus, Mary, and Joseph. It's possible. Gloriously, marvelously possible."

"I'll have to sink a shaft to know for sure."

"Know what?" B.D. and Nels demanded in the same breath.

Nathan dumped the gravel back into his pack. "Whether or not we're standing atop an ancient streambed."

"Yeah, well, who gives a sh—a care about that," B.D. said, "besides a rock-brained geologist?"

"*You* should," Megan answered, trying not to let her voice betray her excitement. "Because if water did course through here eons ago, as sure as the bloomin' world, it carried with it the gold nuggets George Carmack found in Bonanza Creek."

Chapter 16

Megan sprawled on the hillside watching a battery of clouds crawl by. A few yards away, three shovel blades rasped in unison. The elongated mound of white gravel rising behind B.D., Nels, and Nathan looked like a beached whale pup.

She examined her palms; the pads swollen and blistered by a shovel's handle despite cowhide gloves. According to Bessie Fontaine, Megan's former neighbor and disciple of *Harper's Bazaar* beauty columns, the mark of a lady was the suppleness of her hands.

Oh well, Megan thought. At least anyone who's ever seen mine knows I don't sit on them all day.

Another wave of laughter, a sound as rude as magpies on a branch, rose from the creek diggings. The catcalls had begun when she and the boys clambered up the slope that morning with a borrowed dredge loaded with tools, stakes, grub, and fresh water in tow.

"Hey, cheechakos," yelled a scrawny gent with a grizzled beard. "Gold don't fall from the sky like rain, you know."

Another shouted, "Don't sprout from hills like cucumbers, neither."

"Aw, let 'em play," a third said. "If'n it weren't for greenhorns, we wouldn't have no entertainment a'tall."

Megan's indignant companions had bowed their necks. She knew once their tempers were sufficiently primed, they'd cut loose with a flurry of obscene retorts.

"Don't waste your wind, boys," she cautioned. "Those jakes don't know their butts from a hole in the ground as far as bench diggings go."

"Just wait'll we flash some color under their noses," Nathan said, tugging on the dredge rope. "That'll change their tune."

Megan's eyes flicked to the oval gouge the three were excavating. She'd tried to tell them that a test shaft wasn't supposed to be wide enough to park a freight wagon in. The emphasis was supposed to be on depth, not breadth.

Their concerted argument that the more ground they worked, the better the chance of a strike held as much water as a cracked thundermug, but she wasn't going to waste *her* wind either.

She scrabbled into a sitting position. Lord, how the Canadian Yukon had changed. The mountains were higher, the canyons steeper, and the nights seemed so much shorter than they'd been twenty years ago.

"I'm just itching to grab on to a shovel," she fibbed. "Which one of you wants a break?"

"Take it easy, Ma. We'll give a shout when we need you."

An emergence of only three digging tools had already indicated that a distinction between men's work and women's work had been made. Considering Megan's aching muscles, she should have been relieved to be relieved from duty. And might have, had it been her idea.

She evil-eyed the trio of denim-clad targets which presented themselves in a most tempting manner. A swift kick to the dross heap effected a less satisfying, though reasonable compromise. A chirt volcano erupted; a minor avalanche clattered down her boot's vamp.

"Nice tantrum, Ma."

She knelt in the gravel and began pushing stones aside with both hands. The channel reclosed almost as quickly as she quarried it.

"Ma?"

Megan plucked out a brassy lump; cragged and vulgar in contrast to its smooth brethren.

"All that glitters," she said, rolling the nugget between thumb and forefinger, "*isn't* gold."

Nathan squatted beside her. Nels curled over his back. B.D.'s knees snuggled Megan's shoulder blades. Her son broke the reverent silence with, "One nugget does not a fortune make."

"No, but unless you've forgotten everything you ever knew, gold is like roaches in a cupboard. Find one and you can rest assured that there's a passel cowering nearby."

As if a whistle had blown, four pairs of hands bailed pebbles, the stones flying in all directions.

"Easy now," Megan said, "or you'll toss the wheat with the chaff."

Presently, white chirt sprinkled the slope as if a hailstorm had passed overhead. Seven nuggets rested in her palm, none larger than a gooseberry: she'd found a second one, Nathan three, and Nels and B.D. a single one apiece.

Nathan's fist uppercut the air. "Eu-u-ree—" His mouth clamped shut and he aimed a furtive glance at the creek diggings. "How are we going to stake claims without them seeing us?"

"We can't," Megan answered. She hadn't seen such a doleful expression since Peg-leg Hank heard that Seattle's board of alderman was contemplating a prohibition statute.

B.D. yanked the brim of his slouch hat. "Great. No sooner than we pound a stake or two, those yahoos'll scramble up here like Sioux after the Seventh Cavalry."

Rising to her feet, she said, "Some of those sourdoughs are old enough to remember the bench claims in the Cassiar District, but most will just laugh until their buttons pop."

"Ma'am?" Nels said plaintively. "Aren't you taking

all this kind of calm? Or are we getting het up over nothing and you're too kind to say so?"

Megan planted her hands on her hips, threw her head back, and laughed at the heavens. "Eu-u-u-ree-ka-aa," she howled, then cocked an ear to listen as it reverberated along the creek valley.

"Was that answer enough for you?" she inquired of the stunned Swede.

A raspy voice from below yelled, "Didja hear that, Delmer? Why, that purdy lady musta feasted her eyes on me and swooned."

"More likely, she caught a whiff of ya and expired."

"C'mon down here, honey," another miner taunted. "I'll give you something to holler about."

A scarlet flush mottled B.D.'s face. He took a step toward the camp. Megan caught his elbow. "Ignore him, son. He's showing off for his friends more than he's insulting me."

"Maybe you don't mind such talk, but—"

She met his angry gaze. "What that fool says doesn't matter a whit to me. What does is that you'd pound him for saying it."

B.D. grunted. "Damn right I will, if you'll let go of me."

"Yeah, and me and Nels'd wade right into 'em with you, kid," Nathan said, "if the odds weren't about twenty-six to one."

Nels jerked a thumb at the sledge. "The best revenge—not to mention, the least painful—might be to fetch our staking gear and make things official."

B.D. shuffled in place, obviously as peeved at being outvoted as he was by the miner's crude remark.

Nathan said, "Since you stumbled over this bench yesterday, Miss Megan—pun intended—me and Nels think you're entitled to the Discovery, plus one."

She shook her head. "It's generous you are, but it wasn't me that spied those pebbles. I'd have hobbled away none the wiser, if not for your sharp eyes."

"We decided last night that if we found anything, you should have discovery rights," Nels insisted.

B.D. chimed in, "Seems fair to me."

"Well, it isn't and if I hear another word to the contrary, I won't lift a finger to help you stake proper claims. One is plenty for us."

"Us?" B.D. said. "What's this 'us' crap?"

"Listen here, Mr. Soul of Chivalry, I'll thank you to keep a civil tongue in *your* mouth. As for the other, though it's clear you're a mite too big for your britches, you're not old enough to register a legal claim."

Megan realized her mistake instantly. Tempers needed time to cool and she'd only thrown fuel on already smoldering embers. B.D.'s body quavered like a panther, poised to strike. She stepped back, genuinely afraid he was about to slap her.

"And who's to know that unless one of you tells the gold commissioner?" An arrogant smirk defiled his handsome face. "Beulah Livermore sure as hell didn't question my age and she got a better look at me than he ever will."

Megan stared down at the barren ground. So that's why B.D. thinks he's a man. If only Barlow P. were here, he'd divest him of that notion in a heartbeat. Her best friend's drawled response couldn't have been any more distinct had he stood beside her: "Now, boy, jes' 'cause a wren can fly, that don't make him a goddamn eagle."

The auditory illusion prompted a melancholy smile. Barlow P. was the most stubborn, cantankerous, opinionated old coot she'd ever known, but he'd sure had a way of putting things in perspective.

Megan looked up at B.D. "After Nathan stakes Discovery and his second and Nels chooses his claim, I'll step off one for us. As far as I'm concerned, it's yours to do with as you wish."

That hateful glint she hoped she'd never see again

returned with a vengeance. "That's it, huh? Saint Megan's sermon on the mount."

"I didn't write the law, son, and there's nothing I can do to change it."

"Then you don't need my help to comply with it."

The morning passed with precious few words exchanged between Nels, Nathan, and Megan beyond questions and instructions regarding measuring and staking protocols.

When Nels insisted that she take One Below Discovery to spread the partners' claims out as far as possible, she called out to B.D., asking after his approval.

He sat a hundred yards away, knees drawn up and baled with his arms, and showed no sign of having heard her.

"One Below it is," she said, angry with herself and B.D. for ruining what should have been a festive occasion.

It was late afternoon before Nels drove the last stake at his Two Below's southeast corner. Megan stepped back to admire their handiwork. "If there's a squarer measure in all the Yukon, I'd surely like to see it."

She turned to invite her son's inspection. The sledge still rested on the hillside, but B.D. had vanished.

"Nathan, did you see B.D. wander off?"

"No . . ." He frowned. "Truth is, I haven't looked that direction for quite a while."

Megan scanned the slope and the valley beyond.

"I'll bet he just took his broodin' back to town," Nels said. "There's nothing more aggravating than being ignored when you're riled."

She fought down the panic roiling inside her. They'd ignored him, true enough, and Nels was right. Why, at this very moment B.D. was probably whining to Minnie about his iron-hearted mother. It wasn't as if he could run away again. Circle City was the closest settlement of any size and it was two hundred and twenty miles downstream. What was he going to do? Swim?

No. He wouldn't have to. He knew where she'd cached the rest of their grubstake and there was enough of it to buy a steamer ticket.

"I've got to get to Dawson."

"Wait up," Nathan said, "we'll go with you."

"You can't leave the sledge and it'll slow you down too much. Meet me at the boardinghouse."

Megan broke into a jog, her boots slipping and sliding on the bald hillside. Halfway to the mouth of Bonanza Creek, she veered inland, away from the muddy track. She tucked her chin determinedly and promised God she'd do anything if He'd keep her son from leaving. Her prayers alternated with the punishments she'd exact on B.D. when she found him.

Miners called out from the claims and the trail, inquiring what was wrong; if she needed help.

Chest heaving, her teeth clenched against the insect blizzard, she trotted on, her mind focused on the mission and not its miseries. Mud collected on her boots like brown mortar. To knock the soles on a stump would take time she didn't have to waste. It wouldn't do much good, anyway.

Where the creek met the Klondike River, the ridge forced her down onto the road. She weaved around wagons, saddle-bagged dog teams, and human traffic as if the devil himself were nipping at her heels.

She was forced to a complete stop by a hustling congregation with picks and shovels on their shoulders storming toward the creek. Some were dressed in Sunday-go-to-meeting clothes; the sleeves of their oxford shirts rolled above their elbows and vests neatly buttoned. To a man, they wore the sanguine expressions common to spectators en route to a public hanging.

A natty gent in a pinstripe suit and bowler looked at her curiously, then separated from the crowd. "Are you ill, madam?"

"No . . . just gotta . . . get to town."

He favored her with a sly grin. "Ah, you have a claim to register at Commissioner Ogilvie's office, I presume. One perhaps that overlooks the valley?"

Megan stared at him, gasping for breath, unable to comprehend his line of inquiry. "Excuse me?"

"My good woman, don't tell me you're unaware that a strike's been made above Bonanza Creek. Why else would you be running pell-mell for Dawson City?"

She whirled to look at her backtrail. Nels and Nathan were nowhere in sight. They couldn't possibly have beaten her to . . .

Megan clapped a hand over her belly. "How did you find out about the bench claims above the creek?"

"The news roared down Front Street no sooner than Mr. O'Malley filed his claim." He chuckled derisively. "The young man's face was so muddied, at first glance we thought he was colored."

Chapter 17

A rap at the door sounded just as Megan finished tying her boots.

"Someone's here to see you," Minnie announced from the hall. "He's waiting on the stoop."

Megan crossed the tidy room in three steps and turned the brass knob.

Dabs of pink rouge appeared to stand out from Minnie's cheeks. The artifice enhanced the landlady's weariness rather than camouflage it.

She peeked past Megan's shoulder, then clucked her tongue. "I'd so hoped B.D. was the one."

"The one what?"

"The first to sneak in without my hearing him." Minnie scuttled backward to allow Megan's exit. "Mark my words, you'll find that scamp before sundown and when you're through with him, I want a crack at him in the woodshed."

"I reckon the line'll form behind Nels and Nathan. They searched the alleys and dives half the night. With hordes of greenhorns streaming in from all directions, they said it was the same as looking for a needle in a haystack."

Minnie started for the landing. "Well, hurrahing the town is a tradition that simply won't be denied, regardless of age. B.D. will turn up eventually, repentant and sick as a dog on green grass."

It was only a matter of time before Minnie heard the news of B.D.'s "discovery," but Megan didn't offer a correction. Better to let Minnie think B.D. was a wet-eared carouser than a fraud.

"Glory," Megan said, almost tripping on the stairs. "The man waiting for me—he isn't a constable is he?"

"Not by a far stretch. I invited him in, but I think he preferred the porch." She glanced at the foyer. "I'll be as close as the kitchen if you need me."

"Why would I?" Megan stared after her, then at the door. She tiptoed closer only to flinch at the squeaky floorboards.

The glass insert framed a squarish copper brown face. A muffled baritone demanded, "Hey, in der—is you Misseh Megan?"

She eased the door open. A tall, powerfully built native dressed in tight-fitting caribou skin trousers, shirt, and knee-high moccasins glared back at her. "Judge, him done sendet Skookum Jim," he said in guttural Chinook. *"Mika coolie wichet nika."*

Megan repeated one of the few words familiar to her. "George? George Carmack sent you?"

His brow furrowed. *"Mika kumtux Chinook?"*

"If you're asking whether I savvy your language, I don't beyond *klahowya.*"

Apparently he understood her admission, but it didn't please him. He crossed his arms and snarled, "I say, Judge, yeah? Dat's whas I mean so." His glower, which seemed as permanently affixed as his walrus moustache, was more disconcerting than frightening. "Come—fetchet you now."

Megan hesitated, torn between elation that Carmack's cabin had obviously been delivered and wanting to track down her wayward son. Realizing that first things must come first, she motioned that she would follow him.

Due to her throbbing thigh and calf muscles, she had the devil's own time keeping pace with Skookum Jim's leggy strides. Experience had taught her that exercise relieved kinks and strains faster than coddling them, but like gnashing chlorate potash tablets for a sore throat, cures often sounded more agreeable before the suffering commenced than while in the throes of it.

They traversed the length of Front Street's boardwalk. The hide-bound, derby-hatted Tagish never once looked back. If he had, he'd found her scowling at him with a fervor equal to his own.

"Where in Sam Hill has Carmack sited that cabin?" she muttered, her boots sinking in the mire. "Beggars can't be choosers, but I'm not fond of being stuck in the boondocks, either."

Worse yet, she smelled rain. The clabbered sky threatened a gullywasher within the hour. Three Indian boys crab-walking across a roof drew her attention. They tamped layers of moss with their hands and bare feet. When dry, it would form an excellent barrier against ice and cold.

Skookum Jim ducked into the former trading post. No sooner than he disappeared, George Carmack came out and waved her toward him.

"Lady Luck brought a supply steamer by shortly after we finished stacking the logs on a raft," he said. "The captain was gracious enough to pull us into port."

Other than a slight skew to its door and window frames, the building looked no worse for its transport down the Yukon.

George pointed upward. "Tin plate would make a better roof, but those sheets cost a king's ransom up here."

"For heaven's sake, it sounds like you're apologizing. I'm just so grateful to you, I can't get the words out."

He patted her arm. "Same as I told you before, I'd rather it was put to good use than left to ruin. We did have to settle it further down the flat than I'd hoped, but I expect the town will grow up around you before long."

Skookum Jim emerged and stalked over to join them. He scratched at his throat. *"Nika tika hootchenoo."*

"I reckon you've earned some refreshment. Find Charley and tell him I'll be there directly. If you see your sister, don't tell her anything."

The Indian bowed slightly from the waist. "Goodet-bye, white lady," he said, then strode away.

George chuckled. "Much as I'd like to palaver a while longer, it wouldn't be wise to leave Jim and his nephew to their own devices for very long. They have a taste for strong spirits, but no capacity for it."

"Before you go," Megan said, "would you have any paper on you? I left Minnie's in such a rush, I forgot to ask her for some."

"I keep a pocket diary." He patted his jacket. "If you're like my Kate, there's a shopping in the offing."

"You needn't tear any leaves out," Megan said. "Just lend me it and your pencil for a moment."

He regarded her quizzically, but complied. She used the flat of one hand as a table to inscribe:

I, Megan O'Malley, promise to pay George Washington Carmack, the sum of $750 with the entire amount plus three percent interest attached, due and payable one year hence the date of this agreement, 12 August 1897.

She flipped to the next sheet and wrote:

I, Megan O'Malley, promise to pay Joseph Ladue a consideration of $5,000 to lease a plat-ted lot within the confines of Dawson City, British Columbia, Dominion of Canada. The sum is due and payable, with three percent interest attached, one year hence the date of this agreement 12 August 1897.

She extended the diary and pencil. "Now, if you'd be kind enough to countersign the first promissory note and the second in Mr. Ladue's stead?"

George scanned her neat copperplate. "You are a

stubborn woman. None of this rigmarole, much less the indebtedness, is necessary."

"Ah, but it is to me. I couldn't sleep a wink here knowing the value of this building and the land it rests on." She pointed at the pages. "This eases my conscience the same as warm milk soothes the stomach."

His blue eyes probed hers. "My mother died when I was three and my father before I reached eleven. I've earned my keep ever since. I suspect your circumstance were similar."

"I emigrated with my sister at fourteen and we went West a year later. She married and settled down in San Francisco. I swore I'd avoid both those fates and have, thus far."

"But you have a son . . ."

"B.D.'s father died before he was born."

George scribbled a signature at the bottom of both sheets. "That does change my earlier opinion of you, Miss O'Malley."

Her fingers curled into fists, the nails carving crescents in her palms. Rather than perpetuate the assumption that O'Malley was her married name, she'd thought Carmack was trustworthy enough to be among the few who knew the truth.

"I called you stubborn," he said, "which you most certainly are." The diary snapped shut. "But in our short acquaintance, I've discovered you are the most admirable, forthright, and courageous woman I've ever met."

Stunned speechless, she barely managed to shake the hand he extended.

"Do be well and prosper. I look forward to meeting again next spring after my family's grand American tour."

"Bless you, George, and thank you for everything."

He started away, then turned. An ornery grin parted his moustaches. "You know, by the time Kate tires of buying every geegaw she sees, I may well need that seven hundred and fifty dollars."

"I'm a-promising, it'll be in the till when you come to collect it."

"I wouldn't doubt it for an instant, dear lady."

Megan paced their cozy quarters at the boarding-house. To anyone downstairs, her footfalls probably sounded like a horse being halter-broke. She couldn't care less.

B.D. slumped on a rag rug, his clothes too wet from the rain and too filthy from gallivanting to sit on the bed. He'd arrived almost as Minnie predicted: tired, nauseated, and reeking of overnight whiskey, but hardly repentant.

"Think you're smart, do you?" Megan said. "Pulled the wool over Commissioner Ogilvie's eyes and feature yourself a swashbuckler for it. The King of Chee-chako Hill, they're calling you."

"I wanted what was rightfully mine," he told the floorboards. "To bar me from staking a claim because I'm too young is no more fair than that conglomerate taking away The Thimbleful."

"Fair or not, in both cases it's the law. The difference is, I didn't know about that clause in Alaska's mining regulations. You knew full well you were breaking Canadian law—and damned if you aren't gloating about it to boot."

His fingers picked at the rug's braids. "So, you're a saint and I'm a sinner. What else is new?"

"Look at me when you talk to me."

Mud still clung to the roots of his hair and streaked his temples. The skin pouched beneath his bloodshot eyes. At the moment, he looked neither thirteen nor eighteen, but like an itinerant denizen of streets that had no name.

"I was mad as hell, Ma, at you, Nathan, Nels, and the whole bloody world. Recite the law till you're blue in the face if you're a mind to, but it won't make it right. I deserve a piece of Cheechako Hill, same as the rest of you."

"That's not the point."

"It's entirely the point."

Megan took a deep breath to calm herself. Allowing a shouting match to erupt wouldn't solve anything.

"Nathan went out to Cheechako this morning looking for you," she said. "Thanks to the stampede you set off, there isn't a yard of the slope we staked or the one on the other side of Bonanza Creek that hasn't been claimed. Men started lining up outside Ogilvie's office before dawn to wait their turn to register."

B.D.'s shoulder hunched. "More power to 'em."

"I'd agree, except that Katy-bar-the-door rush left no claim for me to file."

"Jaysus, Ma." He stared at her a long moment. "You must really think I'm the scum of the earth. I thought it'd go without saying that whatever I find at One Below is half yours."

She crossed over to the rocking chair and sat down, elbows braced on her knees. "You're impetuous, strong-willed, and stubborn as a mule, but a two-timer? Not once have I questioned whether you'd keep the booty and tell me to go hang."

"If that's the truth, why do you look like death warmed over?"

"Because as it stands we'll be lucky to make a nickel off it before someone figures out that you're not old enough to have filed it. When that happens—*and it will*—it'll be gone faster than you can say Jack Robinson and there aren't any more for me to affix my name to legally."

Instead of the comprehension and alarm Megan expected to see, B.D. exuded a placid malevolence. "I'll ask you again same as I asked you yesterday: how's anyone to know my right age unless you, Nathan, or Nels tell them?"

"Look in the mirror, son! Unless you're planning to wear a mud mask for the next five years, you've got no more hope of passing yourself off for eighteen than I do."

"I passed muster with a whole passel of jakes at the saloon last night. They bought me drinks just as they would any *man* that just struck it rich."

"Wait till they sober up," Megan said. "Besides, if you were so sure of yourself, why'd you disguise yourself like a minstrel showman?"

"Insurance."

"Bullshit."

"Ma!"

"I didn't blister your dainty ears, but I'm two ticks from it." She leaned close enough to risk secondary inebriation. "After all we went through to come here, don't you remember how you felt when you found out Bonanza and the El Dorado were sewn up tighter than a three-day-old corpse?"

"Why do you think I grabbed up One Be—"

"And *if,* upon hearing every blessed claim was taken *and* the outrageous price on Big Alex's fraction," she intoned, "you *then* divined that a Bonanza claim was registered to a thirteen-year-old boy, tell me—God's honest truth—*what would you do*?"

B.D.'s mouth opened, then shut. He scooted backward as far as the bedstead allowed, a vein at his jawline throbbing rhythmically. "I'd bring it to Ogilvie's attention."

"Why, son? Why wouldn't you leave it be? For all you'd know, the youngster might have been the first to find color on that claim. Fair is fair, right?"

His voice raised to a strident pitch. "No! The miner's code says do unto others as you would be done by. He wouldn't deserve it to keep it if he cheated me and everyone else to get it."

His stricken, pleading eyes sought hers. "That's what's going to happen, isn't it?"

"I'm afraid so."

"Oh God, I'm so sorry, Ma." His voice caught, then burst forth in a remorseful torrent. "Yesterday, in Ogilvie's office I was shaking so hard my teeth rattled. Thought he was on to me, sure. When he told me to sign that affidavit, my hand was sweaty—couldn't grip the pen.

"I tore outta there hollering to beat Ned. For the first time in my life, I felt like a bona fide prospector—like I *owned* the damned pot of gold at the end of the rainbow. I knew you'd be mad as a hatter, but thought you'd understand when you cooled off. Figured all I really had to do was cozen the commissioner. Have his signature scrawled on the registration and I was home free and legal."

Megan reached to stroke his matted wavy hair. "My darlin' Barlow David, I do understand. I've known that delirious, dizzy rainbow's-end kind of joy, too. Felt it the first time I held you in my arms, and it courses through me whenever I look at you."

"I wouldn't blame you if you hated me, Ma."

"For being young and foolish? Why, that's where older and wiser comes from." She chuckled. "With the head start you've gotten the last day or so, there's a fair chance you'll be smarter than me by the time you're my age."

A crooked grin erased much of the anguish from his face. "I suspect you want me to pay another call on Commissioner Ogilvie, eh?"

"No, it's me that'll do that."

"I bollixed the claim. I've got to be the one who puts it right again."

Megan reached into her trousers pocket and dug out a silver dollar. She balanced it on her thumbnail, then flipped it toward him. He snatched it from the air and examined it as if he'd never seen such a marvel.

"That's the same consideration I gave Barlow P. to secure the deed to the Russ House Restaurant in Tombstone. Best I can divine, your selling One Below to me should put us in compliance with the law."

"Really, Ma? Are you sure?"

"Not by a long shot. I'm not a-tall comfortable with bending the rules to keep from breaking them outright, either. But we found that claim and staked it, fair and square. I don't see any justice in letting it go on principle."

She settled back in the rocker. "I do believe, ol' Saint Megan's halo isn't screwed on as tight as you thought."

"Maybe I like you better with a dab of tarnish on it," he teased. "Now, scratch out that bill of sale, show me where to sign, and you've got a deal."

"Don't you want to hear the contingencies attached to this bargain before you seal it?"

He grunted. "Something tells me, I'll be happier if I don't."

"Only until Nathan rousts you out at dawn."

"What's he have to do with this?"

"In exchange for him and Nels keeping our little secret and not whaling the tar out of you for fretting your beloved mother unduly, you're going to help them build a cabin at their claim."

"Fair enough."

"And chop and haul them a winter's supply of firewood."

"Yeah, well . . ."

"You'll help them sink shafts in their claims until they hit bedrock. In your spare time, you'll build your own cabin at One Below and sink a shaft there."

"*What* spare time?"

"Evenings, after supper, and weekends when you're not inclined to mosey into town and help me," she answered breezily. "George came through on his promise this morning. I'm moving into his old cabin as soon as Minnie and I scrub the place squeaky."

B.D. rubbed his brow. "God Almighty, what a difference a day makes."

"Five thousand seven hundred and fifty dollars difference to be exact. The sum total—not counting three percent interest—of the promissory notes I gave George for the building and Mr. Ladue for the lot."

She countered his shocked expression with a demure smile. "It appears the One Below had better strike pay dirt in a hurry, doesn't it?"

Chapter 18

"Name, sir?" Commissioner William Ogilvie queried.

The man seated across the desk answered, "Albert Lancaster."

"Country of origin?"

"Califor-nee."

Ogilvie glanced up from the affidavit. "I believe the United States acquired that parcel several years ago, didn't it?" he asked drolly.

"S'pect you're right," Lancaster said. "Seems I read somethin' about it in the newspaper."

Megan stifled a laugh by concentrating on the caribou head mounted near the ceiling. Keen peripheral vision allowed her to study the others awaiting an audience with the Canadian official.

Their eyes flicked from floor to bended knees as they tried to appear lost in thought while eavesdropping on every word exchanged across Ogilvie's paper-strewn desk. The room's three benches, arranged in a U formation, squealed and squawked with their constant fidgeting. Watches were fished from vest pockets despite the mellow tick of the Regulator adjacent to the commissioner's desk.

Megan needn't be a mind reader to know what they were thinking. Why, no faster than Ogilvie completed the necessary forms, it might be Christmas before their duly registered claims made them millionaires.

She identified the assembly's lone male sourdough by his knuckles swollen from years of panning icy streams and skin graven by the elements. He glared at the commissioner as if insulted at not receiving preferential treatment.

Her bemused reverie ended when Lancaster all but pirouetted past her to the door. A youthful Mountie, resplendent in a double-breasted red tunic and dark trousers, pulled it shut behind him. When the benches emptied, the books would close on yet another fourteen-hour day. The guard had been posted to deter eager registrants still milling in the compound.

The commissioner swiveled in his chair to poke a folded sheet of paper in one of the wall-hung cabinet's cubbyholes. He surveyed the waiting area, then crooked a finger at Megan. "Next, please."

She doubted if the visitor's seat ever cooled to room temperature during office hours. The exhaustive record-keeping his job entailed would overwhelm a lesser man, as would the temptation to manipulate claims for personal profit. Like Mountie commanders Charles Constantine and Sam Steele, Ogilvie's tirelessness and unimpeachable character were the stuff of legend.

Megan folded her hands in her lap to hide their shaking. Her breathing quickened. She couldn't be more nervous if about to confess a murder to a priest.

Ogilvie's pen poised above the affidavit. "Your name, ma'am?"

"O'Malley. Megan O'Malley."

Without raising his head, he peered up at her. "Where have I heard . . . ?"

"Oh, I held claims in the Cariboo District many years ago. From what I've been told, some of the old-timers remember me." She gasped. "Not that you're an old-timer, mind you. It's me, that is. Forty-three last May."

Blathering twit, she fumed silently. Show the man what an eejit you are, why don't you?

He leaned back in his chair and stroked his manicured goatee as one would a house cat. "Megan

O'Malley, eh? Now that you mention it, Captain Moore once regaled me with a story of your derring-do. The Miner's Angel, he called you."

"An embroidered version to be sure, since tales only get more colorful with each telling," she replied. "It would have been lovely to visit with Captain Billy, but when I landed at Skagway, he was away. Dyea, I think."

"When was that?"

"The latter part of June, though it does seem much longer ago."

Furrows creased Ogilvie's wide brow. "Poor bloke probably wishes he'd stayed there."

"Why? Nothing's happened to him has it?"

"Nothing mortal, anyway." He snorted, but in a quite dignified manner. "I've come to believe the ancient mariner will address Saint Peter as sonny boy by the time he reaches the pearly gates."

Megan smiled at his remark and felt the tension cording her neck dissipate.

"Apparently," he continued, "you arrived in Skagway a month before the crush. The first steamer with gold-fevered tinhorns stacked to her yardarm landed on July twenty-sixth. A veritable armada has disgorged its human cargo every day since.

"I'm sorry to report the horde has completely disenfranchised our friend Captain Billy. An ex-Indian fighter named Reid appointed himself surveyor and collects a five-dollar fee from everyone desiring a lot—in addition to its inflated sales price. When Reid adjudged Billy's cabin to be in the way of a new road, he was ordered to move it."

"I can imagine the captain's reaction to that," Megan said. "I hope the scoundrel is still reeling from the donnybrook he set off."

"The essence of Billy's reply was lost in the account I heard, but a committee decided to ignore him and commenced ripping his threshold with peevees and handspikes. Not given to turning the other cheek, he grabbed a crowbar and started remodeling its owner's anatomy with it. The committee voted to adjourn forthwith, but I fear Billy won the battle only to lose the war."

Megan sat in stunned silence for a moment. "That's all transpired within the last month or so? I don't doubt you, yet it's nigh impossible to believe."

"For better or for worse, Klondicitis is raging worldwide," he said. "Before the spring breakup, only a few hundred souls had converged on Dawson and all from camps in the vicinity. If Captain Constantine's estimate is accurate, our population now hovers near twenty thousand."

A mournful groan escaped Ogilvie's lips. "God only knows how many thousand are en route over the Chilkoot and White Pass trails, and He isn't telling."

He looked past her shoulder and took up his pen. "My apologies for the daggers being aimed at your back," he murmured. "I daresay we'd better proceed before a mutiny is launched."

"My apologies for carrying on so."

"To the contrary. You listened to my prattle with admirable restraint—a rare occurrence and most appreciated."

Megan adopted a more businesslike posture. "Next time you stroll down Front Street, watch for a signboard that says the PROSPECTORS' HAVEN OF REST. I brew a fine cup of tea and can swap yarns with the best of them."

"Oh? I thought you were a prospector by trade?"

"I am, sir, but not daft enough to rely on it to keep my bread buttered." She slid the contract B.D. had signed toward him. "That's a bill of sale to One Below on Cheechako Hill. I'm in hopes it'll pay handsomely next spring, but that won't put food on the table this winter."

"I confess, my earlier recognition of your surname was from a Barlow David O'Malley filing on it, just yesterday." His dark eyes bored into hers. "As filthy a specimen as ever I've seen, yet his hands were spotless. Is he a relative, perhaps?"

"My son," she stammered. Ogilvie's scrutiny not only rekindled her apprehension, it inflamed it. "Uh—well, I'm sure you know how flighty young men can be. His excitement at staking a bench claim vanished before the ink dried."

"It's reasonable to assume you're acquainted with Mr. Kresge and Mr. Peterson, too." His tone indicated that a statement had been made, rather than a question asked.

"They were kind enough to share their canoe with us after our raft broke up below White Horse Rapids."

"I see." He frowned as he perused the contract. "Everything seems to be in order."

"I'm not a barrister, sir, but this is only a simple transfer of title."

"Yes, though I find it quite unusual that a prospector of your reputation wouldn't have staked a claim of your own."

Megan tensed, her mind searching for a valid explanation. "You're acquainted with George Carmack?"

"I employed George and Skookum Jim as packers when I surveyed the Alaska-Canadian border in '87."

"The 'Haven of Rest' I mentioned? Well, the building was, until a few days ago, George's trading post below Five Finger Rapids. He delivered and reassembled yesterday to house my business. By the time that transaction was done, all of Cheechako Hill was staked, so when B.D. offered to sell One Below, I agreed before he changed his mind again."

Ogilvie didn't so much as blink throughout her tirade. Damned if he wasn't looking at her the same way she looked at B.D. whenever his prevarications fell short of convincing.

The commissioner extracted a sheaf of documents from one of the cupboard's sections and riffled through them. "Despite your son's, er—flightiness, I believe you called it, how fortuitous that One Below will remain in the family."

"Then, you have no objection to transferring the deed?"

Ogilvie removed a paper from the pile. As he folded the sale agreement into precise thirds, he inquired, "Should I have?"

"No, Commissioner." She rose from the chair. "By all rights, that claim should belong to me."

He nodded sagely, then returned the crucial documents to their appropriate slot. "I'll have a copy of your affidavit ready in the next week to ten days."

"Thank you, sir."

Megan fought the impulse to run from his office. She willed herself to walk as normally as trembling knees allowed. Just before she reached the door, the sourdough sprang from the bench and followed her out.

"Had all the dawdling I can take for a while," he said, falling in beside her. "Jes' nursemaidin' a coupla greenhorns to see they dot their *i*'s and cross the *t*'s proper. May be so grateful they'll let me partner up with 'em."

Megan glanced at him and lengthened her strides. The old gent appeared harmless, but she was in no mood for casual repartee.

He dropped back only to call after her, "I don't mean to pester you, ma'am. Just want to ask a question, if I might."

"Yes, what is it?" she asked, her tone more brusque than she intended.

"That O'Malley feller what staked the first bench claim over to Cheechako Hill—he's kin to you?"

Megan's eyes narrowed. "I'm sure you overheard my conversation with the commissioner."

"Yeah, I shore did." He twisted a red knitted cap in his hands. "Kinda wish I hadn't."

Chapter 19

"Ain't no prizes give for second in this man's stampede," Spare-ribs Jimmy muttered.

The blade of B.D.'s pickax gouged a chunk from One Below's tunneled wall. He lay semiprone, cocked up on one shoulder which played hell with leverage.

"Well," he said, "prizes for first have been few and far between, my friend."

"Hey, don't take that for complaining. I like working up here for Nathan, Nels, and you."

B.D.'s tongue swiped grit from his teeth, then he spat. "Lancaster, Millett, and plenty of others are doling out fifteen bucks a day to their shovel stiffs."

Jimmy's chuckle tolled like a church bell within their tight confines. "Inquired at every mine in the valley at one time or t'other. All of 'em said fatten up, then they'd take me on. How I'd do that without a nickel to my name ain't never been explained."

"Yeah, but experienced miners are getting scarce," B.D. said. "Somebody's gonna offer half again as much to hire you away."

"Won't do 'em any good. Why, back in Montana, if somebody'd paid the ten a day I'm gettin' from Nathan, I'd have cut a fandango that Cher Azod couldn't match—even without her scarves. Money don't buy much of nothin' here—not if a dad-blamed radish'll fetch a dollar."

B.D. grunted. "Wouldn't give a copper penny for one of those, anyhow."

He pulled on the pick handle, trying to pry a ham-sized chunk loose. "Only I have noticed something that sells for the same price here as in the Lower Forty-eight."

The crickety rasp of steel biting frozen silt preceded a strained, "Such as?"

B.D. planted his feet and yanked again before answering, "A sportin' woman's favors."

A well-aimed clot of mud plinked off his neck. "You been visiting Paradise Alley instead of your mama like you said you was?"

"Not yet, I haven't, but it sure makes for an interesting shortcut to the Haven of Rest."

"Uh-huh. 'Bout as interesting as a feedlot."

"All right, so most of the Jezebels lean toward husky—"

"Husky, hell," Jimmy said. "Them that ain't whales on the hoof is wasted enough to scare crows from a cornfield."

"Calm down, for Christ's sake. Wish I'd never brought the subject up."

A larger clod splattered B.D.'s earlobe.

"That best be all that comes up within a country mile of Paradise Alley," Jimmy warned, " 'lest you wind up carrying your pecker in a sling. Bad enough that them frails is uglier than a backhouse's basement, they've got every kind of pox a man'd sooner die than catch."

B.D. ducked away as the hunk of jagged permafrost he'd pried on broke loose. "How would you know? Personal experience?"

"My pa died of it last spring. Doc Gandolf said it got in his blood and infected his brain. Rare, but not the first case he'd seen. Since Daddy caught it from a squaw, I bartered pert near everything we owned to a Stick shaman, thinkin' he'd conjure a voodoo cure. His big medicine didn't work on Daddy nor the slut that give him the pox, neither."

B.D. rolled over on his belly and onto his knees.

"I'm sorry, Jimmy. If there's anything I'm good at, it's being six kinds of stupid."

"You didn't know." The gaunt young man took a mighty swing at the wall. "But now you do, so don't be traipsing betwixt them crib rows anymore, you hear?" A wide grin erased his daunsy expression. "Wouldn't put it past one of them ol' cows to throw a loop over a fine yearling bull such as yourself."

"Despite my mother's opinion to the contrary," B.D. said, "you don't need to tell me twice."

"Does rankle a feller to see an ox like Big Alex or that no-account Swiftwater Bill Gates with a sweetheart on each arm."

"You got that right. What do they have that we don't—besides a million in gold piled in a corner somewhere?"

"Money ain't everything, kid."

"Hmmmph. That's what rich people say to make poor folks feel noble."

"Doesn't work worth a shit, either, does it?" Jimmy teased.

"Not hardly."

B.D. grimaced as he scooped muck from the floor and dumped it in a dredge bucket which would be windlassed out and emptied onto the slag heap. The One Below's ratio of pay dirt to dirt-dirt wouldn't be known until the spring wash, but regardless of value, half-thawed permafrost felt like cold horse apples and stank worse than ripe ones.

A couple of chunks of firewood sailed past his nose. They landed dead-bang in the center of the fire at the tunnel's far end. Embers flew every which-a-way.

" 'Preciate that, Jimbo," B.D. drawled. "It was just getting fit to breathe in here."

"Noticed you stopped hackin'. After all these weeks of sucking down soot, 'twas afraid a lungful of clean air'd kill ya."

"It could, sure enough. If the smoke down here

doesn't get me, that smudge factory Nels calls a stove will."

"Tried to tell Mr. College that the flue pipe he rigged wasn't big enough." Jimmy shrugged. "Maybe city slickers is more accustomed to suckin' down pizen. For all we know, their cabin smells as pretty as an undertaker's parlor to them."

B.D. nodded absently while he considered clambering out of the shaft to empty the bucket. It'd take another hour's digging to fill it, but Jaysus, how sweet it would be to stand up straight. To reach for the stars and stretch the kinks from his back.

He groaned low in his throat, then scuttled around to sit Indian-style. Any change in position felt so fine, a workingman could nigh fall to a swoon from it. About the time he decided he'd discovered a better way of doing things, misery broke out in a new place.

The fire they kept stoked to melt the permafrost didn't chase away the cold that seeped through to his bones. Only in the Klondike could a fellow wipe sweat from his brow while suffering chilblains-of-the-butt.

As he hied back with his pickax, the crown of his hat scraped the ceiling's icicle beard. He bowed his neck like a goose on the prod to prevent icy pellets from showering down his collar at every move. While his hat cleared with the next swing, a sharp pain stabbed him between the shoulder blades.

"God Almighty damn," he hollered. "How Ma stays hunkered down here from morning till night every Sunday is beyond me."

"Well, for starters she's short, kid."

B.D. grinned at the craggy wall. "She's also older than both of us put together."

"Miss Megan's spry, I'll grant that. Tough as a hobnail, but a lady to the core. Fact remains, I never envied them circus midgets till I started minin' for a livin'."

"Kind of makes you wonder why more of them aren't prospectors," B.D. said.

"Aw, just because their pins is sawed off don't mean they're shy on brains. They'd be plumb loco to give up a tassled chair in a sideshow tent to turn gopher."

"Does that mean we're crazy to be doin' it?"

"Yep. Crazier still to be doin' it up here in the devil's icebox. Leastways, we ain't alone."

The harmonious ching of pickaxes ricocheted around the cavern for several minutes. B.D. realized that conversation slowed progress, but without it he might as well be working alone.

"I can't help but wonder if I'm digging a hole for Ma to pour good money down. Figure it's even odds whether her Haven of Rest ever shows a profit."

He pried a saucer-sized fragment from the wall. "I don't know why she's heart-set on that godawful name, either. Sounds more like a boneyard than a— a—well, whatever it's supposed to be."

"Won't argue that," Jimmy said. " 'Cept Social Club might get construed for a cathouse same as anything with 'parlor' in it. 'Tis restful there, and smells nice, too."

"Trouble is, Ma's got more divvies working than Big Alex. Those notes she signed to Ladue and Carmack have cost me a few nights' sleep and now Minnie's in for a share, too."

"Miss Megan's smart to specialize in fancy eats 'stead of a real restaurant, though. Joe Juneau and Henry Don Brixey already locked theirs up and skedaddled."

B.D.'s belly began to growl. Nels and Nathan were already rationing their larder, which didn't aggrieve them unduly since they ate like a pair of hummingbirds. When B.D. finished his new home, the belly-cheatin' would end.

"How about those BE GONE OR GO HUNGRY handbills Captain Constantine put up all over town," B.D. said. "Think there's anything to it?"

"Well, a bunch of us were down to toenail clippin' stew and pocket lint puddin' before the river busted up this spring. Judging by how many pilgrims are packed in here now and that them three supply boats· is grounded at Yukon Flats for the winter, I'd say the situation's diresome and gonna get worse."

"How much worse?"

"Depends."

"On what?"

Jimmy tossed another log on the fire. "Don't ask unless you for sure want to know."

B.D. swiveled around. "Damn it, there's few things that rouses curiosity faster than statements like that."

"All right. It depends on how many die of scurvy, meningitis, and new-mon-ee." His bloodshot eyes pegged B.D.'s. "The dead don't eat much."

A shiver coursed through B.D. from head to foot. His mother's oft-related Eight-Mile Creek story provided an unwanted education on scurvy and its symptoms. He checked to see whether Jimmy was watching, then gnashed his teeth. None seemed to wriggle in their sockets. No, wait. B.D.'s tongue explored an upper molar. Jaysus. Wasn't there a tiny bit of give to it? Soon as we quit for the day, I'll borrow Nathan's shaving mirror for a look-see. Damned if getting rich is worth gumming my food for the rest of my life.

Absently, B.D. chipped at the wall with his pick. What was it about somebody asking if you want to know something—and it's forever something bad— that compels a yes. Then the instant you hear the answer, you regret ever asking for it?

A grating sound intruded on B.D.'s mental discourse. He swung back and smote the wall as hard as his awkward stance allowed. The blade sank with uncommon ease.

"The fire's too hot," he said. "This section's thawed enough to be dangerous."

"You're complainin'? This over here's still hard as a glacier." Jimmy scooted over and looked at the blade cuts. "Hit 'er another lick."

B.D. complied, albeit grudgingly. The pick cleaved

a sizable gash. A flap of frozen sediment peeled away in the process. The rent gleamed as bright as snow against the darker permafrost.

B.D. snatched up a candle. Its flame tilted sideward and spat when the pool of melted tallow threatened its extinction. He scarcely breathed as his fingertips traced the field of pebbles chinked with bits of dull yellow.

"The ancient streambed," he whispered. "Dear God Almighty, we've hit it, too."

He swiveled on the balls of his feet. "Go fetch Nathan before my heart jumps clean outta my chest. I know what he's gonna say, but oh, how I want to hear him say it."

Chapter 20

Megan rested her elbows on the counter to brazenly admire the Haven of Rest's main room. She hadn't tired of gazing upon her handiwork during quiet moments after the day's customers departed for Front Street's livelier establishments.

She and Minnie had scrubbed and polished the old post, then chinked every crack in its log walls with moss. They troweled on two wheelbarrow-sized batches of plaster concocted from sand, clay, and water, followed by a coat of whitewash. The stuccolike effect brightened the space, but retained its rustic coziness.

When her former landlady offered the contents of her attic to furnish the Haven of Rest, Megan expected an assortment of castoffs too good to discard in an ash bin, but too scruffy for Minnie's parlor.

Instead, Megan found herself staring at a veritable treasure trove; a few pieces with their price tags still attached.

"I learned the hard way that shopping is no remedy for grief," Minnie said. "Two years ago, after Hugo died, I spent weeks poring over a Sears Roebuck wish book. With the means to buy anything and everything my heart desired and the freedom to simply *have* things simply because I wanted them, I was like a kid in a confectionery shop.

"I had second thoughts long before the steamer load of plunder arrived. The men I hired to lug it from the dock to our cabin outside Circle City ended up carting it back to a warehouse I rented in town."

"But why?" Megan asked.

"I realized I only bought them to spite my husband for having the nerve to up and die on me. I didn't need a ton of claptrap to dust and wax. What I missed was having someone to cook for and fuss over.

"Rumors of the Dawson strike seemed like a godsend. I moved here with the idea that a boarding house would let me get some good out of this stuff and cure my loneliness, too."

She'd cackled merrily. "Misery doesn't love company half as much as widder ladies do, but surrounding myself with evidence of that temper tantrum annoyed me terribly. So, up to the attic it came, out of sight and out of mind."

Megan gazed around the dust-hazed space in wonderment. She'd never been one to feel light-headed at the sight of a parlor suite displayed in a furniture store window, but she couldn't imagine Minnie dismissing so many lovely pieces as claptrap. "I appreciate your letting me look, but everything is much too nice to use at the Haven."

"Another winter under the eaves and it won't be fit for stove wood," Minnie said. "That won't do either of us a bit of good."

"Don't waste your breath trying to spoof me. We both know you could sell it all in one afternoon for twice what you paid."

Minnie took on a banty rooster stance. "I don't want to sell it—to you or anyone else. Having it keeps me humble. What I *will* do is loan what you need for however long you need it."

"It's generous you are to a fault and I love you for it, but I can't let you do that."

"Why not? It's neither a gift nor a favor, Megan. At the moment, I don't need these things, but you do. Someone ought to use them besides the mice that are nesting in them."

"How about a compromise?"

"Such as?"

"What if I take a lay on your things at, say, four percent of the Haven's net? Everything still belongs to you that way and I won't feel like I'm getting something for nothing."

Minnie's pugnacious expression relaxed to a grandmotherly softness. "Two percent and a chair reserved for me when I hanker for a friend to talk to?"

"You'd have that, regardless."

"Then start picking and choosing, dearie, while I round up some vagrants to haul it for us."

Megan smiled at the memory of that odd processional up Front Street. An oak sideboard the men declared "heavier than a dead bull buffalo" now hid the patched area where Carmack's hearth once stood. Green-shaded student lamps rested on the sideboard's side shelves; the light they cast reflected by its beveled plate mirror. A pair of saddle seat rockers and hassocks flanked the massive serving piece.

Minnie couldn't explain what prompted her purchase of a standing desk with a built-in book rack, but it balanced the entry wall as if custom-made for it. Because stationery cost a dollar a sheet or more, the desk's triple drawers held scraps of butcher paper and discarded Mounted Police broadsides for customers to write their letters on.

Two square side tables picketed by box seat panel chairs filled the space between the desk and a barrel-shaped Yukon stove; the necessary, albeit ugly, sheet-iron wood-eater George had installed to replace the hearth.

An oak and maroon leather parlor settee angled from one side of the stove. A matching platform rocker occupied the other; its curved arms always draped by a length of unbleached muslin in Minnie's absence.

Megan had refused the wine-, tan-, green-, and corn-colored Brussels rug that was rolled up like a giant

cigar and propped in a corner of the boardinghouse's attic.

"It'll be mud-splattered and ruined before the
week's out," she'd stated.

"It will not," Minnie argued. "The men'll render
themselves sock-footed in a wink. While the sons of
Adam despise dainty foforaws, most of them respect
beauty and comfort."

"No, Mrs. Walentine. I will not allow something so
beautiful to be destroyed before my very eyes."

That the rug's gorgeous floral motif now carpeted
the Haven's floor proved which of them was the most
mule-headed. As for Minnie's philosophy, B.D. was
the only one Megan habitually scolded for tracking
across it in his boots.

" 'Tis a sin to be so house proud." Megan said with
a sigh. She pushed away from the counter to bank the
stove for the night. "Worse, I suppose, to smell a faint
trace of cinnamon at every breath when I know there's
not a speck of it to be found within fifteen hundred
miles."

She started when the door swung wide. "Are you
closed, Miss O'Malley?" Commissioner Ogilvie
inquired.

"I was about to, but if you'd be kind enough to
slide the bar into its brackets, we'll polish off what's
left in the kettle."

"Waste not, want not, eh?" He smiled and shut the
door against the frigid October wind.

"Not with the Alaska Commercial Company rationing supplies. Why, their warehouses are stacked to
the rafters with goods, but even Big Alex has to beg
for a sack of coffee."

Ogilvie shed his fur overcoat, hat, and gloves, leaving his boots on the grass mat provided for that purpose. "I wouldn't divulge this publicly, but I do
question Superintendent Hansen's 'sky is falling'
panic. My cynical side says it's only to justify his outrageous prices."

He drew a chair from under the table and seated himself. "Yet I haven't forgotten last winter's flour-dusted moustaches and whiskers. Far too many were reduced to gobbling it dry from cupped hands like birds pecking after seed."

Megan set a brimming cup of tea before him, then refilled the kettle from an oak water bucket. Drops sizzled to vapor the instant they splattered on the stove's flat top.

"I suspect it's some of both," she said, placing a saucer of petits fours surrounded by bits of fruit leather at his elbow. "Though it doesn't seem fair, there's a strange sort of equity to Hansen's meting out the stores. God help us all if a nabob like Swiftwater Bill were in charge."

With her hostess duties completed for the moment, she sat down across the table from him, then maneuvered her feet to rest on the seat of an adjacent chair.

She frowned at her stained apron and the greasy streaks bespoiling her gray jersey dress. They both needed sponging before her head creased the pillow. It wouldn't do for the Haven's proprietress to greet the next day's customers looking like a charwoman.

Ogilvie sampled a cake, biting the morsel in two rather than popping it into his mouth whole as most did. His eyes rolled upward and his tongue darted out to fish for crumbs.

"Delicious," he declared. "Tastier than anything Mrs. Ogilvie produces in her fancy kitchen—a treasonous remark I'll deny if ever repeated, of course."

"I won't breathe a word, Commissioner."

He dispensed with the tidbit and reached for another. "My sweet tooth is overwhelming my manners, but I must ask if you'd share your recipe. The garden club my wife presides over in Ottawa would sack the refreshment table if a tray of these were served."

"There's no secret, other than being raised on making something out of not much of anything," Megan said. "Twice a week, I bake boards of thin johnnycake, drizzle it with watered honey, then slice it into squares."

"Well, I'll be." He scrutinized the last cake as if a clue to some unmentioned ingredient might be inscribed on it. "And the candy? Shall I believe you cultivate lemons and cherries in the backroom?"

Megan chuckled. "Not unless they'd take root in my mattress." She pointed at the rows of twine-strung fruit ribbons that festooned the rafters. "I salvaged a cartload of spoiling produce from a waterfront vendor. He sold cheap to save himself the trouble of dumping it in the river.

"After I cooked the pulp, I strained it through a sieve, and dried the paste on platters. The grated rinds add a speck of flavor to the tea and I do sprinkle a pinch into the cake batter."

Ogilvie took a sip from his cup; his pinky aloft as if its joint were arthritic. "You're a most resourceful woman and prospering from it, as I understand."

A subtle inflection in his voice tripped an equally subtle alarm in Megan's mind. The boyish glimmer she'd seen in his eyes while he devoured the plate of sweets had evaporated.

She swung her legs to the floor and rested her back squarely against the chair rungs. "This isn't entirely a social call, is it, Commissioner?"

"It wasn't meant to be at all social. Your hospitality distracted me from its original purpose." He studied his thumb as it whipsawed the cup's handle. "Partaking of it under pretense makes me a Janus of the first rank."

"Your reason must be dire indeed to level such an insult at yourself."

He cocked his head and looked at her. "Miss O'Malley, your compassion only increases my guilt tenfold." He laughed, then added, "A result you assuredly anticipated."

"It's the One Below, isn't it? Something's gone awry."

"We both know something was awry from the outset."

"Do you have children, Mr. Ogilvie?"

"If I didn't, I wouldn't have sympathized with the position B.D.'s impulsiveness left you in. Actually, I understand both sides of the issue. B.D. wants very much to be acknowledged as a prospector in his own right."

"Then what would you have done if your son had pulled such a stunt?"

Ogilvie fiddled with his goatee for a moment. "In all honesty, I'd have been sorely tempted to kill the boy and tell the Lord he'd left town. Once reason prevailed, I'd have proceeded just as you did."

"If that's true, then why are you here?"

"Because a fine old gent by the name of Earl Delacroix knocked on my office door this evening and asked for a private chat. Like you, Earl doesn't have a greedy or deceitful bone in his body. That's why he waited until the last minute before expressing his concerns about the One Below."

Megan almost asked what he meant by 'the last minute,' then realized almost two months had passed since B.D. filed the original affidavit. By Dominion law, if Ogilvie declared it invalid—which was the same as it having never been registered—the claim fell open again in sixty days.

"I'll wager Mr. Delacroix is whittling stakes as we speak," she said. "Especially now that B.D. is bringing up color with every bucket load."

"Earl told me he was ready to cry foul the afternoon you transferred title. Spare-ribs Jimmy Mackinson treated Earl to supper the night you arrived and described the party he'd guided through town. Earl knew B.D. was several years shy of majority, but after speaking to you outside my office, he stayed his protest, though he's brooded about it ever since."

A vague recollection of a grizzled codger waylaying her that day flitted behind Megan's eyes. "Brooded, my a—er, my foot. Is it a coincidence that sixty days is almost up? Hah! I don't believe in coincidences, Commissioner."

Her palm slammed the table. "I lost a silver lode in Pioche, Nevada to that kind of finagling and I'll be damned if I'll lose the One Below the same way."

"Earl doesn't want to steal your claim," Ogilvie said evenly. "Nor does he think it's right for you to own it under questionable circumstances."

"Then come the morning of the eleventh, I'll be on your stoop waiting to reregister it. Surely, that'll put Mr. Delacroix's mind at ease."

Ogilvie shook his head. "Technically, the One Below falls open at a tick past midnight and it must be staked before it can be registered."

"Oh, I see. Delacroix figures to stumble around in the dark and set his stakes before I can? Not bloody likely."

For all her bluster, with temperatures hovering at twenty below, driving new markers in the frozen ground would be tantamount to driving them in solid granite.

"Staking is only one facet of the procedure, as well you should know," Ogilvie said. "Do you also plan to race Earl back to town to be sure you cross my threshold first?"

She laughed bitterly. "I've sprinted the distance once. I don't reckon a second time will kill me."

"If word gets out, Earl may not be the only one vying for ownership."

"Well, I'd rather Captain Constantine didn't post any notices of the event, but if I have to outrun every man jack in the Yukon to keep a claim I damn well already own, so be it."

Ogilvie's chest heaved with a dejected sigh. "I am sorry it's come to this. I've scoured every page of the Dominion Lands Mining Regulations for a loophole or a resolution to absolutely no avail."

Megan studied the table's elongated graining. The

irregular, rather grotesque whorls paralleled her thoughts.

She was angry at Ogilvie for destroying her carefully orchestrated illusion of security. Angry at herself for reacting to B.D.'s boastful man-talk by treating him like a naughty boy. He was both and neither.

Adult men who never reverted to childish antics or deeds were not only rare, but insufferable dullards. Boys too young to button their own britches rattled out insights so keen their mothers ceased to breathe for a moment.

Her anger diverted to Delacroix for letting her believe, lo these many weeks, that she'd dueled with Fate and won.

Ogilvie rose from his chair. "Earl is cut from the same cloth you are. He is an honorable man."

His statement, designed to both reassure and compliment, fell short of its intent. Megan didn't bother to acknowledge it. She couldn't. She was struggling too hard against the tears she refused to shed in the commissioner's presence.

"Captain Constantine will inspect the claim site a week hence, then post guards to prevent any shenanigans," Ogilvie said as he hastened into his outergarments. "On the eleventh, at the stroke of midnight by Constantine's watch, he'll fire one shot."

A frigid blast hurtled inside when the commissioner opened the door. "I sincerely hope to see you in my office a few hours later, Megan. Don't disappoint me."

Chapter 21

Two days later, the Haven of Rest hummed with refugees from winter's first bona fide blizzard.

Megan drew a knife through a board of johnnycake. Its mellow, slightly sweet aroma had kept her customers' noses twitching for over an hour. They'd flock to the counter the moment she finished laying it with the fruit-garnished saucers of petits fours, mugs, and a fresh pot of tea.

Each would sprinkle a third of an ounce of dust onto her gold scale in exchange for a plate of nibblings and a splash of orange pekoe. To receive five dollars a serving for such trifles still astounded Megan, but as long as the men were satisfied, who was she to question such insanity?

What she'd come to call Klondike Dementia also allowed her to "rent" months-old stateside newspapers and water-stained books from Minnie's attic for a dollar per hour, and charge two dollars a page to write letters dictated by the illiterate, the lazy, or those incapable of expressing romantic sentiments when they wielded the pen.

Wind-driven snowflakes blasted through the door behind a sizable gent clad in a full-length marten coat and turban-style cap.

Artemis Blankenship's rocker cricked as he waved a greeting with his pipe. "Hey, Tom, shuck them drift-kickers and come sit a spell. Haven't seen you in a coon's age."

"I would, but I can't stay long," the newcomer replied. He whisked off his cap, then inquired to Megan, "Are you the proprietress?"

"I am."

He nodded slowly while his eyes assessed her from widow's peak to apron waistband. His scrutiny seemed more detached than lecherous, but before Megan could react, the door swung open to admit B.D.

"Sorry I'm late," he said to the stranger without acknowledging his mother's existence.

"Just got here myself a minute ago."

"Well," B.D. said, gesturing toward Megan. "What's the verdict?"

"It's hard to tell, but I'd say her lungs are on the small side."

"I beg your pardon!"

Guffaws erupted from all directions.

"Don't appear that small to me," Eugene Franklin drawled. "Why, my last wife was so skinny, I couldn't tell her shoulder blades from her . . . uh, t'other side less'n the lamp was lit."

Artemis slapped his knee. "If you think that's bad, I—"

"Would hush this instant or take my leave," Megan finished for him.

B.D. escorted the stranger to the counter. "Ma, I'd like you to meet a friend of mine, Tom Lippy. Before El Dorado's Sixteen Below made him a millionaire, he was the physical instructor at the Seattle Y.M.C.A."

Megan eyed Lippy warily. A handsome bloke, she'd give him that, but his unrelenting appraisal reminded her of an undertaker measuring a consumptive for a pine box.

"I apologize for any embarrassment I caused you," he said. "My mind was elsewhere when I made it."

"There's no doubt of that, Mr. Lippy."

B.D. leaned forward to whisper, "Will you simmer down and listen, Ma? Tom's an expert at training athletes. He even acted as an advisor to Gardner Williams, the 1896 Olympics swimmer."

"He competed in the hundred-meter freestyle, didn't he?" Megan inquired.

Lippy ducked his chin. "Yes ma'am."

"And lost, as I recall," she continued. "By about ninety-seven meters."

B.D.'s head whipped sideward. "He did?"

"Yeah," Tom admitted. "He was accustomed to indoor pools. That Grecian ice water in the Bay of Zea dang near froze Gardner solid the second he dove into it."

He directed his gaze at Megan. "I'm concerned about you for much the same reason."

"Me? I can't imagine why."

B.D. glanced over his shoulder. "Because of the race."

"What about it?"

"Jaysus, Ma. Ol' Delacroix may be older than Noah's grandpa, but—he's—uh . . ."

"A man," Megan said, her displeasure evident in her tone.

"B.D., you're not helping a bit," Tom said. "It isn't your mother's gender that worries me."

Megan favored her son with a triumphant smile. By gum, she knew she'd liked Mr. Lippy the moment she'd laid eyes on him.

"Might I ask, what does concern you, then?"

"Quite frankly, much the same thing that put the kibosh to Gardner Williams. Because you spend most of your time indoors, I fear your lungs will seize from the cold."

Megan recalled her first winter in the Cassiar. She and Barlow P. had struck out for Victoria, British Columbia after waiting a month for a break in the weather. At forty below zero, every breath she'd expended seemed like her last, whereas inhaling set her chest on fire.

"I've been too worried about the race's outcome to think about the cold, but with only a few days to prepare, I don't know what I can do about it."

"For starters," Tom said, "I recommend taking brisk walks the length of Front Street four times a day, plus, I'd partake of six small meals instead of two or three larger ones. Beefsteak's the best, but moose will do, plus bread or potatoes, and no sugar. A can of milk every day, too, if you can afford it. Lots of water, if you can't."

"Will you do it, Ma?" B.D. asked. "Please?"

Megan gazed lovingly at the board of honey-sweetened johnnycake. Had she been asked to list her least favorite things, wading snow for exercise, fried moose, and canned milk as a beverage would rank among the top ten.

"If you're sure it'll help me beat Earl Delacroix . . . then, yes. Of course, I will." To herself she added, and if Mr. Tom-the-Physical-Instructor-Lippy knows what's good for *him*, it damn well better.

Chapter 22

Veils of moon-silvered smoke hovered over the snow-covered Bonanza Creek valley; the pallid contrast at once eerie and beautiful. The golden orange glow of miners' cookfires dotted the hillsides. Faint, rounder pocks of amber marked tunnel openings where third-shift miners labored by candlelight.

It wasn't a hardship to work during hours when more civilized people slept. Day had no reckoning deep within the earth's bowels. During winter, the region stateside newspapers called The Land of the Midnight Sun became the Land of the High Noon Moon.

"Are you cold, Ma?" The woolen scarf protecting B.D.'s face muffled his voice.

"It's twenty-five below zero. Heavens, yes, I'm cold."

"Sure you won't wait inside the cabin until closer to time? The kettle's on, and I've saved some of your favorite tea."

"Bless you, son, for your thoughtfulness, but the warmth would do me more harm than good."

A vapor-puffing bear-sized form hastened toward her; the frozen snow crunching with every footfall. "Good news," Nathan announced. "Captain Constantine says five of the other nine contenders gave it up. Said the whole racket was insane and not worth losing toes over."

Megan replied, through chattering teeth, "I tend to agree with them."

"You're not wilting on me, are you?" B.D. asked.

"No, I just wish the captain's watch would tick faster."

"Where's the hammer and claim stake?" Nathan asked.

Megan uncrossed and raised her arms, freeing her mittened hands from the cozy niche where she'd tucked them. One grasped a three-pounder's handle; the other, a wooden marker inscribed with the claim designation and number, her name, the date, the letters *MLP* for Mining Location Post and a number one.

"Same place as the last time you asked," she teased, "and where they're sure to be the next."

"Yeah, well, Nels already told me I was as nervous as a Jezebel on her deathbed."

"Are he and Jimmy feeling any better?" B.D. asked.

"Some, I think. The poultice Miss Megan concocted for their chests is helping them breathe easier."

"It won't for long unless you fix that stovepipe so it'll draw right," she said. "It's a wonder you aren't crouping, too."

Nathan said, "I took care of it this afternoon, ma'am. We now have a flue big enough to serve a blast furnace."

Captain William Constantine's baritone rent the air. "Attention, please. One Below Discovery, Cheechako Hill will fall open to all eligible claimants in one minute."

"This is it," B.D. said. He threw his arms around Megan and hugged her. "I'm awful sorry I—"

"No need of that, son. Just wish me luck."

He pecked her cheek—or an affectionate facsimile due to their scarf-wrapped faces.

"Godspeed," Nathan said, "and may the best woman win."

"I'll give it all I've got."

She started toward the Mountie officer, then turned to call, "Keep a close watch on Nels and Jimmy for me."

"We will, Ma."

Captain Constantine motioned for the dozen or so hardy spectators to move out of the way. Four well-bundled contenders remained. Judging by his red knit cap, the shortest could be none other than her primary challenger, Earl Delacroix.

"Good luck, Miz O'Malley."

"The same to you, Mr. Delacroix."

The other three muttered what she assumed were similar sentiments.

"Nicely done," Constantine said. "For the record, at my signal, you are to hasten to the southwestern boundary of the designated claim and situate a stake at its corner to stand independent of any supporting mechanism. At that juncture, since Commissioner Ogilvie has graciously extended his regular office hours"—a chuckle rumbled forth—"I'd advise you gents and lady to run hell-bent for Dawson. Any questions?"

The five claimants answered in unison, "No, sir."

A pistol shot sufficed as an amen to Megan's silent prayer. The four men took off at a sprint, powdery snow arching from their boots. She chased after them, her eyes riveted on her son's wind-milling arms.

"Hurry, Ma," he yelled.

Availing herself of the others' footprints bogged her down. Megan darted left, adjusting her gait to the slope. She reached the claim's appropriate corner only to ignore B.D.'s command to "Drive in the stake." Time was of the essence, but her competitors were taking turns rather than cosh each other senseless trying to swing their hammers simultaneously.

After one ran for the creek valley howling like a wolf, the next motioned for Megan to step up. "Ladies first."

"Not tonight."

"Go ahead, ma'am," Delacroix urged. "Ain't gonna matter none either way."

"If it does, it wasn't my doin'," she warned, plunging her marker into the snow. "Remember that."

The hammer's impact reverberated clear to her shoulders. Nathan had whittled the stake to a pencil-point sharpness, but sweat drizzled between her breasts before it punctured the ground to a sufficient depth.

"Appreciate the courtesy, boys," she said and lofted the hammer toward B.D. "See you in town."

She paused a moment to get her bearings. Snow magically erased both natural and man-made impediments. The day before, during a scouting expedition, she'd memorized landmarks to avoid such hazards and to divine the shortest, least treacherous route.

Her rhythmic side-to-side lope, akin to a speed skater's, seemed awkward at first. Lippy had suggested she practice it while taking her daily constitutionals, but to repeatedly change from a dress to trousers and back again was too time-consuming and bothersome.

The further she ran, the more grateful she was for his advice to acclimate herself to the elements. Ice glazed the outside of her scarf and the frigid air rasped her throat, but not to any unbearable degree.

Megan thought of her mad dash after B.D. in August. Despite winter's harsher conditions, she felt stronger, more invigorated than she had then. She smiled behind her scarf and pumped her arms even harder.

She stayed to the ridge, where the wind had broomed away some of the snow. The humped rise appeared to ramble on forever before it tapered downward.

An object diagonally ahead and below her caught her eye. The first staker. He'd taken what he'd apparently believed to be a shortcut and was mired in a knee-deep drift,

What a shame, Megan thought smugly. I reckon you should have done a wee bit of scouting yourself.

She waved to a Mountie who stood at attention near

the bottom of the hill. Moonlight darkened his uniform coat to the color of dried blood. He didn't return her greeting.

A series of *whumps* startled her. Two men barreled past. Megan stumbled and almost fell. She regained her balance in time to glimpse Delacroix high-stepping through the snow like a manic drum major.

"Jesus, Mary, and Joseph. I've dropped from second lead to second last in seconds."

What had been only a mild breeze slashed through her outergarments, chilling her to the marrow. Her legs trembled, suddenly lacking the strength to raise her feet. She'd lost the race. Beaten herself with her own stupid arrogance. There was no use going on; no prize awaiting a fourth-place finisher.

Her head snapped up when she heard a beloved voice drawl, "Baby gal, you're jes' burnin' daylight. Best you git to gittin'."

She skidded to stop and wheeled a full circle. The landscape sparkled like tiny diamonds strewn across a vast field of white velvet. No lanky old coot in a crumpled black Stetson stood there grinning back at her.

Megan's heart squeezed in her chest. She hopped a step and took off running. Quit cussin' your mule and wishin' it was a horse, she quoted from memory, her strides breaking crusted snow at every syllable. Either saddle the damned thing or sell it.

Churned footprints blazed her predecessor's trail. In two leaps she cleared Bonanza Creek's humped, icy surface to angle slightly northeast along its opposite bank.

She raced cross-country, legs scissored wide, arms cleaving the air, propelling her forward. At the crest of a knoll, Megan scanned the misty horizon. Moosehide Mountain's blunt nose indicated a two-yard shift east. Without breaking stride, she hesitated before making adjustment.

What if that wasn't Moosehide? The surrounding terrain didn't look quite the same as it had during her

daylit reconnaissance. A bowled expanse where Pure
Gold Creek, a pair of unnamed rills, and Lovett Creek
branched from Bonanza lay between her and the
Klondike River. Even a minor error in direction could
cost an extra mile.

Do it, she commanded. There's no time for second-
guessing.

Vapor from her labored breathing turned her scarf
into a frozen mask. Ice clung to her eyelashes and cast
a ghostly aura over cabin roofs and sluiceworks. The
sled-dog grapevine barked announcements of her passage, but no doors opened to investigate the racket.

As she negotiated the fourth creek, she edged closer
to Bonanza's bank and the road that paralleled it. The
snow was too harrowed by constant use to discern
whether her contenders had passed through or not.

Yellow blocks of light from Belinda Mulrooney's
Grand Forks Hotel beckoned a tantalizing welcome.
Megan's pulse throbbed in her ears. Every ragged
breath seared her lungs.

Gotta rest. Just a minute or two. Warm up a mite.

She shook her head. No. Can't stop. B.D.'s counting
on you. Barlow P.'s watching—maybe David, too. Go
on. It can't be much further.

Her feet had numbed before the race began. Over
its course, the rest of her appendages followed suit.
The cold had turned her into a half human marionette.
She couldn't trust her wooden limbs not to misstep,
so she kept her eyes trained on the ground to guide
them.

An upward glance brought a squint into the distance. Megan thought she was hallucinating. No, there
really *were* torches flickering ahead. Saints be praised,
a crowd had gathered at the Klondike River bridge.

Her slow jog broke to a trot. Cheers rose from
the spectators. A dozen mittened hands waved
encouragement—but not to her.

Four runners, their coats and beards crusted with
ice, converged from her left. Earl Delacroix led the

pack by about three yards; the man at drag staggered like a drunkard.

Megan's heel slammed the gleaming wooden surface a half second before Earl's. Both careened wildly across glazed ice. She clipped the side rail and bounced off, knocking herself and Delacroix to their knees.

She scrambled to her feet. Another contender shoved between her and Earl and sent them sprawling again.

"You scalawaggin' son of a bitch," he yelled.

Red-hot fury shot through Megan. She raised to a crouch and bolted across the bridge. Her eyes pegged the shadowy form less than twenty feet in front of her.

Hollering, stamping townsfolk lined both sides of Front Street; their breath forming a misty fog. Megan's gaze flitted to the outline of the Mountie post and back to the runner. His lead had shortened by half. Then, a third.

They dashed through the barrack gate in a dead heat. The man veered toward the post's largest building—the officers' quarters. Megan punched the air and turned sharply right.

She leaped onto the first step to the commissioner's office. Tripped over the second. Her shins banged the riser. Howling with pain, she hurled herself onto the stoop.

Her mittened fist hammered the latch. The door swung wide and banged the adjacent wall. Light blinded her. She belly-crawled over the threshold. "One Below on Cheechako Hill!"

A heavy body fell on top of her. "One Below on Cheechako Hill!"

Boots clumped across the room's plank floor. Megan peered up at William Ogilvie's blurry black form.

"Silas Finch, isn't it?" he inquired.

The man crushing her grunted, "Uh-huh."

"Well, then, Mr. Finch," Ogilvie replied, "kindly

remove your person from the lady struggling to breathe beneath you. The poor woman's eyes are goggled and I expect she'll need them to sign the claim affidavit for One Below on Cheechako Hill."

Having commandeered Minnie's stove-side throne, Megan sat swathed in blankets, determined to spend this Sabbath doing little more than breathe.

"You're sure you're all right?" B.D. asked.

"I'm perfectly miserable, me boyo." She swiped at her nose with a handkerchief. "Chilled clear through, got a nasty head cold, and feel like a freighter drug me a mile or ten. But I won, by God. And Mr. Lippy, of course."

Her cracked lips curled into a smile. "Even though you wouldn't have bet a plugged nickel on my chances."

"C'mon now, confession's good for the soul," he teased. "You weren't so all-fired sure yourself, were you?"

"Against Earl Delacroix? More confident than not. The other four worried me." She snorted. "Whatever the outcome had been, I figure we O'Malleys learned a couple of things we'd be wise not to forget."

B.D.'s brows met at center. "Like what?"

"For one, they say cheaters never prosper for good reason. They don't."

"Yeah, I know. Nathan's given me his Honesty is the Best Policy lecture already. Twice."

"As for the other," she continued sternly, "forty-three-year-old women have no business running foot-races. If I ever succumb to such foolishness again, please promise you'll shoot me at the starting line."

He laughed and stuck out a hand. "You've got a deal."

"Not so fast, son. There's something more important we need to shake on."

B.D.'s fingers and his expression drooped.

Megan slipped a sheet of foolscap from under the

quilt. She unfolded it, pretended to study its content, then refolded it. "This is a copy of the claim affidavit to One Below on Cheechako Hill. Besides Commissioner Ogilvie's signature, the only name on it that's ever mattered a damn is O'Malley.

She extended the paper toward him. "What about you, *partner*? Is it the only one that matters to you?"

B.D. tried to speak, but could only nod.

"Then I suspect while we're at it," Megan said, reaching to clasp his hand, "we ought to shake on that, too."

Chapter 23

Megan hefted an enormous tureen of stew off the counter. Careful not to let it slosh, she glided toward her guests.

The Haven's writing tables had been pushed together and draped with Minnie's heirloom white-on-white embroidered linen cloth. A brass and a pewter candelabra each held six tapers; their tips a smidge heat-bowed, but serviceable.

Rust-flecked tin plates were interspersed with rosebud-patterned china, Blue Willow, and chipped stoneware. Pink champagne bubbled as merrily in assorted crystal flutes as it did in graniteware mugs and the Haven's teacups.

Each dinner guest not only provided a table service, but also contributed something to the Thanksgiving menu. B.D. quartered potatoes and onions for the stew. Nels and Nathan shot and skinned Arctic hares for its meat. Spare-ribs Jimmy Mackinson simmered crushed bones and skimmed the marrow to make bone butter. Minnie brought jars of pickles and applesauce. Earl Delacroix delivered a sled load of stove wood. Tom and Salome Lippy bought Dawson's last tinned peach pie from the Klondike Bakery, and Commissioner Ogilvie arrived with a dusty bottle of wine under his arm.

Megan placed the tureen at the table's center and lifted its lid with a flourish. William leaned forward to sniff at the billowing steam.

"Do you know how long it's been since I've partaken of a home-cooked meal? Prepare to be ashamed of my gluttony."

"That goes double for me, sir," Nels said. "What ol' Nathan does to flapjacks ought to be against the law."

"Oh, yeah? How about that side of venison you tried to smoke for jerky? We'll never need buy another ax blade in this life."

"What does one have to do with the other?" Salome inquired innocently.

"I truly don't know how he did it, ma'am," Nathan answered, "but my partner charred those deer strips till they were hard as tempered steel."

Earl clinked a butter knife on the applesauce bowl. "Fair warning to all you starvin' pups. First man what slides a boarding house reach under my nose'll get a fork stuck in it."

"Does that include us ladies?" Minnie inquired.

"Now, where I come from, Miz Walentine," he drawled, "a lady don't grab after vittles. She bats her lashes real sweet and asks, 'Pretty please, won'tcha pass them biscuits down this-a-way?'"

Minnie snorted. "Well, take a stab at any part of my person, Mr. Delacroix, and you won't pass anything for a month of Sundays."

Megan grinned at the older couple's banter. What might sound petulant to the uninitiated was actually flirtatious repartee. Minnie had dropped by the day after the race and was fussing over Megan when Earl arrived to make sure bygones were bygones.

He and Minnie laughed good-natured verbal bullets at each other almost immediately and a cease-fire had yet to be declared. A customary indication of love at first sight it was not, but the parties involved weren't exactly conventional.

Megan inspected the table to be sure everything was in readiness, then seated herself. She nodded toward its opposite end. "B.D., will you say grace?"

"Me?"

"Why do ya think me 'n Nels jumped at the corners,

boy?" Jimmy stage-whispered. "That there's the 'amen' chair and you're welcome to it."

Megan laid her left hand over William's and her right atop Earl's distended knuckles. When the fellowship circle was complete, B.D. said, "Lord, I reckon I speak for all of us when I say thank You for the blessings You've bestowed. We've got roofs over our heads, warm clothes on our backs, and Ma's supper smells real fine, but I don't suppose that'd mean much without these gathered here to share it. In the name of the Father, the Son, and the Holy Ghost . . . amen."

Megan raised her head. "That was lovely, son."

He chuckled sheepishly. "Does that mean we can dig in now?"

"Not quite," William said, lofting his wineglass. "A toast, if you please, to Her Majesty Queen Victoria, your American President Lincoln who declared this celebration a holiday, and to our hostess, Megan O'Malley."

Tom Lippy seconded with a rousing, "Here, here."

Megan took a tiny sip of champagne, trying not to pucker at its dryness. Rumor had it that Swiftwater Bill Gates bathed in "French horse water" on occasion. Somehow, that seemed more appropriate than drinking it.

Victuals heaped ten plates with astonishing speed. Conversation gave way to clattering utensils and compliments. Megan savored every bite of the potluck feast, no longer concerned that the stew was long on water and short on meat and vegetables or that the biscuits were flat for want of enough baking powder.

"Prime your fork, Earl," Nathan said as he scooted his tin plate against the tureen. "I'm swooping in for seconds."

Jimmy's head jerked up and cocked sideward. He squinted at the cabin door.

"I'm a-watchin' you—"

"Quiet, Earl," Jimmy ordered.

Megan and her guests froze in midmotion. The

room fell silent. Above the wind's whistle came a faint cry. "Fire . . . *fire.*"

Tableware clanked dishes. Chair legs chafed across the carpet. Everyone dashed for the coat tree.

"What the hell are we gonna use for water?" Earl said. "The river's froze solid."

"We'll figure that out when we get there," Tom answered, struggling into his boots.

Megan grabbed the bucket from beside the stove. "Here, B.D.—take this."

Minnie climbed over Nathan to yank her coat from a hook. "There's six or seven more buckets at the boarding house."

"Where?" Nels asked. "In the kitchen?"

"Leave the fetching to us," Megan said.

William paused at the door. "You ladies had better stay here where it's safe."

"This is no time for chivalry," Minnie bellowed. "Get *goin'.*"

As the men ran out, a smoky, frigid blast rushed inside. Megan jammed a fur hat down over her ears, glancing at Salome Lippy in the process. The young woman's expression reflected confusion and fear.

"We can't go off and leave the candles and the stove burning," Megan said. "Will you tend the house, Salome?"

She nodded with obvious relief.

Megan darted outside with Minnie close on her heels. At the opposite end of Front Street, flames licked at the sky; their orange glow brighter than daylight.

Minnie pointed toward the boarding house. "Meet you down there in two shakes."

Megan waved an acknowledgment. From Pioche to Tombstone, Arizona, every boomtown she'd ever lived in or heard of had been destroyed by fire at least once. Destiny had arrived in full furl in Dawson City.

The smoke's acrid pall stung her eyes and parched

her throat. Crackles, muffled explosions, and hoarse commands grew louder as she neared.

Red-coated Mounties directed bucket brigades stretched from the Yukon's riverbank to Front Street. Despite their valiant efforts, the volunteers had lost the battle the moment it began. They needed pressurized hoses to direct the water and sufficient gallonage to douse the flames, but just like Dawson's predecessors, municipal leaders were too busy building their town to worry about its potential destruction.

Hundreds of people watched the drama unfold in helpless, silent resignation. Every structure in town was wood-constructed; a few, three stories tall. The fire would simply have to burn itself out.

A crew ripped open bales of blankets near the Alaska Commercial Company's warehouse. Another group dunked them in a hole chopped in the ice. When saturated, the blankets were hurled upward to men crouched on the roof, working frantically to protect the structure with a shroud of wet wool.

"How did it start?" Megan asked a bystander.

The man shook his head mournfully. "A dove by the name of Belle Mitchell got riled at another doxy and threw a lamp at her. The whole saloon caught fire in a blink."

Megan willed herself to reserve judgment. Whether a tossed lamp or an untamped cigar was the cause, Dawson City was truly a disaster just waiting to happen.

"Anyone hurt?" she asked.

"Not that I know of, ma'am. 'Tis a Thanksgivin' miracle, sure enough, 'cept it's sure to make supplies scarcer than ever."

He turned away to gaze at the warehouse. "If that goes . . ."

"Don't even think it," Megan said, as much to herself as him.

A brigade now surrounded the warehouse, dashing water on the blankets. Vapor streamed from the men's mouths and curled upward from their clothing. Sub-zero temperatures swallowed the fire's heat. The flames bronzed the volunteers' grim features and those of the spectators huddled nearby.

A young woman on the outskirts of the crowd smiled wanly at the burly man who wrapped a blanket around her shoulders. Megan looked past them to scan the throng for B.D.—then wrenched back again.

"Jesus, Mary, and Joseph," she gasped.

The woman's eyes fluttered. She collapsed against the Samaritan's chest. He wrestled her limp body into his arms, then stood stock-still, apparently unsure what to do next.

Megan hastened over, pointing up the street. "Hey—you! Get her away from the smoke—the fumes."

"Hell, lady, the whole town's afire!"

"Not quite yet, it isn't. Carry her to the Haven of Rest—now."

He glared at her. "Who are you to be barkin' orders at me, by God?"

"The girl's aunt," Megan yelled. "That's who."

Chapter 24

The remains of the festive Thanksgiving dinner littered the table like wilted flowers atop a grave. Megan surveyed the mess, at once annoyed Salome hadn't seen fit to clear the dishes and gladdened by it. Before this night ended, a pearl-diving session in a pan of soapy washwater might be soothing.

Her unexpected visitor coughed into her fist, then took a sip of honey-laced tea. All swaddled in blankets and hunched in a high-backed rocker, she looked smaller and younger than her twenty-two years. A healthy glow suffused her cheeks, but her brown eyes stayed riveted on her lap.

"Cad, is it?" Megan said. "That'll take some getting used to since I've known you as Catherine Ann Dannelly your entire life. With no wedding band on your finger, where, might I ask, did the Wilson come from?"

"The steamer captain was named Hezekiah Wilson," her niece answered quietly. "He treated me as kindly as Captain Jorgenson did you and Mother when you sailed to America, so I borrowed Wilson for my stage name."

"Your *what?*"

Cad jutted her chin in a manner her aunt found hauntingly familiar. "I'm a singer, and I command the highest salary of any entertainer in Dawson City."

How well Megan remembered the auburn-haired little girl who warbled "I'll Take You Home Again, Kathleen" in the Dannellys' parlor. Cathy—as she was called then—hadn't exactly mangled the beloved Irish tune, but neither Megan nor her sister Frances heard any evidence that the O'Malley side of the family had finally produced a balladeer.

"I'll thank you to stop staring at me like that, Auntie Megan. Why, you'd think I just confessed to being a Paradise Alley strumpet."

"And what would you have me do, lass? I know as sure as I'm sitting here that your mother and father have no idea where you are, let alone that their youngest child is a bloomin' dance-hall queen."

Cad banged her cup down on the sideboard. "Don't *ever* use that vile term again." She threw open the blankets. Her scoop-necked delft gown was surprisingly conservative save its midcalf length. The wide gold nugget belt encircling Cad's waist was certainly garish and bordered on vulgar. A miniature pick and shovel flanked a pan filled with tiny mining tools. Nugget chains hung from the belt, each trimmed with trinkets such as a bonbon box and a perfume bottle.

"The customers at the Tivoli and the Orpheum fashioned this for me, Auntie Megan. I'm neither pretty nor wildly talented, but my skits and songs make them laugh and they love me for it."

Cad burrowed into the blankets again. "Yes, I flash an ankle and a shapely calf now and then. A hundred men would pay a small fortune to see all of me except they'd only pay it once. That's the secret. An entertainer has to give a little to keep her customers wanting more."

"It's a dangerous game you're playing, Cathy. Some men don't cotton to that kind of teasing. Others won't believe that's all it is."

Cad's lips bowed into a feline smile. "As I recall, it was you who told me that men are only boys with whiskers. Don't worry. I can take care of myself."

"Your cousin Barlow David said the same thing a few months ago. He learned otherwise in a finger snap."

"Cavorting with a gang of wharf rats is hardly the same as singing onstage for my supper."

"Oh? And how would you know about that?" Megan inquired, her eyes narrowing to slits. If her son knew Cathy was masquerading as Cad Wilson and hadn't breathed a word of it . . . Well, a suitable punishment would come to mind before the time came to exact it.

"Mama read your farewell letter to me," Cad answered. "By her sobs I thought a wake was in the offing."

"Save that to shovel around the rosebushes next spring, me lass. Yammering a priest's ears off, I'd believe. Driving your poor da to the pub with her fuming and stomping, I'd believe. But Frances sobbing over me? Not in this life."

Cad threw back her head and laughed; the kind of throaty, from-the-belly guffaws that proper ladies considered coarse and men adored.

"Now, *that's* the Auntie Megan I know and love. A spitfire with a brogue thick enough to eat with a spoon when she's angry. I haven't seen you in years and was beginning to think you'd become as stodgy as Mother."

Megan groaned in sympathy for Frances. As if helping raise her rebellious younger sister weren't enough, a similar ornery streak had been visited upon her own daughter.

"The girls at school put Florence Nightingale and Elizabeth Cady Stanton on pedestals, but not me," Cathy said. "Those old battle-axes pale in comparison to my favorite aunt's tales of adventure."

"Favorite, eh? I'd be more inclined to preen if you had more than one."

"Given a dozen to pick from, I'd still have chosen your footsteps to follow. Whenever Mother chides me for being just like you, she thinks she's leveled an insult. *I* take it as a compliment."

Well, fancy that, Megan thought. All the while I've

threatened B.D. with a visit to his ironfisted Aunt Frances, she's used me as a bad example for her "wages of sin" lectures.

Something Cathy mentioned recurred in her mind. "What do you mean, follow in my footsteps?"

"Your letter arrived the day before news of the gold strike hit San Francisco. I knew the two combined were an omen. That it was my *destiny* to go north, just as you did."

"Oh, please," Megan said. "Spare me the tragedian's hooraw."

Cathy's mouth puckered into a pretty pout. "I'm *not* exaggerating. I've never felt so—so *overwhelmed.* It was frightening and wonderful and absolutely *right* all at the same time."

She hugged herself, her eyes ablaze with excitement. "There I was, simply dotty from this revelation welling inside me, and at the same instant the entire city went stark raving gold mad. Stores, banks, and shops locked up tight with KLONDIKE HO! signs on their doors. Cable cars stopped running when conductors resigned to join the mob in the streets. Factory workers, doctors, preachers, constables—even seamstresses and typewriters—quit their jobs to fight for standing space along a ship's rail. Thousands jammed the wharfs to clamor for steamer tickets and buy provisions and equipment by the ton.

"Why?" Megan asked. "I've seen plenty of gold strikes in my day—silver, too—but I've never heard of a city going berserk because of it."

"I certainly can't explain it," Cathy said. "Except there's something about the word *Klondike* that inflamed people's passion. Street-corner drummers hawked Klondike boots, and Klondike stoves. Literally overnight, restaurant bills of fare had Klondike soup or Klondike steaks inked on them. Newspaper headlines screamed that magical word in huge black letters and locomotives chugging from Union Station seemed to chant it."

She gasped for air. Her frenzied expression undoubtedly mirrored the horde of fools she described. "You may not remember, but when B.D. was tiny and you were getting ready to leave for Alaska, you gave each of us kids a five-dollar gold piece to save for someday."

"How could I forget? Your mother scolded me for giving such a fortune to Tommy and Ellen, much less Michael, Sean, and you."

"Well, someday finally arrived last July, Auntie Megan. Your gold eagle and the savings it fostered bought my steamer ticket from Frisco to Dawson City."

"So you could become a dance-hall . . . singer."

"For now, anyway." Cathy stretched her arm, splayed her fingers, and waggled them lazily. "Maybe I'll marry a Klondike millionaire and live happily rich ever after. Or maybe I'll just have adventures like you've had and never marry at all."

"And maybe you'll be on the first ship bound for San Francisco, come spring," Megan snapped. "I've listened to your romantic notions of who and what you think I am, and how you've used them to justify your own spoiled, selfish antics—"

"Well! I don't have to sit here and—"

"Oh, yes, you do." She poked Cathy's shoulder; a not-so-subtle encouragement to retake her chair.

"If it's my life you're so damnably eager to imitate, put that imagination of yours to work and conjure what it'd be like to awaken to a gunshot from the barn. Find out your da had chucked the barrel under his chin and pulled the trigger because he just couldn't take watchin' his wife and daughters go to bed hungry anymore.

"Think about your mama lyin' dead in a rotted tatie patch. Closing the same black velvet eyes you looked into for love and always found there. Burying her in the only store-bought dress she ever owned—her wedding gown."

Cathy shook her head slowly, her mouth agape.

"Take care of yourself, can you? How many knives have you felt at your throat? How many filthy hands have kneaded your breasts so hard the pain jolted to your bones and there's not a soul within shoutin' distance to stop him? A rapist needn't have his way to steal a woman's innocence—make her feel shamed and guilty and dirty. Go ahead, risk that part of you that nothing, not even the love—the gentlest touch— of a good man, can ever replace.

"To be me, you'll have to luck upon the finest fellow God ever put on earth and thank Him every day that he's your best friend. Fall in love with another whose name you can never take, then bear his child.

"Live out your days with the certainty that both those men died because they loved you. That you could have married the first and been happy because you were two of a kind. That the second became your lover because he was handsome and virile, yet you knew, deep down, the one time you could have become his wife you ran like hell because he wasn't and never could be the man you truly needed and who needed you."

Megan paused. Emotional exhaustion rolled over her like an ocean wave. Embarrassment at her outburst followed in its wake.

"Despite everything I've told you, Cathy, I'm neither bitter nor regretful. I've been blessed with abounding joys—far too many to tell you."

She chuckled. "Truth be known, I can't divine why I told you any of it unless it's because my history, my memories, and my mistakes are mine—not yours to copy like the prettiest lines from a recitation you admired and then take as your own."

Cathy reached to clasp her aunt's hands. "You're—"

"Not quite finished with this kettle I set to boilin'," Megan said. "I see a different kind of romance sparking behind your eyes. A 'you're so wise and brave' gleam in them. Well, that's as bogus as the rest of your silly notions. If I recognized your trying to squeeze into my shoes it's because I've spent the last thirteen years trying to make B.D. fit his namesakes'."

Cathy studied her for a long moment before a grin crawled across her face. "Are you done now?"

"All but the Hail Marys."

"I love you, Auntie Megan."

"I love you, too, child."

"But Cad Wilson isn't going to stop singing 'Such a Nice Girl, Too' for her supper."

"I suspected as much."

"We are different, Auntie Megan, I know that now. We're also much the same. Your stage is a hole in the ground and the gold you find there is the applause you crave."

"Once upon a time, I'd have agreed with you," Megan allowed. "The reasons I don't now are another story, but it's late, there's an ungodly mess awaiting me, and I reckon we ought to go see what's left of this fair city."

Her niece sprang to her feet. "Good heavens, I'd completely forgotten about the fire. I may not have a stage to sing from or a stitch of clothing besides what I'm wearing."

Megan hugged Cad's gold-girdled waist. "Boom-towns have a habit of burning to ashes and rising from them before they cool. Bar none, the pleasure palaces are always among the first rebuilt, too."

Chapter 25

B.D. winced when his knee scraped the One Below's ice-crusted wall. The sound drifted along the tunnel, as loud as a plane on dry oak. The hum of voices from deep inside the shaft continued without interruption.

Two days into the New Year, his first-shift crew quit to chase rumors of a strike on Rosebud Creek. He'd expected production to drop by half, but not the seventy-five percent decrease he'd noted over the last couple of weeks.

The smoky haze tickled his throat. B.D. swallowed to stanch a cough. The absence of steel biting frozen dirt strengthened his resolve. He couldn't afford one shirker on the payroll, much less an entire crew.

The shaft widened and rose in height. Where he and Jimmy managed to work in what resembled a prairie dog's run, having doubled the manpower necessitated doubling the One Below's head and elbow room.

Candlelight painted gruesome shadows on the concave white-bristled walls. B.D. crept closer. Four men huddled in a circle playing poker and passing around a bottle of hootch. Either it wasn't the first they'd uncorked or the liquor was of an exceptionally potent vintage.

Every muscle in B.D.'s body tensed. He could have sympathized with a touch of laziness. How well he knew the mindless exhaustion of swinging a pick hour after hour. But drinking and gambling on company time was thievery—pure and simple. He'd have respected them more if they'd picked his pockets on the street. At least that kind of stealing required a degree of effort.

B.D. stepped from the shadows. "What do you think this is, the Monte Carlo's annex? Stow those cards and get to work."

"It's break time, boy." Jake Krantzler sneered.

"Not an hour into the shift, it isn't."

Ralph Murdock shrugged. "Don't split your knickers. We'll start in soon as we finish this hand."

"Call two matchsticks," Gene Dalton said. "Raise back three."

Norm Zachs grunted. "Call five. Up it one."

B.D. yanked the fanned pasteboards from Zachs's fingers. "Game's over, I said."

Krantzler scrambled to his feet. "Who the hell do you think you are, barkin' commands like a goddamned field officer?"

"Let's see now. Best I remember, I'm One Below's paymaster, not to mention its superintendent."

"Cocky little peckerwood." Krantzler pushed his coat sleeves above his wrists. "You're over due for a lesson on respectin' your elders, boy."

B.D. backed up a step. "That's the whiskey talking. You need this job as much as I need miners. Don't make me fire you."

"Shit, you ain't got the cods to sack nobody. I'm done takin' guff off'n a runt pup."

Krantzler's fist glanced off B.D.'s jaw. He staggered and tasted the blood oozing from his mangled tongue.

The miner grinned. His massive arm doubled back; ridged knuckles blanched to a creamy white.

B.D. ducked the second blow. He bolted upright before the miner regained his balance. Two rabbit punches to Krantzler's temple sent the bigger man reeling. A bone-crunching haymaker sent him to the floor.

"All right. Who's next?"

Zachs raised his hands palm-side out.

Murdock looked from Krantzler's still form to B.D. "Where'd you learn to fight like that, boy?"

B.D. scotched the first answer that came to mind. To confess he'd only watched Paddy Cummins beat several rivals half to death wouldn't create much of an impression. "Ever hear of John L. Sullivan?"

"Best bare-knuckler that ever lived," Dalton said. "Till Jim Corbett came along, anyhow."

"Sullivan and my ma are cousins," B.D. said. "Johnny gave me a coupla lessons, last time he came through Seattle on tour."

"Why didn't you say so before now?" Murdock asked. "Sheds a new light on the whole situation, boy."

"No, it doesn't. Gather up your belongings and your friend there and clear out, *boys.*"

The next morning, B.D. trudged toward the miners' exchange to post yet another employment notice. Jake Krantzler and his cronies had been the worst of the lot, but One Below was becoming notorious for rapid turnover.

He understood why grown men resented working for someone half their age and why it predisposed attempts to take advantage of him. Except these days flour sold for ten bucks a pound. A long ton of Yukon pride wouldn't fetch a half dime.

B.D. grinned as he flexed his bruised hands inside his mackinaw pockets. Where that bushwah about Sullivan had come from, he still didn't know, but it served its purpose. He hadn't seen hide nor hair of his former crew since they clambered from One Below's tunnel.

"Good riddance," he muttered. "Damned laggards'll never know that's the first fight I ever had in my life. If my luck holds, Ma won't ever hear about it at all."

He looked up the street toward the Haven of Rest. "A hot cup of something would sure taste fine, but I can't drink it with my gloves on and I sure can't take 'em off."

"Didn't hear you," a passerby said, patting his earmuffs.

"Caught me talking to myself, I'd reckon."

Vapor gusted from the man's scarf. "A Yukon winter'll do that to a fella."

B.D. walked on, as amazed by the number of people braving the seventy-below cold as by the town's miraculous restoration.

Six weeks earlier, the section he was passing through resembled Satan's playground; nothing but an expanse of blackened, smoldering rubble and roofless log skeletons disemboweled by flames.

Wise Mike, a pet donkey who'd frequented Dawson's saloons and napped beside their stoves like a giant dog had been the fire's sole casualty. Since Mike had no owner, no real home, and food was scarcer than ever, a kindhearted patron shot the animal rather than let him slowly starve to death.

Due to the lumbermill's total destruction, whipsaw stands were erected to hew logs the old-fashioned way. Bonanza's and Eldorado's sluice boxes were dismantled temporarily to supply nails, which sold for two bits apiece.

By hook and by crook, enough materials were scrounged to rebuild dozens of businesses, including the Pioneer Hotel and the Tivoli dance hall. Their rapid reconstruction undoubtedly saved Cad Wilson from becoming the second fire-related casualty.

B.D.'s cousin, whom he barely knew and would never have recognized, invited herself to take up residence at the Haven until her hotel and place of business were rebuilt. Cad, being a wee bit conceited, willful, and enraptured by her own stage presence, immediately assumed that Auntie Megan would be thrilled to temporarily turn the Haven into a music hall.

Saint Megan assumed her emphatic no would be taken for an answer.

The resourceful Cad then decided that what her aunt didn't know wouldn't hurt her. The news spread by word of mouth that her shows would go on at the Haven every Sunday at two, which coincided with Saint Megan's weekly jaunts to One Below.

One clandestine and highly profitable performance went off without a hitch. The second resulted in Miss Wilson's arrest for violating the ordinance prohibiting such activities on the Sabbath.

Cad thought the entire incident was an hilarious lark. Not only was Saint Megan furious and embarrassed, she replaced allusions to blood being thicker than water with "You can choose your friends, but by God, not your family."

B.D. chuckled at the memory as he approached the miners' exchange. A moth-eaten knot of men stamped and waved their arms while they perused the employment notices tacked to the wall. He edged between them to add his own to the collection.

"Is you O'Malley?"

B.D. turned toward the speaker. A lady's silk scarf wrapped his face like a floral bandage. Jaundiced, bloodshot eyes peered through a slit in the layers.

"Yeah." B.D. sidled away, hoping to escape before the man inquired after a job.

Meningitis, cholera, scurvy, and typhoid were decreasing the population at a four-per-day rate. By the looks of him, the man suffered from at least one of those maladies.

"Heared ya knocked Jake Krantzler inta the middle of next week," the man said. "That true?"

Because news of any stripe jumped from ear to ear at lightning speed, Dawson City was a paradise for gossips, inveterate liars, and the vividly imaginative.

"Me and Jake had a difference of opinion," he said. "Mine prevailed."

"Uh-huh. So, what's this 'bout you'n John L. Sullivan bein' kin?"

B.D. groaned inwardly. "Pure-de-hooraw, mister."

He started down the street at a brisk pace. Every one of those poor devils was too sick to work, but not sick enough to claim a bed in Father Judge's hospital. For all the priest's brotherly loving care, a fair number who entered through the front door were eventually carried out the back.

The help-wanted notice he'd posted wasn't the only one that was likely to go begging. The omnipresent grapevine bleated "Strike!" on a weekly basis and the able-bodied took to the hills under the delirious influence of gold fever.

B.D. stared into the middle distance. Had his temper gotten the best of him last night? Best he could figure, by spring the O'Malleys would be about fifteen thousand dollars in debt, not counting the cost of building the One Below's sluice works. He hadn't asked what color ink his mother used when she reconciled the Haven's ledgers. Common sense said black, but her legendary generosity made red a distinct possibility.

Jimmy was now supervising Nathan's and Nels's duel operation and busier than a bee in clover. B.D.'d worked One Below single-handedly before and would again, starting tomorrow. Trouble was, the amount of gold he'd wash during cleanup was directly proportional to the size of the slag heap from whence it came.

"Buck up, *boy*," he grumbled. "Those four loafers were stealing you blind. Shoulda sacked their asses two weeks ago."

A ruckus on the other side of the street caught B.D.'s eye. Swiftwater Bill Gates appeared to be wrestling with a polar bear cub.

The squat multimillionaire entrepreneur cackled obscenely. "Tussle all you want, honey. I like my women fiesty."

The object of Gate's attention, a native girl clad in white fur from head to mukluks, struggled mightily to extricate herself from his grasp.

Against his better judgment, B.D. hastened over. Gates, only a year and a rich claim's remove from washing dishes at a Circle City hash house, was a notorious skirt chaser; the younger and prettier its wearer, the more brazen his pursuit.

In the spring of '97, he spent thousands of dollars buying up every egg in town to woo Gussie Lamore, a comely strumpet with an inordinate fondness for fresh hen fruit. When he spied the current love of his life on the arm of a handsome gambler, Gates commandeered a café's stove, fried the eggs one at a time, and flipped them through the window to a pack of slavering dogs.

"Haven't had any brown sugar for quite a spell," Gates said, holding his captive's shoulders to the wall. "How much for a little taste, eh?"

"There you are, miss," B.D. said. "I've been looking all over town for you."

She squinted at him, wary, yet she seemed to understand he was trying to help her.

Gates's head whipped sideward. "Who invited you to my party, kid?"

He held his hands aloft as if offering an apology. With the power Gates wielded, he'd make a formidable enemy. He racked his brain for a way to avoid incurring his wrath.

"Don't, uh, kill the messenger, Mr. Gates. Father Judge asked me to find this girl and tell her to report to the hospital. He's afraid those pustules in her mouth aren't healing proper. May need another dose of medicine to set her right."

Every speck of color drained from Gates's moon-shaped face. "You mean she's got the pox?"

"Father Judge didn't say exactly."

Gates shoved her away and wiped his gloves on his

black cashmere ulster. "Thanks, kid. I owe you one."
He stalked off down the street muttering to himself.

"I am very grateful," the girl whispered, then favored B.D. with a shy smile.

A shrug was the only reply he could manage. Lord above, was she ever beautiful. Her hood's rim of snowy fur enhanced her coppery complexion and exotic, slightly Oriental features. But those huge sloe eyes, so liquid brown and heavy-lashed that a man could drown in them.

"My name is Colleen."

"Oh, yeah—well, just call me B.D. Everybody does."

"You are very smart, B.D., to trick that man the way you did. He is evil. I smelled it on him."

"Aw, Swiftwater Bill's mostly a dunce. He'd be the laughingstock of Dawson if he hadn't struck it rich. He is anyway, just not where he can hear it."

Colleen's pert nose wrinkled in disgust. "I liked it here better when it was a swamp."

"You live near Dawson City?"

"Only sometimes. My guardian has a cabin on the far side of Moosehide Mountain."

B.D. shuddered. "No insult meant, but I wouldn't live there if you gave me the place."

"It is ugly, yes, but we never stay there long. Pete is a trapper, so we hunt, trade the pelts, and hunt some more."

Colleen's mantle of fur seemed to make her impervious to the cold, but B.D.'s teeth chattered so hard he couldn't hear himself think. "How about if we find someplace warm and talk some more?"

Her brow furrowed suspiciously. "Where?"

He looked up and down the Front Street. Rationing had closed all the restaurants and cafés. They were too young to patronize a saloon—wouldn't let her set foot in one, regardless.

Jesus, Mary, and Joseph, he fumed. No wonder the Haven's so blessed popular. It's the only place in town where a body can have a conversation without yelling. And it's the last place I want to take Colleen to right now.

An ice-glazed signboard offered salvation. "C'mon, Colleen, before I freeze to death."

She started after him, then halted. "Where are we going, B.D.?"

"To the library."

Miss Tabitha Meriwether-Jones, the municipal librarian, peered over her pince-nez as they entered. She laid her book down on the desk and inquired, "May I help you?"

"I, uh—a collection of Shakespeare's plays," B.D. blurted. "Do you have one?"

His request obviously thrilled the spinster to her marrow. "Why, of course, young man. There, on the far wall, third shelf down."

"Thank you, ma'am."

She graced him with a horsey smile. "The library sponsors a reading from that volume every Tuesday evening. Perhaps you and your friend would like to join us next week?"

"We'll keep that in mind, ma'am."

A half-dozen patrons in various stages of slumber occupied tables at the back of the room. One portly bibliophile had taken the precaution of wedging a pencil between his chins to stab himself awake before he fell to snoring.

B.D. guided Colleen toward a corner table and chairs. The waist-high row of barrister cases would partially screen them from Miss Meriwether-Jones's renowned scrutiny.

Sweat popped out on his brow before he'd shed his layered outergarments. The librarian spared no firewood keeping the narrow, musty room warm. She didn't need to, with Big Alex McDonald underwriting all the library's expenses, including her salary.

After B.D. slid the cumbersome leather-bound book from the shelf, he scooted his chair smack upside Colleen's. Her long black hair smelled of castile soap and strangely enough, lemons.

"Lean over a bit and rest your head in your hand like this," he whispered as he demonstrated. "Now, if we keep our voices down, ol' pickle-puss won't get overly curious about what we're doin'."

Colleen giggled. "You are wicked, B.D."

"I'll have you know it took years of practice to hone this technique. It's about the only useful thing I learned in school, too."

"I went to the Indian school at Fort McPherson for a while. The teachers did not like me because I already knew my letters, arithmetic, and geography."

"Is that where you learned English?" B.D. asked. "You speak it very well."

"Thank you. So do you."

He felt a blush rise up his neck. Colleen smiled and patted his arm. "I am wicked, too. I didn't mean to embarrass you."

"Don't apologize. I deserved it."

"Pete taught me your language. He is American, but has lived in Canada for many, many years."

"It's none of my business, I reckon, but how'd you come to know him?"

She glanced away, a profound sadness reflected in her lovely eyes. "When I was very small, almost everyone in my village died of the smallpox. Pete was wintering with us and tried his best to save my people, but the disease was too strong."

"Three of us children survived. Pete took us in and raised us. The boy, Matthew, is now a scout for the North-West Mounted Police. Ruth lives in Sitka. She married a white soldier and is going to have a baby."

Colleen's full lips parted in a mischievous grin. "They were jealous of me because I am Pete's favorite. That's why he named me Colleen instead of one from the Bible."

"I suppose that was his wife's name—or maybe his mother's," B.D. said.

"No, she was a sweetheart." Her voice took on a dreamy lilt when she added, "Whenever I ask about her, all Pete will say is that a long time ago, he fell in love with a Colleen."

B.D. clamped his jaw tight to stifle a chuckle. Indian or white, young or old, every female he'd ever known fairly thrived on romantic notions; his mother being the only exception to that rule.

One night, he'd wandered through the parlor en route to the kitchen for a glass of milk when he spied pudgy Harold Dirkson, on bended knee, reciting poetry to Saint Megan.

She sat as stiff-backed and glassy-eyed as a mannequin while Harold droned that "love threads every human heart into a skein of gossamer"—or some such horseshit. B.D. had snuck back upstairs, forgoing the milk, which would have undoubtedly curdled in his stomach.

"Did I say something wrong?" Colleen asked.

"Naw, just woolgathering. Yukon winters tend to make a man do that, you know."

"I don't understand that word . . ."

"The library will close in five minutes," Miss Meriwether-Jones announced. Startled moans and shuffling papers sounded from the back of the room. "Please return all materials to their appropriate locations."

Wouldn't you know, B.D. thought. I finally meet somebody close my own age, I'm having the best time I've had in months just talking to her and ziggedy-bang, it's all over but the shouting.

Colleen reached for her coat. B.D. instantly appropriated it. She glanced at him in surprise, then slid her arms into the sleeves.

"I wish we didn't have to go," he said. "Maybe there's somewhere else we could—"

She shook her head. "I wish so, too, yet I should not have stayed this long. My guardian is missing and I must find him."

"What do you mean, missing?"

She breathed a stoic sigh. "Sometimes Pete—well, he tries to be careful, but whiskey is his demon. If he drinks too much, he does not know night from day and forgets to come home."

B.D. nodded toward the librarian, then opened the door. "Can I help you look for him?"

Colleen hesitated. "Pete is not himself when the demon takes him."

"I don't reckon he is, but from what you told me, he's a helluva fine fellow. I'd like to meet him."

She pulled her hood over her head and tucked her hair inside. Her hands disappeared into a pair of white fur mittens. She looked up at him, then slipped her arm through his. "It is very nice not to feel alone."

The simple statement tugged at B.D.'s heart. "Yep," he said softly. "It surely is."

They walked the length of Front Street, pausing at every watering hole to inquire after Pete. None they asked recognized the name or Colleen's description. They crossed to the west side to continue the search. B.D. shivered uncontrollably, but refused her entreaties to leave her and go home.

Shouts echoed from midway down the block. Men poured into the street, shoving at each other and gesturing wildly. B.D. scanned the rooftops expecting to see tongues of flame and black smoke billowing upward. A Mountie rushed past, his neck craned skyward as well.

"Get back—back," someone yelled. "The jake's got a stick of dynamite. He's done lit the fuse."

B.D. and Colleen traded glances. "Wait here," he said. "I'll go see what the clamor's all about."

She pointed at the milling crowd. "Pete may be over there."

"God, you're stubborn."

"He says that, too."

They meandered through the assembly. Colleen inspected faces while B.D. recited Pete's description.

"What's the name again?" asked a rangy gent with a hammered gold eyepatch.

"Pete's all I know. He's about my height, late forties, gray beard—"

"Hell, that sounds like the swamper that's laid siege to the saloon! He drifted in on New Year's Eve and done homesteaded it for nary three weeks."

B.D. looked around for Colleen, but she'd melted into the crowd. "Does he really have dynamite?"

"Biggest goddamn stick I ever saw. Fuse is sparkin' like a Chinese firecracker, too."

B.D. couldn't fathom why, if a lunatic armed with a lighted stick of dynamite really was inside the saloon, everyone was standing around outside waiting to be blown to Kingdom Come.

Rather than pose the obvious, he asked, "What got him so riled?"

"A new barkeep come on duty this morning. Instead of pourin' the old man his favorite breakfast, he told him to clear out. Said swampers weren't welcome no more. The old fella staggered off, then snuck in again later with us owl hoots.

"No sooner than the 'keep spied him, the swamper hopped on the bar rail, waved the dynamite at him, and hollered, 'I'll blow you to hell, you cheapskate sumbitch.' "

"B.D.," Colleen wailed. "Where are you?"

"Right here." He pushed his way to her.

"Pete—my Pete is in there," she cried. "If he does not surrender, the Mountie will shoot him."

B.D. grabbed her hand and pulled her behind him to the boardwalk. A Mountie crouched outside the saloon's window, his revolver's bore pegged against the glass.

Frozen condensation reduced the buckskin-clad figure to an indistinct blur. He appeared to have a formidable build for a man of his years and wore his hair long in a style reminiscent of Buffalo Bill Cody.

The Mountie cocked the hammer back.

"Wait," B.D. said. "This girl is his ward. She'll talk him out of there."

The officer pivoted on the balls of his feet. "No, it's too dangerous."

"Please," Colleen begged. "He would never hurt me."

"Sorry, miss."

Her hand wrenched from B.D.'s. She darted into the saloon. B.D. tore after her.

"Halt—the both of you."

Colleen skidded on the sawdust-strewn floor. She squared her shoulders and marched toward the bar.

The derelict on the business side of it hefted a bottle above a glass. His free hand gripped the counter's edge as one would a ship's rail in heavy seas. Whiskey puddled around the glass despite his concentrated effort.

"It is time to go home, Pete."

A gap appeared in his rusty gray whiskers as his lips stretched into a clownish grin. His eyes averted to B.D., then to the Mountie beside him. "Step right up and have a snort on the house, Sarge."

The policeman raised his service revolver in a two-handed grip.

"Hey, I said it was free, for God's sake."

Colleen started around the bar. B.D. jumped into the Mountie's line of fire and strode forward. He whisked a foot-long cut of bologna from the bar and waved it at the constable. A piece of burnt fuse fell to the floor.

"Here's your dynamite, sir."

Colleen removed the bottle from Pete's fingers. Her arm encircled his waist. "We are gong home."

"No, miss," the Mountie corrected. "He's going to jail."

"On what charge?" B.D. asked. "Assault with a deadly sausage?"

The officer's grim expression relented and he chuckled. "Now that the crisis is past, it is rather humorous, eh?"

"Nobody got hurt, or would have unless he bashed 'em with it," B.D. said. "Me and Colleen'll see him to his cabin to sleep it off."

The Mountie frowned. He holstered his pistol, obviously stalling for time. "Captain Constantine is a stickler for regulation. The bloke is guilty of public drunkenness, inciting mayhem, and I daresay, a variety of other misdemeanors."

Patrons filtered back in, singularly, then in threes and fours. Whispers swelled into laughter when they saw the defused "dynamite" B.D. held.

"Pete meant no harm," Colleen said.

He tapped his chest, then issued a monstrous belch. "Taught that barkeep a lesson, though, by God."

"Who may well press civil charges," the Mountie replied.

"Naw, he's done got sacked already," a spectator informed. "Serves him right, treatin' that old man so shabby this mornin'."

"Nevertheless," the officer continued, "until the matter is resolved, it's better he stays where I can keep watch over him."

"My mother owns the Haven of Rest," B.D. said, his desperation evident in his tone. "She'll put him up. Be glad to. It's only a stone's throw from the post, so you can check on Pete anytime, day or night."

The saloon's regulars chorused their approval. "That'd be plumb Christian of ya, Constable Perkins. Give the ol' swamper a break, why don't ya?"

The Mountie barreled his chest. "I'll hasten to the post and report the incident to Captain Constantine. If he approves, so be it. If not, I will arrest this man within the hour."

"Good enough," B.D. said. He whirled and trotted behind the bar. "Grab ahold of him on that side, Colleen, and I'll do likewise. Let's get out of here before Constable Perkins changes his mind."

They hustled Pete from the saloon amid its patrons' rowdy cheers. The trapper's head lolled and he aimed a bleary gaze at B.D.

" 'Preciate the help, kid, but who the hell are you, anyway?"

"B.D. is my friend," Colleen answered.

"Oh . . . Well, pleased to meetcha, kid."

"Likewise, I'm sure."

The slick boardwalk was difficult to traverse under any circumstances. To more or less drag a burly, inebriated, rubber-legged man complicated the process enormously. Passersby pointed and laughed. B.D. paid them no mind. How Saint Megan would react when they arrived at the Haven of Rest occupied his thoughts.

He couldn't imagine a more inauspicious occasion by which to introduce his new friend and her guardian. Then again, nothing should pave a straighter road to his mother's heart than a down-on-his-luck pioneer with a child in tow.

Okay, so Pete had been soused to the gills for three solid weeks. A fellow had a right to cut his wolf loose now and then, didn't he?

Jaysus Kee-rist, B.D. groaned silently.

He stopped outside the Haven to leverage the trapper as upright as possible. "Brush that hair back from his face, Colleen," he instructed. "Yeah, that's better."

B.D. smoothed Pete's rumpled clothing and fluffed his matted beard. Colleen peeked around him and regarded B.D. with a mixture of curiosity and apprehension.

"It's all right," he assured. "Just tryin' to make him a tad more presentable."

"Ain't much use, is it?" Pete asked.

"Nope. I reckon not."

B.D. eased open the door and craned his head inside. The room was empty, save for his mother. She turned away from the stove, fists automatically digging into her hips.

"Pinch me, I must be dreamin'," she crowed. "If it isn't John L. Sullivan's boy cousin come to pay me a call."

"I'll explain that later, Ma. Got somebody I want you to meet."

He shuffled inside, the trapper and his ward following like cars hitched to a locomotive. "Pete, Colleen, this is my mother—"

"Megan O'Malley," Pete whispered.

She glided forward, her eyes searching his face. An expression of pure joy washed over her own. "Pete? Buckskin Pete Vladislov?"

The trapper shrugged off his escorts and held out his arms to her. She skipped forward, almost falling into them and wrapped her own around him.

B.D. and Colleen turned to stare at each other, their mouths agape.

Chapter 26

Pete's soft groans and smacking lips roused Megan from a fitful sleep. For five days, she'd catnapped in an armchair beside the bed while he wrestled a host of specters only he could see.

Whenever they appeared to him, he thrashed like a madman trying to escape whatever tyranny they threatened. Megan quickly learned that to subdue Pete's flailing arms only increased his terror. Instead, she stroked his sweaty brow and murmured reassurances until the delirium subsided.

More heart-wrenching were interludes when he conversed with thin air; nodding, and chuckling, and gesturing as one did in the company of friends. Blind and deaf to her attempts to intervene, Pete would ramble on, his one-sided repartee completely, horrifying lucid.

Late last night, his fever broke. He fell into the first natural rest he'd had since B.D. brought him to the Haven. Besides Pete's self-inflicted demon, he'd been malnourished, dehydrated, and on the brink of pneumonia.

He rolled onto his back and blinked at the ceiling. His eyes flitted about, obviously seeking a recognizable object.

"Megan, are you there?" he whispered. "Please, let me know it wasn't all a dream."

She threw back her quilt and struggled from the chair. A crick in her neck and lower back stabbed like blunted knives. "It isn't, though you've had plenty enough of them the past several days."

"I don't remember much of anything. By your tone I suspect it's better I don't."

Pete pushed up higher on the pillows. A flinch gave way to a bewildered expression. He lifted the blankets, squinted, then yanked them to his chin. "Correct me if I'm wrong, but I seem to recall being clothed when I arrived."

Megan eased herself onto the side of the bed. Her fingertips traced his forehead. The skin felt soft despite its grainy appearance; cool and dry to her touch.

Pete's hand covered hers, pressing it to his face. A flutter commenced in her midsection. She sucked in her belly and slipped her hand from his grasp.

"After you passed out in my arms," she said matter-of-factly, "Colleen and B.D. carried you to bed, relieved you of your buckskins, and bathed you in cool water to bring down your fever. It took me a day or so to convince her that my nursing skills were adequate and my intentions honorable."

"I haven't been much of a father-protector to that little girl," Pete admitted. "But I love her the same as a daughter. Maybe more so, since I chose her for my own."

He gandered about the room. "Where is she, anyway? Not alone in that drafty old cabin, I hope."

"A friend of mine, Minnie Walentine, owns a boarding house up the street. Colleen is staying with her, swapping chores for rent."

Pete grinned. "I have no doubt she's earning her keep. There hasn't been a paint invented that Colleen couldn't scrub off a wall along with the dirt."

"Minnie said almost exactly the same thing yesterday when she dropped by. I don't know whether Colleen has or ever wanted a grandmother, but she certainly has one now."

Pete's hazel eyes probed Megan's. "You haven't changed a bit. Forever the caretaker, eh?"

She shrugged and looked away. "When I see something needing done, I do it. Is that wrong?"

"How, exactly, is a man in my position supposed to answer?" His chuckle set off a coughing jag that was painful to hear.

As he gasped for enough air to satisfy his tortured lungs, Megan lifted his head and brought a mug to his lips. He took a sip, then gagged.

"What the hell is that? Outhouse punch?"

"It's green oil, Mr. Vladislov, and it'll cure what ails you. Already has, truth be known."

His upper lip curled and he shuddered. "No damn wonder I've had nightmares. I suspect its ingredients are something else I'd be better off not knowing, but I'm compelled to ask."

"Boiling water, dried red sage, rosemary, bee baum and camomile flowers, wormwood, and a pinch of ground valerian root infused with olive oil."

His features contorted more gruesomely with each ingredient. Megan winked, then added, "Wu-nav-ai, the Paiute medicine woman, taught me well those many years ago. I haven't traveled a mile without my satchel of herbs ever since."

"Oh, yes. God help me, had I been spared your witch doctoring," he said, "I might have been forced to resort to store-bought pharmaceuticals."

Megan dabbed his greasy lips with the sheet. "Hush up and rest. That's the second-best medicine I can prescribe."

He grabbed her wrist. "I'd given up on ever seeing you again. Talk to me awhile."

"Later, Pete. You're just beginning to get your strength back."

"I have no right asking favors," he said. "No right to ask anything of you after all you've already done. But please, Megan, stay with me, just a few more minutes."

She'd contemplated this moment at length. Her decision to treat him the same as any number of sick strangers she'd nursed back to health failed to address the fact she'd loved Pete Vladislov, once upon a time.

Back in '77—a lifetime ago, it seemed—she, Barlow P. and Pete mushed across the British Columbian wilderness for two and a half months to rescue the miners at the North Nevada camp above Eight-Mile Creek. Twenty-eight men had succumbed to scurvy and its complications before they arrived. From that point on, the death toll rose no higher.

After the crisis passed, Pete asked her to go with him to "where the northern lights sizzle across the sky in all their glory." Megan refused, having just learned of David Jacobs' marriage to Amanda Meredith. She chose to be a martyr for the love she'd lost, rather than risk her heart anew.

"Please," Pete said, intruding on her reverie. He patted the quilt. "For old times' sake."

She resettled, knowing that to maintain a physical distance, much less an emotional one, smacked of the same kind of fool's game she'd played on herself twenty years earlier.

"Tell me about your son. My memory of our acquaintance is foggy, I'll admit, but he's a strapping, handsome boy, as I recall."

"And is almost fourteen going on thirty-four, to be sure."

"Most are, my dear, when their sap starts to rise. Some say a man's brain never recovers from it."

"No quarrel there, but B.D. cut many a dido before whiskers downed his lip. Sometimes I fear we're too much alike. Others, that we're as opposite as cats and cattle. For the most part, I love him and like him and pray he feels the same for me."

"I'd trade a girl-woman for him, even up," Pete said. "From one minute to the next, I don't know whether Colleen'll be sweet, sulky, or somewhere in-between."

Megan thought it wise to keep silent counsel. The girl's earlier insistence on directing Pete's recovery and casual efficiency showed her to be a veteran of Pete's thirst for spirits. Indians were far less prudish than whites, but Megan had been shocked when Colleen stripped Pete to the skin like an oversized, filthy infant.

"I suppose you've guessed that I named her for you," he said. "After a fashion."

"And to be sure," Megan teased, " 'twas the sweet side of her nature that reminded you of me."

"Actually, her fire and her will to survive. And maybe the shiny, black, plunder-your-immortal-soul eyes you share."

The flutter took wing again. Megan fidgeted to quell it. The time and place for them was past.

"I'll wager that B.D. has connected the names," she said, somewhat primly, "although he hasn't asked about our history. Yet."

"The boy's initials—may I ask what they stand for?"

"Barlow David."

Pete nodded. "For Barlow P. Bainbridge, no doubt, and David Jacobs, I assume. The O'Malley, however, remains intact."

Megan explained B.D.'s paternity with blunt brevity. Pete didn't appear to be scandalized or even startled by it.

"I wonder . . . he mused. "Had Fate allowed those church bells to peal, would you really have vowed 'I do' this and such to ol' Bald Eagle Bainbridge?"

Megan smiled at the nickname. Pete's jealousy and frustration at her best friend's hovering presence had driven the trapper to distraction. "Yes."

"Out of habit, or real love?"

"The best of both."

Pete cogitated for a long moment, obviously reaching the decision not to believe her. "It can't have been easy to raise the boy alone."

"Odd you should say that. B.D. told me you cared for Colleen and another Indian boy and girl by yourself."

"The circumstances were quite different."

"Why?" Before he could respond, Megan raised a hand to halt it. "Because yours were orphans and mine is a bastard?"

"A damnable harsh word to attach to him, isn't it?"

"More honest to speak it aloud than indict him in silence the way you did."

"You're wrong," Pete said.

"So were the children who never chose B.D. for their schoolyard games. I told him the truth as he did to them until scorn taught him to lie."

Pete shook his head. "I sympathize with you and B.D., but I don't deserve to stand in their shade. Even after all these years, you should know me better than that."

She studied his hollowed cheeks, the gray whiskers and hair threaded with vestiges of auburn. Traces of the man she'd known remained, yet had she passed him on the street, she'd never have recognized him. His voice, liquor-scorched though it was, struck the most familiar chord.

"When Matthew, Ruth, and Colleen were small," Pete said, "I stayed near their people, the Athabascans. The children needed to learn the language, the traditions and stories. The women spoiled them. Sewed skins for their clothes and made them a towsack full of bone and hide toys."

He took a deep rasping breath. "Entire villages helped me raise my foster children, yet many a night I prayed to God for His help, too. Unless I miss my guess, you've been mother and father to B.D. without anything to lean on except your faith. If that doesn't constitute different circumstan—"

A strangling cough stole his voice. Paroxysms shook the heavy oak bed from stem to stern. Megan leaped to her feet and pounded his back to loosen the phlegm. He spat into the rag she offered, then fell back on the pillows. Another dose of green oil went down without a struggle.

"I hate this—this weakness," he railed. "You'll find

me up and about tomorrow or hanging from a rafter by a rope."

Megan tucked the covers and lifted his beard from beneath their confines. "I'd already planned on taking you on a tour of the Haven. Staying abed too long will ruin your lungs."

"So much for my being masterful."

"Sleep now, while I fix a bowl of bread soup for your supper."

"I won't eat a bite." The quilt undulated as his legs scissored wide and shut. "A man needs meat to cure what ails him, not baby mush."

"And isn't that a fine howdy-do coming from one who's bottle-fed himself for weeks on end."

"I had my reasons."

"Yes, well, most people managed to celebrate the arrival of 1898 in one night."

"But I'm a drunkard, my dear." His nostrils flared. "That's all an empty shell is good for. Filling up."

That's the whiskey talking, Megan reminded herself. More accurately, the lack of it. His innards crave it; they're clawing for it, and he's got to lash out at something. I just can't let him bully me.

"If it's pity you're angling after," she said, "you won't get any from me."

"I've plenty enough of it for both of us, thank you."

A peevish sigh whistled through Megan's lips. It seemed as if she had three men wallowing in her bed: the derelict quaking with delirium tremens, the sullen brute bent on inflicting more misery than he suffered, and the soft-hearted, ornery, spirited Pete Vladislov she'd loved and never forgotten.

"Do you remember what you told me before you left the North Nevada?" she asked.

He turned his head to stare at the wall. "My recollection begins with kissing you, feeling you respond, and your telling me good-bye. It ends with all the things I should have said or done instead of walk away."

Megan frowned at his snide tone. "You said if I ever found what I was looking for, to grab it in both hands and never let it go, no matter what."

He snorted bitterly. "Pithy son of a bitch, wasn't I?"

Megan's temper flared despite her efforts to contain it. "Make sport if you're a mind to, but I took those words to heart and they've kept me going more times than I can count."

She forced him to look at her and held his head in place. Her eyes bored into his. "It's a damned shame to find out now that all you've grabbed on to and refused to let go of all these years is a long-necked bottle of whiskey."

Chapter 27

Pete lowered the book he wasn't reading. He laid it open across his lap like a napkin.

Megan felt his gaze beckon her own. She flipped a page of Henry James's *The Portrait of a Lady* and feigned interest in a character neither she nor the author liked particularly much.

A month's convalescence had restored Pete's physical and mental equilibrium. A mild cough persisted and he tired easily, but her role had evolved into more of a benevolent warden than a nurse.

He slid the book beside him on the settee and planted an ankle on his knee. Finding the position unsatisfactory, he reversed it. His moccasin's whip-stitched seam drew intense scrutiny. He plucked at one hide-laced loop. His fingernails worried it taut, then repeated the process with sequential stitches.

Megan was as fidgety as he was, but trying to project a calming influence. Good intentions aside, about two more minutes of his nervous flusters would have her ransacking the cupboard for the cooking sherry.

"This is why you drink, isn't it?" she asked, not unkindly. "You can't abide winter's imprisonment. Bending an elbow in a saloon and jawing with other bar-dogs makes the time pass faster."

"You're partly right," he said. "I don't touch liquor during trapping season. Whiskey warms the inner man while the rest of him freezes to death. Can't hope to plug a bear when all of a sudden there's twins in your sights."

"And the other part?"

Pete stroked his moccasin's smooth, moosehide vamp. "Habits are damn hard to break. I took up one to forget another." He grunted. "It didn't work."

"Barlow P. told me he did the same thing after the South gave up the ghost. The war left him with plenty of them to fight by himself."

"Ghosts of one kind or another haunt us all." Pete's head raised and a melancholy smile appeared. "That old coot went to his grave loving you. Hard as I've tried to forget you, I reckon I will, too."

Megan squirmed in her chair, the conversational ground having taken a detour she hadn't expected or wished to explore. Before she could maneuver it away from romantic sentiments, Pete said, "Remember when I got a bellyful of his interfering and stormed out of the bunkhouse?"

"That tantrum cost you a share of my famous biscuits, as I recall."

"Barlow P. came outside directly for a man-to-man about you and Jacobs—"

"Oh? I thought you'd conspired to get out of helping me scour that filthy cabin. Funny how neither of you reappeared until the chores were done."

"Megan?"

"Yes?"

"You're doing it again."

"Doing what?"

"Chitchatting to avoid a serious discussion." Pete fluttered his lashes, then pantomimed balancing a teacup and saucer in his palm. "Simply abominable weather we're having, isn't it, Miss O'Malley?" he minced. "I do declare, it's the worst I've seen since . . . why, since *last* winter."

"Never in my life have I prattled like a biddy." Megan flounced from her seat and toward the counter to mask her amusement.

Pete's arms encircled her waist from behind.

"You've been dangerously close to it the last few days."

Megan leaned against his broad chest and clasped her hands over his. His clean-shaven cheek nuzzled hers. She breathed in the scents she'd always associated with him—shaving soap, tanned leather, and scintillating male musk.

It had been so long since she'd let a man hold her. She thought all those languid, womanly desires David Jacobs had aroused in her had died with him. Their unexpected resurrection made her shiver.

Pete turned her around to face him. Time and dissipation hadn't diminished his angular Slavic features nor tamped the fire in his eyes.

"I also remember a night spent in a snow cave during a howling blizzard," he said, "and awakening with you pressed against me, just as you were a moment ago."

Megan blushed to the roots of her hair, grateful that he ended the reverie without a mention of her drowsy, shameless wriggling before she realized what she was doing.

She extricated herself from his embrace, albeit reluctantly. "I must get crackin' if the Haven is to reopen tomorrow morning."

Pete caught her arm. "I haven't proven myself to you, yet, have I?"

"There's no proving to be done, but to your own self. Changing to please another—any other—is the worst kind of charade."

She proceeded around the counter and quickly assembled ingredients and implements. "A friend of mine in Seattle was smitten with a lady named Pearlina Capshaw. Because Pearlina said she admired scholarly sorts, Hank memorized Hawthorne and Thoreau, kept his hair and jaunty new Vandyke trimmed, and duded up in cutaway sack suits, starched shirts, and silk neckties."

Bowls and utensils danced when Pete hiked himself

up on the counter's far end. "Assuming there's a lesson to be gained here, I'd guess Hank and Pearlina didn't live happily ever after."

"After a few evenings in each other's company, Pearlina told him not to bother calling on her again. He was simply too much like the other beaus who'd squired her."

Megan lifted a half-empty gunny of flour. Only one fifty-pound bag remained. She'd bought her stores before prices shot to twenty-four dollars a pound, but the johnnycakes would be as thin as her shimmy before supply boats docked in the spring.

She glanced at Pete as she cranked the sifter's handle. His bemused expression piqued her curiosity. "Cat got your tongue?"

"No, I'm just waiting until you're up to your elbows in batter."

"Why?"

"So I can say what I intend to say without your dodging me."

"I don't abide ultimatums, Pete."

"Better to give than to receive, huh?"

Megan tossed in a measure of indian meal. "Damned if I didn't like you better when you were sick."

"Well, seeing as how I've worn out my welcome, I'll take my leave." He pivoted on his haunches and scooted forward. "Maybe we'll run into each other again, oh, come 1918 or thereabouts."

"No, Pete!" Flour billowed upward. Her lusty sneeze sent a white cloud mushrooming from the bowl, which fluttered down over her, the counter, and everything atop it.

He slapped his knee and guffawed. Megan tried her best to grace him with a scowl, but dissolved into gales of laughter. He scrambled onto all fours and kissed her dusty nose. "That's what I've missed most. The best tonic in the world is hearing my lovely colleen laugh."

"Away with you while I tidy this mess." She scooped the strewn flour with a spatula blade. "If more merriment's what you hanker for, stop pestering me to rattle old skeletons."

"We share a common past, Megan."

"That, we do. Except I have more on my plate than I can say grace over in the present."

She fetched the kettle from the stove. A surreptitious glance found him glowering into space. "That's what's troubling you, if you'll only admit it," she added softly. "Colleen, B.D., and I all have things to keep us occupied."

"So help me," he warned, "mention idle hands being the devil's playground and I'll dump that bowl of batter over your head."

"Struck a chord, did I?"

"If memory serves, the Gypsy in you is one of your least endearing traits."

Megan pushed a dollop of molasses into the mixture, then licked the long sweetening from her finger. "It didn't take a crystal ball to divine the idea for the Haven of Rest, my friend. Old Man Winter squeezes the life out of the Klondike for eight solid months. For a while, Front Street is like the carnival come to town, but even gambling, guzzling liquor, and cavorting with Jezebels gets tedious eventually—let alone, hearing Cad yodel "Such a Nice Girl, Too," night after night."

Pete swiped at the batter dripping from the bowl's rim. He smacked his lips. "Yeah, but I wouldn't have bet a plugged nickel on your chances of making a go at a tearoom."

"The Haven isn't a tearoom, you lout. It's a social club of sorts. The only place in Dawson City where men can parley without a bloomin' melee of some sort in the background."

Pete shrugged. "Reckon I'll see for myself in the morning. That is, if you remember to remove that QUARANTINE sign from the door."

Megan scowled as she poured the ivory batter into the baking tin. B.D. should have arrived an hour ago. Without a doubt, he was dawdling in Minnie's parlor making cow eyes at Colleen.

Son, she thought, you have until this cake's done to darken my door. While it's grand you have a friend to spend Sundays with, I need an accomplice to help me push mine from the nest.

Chapter 28

"My mother's fourth husband, a sawbones of some renown, once asked me why I chose trapping to make my living," Pete said. The pick he drove into the One Below's wall punctuated his remark. "The answer still hasn't occurred to me, but I'm learning fast why mining never entered my mind."

"If it's that onerous, you can call it quits anytime," B.D. said. "I didn't twist your arm. You volunteered."

"Yeah, well, your mother's concern over your labor troubles inspired me to kill a flock of birds with one rock."

Pete propped his chin on the pick handle as one would a cane, apparently incapable of swinging it and talking simultaneously.

"First off," he said, "it isn't right that you're stuck in this glory hole by your lonesome. Secondly, now that I'm healthy enough to ruin your mother's reputation, but can't abide Minnie's claptrap, bunking with you is a godsend. Most importantly, playing prospector lets Megan think I'm ignorant of her scheme to remove me from liquid temptation."

"I don't follow."

"Her high dudgeon about you getting hurt or sick and no one being the wiser for days? Why, if that wasn't a female flimflam to coerce me into white knighthood and away from the irrigation parlors, I'll eat these gumshoes for supper."

B.D. scratched at his side-whiskers. "Yeah, well, Ma

is an expert at nudging a man in the direction she wants him to go."

Pete chuckled. "You're preaching to the choir, son."

"Maybe so, but I don't need nursemaiding and neither do you. If you truly hate the work, don't do it."

"Nah, I'm too puny and stove up to chase caribou across the tundra. Besides, perseverance builds character. A bushel or two extra won't do me any harm."

"There are worse ways to make a living."

"Oh? Name one."

B.D. shoveled several loads of muck into the slag bucket. "How about chief eunuch at Sweet Molly Marie's House of Delight?"

Pete laughed so hard the pick's blade bounced down the scarred wall. "You got me there." He glanced sideward. "Except you're kind of damp behind the lobes to yank that one out of your war bag, aren't you?"

"I'll be fourteen in a couple of months." B.D. hoped the prideful note in his voice wasn't too obvious, but fourteen definitely had a stouter ring to it. "The thirtieth of April, to be exact."

"Well, I'd say you're a fine example of our species for a fellow your age. Hardworking, responsible, and from what I've seen, there's a respectable amount of horse sense under that mop of black hair."

"Why, thanks, Pe—"

"On the other hand, I remember too well what I spent all my waking hours, and regular interludes of my sleeping ones thinking about when I was a young buck."

B.D. chucked his shovel into a pile of silt. "Let's get something straight. Just because you're courting Ma doesn't give you leave for a birds and bees talk with me."

"I agree."

"You do?"

"Of course, I do. It's not my place to educate you

in such matters even if you needed it, which I suspect you don't."

"I should say not," B.D. lied.

"It is my place, however, to warn you that if you so much as *suggest* anything untoward to Colleen, you'll be imminently qualified for that job at Sweet Molly Marie's before you can whistle 'Dixie.' "

The very idea sent a guilty flush to the boy's cheeks and a shiver down his spine. He wished he could trust Pete enough for a man-to-man about women in general. The trapper hadn't touched a drop of whiskey for over two months, but B.D. recalled the intimacies he'd revealed while in the throes of delirium—including references to his couplings with someone named Anuska.

"Colleen is my friend," B.D. said. "The best I ever hope to have. I'm not blind, but I'd never hurt her like that and I'd kill anyone who tried."

Pete studied him a moment. "I believe you, son." He chuckled wickedly. "That doesn't mean I won't watch you like a hawk, but honorable intentions ought to count for something."

A companionable silence fell between them. A thousand questions rattled in B.D.'s mind, including how honorable Pete's intentions were toward his mother, but the work would suffer if he broached them.

The trapper was no idler. The massive shoulders, chest, and upper arms his chosen trade had visited on him made hoisting a pickax appear effortless. Pete just relished a parley and wasn't about to let anything put the quietus to one.

If only Mother Nature would cooperate, B.D. wouldn't begrudge Pete his gift for gab. But for all the hosannas sung when B.D. and Jimmy hit gravel, there'd been precious little worth humming about ever since.

Because placer gold is heavier than water, it sinks to the bottom of a stream and gradually filters down through the silt, layers of coarse gravel and finer grit to mingle with the black sand deposited atop an impenetrable rock base.

Once he'd struck bedrock, B.D. had relied on Nathan's educated guesswork to determine in which direction the original stream flowed. The object of the "drift" B.D. then dug was to find and follow that elusive, shallow stratum of gold-rich sand. Gravel layers contained two to five dollars-worth of ore per pan, but black sand deposits yielded upward of ten times that amount.

Trouble was, after months of thawing, digging, and hoisting countless bucket loads of muck from the drift, not a speck of sand had shown itself.

How deep should he go before he gave up on this drift and started another? Should he branch a second off this one or backtrack to the main shaft and begin anew?

Nathan refused to advise B.D. further. Expertise in geology notwithstanding, water always follows the path of least resistance. Lord only knew how many crooks and twists and shifts had occurred over the millennium.

"All I can do is wish you the best of luck," Nathan said. "That's what prospecting boils down to: five percent expertise and ninety-five percent serendipity."

Pete's outlook had been considerably more pragmatic. "Sounds like hunting for a fart in a whirlwind to me."

B.D. squinted at a fresh shovel-load of semithawed sediment. It probably contained a compliment of ore particles, but still no sand.

Maybe it'll show before we quit for the night, he mused. Maybe tomorrow. Or the day after.

Rather than permit an "or maybe never" to creep into his thoughts, he diverted them to Colleen; a subject guaranteed to raise his sagging spirits.

She possessed a childlike sense of wonder that delighted him, a sunny disposition that defied the Arctic gloom, and a perceptiveness that astounded him. B.D. liked her as well as he loved her. She was the sister he'd always wanted, boon companion, and sweetheart combined into a jumble of conflicting emotions.

The clock's hands spun as fast as a whirligig during their Sunday afternoon visits, but every tick seemed to take ten during the intervening six days.

A week earlier, while Pete was having supper with his mother, B.D. was so desperate for Colleen's company he dashed into town to invite her to one of Miss Meriwether-Jones's Shakespeare readings.

He'd arrived after Minnie ventured to the Haven to stick her nose into Pete and Saint Megan's fledgling romance, but insisted that formal permission wasn't needed "just to mosey down to the danged library."

Miss Meriwether-Jones's flair for making the bard's lusty soliloquies sound as dull as Latin verb conjugations was compensated for by surreptitious whispering at the back of the room.

The laughing young couple didn't expect to find a three-person vigilance committee waiting for them when they returned to the boarding house. Minnie, Saint Megan, and Pete tried to outshout each other with questions, accusations, and threats.

"Pipe down—all of you," B.D. bellowed. "Those jakes trying to sleep upstairs are gonna think another fire's broken out."

To his surprise, they complied, although Saint Megan looked fit to bust. Or do murder.

"We have done nothing wrong," Colleen said before B.D. could speak his peace. "We work as hard as you do and deserve a . . . a respite, now and then."

"Yeah," B.D. chimed in. "Folks in glass houses shouldn't throw stones."

"What the devil is that supposed to mean?" Minnie snapped.

"Aw, hell, I dunno. Y'all have got me so bumfuzzled, I can't think straight." B.D. took Colleen's hand. "I'll give you the fact that we aren't full grown.

Reckon we should've left a note to let you know where we'd gone, too. Only it isn't fair to expect me and Colleen to pull our weight, then treat us like porch babies."

"Realizing that life isn't fair is part and parcel to growing up, son," Pete lectured. "So is understanding that fear changes to fury the instant the 'all's well' sounds."

"When Minnie came home and couldn't find Colleen," his mother added, "we were terrified something awful had happened to her."

The landlady grinned. "Oh, I figured she was with you, and made the mistake of saying so. Law, did that ever put a hot match to the coal-oil can. You should have heard how your mama and Pete carried on, then."

She cackled. "On second thought, it's best you didn't."

Colleen yawned and patted her lips. "I am tired from a long day." She hiked up on her tiptoes and right in front of God and everyone else in the parlor, kissed B.D.'s cheek. "Thank you for such a very nice surprise."

After she bid good night to her elders, Colleen started for the stairs.

"Surprise?" Pete inquired suspiciously. "What surprise?"

She favored her guardian with her sweetest smile. "For making me feel special enough to come many miles out of his way to visit."

Minnie poked Saint Megan in the ribs and jerked a thumb at Pete.

B.D. hid a smirk behind his hand. The exasperated expression on his mother's face was worth every second of the lambasting he'd received.

"Holy Moses, son." Pete's raspy voice jerked B.D. back to the present. "How are you going to benefit from my wisdom if you haven't listened to a blessed word of it?"

"I—uh, sorry."

"Aw, now you know why the good Lord made earwax. It muffles an old fool's ramblings. Chances are, I'll strew the same pearls before the month's out. Codgers are prone to repeat ourselves, you know."

He reared back and hilted his pick's blade in the wall. A dishpan-sized chunk of earth prized free. B.D. flinched. He could have sworn the ground shuddered beneath his feet at the impact.

"Of course, I may forget the gist till after that fancy-pants soiree your mother's in charge of," Pete said. "If I do, I suspect it'll teach you to listen sharper."

B.D. rolled his eyes ceilingward. "Okay, I'll bite. What pearls do you want to bestow about the Fireman's Ball? Which, by the by, portends to be about as much fun as a public flogging."

"Me and Earl are with you there. We suggested just passing the hat amongst Dawson's hoi polloi to finance the equipment, but *no-o-o-o. Huh-uh-h.* Our women-folk are dithering like hummingbirds in a poppy field over this shindig. Come hell or high water, us fellows are going to jig to their tune."

B.D.'s eyebrows met at the bridge of his nose. "Colleen hasn't said anything to me about it."

"Well, it's nice to know that one of my ladying lessons sunk in and held fast. She's not *supposed* to, kid. *You* are."

"But how was I to know she wanted to go?"

"You, being the man, casts the invite even when you know as sure as sixty that a girl's itching to be asked. Then she either accepts or declines. To get a yes pretty well means yes, unless she only says it to make some fool she's sweet on jealous enough to pop the question himself.

"A no may mean she sincerely doesn't want to go—or leastwise, not with you. Then again, it could mean she's playing hard to get and wants to be begged. Or she's already promised another, but wants to keep you stringing along, though she could be saving you from hurt feelings with a flat-out 'nothing doing.' "

B.D.'s howl echoed through the shaft. "I have to wade all that hokum just to ask Colleen to a dance I don't want to go to in the first place?"

"Shoot, no. I'll admit, I kind of hoped you would so I wouldn't be the only one nipping at the sarsaparilla, but . . ."

"But what?"

Pete waved a hand dismissively. "Really—it's nothing to concern yourself about. Sure as the world, one of the Romeos that's invited her already will take pity on me and refrain from being a bad influence."

B.D.'s heart skipped a full beat. Through clenched teeth, he inquired, "Anybody I know?"

A corner of Pete's mouth curved into a sly grin. He splayed his fingers and ticked off, "Nels, Nathan, Jimmy, Roddy Connors, Ikey Sutro, Constable Perkins—the Mountie who took such umbrage to my little joke with the sausage—Dick House, Shorty McBroom—"

The shovel blade clanged to the floor. B.D. sprinted for the main tunnel.

"Hey, son," Pete called after him. "Where are you off to in such a blazing hurry?"

"Just where the hell do you *think?*"

Chapter 29

Megan gawked at the image reflected in the cheval mirror in Minnie's bedroom. She scarcely recognized the handsome elegantly begowned woman staring back at her in wide-eyed wonder.

The cobalt, sculptured velvet evening dress clung to her like a second skin. A veed panel of black Chantilly lace plunged to her nipped waist; the gusset guaranteed to capture masculine attention, yet exposed the merest hint of her charms.

Beaded passementerie dangled from double-frilled lace epaulets. Chantilly ruffles encircled her wrists, layered her hips, and trimmed the skirt's embroidered straw-colored satin insert. Having declared its velvet train to be useless save as a boardwalk broom, Minnie had snipped off the expendable fabric and hemmed the remainder to street length.

Never again would Megan tease her friend for being a pack rat. The gorgeous frocks she had produced from several trunks and a monstrous wardrobe comprised what she called her "Boston pretties."

Megan couldn't imagine Minnie in the role of society maven, but Minerva Hortense Van Buren Scott had been a force to reckon with before she divorced brutish Manfred Scott and his family fortune to marry penniless Hugo Walentine.

"If Miss O'Malley ever finishes preening," Minnie stage-whispered to Colleen, "you and I might have a turn at the glass before the men arrive."

Megan gave her chignon a final pat and glided sideward. She and Minnie exchanged gratified looks as Colleen stepped forward. Until tonight, they hadn't seen her in anything but a fringed animal skin dress and hide leggings and doubted if she had, either.

Colleen craned her neck toward the mirror like a wary swan, then clapped her hands over her mouth and squealed with delight. "I am pretty."

"No, lass," Megan said, "you are gorgeous."

Minnie realized earlier that hairpins capable of securing the girl's thick raven mane had yet to be invented. Instead, she'd brushed it back from the sides and crown and fashioned a center braid, gathered the loose hair with it, and tied it at Colleen's nape with a ribbon. A few whipstitches attached a cluster of fabric roses snipped off another dress.

Colleen twirled to and fro, giggling at the rustle of sea-foam green silk swirling over her flounced lace underskirt. Cascades of pink, cream, and scarlet fabric roses held a swag of draped silk at her hip and blossomed at the underskirt's peak. A daintier floral streamer trimmed one side of the bodice.

Megan frowned slightly at the gown's sweetheart neckline—rather, at the expanse of bosom it revealed—but as Minnie had quipped, "The best seamstress in the Yukon can't stretch a wolf pelt to fit a caribou."

The two older women smiled as Colleen ghostdanced in front of the mirror.

"The evening bag I made you from that scrap of train," Minnie whispered to Megan. "Did you tuck a vial of smelling salts in it?"

"Heavens, no. Why would I?"

"Because when your son gets a look at her, he'll need a whiff. I'm not so sure Pete and Earl won't pitch into a swoon themselves."

"Pete better have eyes only for me, and unless I miss my guess, Earl won't take his off you for a second."

She took Minnie's hands. "Your gown is a master-piece. I've never seen anything like it."

"I'm partial to it, I'll admit," Minnie said. "The few times I've worn it, I just know I could reach a cupboard's top shelf without straining a muscle."

Her high-necked, maroon-over-beige stamped velvet gown hugged curves Megan didn't realize the older woman had. The folds of a beige sleeveless caftan narrowed at the shoulders, then fell to the floor in graceful, Watteau-style pleats. Her hair, braided and looped into a coronet, completed her regal ensemble.

A rap on the door startled all three women. "There's a coupla jakes in the parlor waitin' for visions of loveliness to appear," Earl hollered.

"Well, how about you, Mr. Delacroix?" Minnie inquired.

"I just want to get this hoedown over with so's I can swaller without my dadblamed collar paring the hide off'n my Adam's apple."

"If that man were any more romantic," Minnie said, "it'd be me needing a jolt of smelling salts."

"Are you ready, Colleen?" Megan asked.

"Oh, yes, ma'am." She started forward, then grimaced. Her fingers traced her gown's bodice. "Pins are gouging me, I think."

"I'm afraid not," Megan said. "Whalebone stays are part of dressing like a lady. Might as well get accustomed to them."

"My people do not use whalebones to splint their ribs even if they are broken."

"Welcome to civilization," Minnie said. "And please, try not to clobber B.D. when he grouses about the hour he spent shaving."

"Which he will," Megan added. "Same as the other two."

Minnie strode into the hall. "Age before beauty."

Megan started out behind her to save the fairest maiden for last. She heard bootheels clop the floor in unison when Minnie entered the parlor.

"Why, you'd give Queen Victoria a run for her money," Pete said.

Earl drawled, "Took the words right outta my mouth."

Megan assumed her son contributed the wolf whistle. She took a step, then whirled. "Tell me, Colleen, do I really look all right? My gown, it's not too fussy, is it? Too dark?"

The girl's eyes widened with surprise. "Do you have wings fluttering in your belly, too?"

"Bigger than an eagle's."

"But you are ol—er, you are not . . ."

"I'm too decrepit to suffer the nervous flusters?" Megan smiled. "I thought I was, too, but it's Pete in there waiting and—well, all of a sudden, it *matters* what he'll think when he sees me."

"Could he be feeling the same thing?" Colleen asked.

"Oh, I'd stake my life on it."

The girl paused, her demeanor somewhat timid as it became during rare occasions when she and Megan were alone. "I am young and foolish, but to care so much about pleasing one another seems more important than how it is done."

Megan gave her wrist a gentle squeeze. "It's a bold lass you are and a better one than you know."

"Jaysus, are you two gonna primp all night?"

"I'm coming," Megan said and gathered up her skirts.

She squinted as she entered the parlor. Minnie had lit a single strategically placed lamp to set the mood.

"Good evening, gentlemen," Megan said. "Beg pardon for the delay."

Her son's jaw came to rest just above the shirtfront she'd flat-ironed that afternoon. Closer inspection found an inch of cuff flared from his suit coat's sleeves; his shoulders and upper arms virtually upholstered in charcoal wool.

"I hadn't realized you'd filled out so much," Megan said.

"Aw, nobody's going to notice us menfolk, anyhow." He lowered his voice to a whisper. "Minnie cleaned up real nice, but she can't hold a candle to you, Ma."

"Why, thank you, son."

"I know now why some call you Angel, Miss Megan," Earl said, " 'cept you're purtier than any I've seen in picture books."

"What a lovely thing to say."

The sourdough's frilly shirt, tapestry waistcoat, knee-length coat, baggy trousers, and Hessian boots harkened back to the era of powdered wigs and muskets, but the man dignified his outfit, rather than vice-versa.

Megan's gaze drifted to Pete, who stood at military attention in the far corner. His silvered hair gleamed in the lamplight; the perfect foil for a jet black frock coat and trousers, boiled shirt, and gray silk tie.

She bowed her head and curtsied. Pete's palm cupped her wrist to bring her upright, then gently to his chest. When lips brushed her cheek, she trembled and closed her eyes to quell the dizziness assailing her.

"When you were twenty-two, I thought you were the most desirable, naturally beautiful woman I'd ever seen," he said, his voice husky with emotion. "I still do."

The wings inside Megan ceased fluttering. But I'm not twenty-two, and this isn't the Casisar, she wanted to shriek. Look at me, for God's sake. Just as I am. I can't compete with the ghost of the girl I used to be. She doesn't exist anymore.

Colleen's entrance gave Megan an excuse to turn from Pete's embrace. B.D.'s rapturous expression ricked his mother's heart. Someday, years in the future, would he impose his memories of this evening on the woman Colleen becomes?

"If we don't get goin'," Earl said, "the band'll be

tootin' 'Good Night, Ladies' afore we shuck our galoshes."

A strangled cry burst from Minnie's lips. She glanced at her gown, then at Megan's. "Good heavens, for all the hours we've spent pluming and sprucing, it never occurred to me until now . . ."

"What is wrong, Miss Minnie?" Colleen asked.

"Our gowns and slippers. How will we ever walk to the Cosmopolitan without ruining them?"

Pete sidled over to tap Earl's shoulder. "They thought they'd picked us for escorts 'cause we're the handsomest yahoos in town. Got more than they bargained for, didn't they?"

"Ain't short no oars in our boat, no-sir-ree."

"Keep it up and you'll be short something else," Minnie warned.

"Unless somebody's stolen them by now," B.D. said as he helped Colleen into her coat, "there's three dog teams out yonder to deliver you ladies to the ball."

"Tried to hire a sleigh big enough for all of us," Earl said. "Pete figured it'd be plumb romantical."

"Only we couldn't afford the horses to pull it," he chimed in. "And harnessing our own shiny selves might've detracted from the romance somewhat."

The men went out to ready the Klondike-style carriages while the women, mindful of their ensembles and coiffures, bundled against the frigid weather.

Eighteen malemutes, yipping and yapping in frantic unison, were audible from inside the house. The noise rose to an ear-splitting crescendo when Megan opened the door.

She skated toward the boardwalk, her flat-soled dance slippers skidding every which-a-way on the treacherous, ice-covered porch. Pete clutched the railing and extended his other hand to her; the dark scarf wrapped around his face already spangled with frozen crystals.

Megan sat down gingerly on the sled, then he swung

her legs around and layered furs over her from her toes to her chin.

She waved to answer his muffled "All set?" The six-dog team, curved tails quivering in anticipation, barked their readiness. The basket wobbled as Pete situated his feet on the runners and grabbed on to the handlebar.

"Hey-up, dogs!"

The paired leaders strained against the harness. In no time, they left their howling compatriots behind, jogging along as if out for a Sunday afternoon stroll.

Megan thrilled at the crisp grate of the runners coasting over the ice; the amber lights streaming from windows and puddling its surface; even the sting of the frigid breeze.

She'd heard rumors of a railroad conglomerate's plan to lay track from Skagway to Dawson. To her mind, such modern transit couldn't compete with sailing along behind a canine-powered locomotive, gandering at the inky sky, the frozen, grotesquely beautiful sea of desolation beneath it, and the ribbon of motionless gray blue river dividing it.

A symphony of wispy light appeared beside a low-hanging copper moon. Megan sat enthralled by eddies of mauve, white, and green arcs. The colors deepened near the horizon, curling into glorious pastel shades as they feathered into the heavens.

The aurora borealis. To many natives the joyful souls of their ancestors dancing across the sky. She wished Pete were beside her instead of behind. It certainly wasn't her first glimpse of the northern lights, but he'd promised to watch them—Stop, she commanded herself. Now who's jumping backward in time and applying it to now?

At Pete's "Whoa," the team halted in front of a two-story log edifice. Frozen condensation caked its windows and rendered the arched Cosmopolitan Club lettering illegible.

Megan wished a more sedate locale could have

hosted the festivities, but as always beggars could not be choosers. Salome Lippy, Belinda Mulroney, and other committee members had solicited donations, but few of Dawson's genteel set would be caught dead in a dance hall regardless of the cause.

Pete darted inside the foyer and returned with the squat man in charge of stabling dog teams in a lean-to shed behind the building.

A chill raced through Megan when Pete whisked back her furry cocoon. He wrapped his arm around her waist and spirited her into the hall just as Earl's sled crunched to a stop behind them.

Despite its highfalutin name, the Cosmopolitan's smoky interior was indistinguishable from any other in Dawson. A long polished bar dominated one side of the room. The mirror behind it reflected customers' faces and the bartenders' backs.

Beyond the saloon area, a smaller room purveyed faro, poker, roulette, and craps round-the-clock, except on the Sabbath. The game room led into the theater with its skimpy curtained stage, a six-box balcony where the Klondike Kings reigned over their less fortunate subjects, and the "auditorium" with moveable benches that doubled as a dance floor.

Opposite the bar, North West Mounted Police constables LeFarge and Smythe stood with their arms akimbo guarding an open whiskey barrel. While Pete dispensed with their wraps, Megan peered between the officers, delighted to see the container was three quarters full of drawstring pokes and loose gold.

"Looks like we'll have a genuine fire department with all the trimmings by summer, doesn't it, Constable LeFarge?"

"Yes, ma'am. Captain Constantine asked me to pass on his thanks for coordinating the fund-raising effort."

"Oh, the idea was mine, but a raft of ladies helped put on this shindig." She laughed, then added, "Truth is, a hard winter should get most of the credit. Why, folks'd pay a hundred a head for anything that smacked of a diversion by now."

"Those that had it would," Constable Smythe agreed.

Pete bounced a hefty hide pouch in his hands, then proffered it to LeFarge. "This should cover admission for us and our four guests."

"But—I—Glory, Pete. Where'd you get six hundred dollars in gold?"

"I withdrew it from the bank, of course."

Her eyes narrowed. "The bank?"

"For Christ's sweet sake, not at gunpoint, which you so obviously suspect. I may have looked like a bum when we remade our acquaintance, but I'm a far cry from destitute."

He took her arm and steered her toward the theater. "It's John Healy at the North American Trading Company who's thirty thousand dollars poorer. He bought enough furs to outfit half of Canada last December."

"If you're so well-off, why is Colleen working for Minnie and you for B.D.?"

"Not to mention, why didn't I offer you money for my keep?" His gaze flicked to the bar. "What was I . . . ? Oh, yes, I didn't offer board because I knew you'd be insulted. Colleen isn't keen on living in town, but is happy at Minnie's and housekeeping makes her feel useful. As for me, I really can't abide hunkering on my duff and I've thoroughly enjoyed getting to know your son better."

"Fair enough," Megan said.

When they sidestepped a clot of partygoers, she noticed a stony set to Pete's jaw. He stared at the glass a man held and licked his lips.

"This is difficult, isn't it?" Megan asked.

"It's nothing compared to how crowded the dance hall will be."

"That isn't what I meant."

"I know," he said. "Except talking about not drinking is as bad as wishing I could. Both keep my mind on whiskey instead of letting it wander elsewhere."

"Such as, to what's become of our friends and family members?"

"B.D. ducked in the door a minute ago. They'll catch up with us, directly."

Dawson City's richest, several of its fairest, and a goodly number of its ladies of ultimate accessibility were packed cheek to jowl in the theater. A fog of expensive perfume, cheap toilet water, sweat, tobacco, hair oil, witch hazel, spilled whiskey, and champagne assaulted Megan's nostrils.

Despite the ribald clamor, all eyes seemed locked on the stage. Presently, Coatless Curly Munro, renowned for his lunatic disregard for the blistering cold, lurched from behind the curtain.

He raised his arms and bellowed, "Hear ye, hear ye. A naughty rumor's been circulating that DeeDee Lovelace has offered to auction the full extent of her unique and varied services for a period commencing tonight through to the spring breakup. Well, gents, I'm here to tell you, the offer's bona fide."

Whistles and whoops exploded from the assembly. Curly glowered at his audience and gestured for silence.

"If you randy types can't control yourselves, we'll forget the whole thing. Miss Lovelace, a most civic-minded young lady, is making the ultimate sacrifice to support this worthy cause. Let's show her some respect."

Megan's temper flared. How dare they turn the Fireman's Ball into a blessed white slave auction?

"Simmer down, little Miss Teapot," Pete said. "The boys'll have their fun whether you approve of it or not."

"But this is ridiculous. No, it's worse—it's *obscene.*"

The man in front of her turned to sneer, "Who the hell are you? DeeDee's mother? She sells herself to

God knows who and how many every night. The only difference is the transactin' ain't usually so public."

Megan had the good manners to wait until his back was turned before making a face at him.

Curly shouted, "All sales has got conditions, so listen up. An amount matching the high bid has to be pledged to the fire department. For those too soused to cipher, that means if she goes for a thousand, another thousand hits the collection barrel afore DeeDee sashays off with the winner. Lastly, she reserves the right to reject the high bidder if she isn't keen on his particulars."

Colleen, Minnie, Earl, and B.D. inched into the room as Curly finished his spiel.

"I came here to dance with the prettiest girl in town," B.D. grumbled. "How long's this going to take?"

"A far sight longer than I can stomach," Megan said.

"Do you want to retire to the saloon?" Pete asked.

She almost blurted yes, without a thought to the consequences. Bad enough that a person could become giddy on the fumes pervading the theater. To ask Pete to dawdle near the bar would be as cruel as offering a man dying of thirst in the desert a cool drink, then pouring it on the sand.

"I'll survive," she said. "Just keep reminding me that it's for a worthy cause."

DeeDee Lovelace's debut met with thunderous applause. The henna-haired partridge tottered to the lip of the stage and bowed; her purple satin sheath struggling to contain her bounteous proportions.

"Five hundred," a high-pitched voice shouted.

"I'll go seven fifty."

"If'n she can cook," a baritone hollered from the back, "put me down for a thousand."

"Double it. I don't give a damn if I starve."

A lull in the proceedings at the five-thousand mark inspired DeeDee to drop her handkerchief. She bent to retrieve it, which increased her assessed valuation by two thousand dollars.

The crowd roared its approval when short, thick-set Roddy Conners' ninety-two-hundred dollar bid was declared the winner.

Curly said, "You understand that ninety-two goes to DeeDee and a like sum to the fire department, don't you?"

"Aye, 'tis worth every penny."

"DeeDee?" Curly asked. "What say you?"

A hush fell over the room. She visibly paled. Conners' unique predilection was apparently known to her.

Six nights a week, from an orchestra's first note to its last, Roddy's favorite partners, sisters nicknamed Vaseline and Glycerine, worked in shifts to keep pace with the Irish hoofer. When he became too exhausted to dance in time with the music, he ponied up his dollar-a-tune anyway and walked his partner around the floor.

"Ninety-two hundred bucks, eh?" DeeDee repeated. Her palms stroked her capacious hips while her lips curved into a provocative smile. "Well, honey, I suppose I could use the exercise."

Amid hurrahs and stamping feet, the parched audience stampeded for the saloon. Pete, Earl, and B.D. wrapped their arms around their respective ladies to prevent their being carried along in the crush.

"Are you still upset?" Pete asked over Megan's shoulder.

"Truth be known," she said, "I caught myself cheering for Roddy."

"Might as well. DeeDee could have done worse than pay the price with her feet."

Megan grinned at him. "And 'lest you forget, it's for a worthy cause, right?"

A rumble and the squeal of unoiled castors presaged an upright piano's appearance on stage. Its maestro

twiddled a few keys and a fiddler and a harmonica
player took up their positions.

The fiddler wedged his instrument under his chin,
sawed off a partial refrain, then launched into a rousing "She Got It Where Dooley Got the Brick."

"Shall we?" Pete asked.

Megan worried her lower lip. "I never learned any
dance but the waltz." She added silently, *and the only
arms I've ever danced in belonged to David Jacobs.*

"Don't wander off," Pete said. "I'll be right back."
He strode toward a set of steps leading to the stage.

Minnie dug a none-too-gentle elbow into Earl's ribs.

"What'd you do that for?"

"I want to dance."

"Cain't. I got the lumbago somethin' awful."

"There's worse ailments a man can suffer," Minnie
warned. Then she whispered in his ear.

Earl's arm winged smartly. "Well, let's have at it,
then."

B.D. and Colleen followed, oblivious to others pair-
ing up for a whirl, much less the older couple's
squabbling.

Swiftwater Bill Gates's keg-on-legs frame swaggered
to the center of the room. His latest nubile conquest
clung to the sleeve of his Prince Albert like a shipwreck
victim clutches flotsam. Brandi Bliss, the fourteen-year-
old singer's ridiculous stage name, gazed adoringly at
her escort, which indicated to Megan that she hadn't
known him long.

Gates ogled Colleen's bosom, which provoked a
glance at her face. The Klondike King looked from
Colleen to B.D.

"Hey, you—kid," he said. "Don't I know you and
that pretty squaw from somewheres?"

B.D. froze. "I—uh, gosh, Mr. Gates, everybody in
Dawson knows you. But us? We're just nobodies."

Gates beamed at the homage paid him. "Couldn't
have said it any better myself, kid, that's a fact."

Megan started when Pete's hand cradled her waist. "Your son is one smart cookie, Miss O'Malley."

"He comes by it naturally," she teased, "from his mother's side of the family."

"Ah, but is she daring enough to steal away to a corner bench with a deucedly handsome admirer?"

"I'll tell you true, my friend. I'd steal away with Swiftwater Bill for a chance to sit down awhile."

Pete led her to where the crude theater seats were stacked. She clucked her tongue at his ingenuity. No wonder he'd been gone so long. Several benches had been rearranged to fashion a cozy alcove.

He wriggled backward over three seats laid parallel to form a chaise-style seat. Mindful of her voluminous skirts, she snuggled into the crook of his arm.

"This is lovely," she said with a deep sigh. "Though I feel like wicked children hiding in the vestibule from the priest."

"Fun, isn't it?"

"Far more than that cattle auction."

"You're not enjoying the party?"

She knew the question had nothing to do with the ball and everything to do with his company. Pete was trying his level best to please her without a drop of liquid courage to either relax or energize him.

"I am now," she said. "It's grand to listen to the music without being smothered by it or a pack of strangers."

He grunted rather indelicately. "Please, do correct me if I'm wrong, but didn't you spend hours fussing and primping to get ready for this shindig?"

"No."

"Well, maybe not hours, but—"

"What time I spent was to make myself pret—er, presentable for you, Pete. Not a bunch of rowdies."

"Do you mean that?"

"Are you fishing or don't you believe me?"

His eyes twinkled. "Fishing."

She twisted sideward. "Then if it's nibbles you're

after, I chose this gown from a dozen Minnie offered because I thought you'd like it best."

"I do, but only because you're wearing it."

"I let her fuss with my hair and dab rouge on my cheeks because I'm all thumbs at such things and I wanted to look pretty—there, I've said it, right out loud."

"For me and me alone."

"Saints be praised, you are the most insufferable—"

Pete's lips met hers in a tender, lingering kiss. When they parted, she didn't dare move; she scarcely breathed, wanting to savor the moment, rather than hasten its demise.

From what seemed like a great distance, a fiddle rived the beginning strain of "Only One Girl in the World for Me."

"May I have this dance?" Pete asked.

"I'd love to."

The refrain began again as they clambered from their corner. To Megan's surprise, B.D. appeared from behind the stage's backdrop.

"Ladies and gentleman, I ask your indulgence to clear the floor for the night's first waltz as a tribute to a very special lady."

"Oh no," Megan said, shrinking away from Pete. "Not in front of everyone. I haven't danced in twenty years."

He held out his arms. His eyes repeated the invitation and dared her to refuse.

The song's lifting melody surrounded her; the fiddler's command of instrument and bow requiring no accompaniment.

Megan slipped her hand into Pete's raised one and stepped into his embrace. Her self-consciousness evaporated along with the memory of her first waltz so very long ago.

They glided within the circle of strangers, friends, and family with the fluid grace of two people who had danced together forever and would forevermore.

* * *

Snow began falling just as the sled team pulled away from the Cosmopolitan Club. Flakes of the plump feathery variety that usually fell in accordance with Old Man Winter's first roar or final one cavorted on the air like faeries up to a bit of midnight mischief.

Megan held out a gloved palm and caught a few for good luck. Superstitious as the Irish were known to be, she'd never heard of snow being a talisman, yet anything so dainty and magical simply must be a charm.

If only I had some vanilla extract stashed in the cupboard, she mused. Why I'm hankering for snow ice cream when it's blanketed the town for months, I don't know, but I'd surely give a king's ransom for a bowl of it right now.

Pete called, "Whoa, dogs," and startled her from her reverie. The leaders barked and tossed their heads, vexed at barely starting a run before hearing the command to end it. Obedience won out, though they pranced a yard or so beyond the Haven proper before the sled's clawlike brake took hold.

Pete's white-sprinkled form loomed beside the sled. He dispensed with the fur robes, scooped her up in his arms, and carried her to the door.

"It's a lunatic, you are," she said, "and crippled you'll be for it."

A sharp kick with his boot sent the plank door swinging wide. He angled his body partially inside to set Megan down on the threshold.

"Wouldn't be proper to take you any further. Not yet, anyhow."

She hastened through the gloom to the counter, where she'd left a lamp and several lucifers with which to light it. Once its mantel glowed soft amber, she started toward a second lamp resting on one of the writing tables.

Pete stepped in front of her. "I think one's enough

to keep us from barking a shin on the furniture. Don't you?"

"Ye—yes, I suppose so."

He helped her remove her wraps and hung them and his own on the pegged rack. Having removed one boot, he tugged at the other, then aimed a scowl at Megan.

"What's wrong, Pete?"

"I just remembered that I can't tarry long enough to ravish you. I've got to meet B.D. and return the dog teams to Jasper Gruening by half-past midnight."

Megan laughed until tears welled her eyes. "Glory, did I look *that* skittish?"

His other boot thumped to the floor. "Pure-de-rabbit-eyed, darlin'."

"Awfully silly of me, considering you stayed here for nearly two months."

"Not necessarily, it isn't." Pete pulled her into his arms. "I was mighty puny, then." His lips traced the sensitive hollow from her temple to her jaw. "But my vigor has been completely restored."

A tremble of pleasure shimmied downward from Megan's nape. The sensation quickened her pulse. A forgotten ache flourished deep within her.

"But it's also true," he said with a melancholy sigh. "I really must be on my way before long. B.D. trusts me with you about as much as I trust him with Colleen."

Megan rested her hands on his chest and gazed up at him, both disappointed and a tiny bit relieved. If their desires were genuine, time would only intensify the passion, not diminish it.

Pete removed the pins from her hair and dropped them to the floor, one by one. Her scalp prickled deliciously as her chignon slowly unfurled.

"I thought I could never love anyone as much as I loved you so many years ago," he said. "I couldn't have been more wrong. The woman you've become is superior in every way to the girl you once were."

He cradled Megan's face in his hands. "I adored that pretty colleen and will always cherish my memories of her, but I fell in love with Megan O'Malley, right here in this room, a few short weeks ago."

She felt no need to ask if he meant what he'd said. His words echoed in his eyes, his tender touch, the glorious intimacy of his loosing her hair.

Could she risk giving her heart away again? How well she knew the joy of loving another and being loved in return. The vulnerability it engendered. The wrenching bereavement of its loss.

Megan smiled up at him, bemused by her own emotional wrangling. Whatever the future might hold, the choice was no longer hers to make.

"Hard as I've tried to convince myself otherwise," she said, "I do love you, Pete, and I will for the rest of my days."

Chapter 30

Megan loosened another button on her shirt and blew down her cleavage. "Much as I cussed the cold, this god-awful heat is a thousand times worse."

"Earl says the mosquitoes are already thick at the mines," Minnie said. Her rocker's runners creaked in time with the Jenkin's Funeral Parlor & Taxidermy fan she waved.

They'd dragged chairs onto the Haven's stoop to avail themselves of the feeble breeze drifting in from the still-frozen rivers. To sacrifice their noses to the reek arising from the mucky street and thawed tidal bank, garbage dumps, and innumerable outhouses was preferable to slowly roasting inside the windowless log building.

It seemed a blessing indeed that the Haven's business had slackened when the snow began to melt in early April, then ceased altogether. Thus far, during this first week of May, temperatures had hovered in the unseasonable low nineties. The very idea of serving customers while attired in that dratted jersey dress soured Megan's stomach.

"How much longer before the rivers break up?" she asked. "The sun shines more than half the day. Birds are chirping nest-building songs and the hills are sprigged as pretty as you please."

"Watch what you wish for, dearie. The Bonanza Creek and Eldorado miners aren't sleeping on their roofs to star-gaze."

Megan sniffed. "The runoff building to a flood

serves them right for having so much sport with us Cheechako Hill types. By golly, Pete and B.D don't have to paddle home after a shift at the One Below."

"The Klondike's crested its banks," Minnie warned. "The Yukon rose two feet just yesterday—ice floe and all. Why do you think Captain Constantine patrols the riverfronts day and night? For exercise?"

"I know. Legend has it that—what? Thirty or forty years ago? The Thron-diuck and whatever the natives called the Yukon back then swelled from an early snowmelt and flooded the valleys for miles. Hmmmph. Doesn't mean it ever happened, nor will again."

Minnie rolled her eyes. "My, aren't we contrary of late. Everybody and their dog is biting their nails to the quick worrying that Dawson City will be washed away, but not you. As I recollect, Noah watched it rain awhile before he started wondering how big a cubit was."

"Oh, everyone's just spring-fevered and fawnching to be part of the world again."

"Seeing as how it got along fine without us, maybe there's something to that ignorance-is-bliss stuff," Minnie said, then chuckled. "I'll bet a dollar to a doughnut, ninety-nine percent of the news we've missed is bad. At this juncture, being apprised of it won't change what's transpired, anyhow."

"Those *New York Heralds* Sid Grauman brought in by dogsled weren't worth two dollars apiece, sure enough," Megan said. "That boy does know how to hustle a sawbuck, though. I'll give him that."

She squirmed, then propped her trousered legs against a post. Ladylike decorum be damned. The first passing male who looked askance at her could rig himself up in a corset, petticoats, cotton hose, drawers, and a wool dress. An hour's worth of that nonsense should alter his perspective on which was the weaker sex.

"About the only thing I miss about big-city living is skulking out on the porch for the daily newspaper,"

Megan said. "The sweet, solitary ritual of sipping fresh coffee and breathing in the wondrous aroma of ink."

"Won't be long before that craving is satisfied. The first week of June or so the steamers will start landing from St. Michael with no telling what kind of greenhorns aboard. I'll bet Sid will have Dawson papers to hawk soon enough."

Megan frowned at the perpetual procession ambling up and down the boardwalk on both sides of Front Street. Hammers banged and saws grated from daylight to dark. Buildings of every size and description were springing up in anticipation of the rumored influx.

Apparently, she and Colleen were the only two who perished the thought of the Klondike Stampede, which Cad told her the *San Francisco Examiner* had tagged last year's stateside exodus.

Minnie whapped Megan's elbow with her fan. "Cheer up, before all that ugly sticks to your face permanently."

"Very funny, Mrs. Walentine."

The older woman's expression reflected concern, affection, and frustration. "You've been contentious and irritable since the Fireman's Ball. Frankly, I'm at a loss to understand why. Brooding isn't your nature."

A snide retort sprang to Megan's lips. She stifled it, at once surprised and ashamed by her instantaneous annoyance.

" 'Tis a cranky ol' hag, I'm becomin'," she sing-songed. "May'n't be I always was, but me grace is fadin' like me charms."

"Spouting blarney won't cure what ails you."

Megan favored her with a wan smile. "It's easier than admitting I've got one foot in the past, the other in the grave, and straddling the future."

Minnie's nose twitched after the breeze like a hound's. "Dung flows downhill, sure enough. Quite a pile of it's collecting on this porch all of a sudden."

"You're going to pester me until my troubles weigh you down, aren't you?"

"That's what friends are for, dearie. Not for fixing what's broken or to give unsought advice, but purely to listen. Most times, all a chafed soul needs is to be heard."

Megan fingered the mended rent in her galluses. "It's only a little of everything and a lot of nothing that has me daunsy. And don't think being daunsy doesn't perturb me in itself."

"By your restlessness, I'd hazard a guess that the shine wore off the Haven quite a while ago."

"It did. Much as I love listening to the men swap yarns and such, I didn't come to the Klondike to bake johnnycake and pour tea."

"Plying the prospector's trade on Sundays isn't enough, eh?" Minnie asked. "Haven't done that in quite a while."

Megan shook her head. "I told B.D. the One Below was his and I meant it. It's been hell watching that boy work himself half to death and not wading in to help, but he wouldn't see it that way."

"Could you blame him?"

"Not a'tall. Fact is, I admire his gumption. I've heard the guff he's taken off his shovel stiffs—not from him, mind you. He's earned the right to straw-boss that mine without his mother breathing down his neck."

"Why not—" Minnie groaned, then added, "Never mind."

"What'd you start to ask?"

"A stupid question. I wondered why you didn't venture off and find your own claim, then remembered Dominion law only allows one in the district per person."

"One discovery claim," Megan corrected. "My name being on One Below's affidavit doesn't prevent me from buying another. Being in debt to my earlobes is what puts the quietus to that notion."

"Logic doesn't cure the itch, though, does it," Minnie stated, rather than asked.

"Only makes it worse."

"How about Pete working at the mine? Does that bother you?"

Megan grinned. "Oh, I might kindle envy if I let myself, but it's a godsend for him and B.D.—another reason why I stay away. Two is fine company, but three's a crowd. Somebody's destined to be odd man out and resent it."

"Having been wed to a prospector—God rest him—I do understand why it's vexing to watch your pickax gather cobwebs in the corner," Minnie said. "Having been meddlesome since I got tall enough to peek through keyholes, I suspect Pete accounts for the other half of your upset."

"He does."

"He's loved you forever."

"I love him, too, and trust him more the longer he's sober." Megan sighed. "Strict temperance, I'm not. I'm Irish to the core and pubs were my da's and cousins' second homes. But if a man's in his cups, it's easy to believe anything he says is liquor talk."

"Far be it for me to defend Pete, but from what Colleen's divulged, he never drank himself blind-staggered more than once or twice a year."

"Which to my mind makes for a dishonest drunkard. Along about the time the last binge is forgotten and you start convincing yourself he's finished with cutting his wolf loose, he totters off to a saloon and Katy bar the door."

"Maybe Pete's through with that nonsense."

"Could be, but even if he is, we're too old for romantic fancies," Megan said. "Such foolishness is for the young."

"Oh, I see. Like B.D. and Colleen, perhaps?"

"I should say not! Friendship and a pinch of puppy love is grand, but B.D. must finish his education and he can't here in the Yukon. Colleen is too bright to forego proper schooling herself if she's to make her way in the world."

Megan crossed her arms below her bosom. "If their feelings are true, B.D. can send for her after he graduates from the university."

"You've discussed these plans with him, eh?"

"B.D.'s aware of how I feel."

Disapproval etched every crease in her friend's pursed lips. In profile, she resembled a wizened bulldog whose supper hadn't agreed with him.

"For heaven's sake, Minnie. It isn't as if I'm ignorant of youthful impetuousness. Had I listened to my heart and married David Jacobs in Pioche, we'd have been mired in misery before our first anniversary."

The older woman carefully laid the fan in her lap, swiveled sideward in her chair, and clenched its arm in her bony fingers. "Remember when I said a friend doesn't give unsought advice?"

"Uhm—hmmm."

"Well, that doesn't include opinions, and I have a couple or two of them for you, Miss Dowager-Queen-of-Hearts O'Malley."

"I beg your par—"

"Hush up, and I don't mean maybe."

Megan's jaw snapped shut so hard her molars clicked.

"From what you've told me, age had nothing to do with what transpired with David. You were no better suited in Pioche than you were a decade later in Tombstone. And you damn well knew it, second time around, or you wouldn't have torn off to Baja on that prospecting expedition to get away from him for a while.

"As Fate would have it, being locked up in that Mexican jail forced you to acknowledge your own mortality. Scared you spitless. A woman with half your grit wouldn't have survived. All the same, no sooner than you returned to Tombstone, you ran pell-mell to your handsome knight in shining armor, having convinced yourself that only he could make you feel safe and alive again."

"I've never denied that," Megan said.

"But what you will *not* admit, even to this day, is that after brushing upside the Grim Reaper, you weren't about to dillydally another ten years and risk dying a virgin."

"Minnie!"

"Well, it's true! And ever since Jacobs went to his reward, you've intentionally sought the company of men you've liked well enough, but who didn't arouse you as a woman. Penance for unbridled passion."

Minnie grinned slyly. "Ah, but Mr. Vladislov upset that neat little apple cart, didn't he? That's what this 'too old' hooraw stems from. You not only love him, you want him in your bed at least as much as he's panting after you."

"I have never in my life—"

"No, dearie, you've *never* for far too long at a stretch in your life," Minnie stated. "There's nothing in the world like a fine frolic between the sheets to improve one's general outlook." She winked. "Ask Earl, if you don't believe me."

Megan gasped so violently, she choked. "You and Earl—you're—oh my God in heaven."

Minnie laid her hand over Megan's and squeezed it gently. "No man or woman is ever too old as long as there's love and desire between them. What could possibly be wrong with that?"

"Nothing," Megan answered softly. "Absolutely nothing."

"But . . . ? I know another shoe is poised to drop. I can hear it in your voice."

A nervous chuckle rattled up Megan's throat. She felt nearer Colleen's age than her own; equally reassured and discomfited by a more intimate conversation than she'd ever had with anyone, including her mother and older sister.

She was painfully aware that behind her independent spirit and lust for adventure lurked a childlike naïveté and profound sexual ignorance.

"I can't—I mean, how do I . . ." Megan almost howled with frustration. "B.D. and Pete are working eighteen-hour days to build a sluice works and shovel out as much of the drift's black sand as possible before the washing begins.

"The few times Pete's dragged over for supper lately he's been so exhausted he's all but taken a header into his plate, but even if he were perky as a bull moose in a willow bog, what am I to do? Greet him at the door in my shimmy?"

Minnie slapped her knee and cackled. "That'd send the blood rushing from his head. May even try that one on ol' Earl sometime."

"I'm seeking advice, *friend,* tough as you're making it to ask for."

"Just relax, dearie. Enjoy Pete's company whenever you can. When the time is right for both of you, nature will take its course. All you really have to do is let it happen."

Hours later, Megan was roused from a fitful sleep by boots pounding the boardwalk and voices shouting, "The ice is going out!"

She scrambled from bed; her socked feet searching out the galoshes she'd placed beside it. Like most of Dawson's citizens, she'd slept in her clothes in expectation of that clarion call.

Groggy and bleary-eyed from a night of imaginary lovemaking, as Megan rushed to the door, she cursed Minnie for planting those enticing seeds in her surprisingly fertile mind.

Hundreds of anxious men had milled along Front Street every night for a week, terrified that the old-timers' flood prognostications would prove correct. Now they and countless others assembled above the town to stare across the Yukon River's dark, splotchy surface.

The pressure from runoff flowing into the river from lesser streams had gradually heaved its vast ice mass at center until it resembled the crown of a road. Water channeled from the apex across the ice toward shore. A few yards of silty bank separated the city from imminent disaster.

Megan spied Captain Constantine's distinctive silhouette: feet spread, fists situated on his hips, and arms winged wide as if to warn the river not to truck with Her Majesty's renowned police force.

A crackling, monstrous roar hove from the river; the concussion as loud as a dozen thunderbolts crashing at once. The crowd tottered backward a step en masse.

The Yukon's ten-foot-thick ice cap tore loose from its tenuous moorings at shore, forced into motion by the current raging beneath. The center split asunder. Jagged glacial slabs whirled and heaved. Collisions sent fountains of black water spewing skyward.

Every instinct commanded Megan to retreat as the awesome spectacle unfolded. She watched in horrified fascination as the mighty river, freed from its long hibernation, crept ever higher up the bank.

Where the channel narrowed and curved, the swift current hurled greenish floes as large as cabins well beyond the shoreline. The massive blocks hissed and steamed and crashed to land along the shallow escarpment along Front Street. Megan shuddered as she recalled the vitriolic remarks of those who'd wintered there in tents before Constantine ordered an evacuation.

The river crested, hesitated, then spilled over the embankment. Megan glanced down at her boots, suddenly aware of water lapping above her ankles.

Screeching cries of *"Chee-cha-ko!"* burst from the men on the bank. They waved frantically at a boat with five passengers and their yapping dogs gamboling amid floating ice blocks.

"Glory hallelujah," a man near Megan shouted. "The world's finally comin' to us."

"Gotta be one of them tinhorn tubs outta Lake

Bennett," another agreed. "Onliest time them lame-brains is welcome is when they know somethin' we don't."

The first drawled, "It'll take about three minutes afore their ignorance shines through. Problem is, then we're stuck with the sumbitches for the duration."

Concern for the town's survival changed instantly to excitement at the prospect of news from the outside. Megan was carried along the shoreline to follow the craft's progress.

Presently, the bowman threw a weighted rope toward the bank. The craft was no sooner beached than its passengers were hounded for information. A rousing groan of disgust met their admission that not only were they old-timers, their point of departure was the Stewart River, a scant hundred miles upstream.

"Chee-cha-ko!" echoed from the hills. Megan surprised herself with a return trot up the bank accompanied by what appeared to be Dawson's entire population.

The Peterborough canoe that inspired the clamor skidded to rest a few yards from her. Again, the passengers were of a pioneer stripe, but had traveled through Lake Bennett shortly after the New Year began.

A wiry, beetle-browed man motioned for quiet. "Leander Monk's the name, late of Alaska and destined for hell."

Laughter rumbled through the expectant audience.

"When I finish my tale," Monk continued, "you'll call me a liar. 'Preciate it if you'd set the record straight with the Almighty when it's proven gospel."

Megan asked, "Are there really a couple of thousand people at Bennett, Mr. Monk?"

"No, ma'am," he drawled. "Nearer thirty-five thousand, if you include those roosted on Lake Lindemann, Laberge, and Tagish Lake as well. Tents stretched as far as the eye can see—the twenty-pole circus variety to canvas lean-tos. Got everything from churches to privies to flocks of soiled doves in 'em.''

"Ain't a tree big enough to tether a gnat left in that country. Whipsaws screeched all winter cutting planks for boats. More'n one partnership that endured the trail busted up permanent over that chore. Why, a coupla fellers sawed their dredge in two and started choppin' flour sacks before a Mountie put the kibosh to 'em.''

"Just what we need," a voice in the crowd bellowed, "a horde of tenderfeet descending upon us."

Monk's head wagged slowly. "Make no mistake, those folks are a scruffy lot, but ain't nary a tenderfoot amongst them no more. The Mounties posted themselves at the top of Chilkoot and White Pass and wouldn't let anyone with less than fifteen hundred pounds of supplies over the border—takes thirty trips or better to cache that much at the top. Then they lived like hutched rabbits for eight months, whanging together boats to bring 'em to this Promised Land."

Monk chuckled, but with scant humor. "Well, no insult meant to y'all, but I'd weight any one of 'em's grit against any one of yours."

"Glad to hear it," a listener declared. "I just hope those overnight sourdoughs know how to swim. From the look of things, they'll need to."

The wall of humanity behind Megan disallowed a view of Front Street. She wove between the men still entranced by Monk's speechifying and struck out for town. Every step mired her ankle-deep in cold, soupy mud. The greeters whistled and cheered the arrival of two more boats. Megan didn't bother to cast a backward glance.

What percentage of Dawson's citizenry hadn't witnessed the ice breakup were now on the boardwalks, pointing at the flooded street and jabbering like magpies. In low-lying sections, water washed over the plank walk and spilled into doorways.

Megan made a beeline for Minnie's, mentally framing an argument to convince her friend to seek refuge on higher ground. She found Pete and B.D. in the parlor, bundling provisions, house goods, and keepsakes in knotted sheets.

"We're taking you to the cabin at the One Below, too, Ma," her son ordered. "Won't do a bit of good to raise a donnybrook."

Pete jerked a thumb at B.D. and grinned. "Bossy son of a soldier, isn't he? Can't imagine where he gets it from."

"Where are Minnie and Colleen?" she asked.

"Upstairs," B.D. answered. "They're stashing what we can't haul and they don't want to lose in the attic."

A hollow sensation racked her midsection. "Do you think the flood will get that deep?"

"It could," Pete said. "You'd better drift down to the Haven and collect your treasures while we finish here."

B.D. nodded toward the settee. "Take that stack of sheets with you and fill their middles with perishables and such. Me and Pete'll rope them up to the rafters."

Megan grabbed the linens and raced for the door. When she opened it, a tongue of brown-green water purled over the threshold. She ran for the Haven.

Four inches of bilious, stinking floodwater covered the stoop, where yesterday she and Minnie had palavered for hours. She reeled at the stench already permeating the cabin's interior.

Trickles of scarlet, blue, and green bled from the edges of Minnie's beautiful rug. A nasty skim of flour and meal swirled from behind the counter. Megan's temples throbbed; needles converged at her brow. She staggered, then said, "No time for the vapors. Save what you can and leave the rest to the Yukon."

Like a madwoman, she dumped baskets of letters her customers had entrusted to her into pillowslips and ferried books and Minnie's pricey lamps and geegaws to the countertop. She sloshed behind it and wailed at the destruction already wreaked on her precious stores, salvaging only a tin of molasses, a partial case of canned beans, and one bag each of tea and coffee.

Megan darted into the bedroom alcove. She threw her meager wardrobe atop the bed quilt, pausing to glare at the despised gray jersey dress. It joined the heap of unmentionables, socks, the treasured pair of silk galluses, and the spare prospector's outfit.

She bent to yank a rope-handled wooden box from beneath the bed. A knifelike pain stabbed her lower back. With an agonized yelp, she fell to her knees in the murky water.

"Ma?" B.D. hollered from the front room.

"Here," she answered feebly.

Wading footsteps rippled the water around her thighs.

"Jaysus, Ma. Can't you dispense with the novenas till we get to One Below?"

"I'm not prayin'. I wrenched my back trying to heft the Haven's till from under the blasted mattress."

B.D. reached in front of her and drew out the box. "You mean this is full of gold?"

"Half full, maybe."

He grunted as he lifted it, then started out.

"Barlow David O'Malley. I will thank you to set that damned box down and help your mother to her feet."

A rosy flush raced up his neck. "Oh—well, sure."

He grasped her under her arms and brought her up slowly. Megan winced as she straightened.

"You're hurting real bad, aren't you?" B.D. asked.

Pete splashed into the room. "Hurt? What happened?"

Megan took a tentative step, then another. "I put a hitch in my get-along. No cause for alarm."

"Here, darlin', I'll carry you—"

"Like hell you will. Get to hauling stuff up to those beams before everything floats clear to Circle City."

B.D. nudged Pete. "A fairly good sign that her demise isn't imminent, wouldn't you say, old chap?"

Megan limped into the main room. Townsfolk hustled past the door, bearing armloads of their possessions. She goggled at the sight of a gaudily dressed woman paddling up the street in a birch canoe.

"Oh, my God," she said. "What about Cad? We must see that she's safe."

"Nathan, Nels, and Jimmy got to the boardinghouse just as we left to come here," B.D. said. "Jimmy volunteered to check on Cad, though I'm sure she has more rescuers than a potentate's favorite concubine. The other two escorted Minnie and Colleen to the cabin."

"What's to be done here?" Pete asked. "This water stinks of sewage and I want out of it."

Megan scanned the room for any small items she might have overlooked. "Most of the supplies are ruined. I'll tie up what's left while you hoist the rug to the rafters."

B.D. glanced at the floor. "Sorry, Ma, but it's already wetter than sop. If the weight doesn't snap the ropes, it'll cave the roof."

"Oh, now," Pete hedged, "I reckon we could try."

"No, B.D.'s right. A carpet isn't worth it." She unfolded a sheet. "Not much here to trouble with, I guess. If one of you will bundle the pillowslips into the bed quilt, I'll tie up the provisions."

"Sure that's all you want to take?" Pete asked softly.

"Oh, it's egregious to leave so many things behind." She focused misty eyes on the pouch she had devised. "But all that's truly dear to me will be safe atop Cheechako Hill before midday."

Chapter 31

B.D. hiked muddy clothes onto one of the cabin's top bunks, then sat down on the lower one to draw on his boots.

"If your mama was still here to see that," Pete said, "she'd have a jumping cat fit."

"Don't I know it. It's taken nearly a month to get this place liveable again after those females rampaged through."

He stood to tuck his shirttail into his jeans. "I thought the flood was a disaster, but it didn't hold a tall taper to the damage they wrought."

"Oh now, Megan, Colleen, and Minnie just did what a woman's prone to do—turn a man's castle upside down, sideways, and inside out, then tell him how much better he likes it when she's done."

B.D ran his fingers through his damp hair. "Still taking Ma's side on things, eh?"

"What's that supposed to mean?"

"I suppose you've forgotten her ordering me to shuck my boots whenever I came inside—to my own cabin, mind you. And you giving me the evil eye for arguing with her. Then there's her making me wash gravel the way *she'd* always done it. And you agreeing we ought to."

Pete looked up from sharpening his straight razor. "Sorry if your nose got skinned, son, but the fact remains, she *is* your mother." He hoisted the leather strap. "Mine provided my first introduction to this appliance the one and the only time I hollered at her. I suspect that's why my butt burns when you smart-mouth yours."

"You weren't trying to daddy me?"

"Naw. Be real strange for any man not to disagree with his mother, now and again. But if he can't speak his peace without raising his voice, then to my mind even if he's right, he's wrong."

Pete's gray whiskers vanished beneath a thick layer of shaving soap. His slavish devotion to tonsorial ritual indicated a belief that the discussion had ended.

"Colleen doesn't like it when Ma yells at me, either," B.D. stated. "Or when you stand up for her."

Pete twisted his head and slid the blade up his lathered throat. "My ward has made those feelings quite well known."

He squinted into the shard of mirror propped on the table, grunted, and then repeated the process. "Colleen has also been told to keep a civil tongue in her head."

The trapper wiped the razor on a rag. His upper lip curled over his teeth to flatten the next shaving surface. B.D. caught himself aping Pete's expression.

"What we have here, my boy, is a classic battle for territory. It's common amongst all animals, but the kind that ambulates on four legs isn't as peevish about it as us bipeds."

B.D. plopped down on a stump, anchored an elbow on the table, and settled his chin in his palm.

"What's the matter?" Pete asked. "That bath take the starch out of you?"

"Nope. Seeing your kisser arrange itself into Wise Old Solomon's means a siege is due. Might as well make myself comfortable."

"I expect you'll hear plenty of Independence Day sermons in town today." Pete splashed his face with water from a cook pot, then patted the drips with the rag. "Mine, however, is damned eloquent for its simplicity."

Rather than continue, Pete strode across the room

to fetch the new buckskin shirt Colleen had made him. The hide was butter soft, heavily fringed at the seams, and draped Pete's muscular build in a way even B.D. admired.

That didn't prevent the young man's fingers from drumming the plank table like hail on a tin roof. Pete didn't strew pearls of wisdom until he was good and ready.

Presently, he asked, "Remember the evening your mother and Colleen bared their claws over you, and I took Colleen for a little walk outside?"

"Mostly, I recollect being stuck in here with Ma."

"Well, I'll tell you what I told Colleen, then: Be loyal to one another. Protect and defend one another. When she hurts, feel a twinge in your gut."

Pete's eyes turned stone serious. "But what you young'uns must understand and respect is the fact that me and Megan share the same kind of bond."

B.D. averted his gaze to the rows of empty, moss-chinked pickle jars which served as panes for the cabin's lone window. He studied the bowed, opaque barrier and the faint patch of light it cast on the floor. His lips spread into a lazy grin. "You mean me and Colleen don't hold the patent on boon companionship like we thought we did?"

"Not hardly. And that tracks straight into a subject I'd planned to discuss with you before we repair to Dawson."

"But the hooraw's gonna start at midnight. Slow as you're primping, it'll all be over before we get there."

"Be patient, son." Pete reclaimed the other stump. "I just need a second to steady my aim."

Curiosity lapsed into concern when B.D. noticed how the trapper's hands trembled as they cradled his coffee cup. A sense of foreboding chilled the boy to his marrow. Was Pete sick? Or maybe . . . B.D. wouldn't allow himself to finish the thought.

"I reckon you know how much I love your mother," Pete said softly. "From what she tells me, it's mutual.

I plan on asking her to marry me today, but I want your blessing, first.''

The breath B.D. had been holding escaped with a loud *whoosh*. "Jaysus, is that all?"

"What the hell do you mean, 'Is that all?' I've never proposed to a woman in my life, much less asked her male kin for her hand. My innards have been strictured something fierce ever since I made my mind up to do it."

"Well, from all the twitches and moans, I thought you were gonna tell me you were dying, for Christ's sake."

"One of us still might," Pete said, "if he doesn't get to yeahin' or nayin' pretty damned quick."

"Does Colleen know?"

"She does. Got pickle-faced a minute when she thought that might make you and her brother and sister. I set her to rights on that." Pete frowned. "Maybe I shouldn't have. She looked entirely too damned happy when I did."

"But will I gain a father in the bargain?"

"Truth be known, I think it's plum sad how that word puts your teeth on edge. Best I can promise is I'll always be there when you need me. I may be compelled to kick your ass if you get too far out of line, too. If that's how you define fatherhood, well, you can't say I didn't give fair warning."

"Ma's never been keen on the idea of holy wedlock."

"Neither was I, until about six months ago."

"What are you going to do if she turns you down?"

"Keep asking until she changes her mind or shoots me to shut me up."

B.D. hesitated. "I only admitted this to myself a while back, but Megan O'Malley truly is one helluva woman. From where I sit, she's met her match in you." He stuck out his hand.

Pete clasped it in both his own. "Your approval means the world to me, son."

His shoulders sagged a bit and sweat glistened his brow. As much to himself as B.D., he said, "Now, if I can just wrangle a yes out of your mama, this Independence Day'll be a happy end to mine."

Chapter 32

"Do you remember your first carnival?" Megan asked Pete as they strolled along Front Street.

"The county fair is about as close to one as I ever got. Roasted peanuts, lemon ice, mule-pulling contests—pretty heady stuff for a boy of six."

"The traveling show that circuited through Tombstone didn't come within a rock's throw of my imagination. I was a woman grown, but as disappointed as a child." She made a sweeping gesture with her hand. "Other than a sore lack of dancing bears and elephants, this is a bloomin' dream come true."

"Which would've busted had Colonel Steel acted like a stiff-necked royalist," he said. "Constantine may not be as hard an act to follow as I thought."

"To celebrate Canada's Dominion Day and the Fourth of July together was a mighty shrewd compromise," she agreed. "Funny how fast people forget that Dawson may be overrun with Americans, but isn't part of the United States. Riot talk was all over town a few days ago with rumors the Mounties wouldn't abide an Independence Day party. Why, I'll wager not half of these jakes could tell you how many stars spangle their beloved banner."

Pete hugged her arm against his ribs. "Since you're neither fish nor fowl, my lovely colleen, what are you celebrating this sunny, ungodly humid morning?"

She smiled, extended a hand, and ticked on her fingers: "The flood sparing the Haven, though I'm still scrubbing up the muck it left behind. Moving back there before I strangled my son or your daughter. The warehouses fit to bust with provisions and goods. Scraping together enough gold to pay our debts and Canada's ridiculous twenty-percent royalty, plus stock the cupboards, buy my new dress, and some left for the bank to safekeep."

"Umm-hmm. Anything else?" he wheedled.

"That's quite a lot, isn't—oh, yes—I suppose spending the whole day with you rates mention."

He clapped a hand over his chest as if a bullet had lodged there. "Dear lady, your enthusiasm nigh overwhelms me."

A blast, like a cannon's report, rent the air. Megan pivoted left and right, searching for the source of the explosion. A second, then a third boomed from different directions.

"They're firing the anvils," Pete yelled.

Megan ducked as another salvo commenced. "They're what?"

Pete cupped his hands around his mouth. "Fourth of July tradition. Heap blasting powder on an anvil, set another on top of it, charge the powder with a red-hot poker, and *ka-pow*."

The tens of thousands crowding the street erupted in cheers; the hullabaloo louder than the concussions. Confetti rained from rooftops and bunting-draped balconies. Rifle shots filled the lull between the anvil cannonade.

Jesus, Mary, and Joseph, Megan thought. It can't be much past five o'clock in the morning. What in blue blazes will these lunatics be blowing up by noon?

Yet she knew the hoopla wasn't rooted in adoration of Queen Victoria or of red-white-and-blue patriotism borne of Commodore Dewey's rout of the Spanish fleet at Manila Bay. The fanfare symbolized the Klondikers' conquest of deprivation, unfathomable physical and mental hardship; the death-defying travail of mountain passes, glacier fields, fiendish rivers, and bone-cracking cold.

Scores of fresh graves humped the cemetery at the foot of Moosehide Mountain, but contrary to the doomsayers' predictions, none had died of starvation. Typhoid, acute dysentery, scurvy, hypothermia, and meningitis claimed most, whereas a couple of doxies had used strychnine to permanently mend a broken heart.

"Look out," Pete shouted. He yanked her in front of him and hooped his arms around her waist.

A howling canine stampede dodged between the sea of human legs, knocking dozens of celebrants to their knees. Large and small, long-haired and short, the white of every dog's eyes gleamed in the sunlight as hundreds of them made a mad, concerted dash toward the river. Without hesitation, they leaped into the water and paddled in a V-formation like geese migrating south for the winter.

Pete leaned over her shoulder. "I do believe man's best friend just threw him over for some peace and quiet."

"Much more of this donnybrook and I'll be paddling after them."

"The Mounties'll put the kibosh to it, soon enough."

She angled her head to look back at him. "Uh, Pete?"

"Ummm?"

"I think the dogs are gone."

"Is that a nice way of asking me to turn you loose?"

"It is."

He grinned, planted a quick peck on her cheek, then complied.

Megan socked him playfully in the shoulder. "What manner of man are you, taking liberties in public?"

The handsome devil reeled her tight against his chest. "The kind that loves you and wants you for—"

A finger tapped Megan's shoulder. She whirled, breaking Pete's embrace in the process.

"Gamaliel!" She flung her arms around the towering Negro's waist. "Is it truly you?"

"None other, Miz Megan. Lawsy mercy, how I found you smack in the middle o' this jubilee I'll never know."

"Is Plew here, too?"

"Nah, he stayed up to White Horse to mind the saloon. I ain't lyin' nor braggin' neither, but we're raking in gold and cash money faster'n we can count it."

"Pardon me, mister," Pete said, sidling beside Megan. "I don't believe we've been introduced."

Megan glanced at him, perplexed by the anger in his tone, but proceeded to do the honors.

"I should've realized who you were," Pete said. "B.D.'s told me all about you."

"Where is that boy?" Gamaliel surveyed the crowd, his chin on a level with most everyone else's crown. "Did y'all stake yourselves a good claim? And what's come of Nathan and Nels?"

"Proud to say we have neighboring bench claims on Cheechako Hill. Paying ones, too," Megan said. "B.D. has worked like a Trojan all winter, hasn't he—"

She looked around, only to discover that Pete had disappeared. "I, uh, guess you'll have to take my word for it."

Gamaliel's brow furrowed, but he responded as if no interruption had occurred. "Nothin' like sweat to hone the chip off a boy's shoulder. I knew B.D. was a keeper. Jes' needed something to want more'n he wanted to make trouble."

Megan smiled. The passage of a year hadn't dulled Gamaliel's memory or his perceptive powers.

"As for the others," she said, "Nathan shipped most of his profits to Frisco, but Nels invested his in the 'Flyer' line—a fleet of two spanking new steamboats to make runs between Seattle and Dawson."

"Why, with tinhorns swarmin' in like flies on fatback, Nels'll need a one o' them great ol' big ships to tote his money in afore you can say 'Land Ho.' ''

"Well . . .'' Megan grimaced. "Last we heard, his *Bonanza King* made it as far as St. Michael without a hitch, but the *Phillip B. Low* isn't faring quite as well. She's taken on water so many times, people have started calling her the *Fill Up Below.*''

Gamaliel's laughter boomed above the noise of the crowd. "Poor feller. Nels is quiet-natured, but sure as Sunday, that kind of spoofin' sets his kettle to boil.''

He squinted toward the Monte Carlo. "Yer friend's headed back this way. 'Spect I'd best git. Want to find B.D. and the others afore I catch the steamer back to White Horse.''

"But you just got here.''

"I can't leave Plew to manage by hisself for very long. Jes' come to town to fetch a load of supplies. Didn't even think about it bein' the Fourth.''

"Please, promise you'll meet us for supper at the Arcade. B.D. will be there and some new friends I'd love for you to meet.''

"Oh, I dunno. Don't figger that Pete feller'd take kindly to it. Man'd have to be blind as a tater not to see how sweet he is on you.''

"I can't explain why Pete acted the way he did, but fact is, I'm very fond of him, too, and I truly want you to get to know him better.''

"If'n you don't mind me askin', how's B.D. feel about you and him?''

"They've mined One Below together for months and I do believe, if forced to choose between me and Pete, B.D. might cast his poor old mother aside.''

Pete declared from behind her, "No doubt about it, uh—Gamaliel, wasn't it?''

"That's right, sir.''

"Hey, no need for formality among friends is there?'' Pete said. "Beg pardon for my hasty departure, but I really needed to see a man about a horse.''

Gamaliel grinned at the euphemism for a visit to

the privy. "I s'pect there's fellers lined up for a mile round his barn, too."

Tension drained from Megan's neck and shoulders. A mild case of the backdoor trots would account for Pete's uncustomary jitters, distraction, and several unexplained absences. It was a shame he didn't feel well, but a glass of seltzer or sarsaparilla should set him to rights.

"I've invited Gamaliel to meet us at the Arcade this evening, Pete."

"I was just about to do so myself. Is four o'clock too early for you? With this crowd, tables may be at a premium."

"My steamer don't pull out till eight, so's that suits me mighty fine. Thank you kindly, and I'll see y'all there."

As Gamaliel melted into the milling horde, Pete said, "You know, I haven't been inside the Haven since the deluge. Why don't we mosey down there and escape this turmoil for a while?"

"You really *don't* feel well, do you?"

"Me?" His normal baritone rose a full octave. "Why, I've never felt better in my life. What gave you the idea I was sick?"

"For one thing, you're sweating like a lawyer on Judgment Day. Plus, devouring peppermint candies, and twice, I've found myself talking to thin air."

Pete shook his head, chuckling. "I don't reckon a raging sweet tooth, the thermometer nudging eighty, and guzzling iced tea by the gallon might have a similar effect."

"Oh. Well, I suppose it could—but why do you want to hie off down to the smelly old Haven?"

Pete's hands raised in surrender. "I don't. Wouldn't go there if you paid me. Huh-uh-h-h. Uck-phooey."

Megan laughed at his antics. " 'Tis too many beans you've eaten this winter, Mr. Vladislov."

"Yeah, well, since questions concerning my health have been answered, what's your pleasure, madam?

Take in a show at one of the pavilions? Gorge ourselves on Rock Point oysters, Saratoga chips, Bengal
chutney, and sherbet?"

"Lord above, we'd both taste our socks after a combination like that."

His mouth compressed into a thin line. "Your wish
is my command, dearest. Apprising me of one or three
of them would be much appreciated."

Megan grinned. "Do you want to know what I'd
like to do?"

A distinct ruddiness suffused his complexion.

She continued demurely, "Stroll along nice and
slow, taking in the sights and sounds until it's time for
the parade."

He winged an arm. "Actually, that was to be my
next suggestion."

"You're a tetchy old devil, but I do love keeping
company with you."

His arresting gaze released the now-accustomed
flurry in her middle. "And why do you think that
might that be?"

Suddenly as shy as a schoolgirl in the throes of a
crush, she whispered, "Because I love you."

Pete's expression mirrored his own emotional di-
shevelment. "And I love you, darlin'. Very much."

They set off at a leisurely pace, enjoying the rare
contented silence borne of not forcing conversation
for conversation's sake.

Megan reacquainted herself with the town she'd
lived in for almost a year; so many facades as unfamil-
iar to her as the faces passing before them.

Although most of Dawson's business district had
been under five feet of water at the time, Gene Allen
had founded the first newspaper, the *Klondyke Nugget,* with the *Midnight Sun* vying for readers within
days.

A few weeks ago, a crowd gathered at the Yukon
Telegraph Company's office in the Dominion Hotel to
hear the first hello gargle over telephone wires strung

from its main office in two-miles-distant Lousetown. None questioned the necessity of telephone service any more than they did a local merchant advertising a limited supply of mammoth tusks.

A battery of new saloons, bawdy houses, dance halls, opera houses, brothels, and gambling dens supplied every sinful diversion a man could endure. In addition to Father Judge's Roman Catholic church, opportunities for repentance were now available for disciples of the Church of England, the Methodists, Presbyterians, and Salvation Army.

The Canadian Bank of Commerce not only ended the Bank of British North America's monopoly, it immediately issued a million dollars-worth of paper money. When miners discounted their gold in exchange for the more convenient banknotes, currency from almost every country in the world started to circulate, including aged Confederate notes and bills. Rumor had it that an accommodating Bank of Commerce clerk had cashed a three-dollar check scrawled on a six-inch square spruce plank with a nail driven through it.

Pete distracted her reverie by asking, "Are you hungry, darlin'? Thirsty?"

"Some of both, now that you mention it."

"Why don't you wait here while I fetch us something? No sense in both of us getting trampled."

Megan scooted inside in the framed shell of what would become Gandolfo's Produce Market. She scanned Front Street's undulating human sea, hoping to spot B.D., Colleen, Minnie, or Earl.

In one month, Dawson had become Canada's largest city west of Winnipeg; the population nearly equal to Seattle, Tacoma, and Portland. To Megan's mind, the unprecedented influx was like a whale that had swallowed the old-timers in one monstrous gulp.

As Leander Monk had foretold, an armada of hand-hewn and canvas-rigged scows, rafts, arks, junks, catboats, and outriggers landed along the town's swampy beachhead. By early June, steamers docked cheek to jowl along the waterfront to unload passengers, animals, liquor, hay, foodstuffs both plain and fancy, and merchandise rivaling anything on New York City's Fifth Avenue.

Similar to the hollow-eyed wraiths who sailed from the upriver tent cities, those who'd steamed in via St. Michael weren't particularly interested in gold mining. Most sought escape from a shady past, a humdrum existence, or a bleak future.

Only yesterday, B.D. had fumed, "I'll be damned if I can feature what induced these fools to come here. They knew when they started out that the creek claims were staked two years ago and the bench claims in '97. All they do is shuffle along like sheep. No money, nowhere to go, and no place to live save in a scrap of tent canvas or a doorway."

Megan was no closer to divining an answer now than she was then. Tomorrow, when the makeshift pavilions were knocked down for their lumber and nails and yards of bunting waved in forlorn effigy for a ribald celebration, the listless, aimless shuffle would resume.

Too many changes, too fast. William Ogilvie had repaired to Ottawa and Megan missed him terribly. George and Kate Carmack and their clan had returned for the spring cleanup, soon to depart again for California. He'd come by the Haven to let her make good on her debt and tell her that Joe Ladue's note would have to be retired by forwarding a draft to the States.

Joe had rambled the Yukon for thirteen years to marshal enough gold to ask his wealthy sweetheart's father for her hand. He'd finally claimed his patient bride, but happily ever after only lasted a few weeks before consumption made the new Mrs. Ladue a widow.

Megan thought, how badly I want away from here. Want to dip a gold pan where I can hear the creek trip over its rocky bed. Pete, B.D., Colleen, Minnie—I can *feel* their restlessness, but we're all fearful of admitting it. Maybe it's time I do. The idea of spending another winter in this madhouse of a town makes me cringe.

Pete loomed in front of her. "Now, who's looking a mite peaked around the gills?"

"Oh, don't mind me," Megan said. "I'm just disparaging this sprawling, ugly city that used to be a nice little town—what? A whole month ago?"

She nodded her thanks for a fritter and a paper cone of fruit juice.

"Civilization has never appealed to me, much less Colleen," Pete said. "She's torn between her attachment to B.D. and a strong hankering for her people and 'to breathe the free air, not what others have used and thrown away.'"

"Colleen does have a knack for slicing through to the marrow. I admire that."

"You're alike in that way. My tongue always clabbers when I need it the most."

"Maybe you don't lubricate it enough," she teased, hefting her cup.

His mouth fell open. "But—I—how did you . . . ?"

Before she could remark on his reaction, B.D. and Colleen bustled up behind him.

"We saw you down the street," Colleen said.

Pete visibly paled. "You did?"

B.D. glanced from Megan to Pete. "The celebrating's kinda getting out of hand, isn't it?"

"Not to my mind, it isn't," Pete replied. "A man has to relax once in a while, you know."

"Has the heat unhinged me or is there something going on that I'm not privy to?" Megan inquired.

"The parade's about to begin," B.D. said. "Mind if Colleen and I stay around and watch with you?"

"Of course we wouldn't," Megan said, though Pete's expression reflected a sore lack of enthusiasm, perhaps due to the staring contest between him and Colleen.

Megan stamped her foot. "What in blue blazes has gotten into everyone?"

A bugle's trill parted the revelers congregated on Front Street. People fanned out and jostled onto the boardwalks. B.D. and Colleen sidled to Megan's left, with Pete on her right. He shrugged and gave her a lopsided grin.

Courtesy evaporated as Dawsonians wrestled for a vantage point. A buxom young woman wearing a tricorn awash with patriotic plumage and ribbons wedged her parasol, then her person, between Megan and Pete.

Megan's scathing glare failed to ruffle the intruder's feathers. Rather, her feline smile had "I dare you to make a scene" written all over it. She turned to Pete and drawled, "I simply *adore* buckskin on a man— particularly one as tall and broad-shouldered as you are. It's so—so divinely *rugged*."

Pete puffed out his chest. "You think so?"

"Oh, indeed I do." The hussy's fingertips stroked his hide-clad forearm. "Goodness me, it's as soft as velvet."

Megan snarled inwardly. Judging by the moronic look on Pete's face, if he had a tail, he'd be wagging it ninety to nothing.

Deafening applause greeted Captain Jack Crawford's appearance at the head of the parade. The famous frontier scout—also a devotee of buckskin, Megan noted—owned The Wigwam, which dispensed assorted wares ranging from hay to ice cream. Crawford's talent for composing on-the-spot poems about virtually anything or anyone had endeared him to the townsfolk.

A Mountie color guard, resplendent in their scarlet tunics, wide-brimmed hats, high boots, and dark trousers marched hayfoot/strawfoot in precise unison. That the American contingent was neither as uniformly dressed nor drilled didn't matter to the multitude who snapped a salute when Old Glory fluttered by.

Megan's gaze drifted casually toward Pete. She couldn't see past Lady Liberty's cantilevered bosom. Oh, what I wouldn't give to be a few inches taller, she mused. Among other things.

Colleen tugged her sleeve and pointed. "Did you know Cad would be in the parade?"

A horse-drawn wagon rigged like a sailboat rumbled past. The Belle of Dawson in all her golden-girdled splendor clutched its fake mast and belted out her trademark song.

"No, I didn't," Megan said, "but I'm beyond being surprised by anything that girl does."

An assortment of conveyances lumbered behind Cad's barge. Every wheeled vehicle, horse, mule, and ox in town must have been conscripted for the event, along with a bevy of comely females to decorate them.

The pageantry gave way to an unadorned buckboard bearing one of the city's new steam-engine pumpers, followed by volunteers in cut-off Union suits, pulling the two-wheeled hose cart.

The town council hadn't yet hired any firemen to operate it, but everyone cheered the equipment they prayed would never be needed. Their applause changed to rhythmic claps for the final attraction: Ikey Sutro's roving street band.

Sutro, a pawnshop owner who leased hocked instruments to other musicians by night, played a hand organ with relative proficiency. His cornetist, however, possessed far more volume than skill. The drummer kept time to his footsteps instead of the music, and the cadaverous fiddler looked as though every note would be his last.

As was his custom, Sutro's trombonist scurried ahead of the other musicians, stopped, then grinned at them in triumph before scatting into the lead again.

Megan unleashed a weary sigh. Her legs throbbed from standing in one place for almost two hours. A breezy spot with a chair, an iced drink, and enough privacy to loosen her corset stays sounded like heaven.

She was poised to circumnavigate the hussy beside her and retrieve Pete when B.D. said, "Damn it, I'm gonna kill him. Swear to God, I will."

"Who?" Megan asked. "What's wrong?"

Above the laughter of the dispersing crowd, a raspy baritone warbled, "I courted her for beauty, an' Molly was her name . . ."

B.D.'s face was as livid as Colleen's was pallid. He grabbed her hand and they stormed into the street.

Lady Liberty stabbed the air in front of her. "As you can no doubt hear, Mr. Vladislov excused himself quite a while ago. What a pity for all that hand-someness to be wasted on a drunk who can't carry a tune in a bucket."

Megan's heart plummeted. She shoved her way through the spectators huddled around her son, Col-leen, and a rubber-kneed Pete.

"You've been sneaking whiskey all day haven't you?" B.D. hollered.

"Jes' tryin' to keep up my courage, son. Had a cou-ple too many whilst I was waitin' for the right mo-ment." He hoisted the half-empty bottle clenched in his fist. "Barkeeps ain't baptized the new stock yet. Stuff 'bout knocked me on my ass 'fore I knew wha' happened."

The tears streaming down Colleen's face turned Megan's sorrow into stone-cold fury. "I despise you for what you're doing to this girl. Colleen was begin-ning to trust you again. To hope you cared more about her—about all of us—than five damned dollars-worth of liquor."

"I'm sorry, Megan. Surely to God I am." Pete stag-gered toward her, his rheumy eyes pleading for for-giveness. "Won't happen again. Never. Promise you, that"—he reeled around—"promise you, too, Colleen. And you, son."

The desperation in his voice wrenched Megan's very

soul. Pete needed her help; another chance. She wanted desperately to give it. Maybe this time . . .

Her gaze shifted to the amber bottle he held. She stared at his fingers curled tightly around its neck. The taut, whitened knuckles showed no sign of slackening.

Pete raised his other hand and reached out to her. "Don'tcha you know how much I love you, darlin'?"

"I do now." Megan brushed past him. She gathered Colleen in one arm, B.D. in the other, and walked away.

Chapter 33

A knock sounded on the Haven of Rest's door. Megan's heart skipped a beat, then pounded. Thinking it must be her son, she bolted from the rocker where she'd been dozing.

Her eyelids fluttered at a rush of wooziness, yet the sensation cleared her head. It couldn't be B.D. He wouldn't bother knocking.

"Who is it?" she asked.

A merry voice replied, "Dash it all, I've forgotten the password."

Megan groaned softly as she lifted the wooden bar. She was in no mood for Cad's prattle, but there was no escaping it.

Her niece whisked inside, her coral taffeta gown rustling like autumn leaves. "I'm sorry it's so late, but I simply had to share my news, Auntie Megan."

Cad glanced around. "Mercy, it's dark as a cave in here. Mind if I light the lamp on the table?" She'd raised the globe and struck a lucifer before Megan had a chance to protest.

"Come, sit down," Cad said, having availed herself of a chair. "You'll be glad you did when you hear what I have to tell you."

Her niece scooted the lamp closer. She slid her left hand from beneath her right and presented the former with a dramatic flourish. Her ring finger drooped under the weight of two carats' worth of pear-cut diamond flanked by graduated triple baguettes, mounted on a band of satin-finished gold.

"Best not let that too near the flame," Megan said. "It'd leave a fair-sized puddle when it melted."

Oblivious to her aunt's sarcasm, Cad reeled back her hand to gaze upon the sparkling bauble as one would a firstborn child. "Isn't it the most beautiful engagement ring you've ever seen?"

"It's the most audacious, to be sure."

"And there's not another exactly like it, anywhere in the world. The cost is prohibitive and diamonds with this degree of clarity are *extremely* rare."

Megan's lips turned up in a bemused smile. "You sound like quite an expert on the subject."

"Would you believe, in all of Africa only one mine—the Kharmaja-something-or-other—produces stones of this quality? It has something to do with carbon, but I disremember what."

"Umm-hum." Megan sat back in her chair. "It's very pretty and I can see you're quite proud of it, but is that all you came by to tell me?"

Cad stared at her for a long moment. "I—I thought you'd be happy for me, Auntie Megan."

"I might be, if I had the foggiest notion who it is you intend to marry."

Her niece burst out laughing. "Good Lord, you must think me a perfect dunce. Especially since I'm getting married tomorrow morning and sailing for the States in the afternoon."

"Those do seem rather important details to leave out."

"Yes, well, I guess William Congreve was right when he said, 'Love's but a frailty of the mind.' "

Megan snorted. "As I recall, he also said, 'Married in haste, we may repent in leisure.' "

"Oh, don't be such a sourpuss. Sol and I met weeks ago. The day he arrived in Dawson, as a matter of fact. He's an *extremely* successful jeweler in San Francisco, which should please Mother and Papa, and has a palatial home on Russian Hill, no less. Sol's first wife died last year and he was just beginning to emerge from mourning when we bumped into each other—literally—during intermission at the Opera House."

Cad took a deep breath and sighed dramatically. "We knew the instant our eyes met that we were destined to be together."

"Sol?" Megan repeated. "Surely not Sol Lichtenstein."

"You're acquainted with him?"

"Enough to know that if your eyes met, he must have been standing on a box at the time."

"Auntie Megan," Cad wailed, "you're disparaging the man I love. Sol may be short-statured, but he's kind, and generous, and most of all, he makes me feel so very *special*."

"He isn't Catholic."

"More to the point, he *is* Jewish."

"Marry outside the faith and Oran and Frances will lynch him and deliver you to a convent—or an asylum—in two shakes."

"We'll be lawfully wedded and God willing, I'll be carrying Sol's child before we arrive in San Francisco. Oh, I don't expect them to welcome him with open arms, but love will win out."

"Uh-huh. I suppose it doesn't hurt that he's rich as Croesus to boot."

Cad's welling tears evaporated instantly. "You're just jealous because you and Pete had a falling-out. You're miserable and bitter and simply can't *stand* for anyone else to be happy."

A lump swelled in Megan's throat. She trained her eyes on the lamp's steady flame. "You may be right, Cad. I'm not a'tall sure I could feel happiness for anyone right now."

Her niece edged her chair closer. "I'm sorry for what I said, truly I am. I've seen B.D. and that Indian girl searching for Pete. B.D. looks a decade older than he did at the parade."

"The past ten days haven't been the easiest any of us have ever spent," Megan said. "We hoped Pete

would come home of his own accord. Even Colleen
agrees that rescuing him time after time was a mistake,
well-intentioned though it was. Our resolve lasted a
week."

"I take it they haven't found him?"

"Minnie, Earl, B.D., Colleen, and I have scoured
every inch of Dawson. Apparently no one's laid eyes
on him since that Fourth of July fracas."

"What about the Mounties?" Colleen asked. "Won't
they help?"

"Before we notify the police, B.D. went to check
Pete's cabin on Moosehide Mountain. Colleen is furious with B.D. for not taking her with him, but he
insisted on going there alone."

Megan pushed up from the table and paced the
floor. As much to herself as Cad, she said, "Except
he's been gone longer than I expected and he acted
so peculiar before he left. He kept muttering about
the mountain being evil. How he hated the scar on
its flank."

"Maybe there's a superstition attached to it that
Colleen told him about and it gave B.D. the willies,"
Cad suggested. "Heaven knows the Yukon is crawling
with legends about phantom wolves, frozen corpses
resurrecting in the spring—all kinds of spooky stuff."

"Though I'm not as well versed in Athabascan lore
as Tlingit, I've never seen a moose totem, which is a
fair indication there's no big medicine attached to
them. Besides, if there were, Colleen wouldn't have
spent an hour there, much less several winters."

Cad shrugged a shoulder. "I know B.D. is terribly
fond of Pete. Maybe he's so worried, he can't think
straight. Who knows? He might even feel responsible
for Pete's disappearance for some unknown reason."

"No, B.D. blames me for that. Says if I'd stuck by
Pete when he needed me most, none of this would
have happened."

A pounding on the door brought startled gasps from
both women. Megan dashed across the room and flung

it open. A bearded man clutching a tattered slouch hat stood on the stoop.

"You Miss O'Malley?"

"Yes."

"Your son sent me to fetch you to Father Judge's hospital. Said to tell you Pete Vlad—somethin' or t'other—is hurt bad."

Megan gripped the door facing. "How bad?"

The messenger sucked his teeth. "I ain't no doctor, lady, but it looks plumb mortal to me."

The messenger stopped a few yards from the two-story log hospital's screen door. "If'n you got a hankie, I'd hold it 'neath your nose. It stinks pretty raw inside."

Megan motioned him onward. "I've been around sickness before."

He scowled, then shuffled forward. "Just don't holler Dan Bob Beecher when you starts pukin'. I ain't swabbin' up after you."

Megan flinched at his gruffness. She knew Father Judge had to rely heavily on male orderlies one remove from vagrancy to care for his male patients. Seven Sisters of St. Ann had answered his call for help, but none were trained nurses. Between staffing the second-floor women's ward, plus kitchen and laundry duties for the hospital's one hundred and fifty total patients, their stamina was pushed to its maximum.

A dense mat of black flies and mosquitoes clung to the door's screen. When Beecher yanked it open and held it for Megan, fully half the insects swarmed inside.

Three rows of cots lined the walls and center of the room in a barracks-style formation. Most of the sheet-draped bunks were occupied. Some patients moaned and writhed in pain and delirium. Others lay comatose or in a drug-induced stupor. The stench of urine, excrement, pus, and vomit permeated the still, muggy air.

Megan staggered a step and clapped a hand over her nose and mouth. Beecher favored her with a smarmy leer.

"Take me to Mr. Vladislov's bedside," she commanded. "Now."

The orderly's hobnail boots thundered on the plank floorboards. An emaciated Negro screamed at the noise. His splayed fingers gripped his skull as if to keep it from bursting or to crush an unbearable agony.

"What's wrong with him?" Megan asked.

"Meningitis," Beecher said. "Already got the holes dug for him and two others. Prob'ly need 'em afore mornin'."

"How can you be so heartless?"

Beecher whirled on a heel. "Save your sympathy for your friend. He's got a slim chance of livin'." The orderly jerked a thumb at the Negro. "If'n that poor bastard was a dog, I'd shoot him. Bein' human means he's gotta wallow in his own shit and suffer till he dies."

"I'm sorry, I didn't re—"

"But you're right." His smile, a hideous gap-toothed contortion, was the stuff of nightmares. "I am a heartless sumbitch and don't you fergit it."

B.D. appeared behind the orderly. "Leave her alone, Dan Bob."

"Not till you gimme my money."

B.D. thrust out a folded banknote. "There'll be more if Pete pulls through. Tell the others the same goes for them."

Beecher pocketed the cash and walked away, his footfalls intentionally heavy.

B.D. hustled Megan back down the aisle. "Dr. Pennington just took Pete into surgery. Might as well wait out yonder where we can breathe."

"Please, tell me what happened."

He shook his head and pointed to the door. His waxy complexion glistened with sweat. He steered them to a stacked woodpile and slid down it into a boneless sprawl. Megan knelt beside him and finger-combed the wet hair from his brow. She recoiled at the splotches of dried pus and blood on his shirtsleeves and trousers.

"Pete didn't take any whiskey to the cabin," B.D. said, his voice coarse and grim. "Spent several days thinking about how he's failed himself and all of us. Before he asked for another chance, he needed the strength and solace he'd always gotten from living off the land. He grabbed his rifle off the pegs. Either fell, or he dropped it—doesn't know which. It went off. Blew his leg to smithereens.

"He used his belt for a tourniquet. Kept passing out from the pain, but knew he had to get help. Fashioned a stick for a crutch and hobbled a little ways, then it snapped and sent him careening down the face of that goddamned mountain."

Tears trickled down B.D.'s cheeks; not the sobs of a boy, but the silent anguished kind a man sheds in private. Megan allowed him that by looking away.

"He was belly-crawling through a ravine when I found him. Burning up with fever. Leg swelled twice its size. Putrid, and greenish black." B.D.'s voice caught. "All Pete thought about was getting off that mountain. Praying somebody'd find him. He left the tourniquet on too long—too tight."

Megan rocked on her haunches. B.D. hadn't brought her outside because he was nauseated from the hospital's sights, smells, and degradations, or to spare her from them.

Her son hadn't wanted her to hear Pete scream when the doctor amputated his gangrenous leg.

Chapter 34

Megan sat in a straight-backed metal chair beside Pete's bed, alert to every sound, movement, and respiration. The chloroform he'd received during surgery should have worn off by now. She told herself the heavy jolt of morphine to suppress the pain had knocked him senseless, but only half believed it.

She'd sent B.D. home with Minnie and Colleen hours ago. None had wanted to leave her there alone, but Megan insisted. The hospital's cots rested hardly a chair's width apart, nor was there space at their feet for loved ones to stand vigil.

After dragging Pete for miles on a travois, only to be told Dr. Pennington's verdict, B.D. was on the brink of collapse himself. He needed Minnie's grandmotherly pampering and to pour his heart out to Colleen.

The doctor's litany of Pete's afflictions echoed in Megan's mind: raging infection, blood loss, malnutrition, dehydration, exposure, and wholesale trauma from the amputation.

Pennington allowed that the trapper's overall physical condition was in his favor, yet the physician's grim demeanor transmitted scant hope for recovery.

Megan was grateful for the doctor's surgical skills at the same time she resented his pessimism. Hope didn't cost a nickel, but paid enormous dividends to those sore in need of a glimmer of it.

Pete's head jerked from side to side. He mumbled incoherently. Megan leaned closer to whisper, "I'm here, Pete. Everything's going to be all right. I promise you, it will."

His stubbled beard, complexion, and greasy hair were a uniform shade of gray; his flaccid lips swollen, and coated with a whitish film. He moaned, and his bare shoulders twitched spasmodically before he slumped into the pillow.

Megan chafed his wrist to express her love, confirm her presence, and monitor his rapid, thready pulse. Memories of Barlow P. Bainbridge and David Jacobs haunted her. They, too, had loved her. She'd blamed herself for their deaths and never vanquished the guilt, though the passage of years had dulled its ache.

The pain etched on Pete's face; the rusty blood that seeped through the sheet from his bandaged stump refueled that oppressive remorse—fortified it, like purified iron strengthened steel.

It's true, Megan thought, I've avoided men who attracted me, but Minnie was only half right about the reason why.

Her fingers grazed the contours of Pete's wrist, then the sheet's coarse weave, and curled into a fist in her lap. Maybe the crones gathered round the well back in Rathcormac weren't spiteful hags. Maybe the banshee does follow those whose names begin with an *O* or a *Mac*.

From behind, Father William Judge's soft voice assured her, "Mr. Vladislov could have no better champion than the Angel of the Cassiar."

At forty-five, the bespectacled Jesuit priest known as the Saint of Dawson better resembled a man nearing the allotted three-score-and-ten, yet his energy rivaled that of a ten-year-old boy's.

"I'm not so sure of that," she said. "Or maybe God's willed more on me than I'm strong enough to endure."

"Is it a vengeful God you believe in? One that smites down his lambs with impunity?"

"I don't know, Father. At the moment I don't know what I believe."

"Well, child, I'll grant that fear of the Lord fills more pews than unwavering faith. But while God made us in His image, he bestowed upon us any number of failings and frailties. If He hadn't, what need would we have of Him?"

Megan pondered the question and her knowledge of the man who'd posed it.

The folds of his patched, threadbare cossack couldn't disguise the frail body beneath it, yet he exuded a radiance that one admirer described as making people feel a little better that they belonged to the same race.

He'd single-handedly built his first church from the ground up, carved its altar with a penknife, and fashioned pews from hewn planks and stumps. No sooner had he finished, the chapel burned to the ground. The intrepid padre raked away the rubble, gathered his tools, and began construction on its replacement.

Judge accepted donations from several Klondike kings, the proceeds from auxiliary bazaars and other fund-raisers, but refused to collect pew rent or pass the plate during church services.

"The Lord will provide," he said. Thus far, He had.

When one day's influx of patients outstripped his new hospital's bedding supply, three bales of blankets had mysteriously appeared on the doorstep. An early snowstorm brought another scourge which forced the opening of the second floor before its roof was on. Lo and behold, the weather abated until the shingles were securely in place.

Megan stared at the gold cross that dangled from a cord encircling Father Judge's waist. "I guess I can stew to a fare-thee-well and place blame wherever I see fit, but it won't grow Pete a new leg."

"By your tone I'd say you doubt that a priest ever experiences a crisis of faith."

"Some might," she said, "but I wouldn't believe it

of one who doesn't just preach 'love their neighbor,' but practices it every minute of the day."

The sleeve of his cossack waved like a black wing as his arm swept the room. "These are all good men. Someone's beloved son, brother, husband, or father struck down by diseases we lack the knowledge to prevent and can't always cure. Some, like your Pete, have grievous wounds that have left them maimed or crippled."

He paused, his stoop becoming more pronounced. "The suffering of each and every one of them tests my faith, child. I'd despair mightily if your good man's fate didn't test your own."

Three hours later, Father Judge performed the sacrament of last rites over Pete.

By five o'clock the next morning, Megan was spooning diluted beef tea through Pete's lips. His semilucid rally lasted until a little before noon, when he lapsed into unconsciousness.

The pattern of revival, sustenance, depletion, and coma continued as July faded into August. The seesaw effect of morphine versus pain ransacked Pete's mind. His grasp on reality was as stable as sand in a slotted spoon.

B.D.'s bedside visits shortened in duration and gradually ceased altogether. Megan understood that her son couldn't abide Pete's moribund condition. For many, the murky realm between visible improvement and death was more frightening than death itself. No appropriate emotional release availed itself. Grief was as premature as confidence that a recovery was imminent.

Minnie and Colleen spelled Megan during daytime hours, but night found her posted in her chair, guarding Pete against the banshee's nocturnal keen and Dan Bob Beecher's and the other orderlies' chicanery.

Had he known, Father Judge would have been appalled by the extortion and cruelties they perpetrated on the patients. Money was begged or borrowed from the dying and stolen from the dead. Claims were transferred to supposedly prevent their being declared abandoned and restaked.

Brandy and whiskey prescribed to relieve typhoid's miseries moistened the caregivers' throats rather than the invalids'. Window sash weights used for traction were jostled for the pure sadistic hell of it. Though an argument might be made that an extra ounce of carbolic or turpentine in bathwater increased its disinfecting properties, its application to lesioned skin was tantamount to being immersed in liquid fire.

Week after week, Megan observed, protected, and fumed in silence. Reporting the chicanery to Father Judge or the Sisters would end Dan Bob's and his crew's careers as male nurses, but their replacements would be no more compassionate—perhaps, even less so—than they. The duties they performed in exchange for bed and board were loathsome and thankless. Most of Dawson's unemployed or unemployable vastly preferred to beg for scraps and call an empty packing crate home.

In the wee hours of September eleventh, Megan thought she was dreaming when Pete's gravelly voice drawled, "Hello, darlin'."

She raised from the chair ever so slowly, fearful that her eyes and ears were playing cruel tricks. She leaned over him, her hand brushing his cool brow, then gliding down his bristled cheek to cradle it.

How many hours had she spent waiting for this moment; imagining its sweetness and the words of love and joy she'd whisper when assured he'd hear her, only for them to evaporate and leave her tongue-tied.

"I've been sick quite a while, haven't I?"

"Two months by the calendar." She smiled. "Strange, but all of a sudden, it doesn't seem nearly that long.

Pete raised his arm to draw her near. It dropped like a stone to the mattress. "Weak as a kitten. Not partial to it, either."

"Soon as we get some meat back on those bones, you'll be your old self again."

"No, I won't. Not sorry to say, Pete Vladislov is gone for good." He took a ragged breath and flinched.

"Save your strength until there's some to spare," Megan said. "There'll be time to talk later."

"Uh-uh. Want to tell you, I know I bollixed things as bad as a man can. By the grace of God and a long-handled spoon, I got a second chance. Not going to waste it."

The hospital ward's noises and odors ceased to exist as she stroked his beloved face and gazed into his eyes. "I love you, Pete, just as you were, just as you are, no matter what tomorrow may hold in store. There's no demon we can't conquer together."

A wan semblance of his lopsided grin appeared. "Might sound plum bogus after the fact, but I swear I concluded that myself—right before my bonehead stunt with the rifle."

His hip nudged Megan's. The crow's feet at his eye corners deepened as his lips parted into a full-fledged smile. "Reckon the doctor did a crackerjack job of digging that bullet out. Leg's a mite stiff, but it doesn't hurt to wiggle my toes or anything."

Her head whipped sideward. Pete's left foot remained motionless. She stared at it, feeling as if an anvil were crushing her chest.

"Wiggle them, again, Pete."

"What do mean, again? I'm still doin' it." He chuckled. "Be forever beholden if you'd scratch the itch behind my big toe. Too flat-of-my-back to do it myself."

Megan sat paralyzed, unable to tear her eyes away from the shrouded, abbreviated hump. Pennington had amputated Pete's right leg above the knee, leaving a flap of skin to stitch over the gaping wound.

Mary, Mother of God. How can he feel toes that no longer exist? A violent tremor racked through her.

"Megan? Is there something wrong? Please—look at me."

She balled the fabric of her skirt in her fist, forcing herself to mask her inner turmoil with a composed veneer.

Pete slid her other hand from his cheek and clutched it in both of his. "You can't hide from me any better than I can from you."

"Never could," she said. "I think that's why I didn't go north with you way back when. Even then, you knew me better than I knew myself. Damned discomfiting, as I recall."

"What's wrong with my leg." His monotone framed a demand, not a question.

"Oh, Pete, I don't know how to—"

"Straight up, that's how."

Megan cocked her chin, willing her tears to recede. "By the time B.D. found you, gangrene had set in. Dr. Pennington had no choice but to amputate."

Pete's eyes closed. He lay completely still for a long moment. His breathing quickened. Megan felt the mounting panic course up his chest.

"The doctor saved your life, Pete. That's all I care about. You're alive and you're going to get well."

He rolled away and onto his shoulder, then struggled up on an elbow. It was a slow, agonizing process. Megan wanted to help him, but instinct warned her away.

He peeled back the sheet. His fingers spidered along his thigh until their tips touched the bandage. Shaking as if palsied, he examined the layered cotton strips as scrupulously as a blind man does a house number.

With a strangled cry, Pete lay back on the mattress. His features set in a rigid mask and he squeezed his eyes shut as a very personal, private battle within himself commenced.

Megan smoothed the sheet over him, then sat down in the chair. She laid her hand on his, neither expecting nor receiving a response.

She would be there when he needed her. It would suffice.

Chapter 35

An indignant growl rumbled from the gray wolf's throat. The trap's saw teeth clamped his right back hock, gnawing through fur, skin, and gristle to scrape bone.

The wolf yanked against its grip. Anchor chains clinked loud in the snow-blanketed silence as did the animal's agonized, enraged yips.

It licked its chops; the saliva thick and uncommonly warm. The wolf sniffed the air, but caught no scent of the pack.

The animal hunkered down on its belly, then curled into a crescent. The blood matting its fur and second thigh smelled much like the metal that shackled it. The wolf bared his fangs and began chewing himself free.

Pete jolted awake. His pulse hammered in his ears. Sweat poured down his temples, his ribs, the veed channels at his thighs.

Moans echoed in the gloom. Foul stinks invaded his nose; suffocated him. His head pivoted right and left; his vision myopic and blurry.

Remnants of his nightmare dazed him. Nothing he saw, smelled, heard, or touched begat a calming familiarity. He whipped onto his side and sprang from the bed.

He landed spread-eagled on the floor. The impact crushed the air from his lungs. A cold draft prickled his clammy skin.

The gates in his brain cracked open. Pete knew

where he was and why. A grim smile stretched his lips at the irony of being terrified by a nightmare that was far less horrific than reality.

He splayed his fingers and pushed up from the floor. Drawing his remaining knee under him in a half crouch, he tottered awkwardly on the ball of his feet. No good. The stump skewed his balance. He felt stupid, helpless. . . .

Crippled. His treacherous mind screamed the word repeatedly. It mocked him. Taunted him. Flashed images of every poor son of a bitch he'd ever pitied.

He saw light at the far end of the room. Dan Bob or one of the other simians doing a bed check. Damned if they'd find him groveling on the floor.

Pete rolled onto his buttocks to face the cot's end rail. Scooting forward, he gripped its curved topmost bar. Left leg bent, foot planted for leverage, he pulled himself upright. His arms and thighs, once as strong as corded steel, trembled with exertion.

He bent over the end of the cot, teeth clenched against the nausea churning his gut. The orderly's footfalls reverberated through the floorboards. If only the room'd stop spinning. . . .

Pete's eyes flicked to the chair. Empty. No flame danced atop the stub candle resting on the crate in front of it. Megan hadn't come. He should have realized it sooner. She'd have helped him, soothed him, promised again that nothing had changed; that everything would be all right.

I don't need her. He hopped to the side of the bed. Don't need anyone. I won't be a burden—a millstone.

The therapeutic herbs Father Judge used to stuff the mattresses crackled when Pete grabbed handfuls of its ticking cover. On a level with his waist, he could neither leverage his weight off of the floor nor maneuver his knee high enough to crawl onto it.

The lantern Dan Bob swung cast macabre shadows across his cragged features. "Hey, Crip. Out for a stroll?"

Pete bobbled on one bare foot.

"Get your bony ass back in that bed," Beecher ordered. He lifted the lantern higher, illuminating a smarmy grin. "Oh, can't do it, can ya? Needs your lady crutch, don't ya, and she ain't here."

Pete splayed his fingers on the saggy mattress. He lowered himself to a semisquat and he hurled his body forward. He panted hard, each breath filling his nostrils with his own stench that permeated it and the cloying smell of leaf mold.

Beecher's guttural laughter echoed through the room as Pete wallowed and squirmed toward the pillow.

"Ain't crawled since you was a baby, has ya, Crip? Oughta be real glad you ain't forgot how 'cause you ain't ever gonna walk on two legs like a man agin."

Chapter 36

Megan slogged through black-flecked snow toward the hospital. Even on the outskirts of town the reek of charred wood and steaming ashes harried her nose.

The previous Friday afternoon, hot-tempered Belle Mitchell had hurled a lamp at a rival, just as she had eleven months earlier on Thanksgiving night. The doxy's fit of pique had leveled its flash point, the Green Tree Saloon and Hotel, plus forty additional structures before townspeople and the Mounties curtailed the flames' voracious appetite.

The fire-fighting equipment paraded down Front Street on Independence Day had proven, as Megan heard another bucket brigadeer remark, "Worthless as tits on a boar hog." For all the hoopla surrounding its acquisition, the town council had yet to feel a compelling need to hire any men to assemble or operate it.

Minnie's house and the Haven were spared again, but smoke inhalation and exhaustion took a debilitating toll on hundreds of volunteer firefighters, including Megan. She'd spent two days sipping herbal tea, coughing up dark mucous, fretting about Pete, and castigating the tempestuous Miss Mitchell and the collective stupidity of Dawson's city fathers.

Megan felt considerably better when she'd risen on this gloomy, gray Monday morning. The further she walked, the more her lungs burned from exertion. Hardly a year had passed since she had raced through waist-deep drifts to reclaim One Below. Today, a mere five-inch accumulation weighted her feet like iron boots.

She glanced up at the long log building. It's a sniveling sissy you are, Megan O'Malley. There's man in a bed up there who'd cut a merry caper in the slush if he had two legs as sound as yours.

Megan pushed the door open with her shoulder, whisked through, and shut it to stanch the draft. She sucked in her lips, trying not to gag. In the three months Pete had been hospitalized, the faces staring at her from the cots had changed regularly, but the sickroom sounds and smells remained constant.

Yugo Siroczki, a swarthy attendant whom she admired about as much as Beecher, beckoned to her from a bed along the wall. She hesitated, then answered the summons.

"Ain't seen ya for a spell, Miz O'Malley," he greeted as he wrung a rag over a tin basin. "Thought you'd got wise and give up the ghost."

She turned her head away when she realized the orderly was bathing a naked old man. The wizened gent startled when he saw her and tried cover his privates with his hands.

"Someday it'll be you lying helpless, Siroczki," she said. "The circle always comes round."

"Aw, 'tain't nothin' there you ain't seen a hundred times afore," he sneered. "More of it, too, I'd bet."

She started down the aisle.

"S'posed to tell ya the padre wants to see ya in his office," the orderly called after her. "Ol' Crip, he's done gone."

Megan squinted toward the far corner. The bed Pete had occupied held a short blond fellow curled up on his side, retching.

She ran for the doorway leading to Father Judge's study. Her pounding jarred the crucifix affixed to the priest's door.

"Father? It's Megan O'Malley."

A muffled voice answered, "Come in, child."

When she entered the tiny room, he was chafing his face with his hands. Tufts of hair horned from his scalp and stubble shadowed his cheeks, upper lip, and chin.

"Yugo told me Pete was gone."

The priest sagged into his desk chair. "Yes, he is, though I assure you we did everything we could to prevent it."

"No!" Megan's knees buckled. She grabbed the edge of the desk. "How, Father? Please, no—he can't be—"

Judge hastened around his desk and guided her to a rickety side chair. He knelt beside her, his eyes anguished and sorrowful. "Dear child, I should have asked you to wait outside until I got my wits about me. Pete has only left the hospital, not this life."

Megan blinked. Her mind, still spinning from one shock, seemed incapable of grasping a reprieve.

"I talked with Pete at length the past two nights," the priest continued. "He was noticeably ill at ease—frightened—of letting sleep overtake him, which isn't unusual for recent amputees."

"It's my fault. I should have been with him."

"No, Megan. Pete's dependency on you, Mrs. Walentine, Colleen, and the staff already infuriated him. He isn't one to resign himself to an infirmity. Why, during a bedcheck Dan Bob found Pete trying to walk. It took no small amount of coaxing to induce him to retire."

Megan scowled at what Beecher's style of coaxing likely entailed. "You said Pete left the hospital, but when? And where has he gone?"

Father Judge stood and extracted an envelope from his cossack's commodious pocket. "The morning after the fire, Pete bid me farewell and asked me to give you this. I pray it contains the answers you seek."

Megan took the envelope. As she turned to leave, she jerked her head sideward and coughed; a punishing hack that left her wheezing and slightly dizzy.

The priest laid a hand on her shoulder. "Dr. Pennington should arrive at any moment. Please, allow him to examine you."

"I'm not ill, Father. Just too old to play fireman."

"Then you must promise me you'll go home and rest."

She glanced at Pete's letter. "Yes, Father. I will."

A bare wisp of a smile appeared. "My dear Miss O'Malley, for an Irish Catholic, you're the most unconvincing liar I've ever encountered."

Megan resisted the impulse to tear open the envelope the moment she emerged from the hospital. She wanted privacy to absorb Pete's words, which the burned-out refugees camped nearby in tents and sharing communal kettles of soup hardly afforded.

Naturally, she encountered any number of acquaintances eager to cuss and discuss either the fire, or the finance committee formed to underwrite the cost of a proper fire department, or how quickly Dawson was resurrecting itself, or all three.

Megan's coughing jags, both real and feigned, extricated her from these subzero tête-à-têtes in relative haste. Judging by the men's compassionate expressions, rumors of her imminent demise from consumption should bring a procession of covered-dish and advice-bearing matrons to her door within hours.

She at last found sanctuary inside the Haven, dropped the bar into its brackets, and hung her heavy coat on the peg. With Pete's letter clutched in her hand, she stoked the stove to chase the chill from the room. Then pulled a rocker near it and shook out a lap robe. She filled the kettle and set it to boil.

As Megan gandered about for anything else in need of her immediate attention, her shoulders sagged. A pent-up sigh escaped her lips. She sat down in the rocker and stared at the parchment envelope, now creased and smudged at the corners from handling.

"Odd that such a flimsy little thing has the power to scare me so," she said.

The realization that twenty-seven years ago she'd addressed a similar envelope to David Jacobs the day after a fire destroyed much of Pioche, Nevada struck her like a voice from the grave.

David never received her second letter of farewell, written a decade later and posted to San Francisco, where his wife had been hospitalized for a chronic heart condition. His unannounced return to Tombstone and his discovery of Megan's pregnancy and engagement to Barlow P. led to a jealous rage that left both men she loved most in the world dead on the One Eyed-Jack Saloon's grimy floor.

A more recent memory flickered in her mind's eye. An hour ago she'd warned Yugo Siroczki that the circle always comes round. Her thumbnail pried the flap loose. "Please, Pete, don't tell me ours has spun full."

She scanned the copperplate lines, not particularly surprised to find the rough-and-tumble trapper's penmanship as neat, uniformly slanted, and scroll-embellished as a master scrivener's. Its closing gave her the courage to avert her gaze to the beginning:

My darling Megan,

It seems a lifetime ago since I walked away from you on that budding, beautiful spring morning in the Cassiars. Though I have no right to ask you to wait for me until I am strong enough and able enough to walk into your life again to stay, I promise you, that day will come.

I love you,
Pete

Chapter 37

Nathan Kresge's finger tapped the bill of sale to the One Below. "I'd say you're starting the New Year the best way a fellow can."

"Older?" B.D. asked. "Wiser, maybe?"

"Try a hundred thousand dollars richer on for size, kid. Not counting what you already have stashed in the Bank of British North America's vault."

B.D. grinned. "Ma might take exception to that, considering it's her name on the deed transfer and the bank's ledger."

"Only because the law says you're still too wet behind the ears to affix your John Hancock to them," Nathan reminded. He whistled through his teeth. "Wish you'd heard your mama give David Doig six kinds of hell when he respectfully declined to divvy the spoils into separate accounts. Doig may have won that war, but I'll bet he couldn't hear thunder for a week."

"Aw, Ma's mellowed considerably since we came north. Damned if she hasn't gotten smarter about some things, too."

Nathan leaned back in his swivel chair and winged his arms behind his head. His tastefully appointed Cheechako Mine and Metallurgy office was a huge remove from presiding over the stern end of a canoe, but success hadn't gone to Nathan's head. Clad in his customary wrinkled flannel shirt and pilled wool trousers, he looked more like a Klondike pauper than one of its princes.

"Megan sure turned the tables on me," he said.

"I've tried to buy One Below practically since we staked it, then all of a sudden, she tossed a yes back at me. Was primed to launch my usual argument before I realized the wind had changed direction."

B.D. recalled her broaching the subject when he walked her to the Haven after a rather pensive Christmas dinner at Minnie's. Because she'd been restless and moody since she'd received Pete's letter and B.D.'s thoughts were centered on Colleen, stolen kisses, and the carnal fantasies they provoked, he'd paid scant attention to his mother's contemplations.

"Knowing Ma, her mind was made up before she ever talked to me about it."

Nathan eyed him curiously. "Well, it's kind of like closing the barn door after the horse runs off, but I can't help wondering, why now? You finally found a couple of crews who aren't out to rob you blind or beat you bloody, got three drifts working, a right prosperous-sized slag heap piling up . . ."

B.D. shrugged. "Ma just isn't greedy, and she's hell for playing the odds. We all know the black sand's going to dribble away eventually. Paying miners to bring up muck that only washes five or six dollars to the pan is the same as pouring every ounce we've got in the vault back into the hole it came out of."

"She's right, too," Nathan said. "That's why I'm setting up a hydraulic operation come spring. Machine extraction is cheaper, more efficient, and doesn't get sick, drunk, or meet on the sly to organize labor unions."

"Dawson's getting almost civilized, isn't it? Next thing you know somebody'll lay tracks for a trolley up and down Front Street."

"Oh, you're way behind the times, kid." Nathan shuffled through a stack of papers on his desk, then pitched a brochure across it. The lavish color-plate depiction of a Daimler motorcar on its cover made B.D.'s mouth water. From the headlamps glaring at its bulldog prow to the jaunty rumble seat suspended behind and above its wagon-sized rear wheels, the horseless carriage exuded power, speed, and an enviable measure of pretension.

"If Big Alex has his way, we'll have macadam streets and sidewalks before freeze-up next winter," Nathan said. "And if Nels can keep his damned steamer afloat, there'll be one of those beauties with my name on it unloaded at the wharf in June."

B.D. stared at the illustration and imagined a fleet of motorcars sputtering past the rough-hewn log saloons, stores, bawdy houses, clustered tents, and ramshackle cabins; their bulbed horns squawking at pedestrians, freight wagons, mule teams, and sled dogs.

He laid the brochure on the desk. "I suppose progress can't be kept at bay forever, can it?"

A youthful flow of enthusiasm softened the creases deprivation and hardship had etched on Nathan's face. "My boy, when the new century dawns this time next year, this city'll be known as the Paris of the Yukon."

B.D. plastered on what he hoped resembled a smile. "That'll really be something, all right."

A knock on the door preceded Olive Dunleavy, Nathan's typewriter, poking her head into his office. "Mr. Galvin is here to see you, sir."

"Be right with him," Nathan said, chuckling after she shut the door behind her. "Every time she does that 'sir' business, I expect to see my father skulking behind me. Things have sure changed since we met up at Fortymile, haven't they?"

B.D. rose from his chair. "Changed a heap in the last few minutes with my demotion from mine owner to shovel stiff."

"Do you really want to work for me at the Cheechako? Don't get me wrong, with Spare-ribs Jimmy off on Nigger Jim Daughtery's stampede, I'm lucky to have you take his foreman's job, but it isn't as if you need the money."

"What else is there to do until the thaw besides

stroll Front Street with the scarecrow boulevardiers? Ma doesn't open the Haven but two or three days a week. She doesn't want a butler and I've heard those sourdoughs' stories told about sixteen times apiece, anyhow."

"How about Colleen?" Nathan winked in a quite rakish manner. "I'll bet she'd love to, er, see more of you."

B.D. gripped the doorknob. "She's the reason I've got to have a job, old friend. Keeping myself tired— real butt-dragging tired—is the only way I can hash being with her. Even then, not for very blessed long."

"Are you telling me, after all this time, you haven't—"

B.D. let the door's slam serve as his answer. Five strides took him through the outer office and onto the boardwalk. He'd put a full block behind him before the sixty-below-zero temperature cooled his flaming cheeks.

Jaysus, if everybody assumed he and Colleen were having relations, why the hell was he torturing himself? She'd made it pretty clear that she was hankering after him as bad as he was for her—leastwise, as much as a lady hankered after such things.

It couldn't be healthy getting all worked up for nothing, time and time again. Might be bad for Colleen, too, for all he knew.

And besides, Pete wasn't around to kill him for it.

Nor had his mother heard about his visit to the pharmacy a couple of weeks earlier, as she wouldn't have kept his purchase of protectives a secret. Jubal Ward, the owner, called them "tickets to Paradise," thinking B.D. was fawnching for a crib whore.

He wasn't sure yet whether he was glad or depressed Ward had confided that the devices weren't exactly armor against disease or other complications— after he'd paid for a package of them, of course.

"There's only one way I know of to fend off every kind of dire consequence," the clerk said.

B.D. had tried his best to appear nonchalant. "Oh? And what might that be?"

"Keep your pecker in your pants between visits to the privy."

Easy for him to say, B.D. thought. Fat as he was, he probably hadn't seen his for fifteen years. He gazed off into the middle distance, waging a heated argument with himself. Not having resolved it before he reached Minnie's house, he commenced to pace a trench in the snow at the end of the footbridge.

I loved Colleen as a friend, first. 'Course it isn't like I ever missed the fact she's a girl. A beautiful, sweet-smelling girl . . ."

He groaned and his pace slowed as her image shimmered in his mind. With big, soft—"

"B.D.?" Colleen called from the porch. "What are you doing?"

"Uh, nothin'. Really. Not nary a thing."

"Come inside this minute. Your face is burned red from the cold."

He didn't bother to correct her assumption as he peeled off his mackinaw, boots, fur cap, and gloves. The parlor felt stifling in contrast to the frigid air outside, but no boarders, much less the boardinghouse's owner, greeted him from the settee.

"I did not expect to see you today. But I hoped very much I would."

"Where's Minnie? In the kitchen?"

"She went to Miss Megan's for a commissioner's meeting. Some of the firemen quit because they are not being paid."

"Squeezing money out of the town council might take a while," B.D. said. He glanced at the ceiling. "I s'pose there's a renter or three dawdling upstairs."

An impish grin appeared. "No one is here except us. For once, we have the whole house to ourselves."

"Oh shit."

She stared at him as if he'd left his brains on the stoop.

"Maybe I'd better not stay, Colleen."

Raising on tiptoes, she curled her arms around his neck and kissed him lightly on the lips. "Why?"

When he pulled her to him, her full breasts flattened provocatively against his chest. The tremble within him reverberated in his voice. "You know how Ma and Minnie feel about us being alone together. They're afraid of what'll happen. Damn 'em, they're right."

Colleen gently rubbed her pelvis against his erection. "I am ready," she whispered. "You are ready. It will not be bad for you, this time."

"What do you mean, bad? Much less, this time?"

A pinkish tinge colored her cheekbones. "You told me you tried to make love to that Beulah woman, but could not, and how awful you felt after. I think it made you afraid. It won't be bad with us. It will be beautiful, I promise."

B.D.'s love for her surged through him and almost staggered him. He gathered her in his arms and rocked her from side to side. "No, it won't, Colleen, and not because I'm a couple of years older. I love you and I want you so bad I hurt inside, but we can't give in—not yet."

Tears welled in her dark doe eyes. "I do not understand. Why is it so wrong if we love each other? Because we are not married? That is your law, not the belief of my people."

Before attempting an explanation, B.D. guided her to the settee. They sat at right angles, close enough to touch, but distant enough to allow him to think straight.

"If that were the only thing putting the quietus to us making love, I'd marry you this very second. Plan to someday, if you'll have me. Sometimes I wonder if that's all people want when they plunk down their five bucks at the justice of the peace's office—salvation from mortal sin and a license to make love all rolled up into a square piece of parchment."

His hand glided over her breast and down to her belly. "Problem is, that piece of paper may make what we're panting for nice and proper, but neither of us is ready to have a child." B.D. chuckled deep in his throat. "And randy as I am, we'd get us one the first time."

"You do love me, don't you?"

"Well, if you hadn't figured that out before now, I must not be half the Romeo I thought I was."

Her chin rumpled into a pout. "I am serious, B.D. Pete told me a man must respect a woman before he can truly love her. He said that was the difference between your father's feelings for Miss Megan and Mr. Bainbridge's—why she chose Barlow for your first name. Mr. Jacobs loved your mother, but Mr. Bainbridge respected her *and* loved her."

B.D. stared into Colleen's eyes, their glossy depths like mirrors enabling him to look inside himself.

"Pete's wiser than I gave him credit for. I've wondered my whole life why Barlow came before David. Ma told me that's how it popped into her mind when I was born, but I don't think even she's ever realized *why* it did."

"What makes me happy is to see how much Miss Megan respects Pete."

"See? How? He's been gone for four months. All I see is her getting more fractious every day."

"With her whole heart, Miss Megan wants to find him to be sure he is well, but she does not look. By asking her to wait for him, he asked her not to search. She has respected that."

B.D. shook his head. "Jaysus, I do believe wisdom runs in your family. Maybe if I hang around with you long enough, some of it'll rub off on me."

"It's a bold lad ye are and a better one than ye know, O'Malley," Colleen said in a perfect Irish brogue.

"Well, I'll be—"

She raised a finger to silence him. "And even if you

are the most handsome man in the Yukon, I will try very, very hard not to tease you anymore. We are special friends now and I will dream of someday when we can be lovers."

"And we will be, baby gal," he said huskily, then drew her into the crook of his arm and kissed her to seal the promise.

Chapter 38

Soap-milky bathwater sluiced from Megan's body when she emerged from the tub. Steam wafted from her forearms at the same instant gooseflesh prickled her skin. She'd set the tub as near the stove as she'd dared, but late April's frigid wind seeped through every eroded chink in the Haven's walls.

In Seattle, purple and white crocuses and a few impetuous daffodils had probably reared their petaled heads at the sun, but Old Man Winter's grip on the Klondike hadn't eased a fraction as yet. As Megan buffed her skin dry and warm with a length of toweling, she wondered if spring fever were rooted in an eagerness for winter's end, or fear that by some mystical oversight the warm seasons simply wouldn't arrive as scheduled.

Of one fact she was sure: The Yukon exacted a harsher punishment on its pioneers than on their children. Oh, she'd nodded along with many a sourdough's observation that encroaching civilization had mucked up the weather, but she knew, just as they did, that accumulated birthdays were the real culprit.

How she could explain away her midday, wing-and-a-prayer ablutions posed a thornier dilemma. Not to mention, what manner of lunacy caused a woman to flat-iron the creases from a dress she wore in July when slushy vials of unbaptized whiskey indicated a current temperature of approximately forty-five below zero?

For Megan to cite a gut-level intuition as reason

enough to close the Haven on a profitable Saturday invited regular dosages of laudanum, bed rest in a darkened room, and loved ones trading whispers out of her earshot.

Especially, she admitted, since two earlier hunches had proven the O'Malley family tree's true dearth of Gypsy blood.

Her tobacco brown robe itched like horsehair, but hugging herself in its woolly folds soon quieted her shivers. She bent at the waist to chafe the excess water from her hair with the towel.

An unbidden, droning chorus of discouragements shoved Megan's wishful fancies into a mental ash bin. She tried to ignore the familiar, albeit affectionate, concert, but had no more success now than when the opinions were originally voiced.

In February, Earl had encountered Pete outside Belinda Mulrooney's hotel in Grand Forks. "He couldn't talk for yawnin'," Earl reported. "Just stood there shakin' the screws loose in his crutch whilst his eyes and nose drizzled like faucets."

Fond as he was of Pete, Megan's old rival for the One Below couldn't keep silent and watch her pine after an incurable drunkard that "wasn't worth the powder it'd take to blow him up with."

By March, her son's faith in Pete had eroded as well. "He pities himself a helluva lot more than he loves you or Colleen." B.D. hadn't included himself, but the bitter edge in his tone expressed his own feelings of betrayal.

"Back when we worked the mine together, Pete told me his barfly buddies would never believe that a fellow who drank like he had a hollow leg could turn teetotaler. Damned if Pete didn't end up with one for true."

"I know you're hurt, B.D., but I won't brook that kind of cruelty."

"Jaysus, will you give it up? Pete didn't crawl into a hole to heal. He did it to spare us watching him drink himself to death. Forget about him. He's not good enough for you by half and never will be."

"What about Colleen?" Megan asked. "After all Pete's done for her, has she cast him aside, too?"

"She's aware of his faults same as you—probably more so—and will always love him, regardless. Except what she's known for a long time, and what you can't seem to get through your thick Irish skull, is that she can't depend on him. For a daughter to accept that is one thing, but you? After all these years taking care of yourself, why in God's name would you want a man like Pete?"

Minnie's sojourn to the Haven a couple of weeks ago took a different tack. After a few minutes of strained chitchat, she'd announced. "As soon as the river breaks up, Earl and I are sailing for Boston, then on to Europe for a grand tour. At our age, squeezing a penny till it bleeds is long on optimism and awfully short on common sense."

"Earl's finally talked you into marrying him?"

"No. I finally talked Earl into leaving Dawson before the airs it's putting on get too thick to breathe." She chuckled wickedly. "Oh, I might rattle off another 'I do' someday, but it took a while to become accustomed to Walentine, let alone, spell it. And if Minnie Delacroix doesn't sound tarty as a whorehouse madam, I don't know what does."

Megan grinned, both at her friend's remark and at the possibility of trading her surname for Pete's. To be sure, Megan Vladislov staggered rather than rolled off the tongue. It sounded foreign in all senses of the word.

"Earl and I won't take no for an answer," Minnie said.

"An answer to what? It appears I was gathering wool and missed the question."

"I haven't asked it yet. Now that I have your attention, we want you and B.D. and Colleen to go with us. We'll tarry in Boston long enough to take in the sights and fill a dozen steamer trunks with a wardrobe befitting our *nouveau riche* station, then gad about London, Paris, Athens, Rome . . . Why, I just realized how marvelous it would be for B.D. to visit Ireland."

Megan's chuckle held only a mere hint of humor. "When we came to America, my sister and I lived in Boston. I hated every bloody minute of it."

"Of course you did, but a tenement flat in Shantytown is a world away from a suite at the Hotel Drake."

"No quarrel here, seeing as how I was that marble mausoleum's first elevator operator. Damned if I'll ever set foot in it again, either."

"You're picking nits, Miss O'Malley. Think of what an opportunity this is for Colleen and B.D to see places they've only read about or, in your son's case, the beloved homeland you've told him about."

"B.D. gives not a fig about Ireland and I want to remember it as it was when I left, not lament what it's become."

Minnie's lips pursed in a thin, frustrated line. "It wouldn't matter where we were bound for, would it? Texas or Timbuktu, you'd spout a fistful of excuses, reasons, and quibbles without once saying, flat out, that you've vowed to sit a vigil for that one-legged boozehound and wild horses won't drag you away from him."

"I'll tell you, same as I did B.D. Whatever Pete has done or not done, he doesn't deserve that kind of talk and I won't stand for it."

Minnie's birdlike shoulders sagged. "Oh, I apologize. To you and to him, except . . ." A gnarled finger seesawed under her nose. "I never yearned for a daughter. I suppose the good Lord had wisdom enough to send the stork to another's doorstep, but I've come to love you the same as I would my own child.

"These past months, I've watched you go about your business, doing your utmost to hide the hurt gnawing at you. When I wasn't admiring your steadfast loyalty, I cussed your damn fool stubbornness and stupidity a blue streak. You say you can't abide my condemning Pete. Well and good. I *won't* abide leaving you cooped up in this cabin waiting for him or for eternity, whichever might come first."

Megan paused to allow her friend a moment to compose herself. Minnie didn't shrink from saying what was on her mind and in no uncertain terms, but to express heartfelt sentiments, particularly those she'd obviously contained and grappled with for weeks, must have been as exhausting as it was a relief.

"What you and Earl and B.D. and Colleen see as a log prison is for me a sanctuary," Megan said. "For all the hours I've conjured images of Pete, missed him, worried about him, and felt my breath catch whenever a tall, burly gent swings the door wide, I've already decided when the ice goes out, I'm going with it whether Pete comes with me or not."

"Where?" Minnie inquired, her face a study in skepticism.

"I've booked passages on the steamer *Merwyn*, which should be off-loaded and ready to board for St. Michael by the sixteenth of June. Banker Doig has promised to crate our gold on deposit by no later than the tenth. Mid-July will find us, part and parcel, in San Francisco."

Minnie snorted. "As I recall, you've lived in Frisco twice and despised it nearly much as Boston."

"I do, but Colleen will have several respectable female seminaries to pick from. As for B.D., he will be attending Leland Stanford Junior University next fall."

"I don't suppose he knows anything about your plans for him?"

"He most assuredly does," Megan shot back, "and not a bit taken by them, either. He said I forced him from what he thought was his home only to find it here in the Klondike, and is not going back to the States under any circumstances."

Minnie chuckled. "He may be somewhat more difficult to shanghai the second time around. Or maybe you'll trick Colleen aboard and use her for bait?"

"Actually, I appealed to B.D.'s horse sense with a gentle reminder that he's still three years shy of the legal age for filing a claim."

"Gentle reminder, my eye. A Hobson's choice is more like it. Oh, I can just hear you telling him he could break his back on Nathan's payroll for the duration or bide his time strolling Stanford's manicured grounds with his nose in a book."

"Well, that's the gist of our discussion, though I was certainly more tactful when I presented it."

"And he agreed?"

"Not in so many words," Megan hedged, "but he hasn't launched another argument."

"All right, then, what about you? Think morning mass with your sister and planning bar mitzvahs with Cad will keep you occupied?"

Megan chose to ignore the snipe. "Once the children are situated, I'm off to New Mexico. While I'm finding a speck of gold to swing a pick at the sun'll thaw my bones."

"Umm-hmm." Minnie angled back against the chair, arms crossed at her chest, and aimed a shrewd, lingering gaze directly at Megan. "Sounds as if you've put your house in order no matter what the near future might bring."

"Other than selling the Haven, yes, I believe I have."

"Which you'll do shortly before the *Merwyn* pulls up anchor."

Megan looked at her quizzically. "For heaven's sake, your things won't be sold with the property, if that's what concerns you."

"Not in the least, dearie. What I'm wildly curious

to know is how many fares you've booked on that steamer."

"Four," Megan said as she straightened to finger-comb the damp strands of hair from her forehead. It was the same answer she'd given the day Minnie broached the question.

Strangely enough, rehashing the nay-sayers' litanies had the opposite effect she'd expected. Instead of feeling all the more foolish about closing the Haven, bathing, and dressing for a caller because every instinct assured he would come, her resolve had been strengthened a hundredfold; her belief in Pete and their love for each other intensified.

"Like Gamaliel said, a body's gotta have faith. It's the onliest thing that'll get you through this life."

The filmy summer frock slid easily over her chemise and petticoat—more so than it had the last time she'd worn it. A draft traced her cleavage and sent a corresponding shiver down her spine. She bent double again to brush her hair dry before she caught her death. The stove's heat felt toasty to the brink of scorching on her nape and back while the rest of her chilled.

Megan decided that someone could make a million inventing a spit attachment so lunatic female pioneers needn't risk partial chilblains to finish their ablutions.

A light tap at the door startled her. She listened intently, but heard only rumbles on the boardwalk. The ornery leprechaun in her brain giggled gleefully at having cozened her again.

A forceful pounding rattled the bar in its brackets. Megan took a step, halted, distrusting her own ears, then rushed to yank the brace from its supports.

Pete's eyes shone more brown than green as he stood framed by the doorway. A walrus mustache now adorned his upper lip, yet his long silvery hair still suited no fashion dictate save his own.

She prayed for this moment for six agonizingly long months. In a hundred nights' dreams she'd fallen into his arms, laughing and crying in the same breath, her heart bursting with joy.

Her anticipated jubilance flared and died in an instant. She shook with anger; a rage so intense she was impervious to the wind ruffling her skirts.

"Am I too late?"

Megan didn't trust her voice to reply. A sweeping motion proffered an invitation inside. She strode across the room to the settee, allowing the door's scrape and the bar's thump to indicate Pete's acceptance of it.

She settled into a stiff, regal posture, literally and figuratively bracing herself for a confrontation. Her head snapped up at the sudden realization that no crutch or cane aided his entrance. Her gaze fixed on his glossy, custom-made boots; the trouser legs bloused around their tops.

Pete turned toward her. He shifted his weight left. His right leg swung forward in an arc. Leaning slightly right, his left advanced in a rolling, well-practiced maneuver. A limp unbalanced his gait, but lacking foreknowledge that he'd acquired an artificial limb of some sort, she'd have never guessed his right leg had been amputated above the knee.

He grunted when he sat down beside her. His artificial leg jutted straight out and he kicked a hassock sideward to prop it.

"When I told you I'd walk back into your life, Megan, I meant it. Of course, it took a while longer than I'd reckoned before Li'l Peggy fit right and I learned to trust the ol' girl not to buck me off."

"You named your—your limb?"

"Had to call it something beside hair-curling words. Marvin Masters, the cabinetmaker who fashioned it, suggested Li'l Peggy."

"Good as any, I suppose."

Megan fidgeted under the strain of conflicting, confused emotions. The disparity between the man she last saw in a hospital bed and this impeccably dressed fellow showing scant sign of ever having been sick a day in his life was too much to absorb.

"Much as I hoped you'd latch on to me and kiss me till I begged for mercy," Pete said, "I suspected you'd be angry with me."

"You did?" She averted her eyes. "Well, it came as quite a surprise to me."

"Why wouldn't you be? I stole away from the hospital, hid out for months on end trying to muster up something resembling my manhood, only to arrive unannounced and maybe unwanted on your stoop?"

"If only you'd written me again, or gotten a message to me that you were all right, the wait wouldn't have been nearly so hard."

"Do you really believe that?"

Megan hesitated, then shook her head. "But I would have known you hadn't forgotten me."

"Had Dr. Pennington divested me of my head, I couldn't have forgotten you, darlin'." His arm curled around her shoulders. "What I have to say isn't an excuse or to beg forgiveness. Only to explain how things were, which wasn't how I anticipated they'd be."

He massaged his right thigh, a pensive gesture cultivated years before surgery had rendered it therapeutic.

"We both know whiskey had a more powerful hold on me than I'd admit. When it made a believer out of me on Independence Day, I quit. Not for you, but because I'd lost all respect for the man I'd become. I've stayed sober for the same reason."

"You haven't had a drink since the Fourth of July?" Megan asked.

"Well, the sixth, maybe. Seventh at the latest. Didn't happen to have a calendar on me at the time."

"But Earl said he saw you a couple of months ago . . ." Megan stopped herself, realizing the insinuation she'd made.

"He did, and I was in a mighty bad way, but I wasn't drunk. Doc Pennington didn't tell me morphine was a slavemaster, too, and twice harder to kick. That crystalline god of sleep numbed the pain, but left me so dim-witted and weak, I couldn't think straight enough to realize what it was doing to me for quite a while. Soon as I did, which was about the time Earl and I ran into each other, the drug went out the window, too."

Megan reached to caress his cheek, but he caught her hand and lowered it. "Think about what I'm telling you. I'm a confessed drunkard and a morphine addict. Between the donation I made to the hospital and my expenses the last months, I'm also about two thousand dollars from destitute.

"Humble I'm not. I'm damned proud to walk on two legs instead of giving in to being a cripple, but I can't navigate cross-country in this rig. How I'll earn a living, I don't know, but it won't be from trapping. I'm going to miss that, darlin'. I already do. I'm sure to get surly now and again, longing for the only way of life I've ever known."

His eyes met hers and held them. "Reckon what it boils down to is that I'm one sorry son of a bitch and will probably get sorrier as time goes on, but I love you, I need you, and I want you for my wife."

"At your side, for better and for worse?"

"I'll never leave you alone again. I swear it, now, and will before God tomorrow morning."

"Tomorrow?"

What would B.D. think? And Minnie? Certainly that she'd lost what little mind she had left. Poor Frances had waited over twenty years to stand up for her baby sister at the alter. She'd have screaming conniptions when they docked in San Francisco and Megan introduced Pete as her husband.

Frisco—Lord above, she hadn't even told Pete about the *Merwyn* or Colleen and B.D.'s schooling. . . .

Megan reared her head back and laughed. "Is dawn too early to roust a priest?"

"Does that mean yes?"

She answered with a gentle kiss. His soft lips were as needful and hungry as her own. Passions and desires too long contained obliterated the outside world and everything in it. Never, never had she felt like this before. She didn't want just to be made love to. She wanted Pete. All of him.

Megan loosened the buttons above his vest and her hand delved inside. The sensual textures of warm skin and thick, coarse hair feathering between her fingers heightened her arousal.

He cupped her breast and she moaned at his touch, wishing their clothes would simply melt away, freeing them to explore, caress, and discover in languid repose.

She slipped from his embrace, stood, and reached out to him. "I want you."

The hassock skittered away and he struggled to his feet. He kissed her brow, her cheekbones, her mouth. His thigh pressured hers. She took a half step backward, then another; his prompting strides jerky and awkward until she matched his rhythm for a slow, walking waltz to her bedchamber.

Voile and flannel, lace-trimmed white cotton, and dark wool strewed the floor. Megan crossed her arms at her hips, to clutch the billowy folds of her chemise and peel it over her head. She started to fling it atop the pile, then hesitated.

She was suddenly aware of her heavy breasts sagging against her ribs. Her rounded belly and its dashed, pale scars of pregnancy. The clabbered skin at her thighs, once as smooth and supple as cream.

Megan held the filmy cotton garment in front of her like a shield. She wanted so desperately to be young again and flawless and beautiful for him. Even in the muted light, Pete couldn't help but see every mark the years had inevitably wrought.

Peering from beneath her lashes, she saw him avert what could only be described as an admiring gaze. She dropped the chemise and clambered beneath the quilts, tugging them to her chin.

Pete quickly turned his back. She ogled the muscles rippling across that broad, alabaster plane. The powerfully built man undressing before her was not the old friend she'd nursed and bathed while in the throes of delirium.

Tomorrow, he would be her husband, but tonight, he would be her lover. A shiver raced the length of her.

He cursed as he grappled with the narrow belt that spanned his hips just below his drawstrung drawers. The leather straps descending from it were riveted to a sleevelike affair which secured his stump to the artificial limb. He hobbled to the edge of the bed and heaved himself onto the mattress.

As a rosy blush crept up his neck, he bowed his head. "Darlin', I—well, I feel awful beat up, broken down, and ugly as homemade sin all of a sudden, and it isn't just because of Li'l Peggy. Could you, maybe—"

She turned to face the wall. Her fingers traced a dimpled thigh, the creases lacing her belly, her breast. Pete wanted her, exactly as she was, as much as she wanted him.

The blankets furled and the bed jostled beneath his weight. She lay back on the pillow, her open arms begging to be filled. He molded his body to hers and kissed her, then raised himself to look into her eyes.

Pete took her hand and guided it down his hip, along the sculpted muscle of his thigh to its end. The skin was welted and rough in places; smooth and satiny in others.

"I had to know if you'd be repelled by it," he whispered.

She caressed the stump with gentle, circular motions. "To me, it's simply as much as part of you as"— she slipped her hand from his, let it ramble provocatively upward, then murmured—"this." Pete's eyelids fluttered and he groaned with pleasure.

Ever so slowly her fingertips explored the wiry tuft above his loins. "And, this." She traced the rippled skin at his midsection. "And, this." She followed the valley of his chest, repeating her chant until she reached his lips.

"I love you, Pete. Every inch of you, inside and out. Nothing has changed that and nothing ever will."

Chapter 39

Megan jolted awake. Impenetrable darkness met her blinking stare. Pete stirred beside her, then mumbled in his sleep.

The Haven's door exploded open with an ear-splitting boom. Amber light glanced off the bedroom wall; the shadows it threw veiled in a smoky haze. Footfalls pounding across the front room.

She and Pete jerked upright. Megan clutched the quilt at her throat to hide her nakedness.

"Fire," B.D. yelled, his silhouette, outlined by the lantern he held aloft, filled her bedchamber's doorway. "The tow—" His eyes flicked from her to Pete. "What the *hell's* going on here?"

Megan coughed against the smoke boiling in behind him. "Our clothes, if you'll step out and take that damned lantern with you."

"But—you—he—"

"Damn it, son," Pete shouted. "Do as you're told."

The light and its bearer disappeared. Megan and Pete scrambled from the bed. Having no time for petticoats and frills, she yanked open a bureau drawer and grabbed a shirt, dungarees, and socks. Her fingers grazed the cold brass clasp of Barlow P.'s galluses. She glanced at Pete, then closed the drawer, leaving the past where it belonged.

A crackling roar, terrified voices, and dogs' frenzied howls blasted through the walls from Front Street. The holocaust was bearing down on them, fast and furiously.

Megan fought down panic. She remembered too well the doomsday bellow of wind-whipped flames as they devoured most of Pioche, Nevada, and Tombstone, Arizona. By the sound alone, she knew the earlier two Dawson fires had only been dress rehearsals.

"The roof's tryin' to catch, Ma," B.D. shouted. "Get out—now!"

Thumps and anguished grunts came from Pete's side of the bed. "Shit. Can't get this goddamned leg on right."

"Leave it," she said. "Lean on me."

"No, please. Just help me."

Megan knelt on the piled clothing and secured the rounded brace between the upper cuff and the wooden shoe stretcher attached like a foot.

Pete wrenched the support belt tight and buckled it, then leaped backward on the bed to ruch up his trousers. While he fastened them, Megan shouldered his left boot home. The right caught on the rigid false foot.

"Go ahead," he said, grasping its mule ears. "I can get it now."

Megan stood, but made no move to leave him. Pete forced the boot on with a sharp rap to the floor. He took her hand, and they half walked, half ran into the front room.

"Take to the street, son," Megan ordered, ducking the embers that rained from the ceiling. She shagged her own boots. Pete jerked their coats from the pegs. Not pausing to don either, they followed B.D. into the inferno raging outside.

"Where's Colleen?" Pete yelled.

"Down near the river with Earl and Minnie. Y'all find each other and stick together. I'll find you when my bucket party's over."

Pete's expression registered concern as well as envy for the two good legs B.D. possessed. Megan knew resignation to his disability would never come easy for him any more than it would for her if circumstances were reversed.

She stepped into her boots, then shrugged on the mackinaw Pete held open for her. Smoky gray tendrils curled from under the Haven's eaves. A lump lodged in Megan's throat. Those rough-hewn walls had been her sanctuary in myriad ways and only hours earlier, when she and Pete had made love with such passionate abandon.

She swallowed hard, content in the knowledge that while nothing could be done to save it or its contents, the memories it contained were hers to keep forever.

"I don't mind telling you," Pete said, nodding toward the Haven, "I feel pretty damned helpless at the moment."

She turned and took his arm. "Don't. There's not a thing inside that building worth a second's grieving."

"Appears our nuptials might be delayed a day or three, though."

She shook her head. "Not unless every priest in Dawson takes to the hills, it won't. Come hell or high water, I want Trinity Sunday to be my wedding day."

"Then it will be, darlin'. Especially seeing as how your son's already caught us practicing the honeymoon."

They started for the riverbank without a backward glance at the Haven. Thousands of burnished faces watched in horror as Dawson City crumbled before their eyes.

Megan heard one remark, " 'Leastwise, 'twas Helen Holden what sparked this 'un, 'stead of poor ol' Belle Mitchell."

The man beside him snorted. " 'Spect we oughta have the council pass a law agin whores havin' lamps in their boo-da-wars. Most of them doves is purtier in the dark anyhow."

Minnie's boardinghouse had already been reduced to a charred skeleton, as had the Aurora Café, the Tivoli, and ironically, Harry Ash's Northern Saloon.

Steam condensed into an icy fog that enshrouded the entire city. Flames roared from building to building, their orange-red peaks zigzagging upward like reverse lightning bolts. Airborne sparks mushroomed into fiery tongues, consuming tinder-dry peat roofs, planed lumber, and log walls in minutes. Windows burst from the heat, showering glass fragments like spangled snowflakes. The whiskey river rippling over the Yukon Saloon's threshold and onto the boardwalk froze instantly into a brownish, glossy skim.

The *whoosh* of toppling structures echoed up and down Front Street. Behind dance-hall row, capricious flames leapt atop Paradise Alley's cabins and cribs. Naked, shrieking prostitutes ran from their shanty Sodom into the arms of good Samaritans who ripped off their own coats to clothe the terrified women.

Scores of men carrying foodstuffs, furniture, crates of liquor, paintings, and even a stuffed moosehead scurried from buildings in the path of the inferno to dump their wares along the marsh, then race back for another load. Horses harnessed to wagons and sleighs to transport heavier items whickered and pranced in place, shying from the noise and flames.

Ax- and sledgehammer-wielding volunteers hacked at structures in a vain attempt to create a firebreak. A burly gent carrying a can of kerosene in one hand and a bucket of sawdust in the other rushed past Megan, knocking her off balance. Others toting similar burdens converged and veered toward the river.

Where in God's name are the firemen, she thought. Her stomach took a sickening lurch when the answer resounded in her mind.

After the freeze-up last October, two steam engines equipped with huge boilers had been stationed on the river ice and covered with double tents. A five-man crew worked in round-the-clock shifts to keep the boilers stoked. A large hole cut through the ice to the flowing water below would provide a ready supply for the engines to pump through the boiler and into hoses in the event a fire erupted.

Except two weeks earlier, the hundred newly trained department members asked the town council for a long overdue wage increase. Over Megan's and other concerned citizens' protests, the request was denied.

The firemen voted to strike. By the next morning, without their guardianship, the boiler fires shriveled and died for wont of fuel. Last week, the access hole in the river refroze into a ten-foot-thick slab of solid ice.

Megan started when someone yelled, "Them fellers've burned through to the river." A hurrah went up from the milling spectators. Four Mounties waved their arms, ordering the crowd to fall back.

An army of volunteers vaulted up the bank, cradling a saggy length of hose. They stretched the white canvas tube across the road and pointed the nozzle toward the smoldering, vulnerable Monte Carlo Saloon.

"Throw the pump!"

While flames crackled and popped all around, and the merry chug of steam engines drifted inland, a reverent silence fell over the assembly. All eyes were fixed on the brass nib at the end of the hose.

A feeble trickle spurted from the nozzle. A loud *r-i-p* rent the air. The engines' pressure had forced unheated river water into the hose, which froze almost immediately, shredding the canvas line like so many steam-driven knives.

"God have mercy on us," a man shouted to Captain Starnes, the police commander. "What'll we do now?"

Pete cupped his hands around his mouth. "Blow up the buildings in front of the fire."

Starnes punched at the air. "Yes, by Jove. But we'll need powder or dynamite. A goodly amount of it."

Another voice in the crowd yelled, "There's a fifty-pound box of Giant powder at the A.C.C. Warehouse A."

"Sergeant-Major Tucker," Starnes said. "Take a dog team and go fetch it."

The young Mountie's eyes widened, but he snapped a salute and a curt, "Very well, sir."

Tucker's sled hadn't traveled half the distance to the warehouse when an explosion rocked the ground. The force of the blast hurled Pete into Megan. In turn, she slammed into the kettle-bellied gentleman behind her. A dull yellow arc spewed skyward. Men pushed and shoved, fighting to escape what looked like a rooster-tailed flume of fire descending upon them.

Pete flung his coat wide and drew its front panel over Megan's head. Something pelted down like hail. A strange, sandy grit mixed with pebbles littered the ground around her boots. The crowd's terrified shrieks changed to laughter.

She knelt and picked up a chunk. As she regained her feet, she stared at the gold nugget pinched between her thumb and middle fingers.

"The vault," Pete said flatly. "That goddamned monstrous, triple steel-walled, guaranteed fireproof vault just blew to hell and back."

Megan's heart slid to her boot tops. "Which vault?"

"The one that held every blessed dime we have in the world, darlin'," he said. "The Bank of British North America's."

Hundreds of people dropped to their knees, scrabbling on all fours on the frozen street plucking nuggets, gold watches, and molten clusters of jeweled stickpins, rings, and bracelets as one would strawberries from their vines.

By daylight, every man jack with a gold pan would be prospecting between the boardwalks. Front Street wasn't exactly paved with gold, but the vault's largesse had effected a close second to that fabled El Dorado.

Megan stood stock-still, her thoughts riveted on the months of back-breaking labor B.D. had endured. Her long hours at the Haven of Rest. One Below's fifty-thousand-dollar sale price. Every ounce of it gone in a blink.

Nathan had advised her to ship some of their take to San Francisco, but she'd demurred, partially due to Pete's accident and because she couldn't feature waving a fond, hopeful farewell to their hard-earned money.

Now, only a few months short of having spent three years in Dawson, she and B.D. had less than they had when they'd arrived: nothing but the clothes on their backs.

Her tears froze into slender rivulets. Ice beads weighted her lashes. The cold rasped her throat with each wrenching sob.

Pete took her in his arms and held her. "Hush now, darlin'. I know it's a helluva fortune you've lost and how hard you and the boy worked for it, but it's only money. Something'll turn up and set things to right. It always does."

A chuckle rumbled up his chest. "Father Judge believed that the Lord would provide and you can't say results didn't bear him out. I reckon it can't hurt to take a leaf from his book."

She sniffed, then scrubbed her face on the downy fur of his lapel. "Since when did you get religion?"

He lifted her chin. "The day I fell in love with the Angel of the Cassiar."

"Oh—Jesus, Mary, and Joseph. It's full of blarney you are and more of it than a low-born paddy."

Icy crystals sprinkled from his mustache when he grinned. "That's the spirit, old girl."

The return of Sergeant-Major Tucker's sled saved Pete from a thrashing and temporarily stayed the scavenger hunt. The Mountie saluted his commanding officer and said, "The box of dynamite you wanted, sir."

Starnes turned to address the crowd. "Are there any miners here who know how to use this powder?"

A chorus of "Aye, aye, sir," chirruped from a group

of South Africans known to be as familiar with lighting fuses as most men were with holding a lucifer to a hand-rolled's twisted tip.

"You there—McMahon, isn't it?" Starnes said, pointing to one lanky volunteer, "and Thilwall, Armstrong, and er, Olsen, I believe it is. You lads take the box and blow up the Aurora, Alex McDonald's building, and the Temenos."

The demolition crew raced for the sled. Without breaking his stride, McMahon snatched up the dynamite like a crate of barred soap and tossed it to Olsen, who shuttled it off to Thilwall.

"I think it wise to put some distance between us and those powder monkeys," Pete said, grasping her elbow. "Let's find Minnie and Colleen. Soon as B.D. joins us, we'll make for Grand Forks. Unless Belinda's turned her hotel over to the refugees, I still have a room there."

"Is it big enough to squeeze in a priest, too?"

"As long as he sticks with the 'Will you take' and 'love honor, and obey' parts and leaves out all the damned kneeling."

"Well, if you don't have to kneel," Megan argued, "I shouldn't have to obey."

"Didn't reckon you'd let that one slide." A dramatic sigh brought vapor billowing from his lips. "Oh, all right. If I have to settle for best two out of three to make an honest woman of you, so be it."

She paused at the crest of the riverbank, wrapped her arms around his neck, and kissed him possessively, passionately, and thoroughly.

In quick succession, three explosions jarred the earth. The concussions were felt by every man and beast within a two-mile radius—except for a pair of middle-aged lovers locked in an embrace near the Yukon River's frozen shoreline.

Chapter 40

A sultry, mid-June breeze ruffled B.D.'s hair as he leaned against the *Merwyn*'s deck rail. He aimed a wry smile at the dark, distinctive blemish on Moosehide Mountain's flank and wondered how he'd allowed something so benign—even farcical, truth be known—to give him such a bad case of the willies.

He turned his attention to Dawson City's ratchety skyline. Only eight weeks before, fire had destroyed every structure between Belinda Mulroney's blanket-draped Fairview Hotel and the scorched but reparable Monte Carlo Saloon. Despite the total loss of a hundred and seventeen buildings worth in excess of a million dollars, the boomtown pulled itself up by its bootstraps once again and started reconstruction before the ashes cooled.

According to Nathan Kresge, the fire was a godsend for the civic-minded and town-proud. With most of the old hewn-log monstrosities reduced to little more than fond memories, their replacements would boast the dressed lumber exteriors and plateglass windows apropos to an up-and-coming metropolis.

Tabitha Kelsey, the seamstress who'd purchased the Haven's vacant lot, was a prime example of the city's snooty new attitude. The venerable couturier, as she preferred to be called, erected what B.D. referred to as a titty pink board-and-batten wedding cake from which to sell her overpriced faux-Parisian fashions.

Where once canvas tents and shacks dominated residential areas, neat gingerbread-trimmed houses with bona fide parlors, parlor rugs, and parlor-sized baby grands lined Dawson's die-straight, honest-to-God sidewalks.

Just as Nathan predicted, Front Street was being graded to accept a smooth coat of macadam. A sanitary sewer project was underway. More new school bell towers and church steeples spiked upward every day, and the Anti-Saloon League had more members on its roster than the Elks, Masons, Pioneers of Alaska, and Knights of Columbus combined.

The *Merwyn* creaked and groaned beneath its load of two hundred passengers. Before they docked in St. Michael at month's end, B.D. reckoned he'd be more than ready to board the larger, somewhat more luxurious *U.S.S. Yukon* for the brief, diagonal jaunt across Norton Sound.

Much as he'd ranted and raved about the bank's supposedly impregnable vault belching three years' work to the winds, the gentle hand of Providence must surely have intervened.

Overnight poverty had pretty well assured his absence from the hallowed halls of Leland J. Sanford Junior University, nor would Colleen be sequestered seventy miles away in what constituted a glorified convent.

Instead, without applying much arm twisting he'd convinced his mother to chase after rumors of a strike at Nome, Alaska Territory. As was their nature, she and the other sourdoughs scoffed at the notion of a gold-strewn beach where a few rocks of a Long Tom would put its owner on Easy Street, yet some mighty familiar faces were crowding the deck behind him.

The one he most admired tilted toward the sun to bask in its gentle, early-summer caress. Colleen's hair shimmered with blue-black highlights. The radiant smile she reserved only for him flashed brilliant white.

"It makes you very happy to leave Dawson City," she said.

"Like Ma says, the dog has had its day. There's a

whole lot of folks I'm going to miss—Gamaliel, Nathan, Nels, Minnie, Earl, and Spare-ribs Jimmy among them, but as long as you're with me, I don't expect I'll suffer overmuch." His arm encircled her shoulders, then he pointed to the blissful couple holding hands nearby. "Besides, with you along, I'm not the only third wheel butting in on their honeymoon."

Colleen eyed him oddly. "But Pete and Megan have been married for two months now. At their age, surely, *that* ended a long time ago."

B.D. chuckled. "Baby gal, by the look of them, I don't think it ever will. Why, if one of us falls overboard before we get to Nome, it's sink or swim. I don't suspect either of them'd notice for quite a while."

"Sifting sand on the beach sounds like much more fun than burrowing a mine hole into a hill. Do you really believe we will get rich there again?"

"Maybe," B.D. said. "And then again, maybe not. For a bona fide natural-born prospector, it isn't the finding that stirs the soul. It's the seeking."

He paused and glanced at his mother and stepfather, then added, "That is, if it's gold you're after."

Author's Note

The West was by no means crowded during the late 1890s, but is surely felt that way to the gunfighters, gamblers, grifters, and drifters who'd outlived their era, and to the young men born a generation too late to expect much firsthand experience in rootin', tootin', or shootin'.

When news of a huge Klondike gold strike blared from newspaper headlines, it was manna from heaven for the "Old West's" graying icons and youthful wanna-bes alike. Gold was more of an excuse men used to justify joining naturalist John Muir's aptly named "horde of fools." Otherwise, by about ten miles north of Skagway, where Paddy the mule took his tragic four-hundred-foot swan dive, the lure of instant wealth would have surely lost its appeal.

According to Pierre Berton's *The Klondike Quest,* "Three thousand horses were to die on the White Pass trail that winter (1897). Their rotting cadavers could already be seen strewn along the gravels of the Skagway River, a pitiful hedgerow of carrion leading upward toward the summit of the pass."

To emerge at trail's end relatively unscathed meant camping on the shore of Lake Bennett in a tent for seven or eight subzero months while endeavoring to build a boat or raft capable of negotiating six hundred miles of the Yukon River, including Miles Canyon, Squaw Rapids, White Horse Rapids, Five Fingers Rapids, and Rink Rapids. The only working knowledge most Stampeders had in regard to boat building or river navigation was likely gleaned from memorable passages of Mark Twain's *Life on the Mississippi, The Adventures of Huckleberry Finn,* or *The Adventures of Tom Sawyer.*

Yet they came to Dawson City and kept coming by the tens of thousands; wide-eyed tinhorns, gimlet-eyed vice-lords, and kohl-eyed ladies of ultimate accessibility. As was true of any boomtown, the latter two groups mined trouser pockets faster and with far less effort than shovel stiffs extracted pockets of placer gold from the earth's perpetually frozen bowels.

Pound for pound, more characters frequented Dawson City in its almost exactly three-year heyday than the amassed glitter dust dredged from Bonanza and Eldorado Creeks and the bench claims above them.

The primary players in *Klondike Fever,* Megan and B.D. O'Malley, Pete, Colleen, Minnie, and Gamaliel are fictional, although just as in *Trinity Strike,* Megan was based to some degree on pioneer prospector Nellie Cashman, who owned The Prospector's Haven of Rest in Dawson City.

Nathan Kresge, Nels Peterson, George Carmack and kin, Big Alex McDonald, Swiftwater Bill Gates, Spare-ribs Jimmy Mackinson, William Ogilvie, Coatless Curly Munro, Roddy Connors, Ikey Sutro, and a host of others were real, as were most of the anecdotes surrounding them.

The race Megan ran for One Below was inspired by a similar incident that occurred in November 1896. The two competitors, a Scotsman and a Swede, reached the Mountie compound at Fortymile in a dead heat. Alas, the Swede's wrong turn toward the officer's quarters rather than the commissioner's office cost him ownership of Sixty Above on Bonanza. Ironically, the claim was one of the few along Bonanza Creek that never paid a plugged nickel's worth of gold.

The "explosive" bologna incident was also authentic and entirely too delightful for the author to ignore.

Two of Dawson's fires depicted in *Klondike Fever*

were credited to (or blamed on) a temperamental dove named Belle Mitchell, with the third and most destructive started by another nonvirtuous frail, Helen Holden. What a sight to behold it must have been that frigid April night when the Bank of British North America's superheated vault exploded and spewed hundreds of thousands of dollars worth of gold dust and jewelry to the four winds.

By virtue of its widespread destruction, the Trinity Sunday fire spelled the end of Dawson City's frontier flavor and the beginning of a more cosmopolitan city; an "airy" improvement that left a sour taste in many a pioneer's mouth. No sooner than steamers arrived that June with a fresh influx of greenhorns, adventurers, and (God forbid) tourists, the old-timers stampeded *from* Dawson City, bound for the rumored mother lode awaiting them at Nome, Alaska Territory. In a single week in August 1899, eight thousand people left Dawson City, never to return.

Few of the Klondike Kings managed to hold on to their fortunes. Nathan Kresge sank his proceeds into a barren mine in Oregon and died while on relief in Seattle. Nels Peterson lost nearly a hundred thousand dollars trying to keep his Flyer steamship line afloat, which eventually ruined him.

Tom Lippy supported any number of shirttail relations, donated thousands to various civic causes in Seattle, and lost the rest due to ill-fated investments.

Big Alex McDonald wound up land-poor, cashless, and died of a heart attack while chopping firewood outside his Stewart River area cabin.

Swiftwater Bill Gates, a cad of the first rank, married several teenaged comelies, including his own niece, but frequently forgot to divorce one wife before wedding her successor. Two of his mothers-in-law chased Gates all over Alaska and down the Pacific coast, where he was jailed for bigamy, then released after being bailed out by the same mother-in-law who filed the charge against him. He died in Peru in 1935 after supposedly finagling a twenty-million-acre silver mining concession from the government.

George Carmack abandoned Kate in 1900, due to her inability to adjust to the "civilized" world, which led to her numerous drunken brawls, incarcerations, and an eventual return to her people at Caribou Crossing on Lake Tagish. Carmack remarried soon after and lived happily in Vancouver until his death in 1922.

Tagish Charley sold his mining claim in 1901 and moved to Carcross, where he operated a hotel. One summer's day, during a drunken spree, he fell off a bridge and drowned. Skookum Jim's royalties from his mining interests amounted to ninety thousand dollars annually, but he was obsessed with finding a rich quartz claim and traversed the north country, seeking his own personal mother lode until his death in 1916.

Roddy Connors, the epitome of a dancing fool, spent his entire eighty-five-thousand-dollar fortune on dollar-a-dance girls.

For richer or poorer, for better or worse, the Klondike Stampede was a bona fide phenomenon. Whether greed, a hunger for adventure, or some sort of mass dementia inspired so many to leave hearth and home to go north in droves, those who lived to tell their tales did so for the rest of their lives.

The experience proved to be a springboard for Jack London's and Rex Beach's literary careers, as well as poet Robert Service. Tex Rickard promoted amateur boxing matches in the Klondike and went on to become the manager of Madison Square Garden. News butcher Sid Grauman invested in a moving picture house in Dawson, later moved his base of operations to Hollywood, and build another establishment known worldwide as Grauman's Chinese Theater.

The mayor of San Francisco during its devastating earthquake was a Klondiker, as was a senior, seven-term senator from Nevada. In the 1930s, a Speaker of the Canadian House of Commons and the Premier of British Columbia were both Stampeders.

In *High Jinks on the Klondike,* author Richard O'Connor lent the perfect footnote to this unique, albeit short chapter of our history: "Never before or since have so many American men had such a hell of a good time, without the perils of war, provided they stayed fairly healthy and had a fair amount of luck."